WINTER IN A SUMMER TOWN

Also by Gene Ritchings

Frankenrocker

The Reckoning of Adrienne Monet

Praise for *Winter in a Summer Town*

Eddie Bonneville, the protagonist in Gene Ritchings' new novel, "Winter in a Summer Town," is an authentic, vivid depiction of a modern journalist…Only a journalist who has survived years of the field's unkindest cuts could create a character like Bonneville, whose innocence is peeled away in aching layers as he navigates what he believes will be the story that makes his career… Ritchings has written a novel in which the story of a young man's personal and professional coming of age is a mirror of its times, an oracle of its country's future and a vivid tableau of our present.

The Toledo Free Press

The author's protagonist is a reporter whose interview with a local mobster rocks a small Shore town to its sandy core. Quite the summer read.

The Asbury Park Press

"Winter in a Summer Town" relates the coming of age of a young reporter and the loss of small-town innocence of the Jersey Shore itself, and takes the reader back to an era when news was written on typewriters in smoke-filled newsrooms… The novel is filled with the places and people of the Jersey Shore, like the legendary Upstage Club where the Asbury Park music scene was born, the original Inkwell coffee house in Long Branch, the boardwalks of Point Pleasant and Seaside Heights, and a mob graveyard in a Jackson Township chicken farm. The reader meets cynical politicians, gangsters, hard-working journalists, and even the denizens of the Pine Barrens.

The Hudson Reporter

Jersey Shore native Gene Ritchings' "Winter in a Summer Town" will keep readers turning pages.

The Star Ledger

WINTER IN A SUMMER TOWN

The Education of a Young Man

GENE RITCHINGS

Rebel in the Rubble Books
New York

Winter in a Summer Town is a work of fiction. All incidents and dialogue, and all characters and locales are products of the author's imagination, used fictitiously, and are not to be construed as real. Any resemblance to actual events, locales, or persons living or dead is entirely coincidental.

ISBN   979-8-9985997-3-6

generitchings@gmail.com

For Lauren

A good many things go around in
the dark besides Santa Claus.

Herbert Hoover

Eddie sat slumped in his corner, staring at his opponent across a boxing ring flooded with bright, merciless light. In the smoky, malevolent universe surrounding the ring the bleachers rumbled as the crowd out there in the dark, hungry for more fighting, stomped their feet, whistled and cheered, and drowned out the sound of the downpour drumming on the roof of the high school gym.

He was exhausted. His legs kept shaking and his head kept pounding. Voices out of the darkness urged his opponent on. Across the ring Brian Rollins danced out of his corner and waved his gloves. His face, the kind girls liked to call "foxy," was barely marked. Rolly said in today's Asbury Park *Evening Press*—with a handsome smirk for the photographer—that tonight he would take the championship away from Eddie, his first step toward the day he would win a gold medal boxing for America in the Olympics. Nobody had bothered to interview Eddie, though, and that insult, plus Rolly's boasting, had propelled him into this fight really pissed off. Now, anger was all he had left to keep him going until the final bell.

Eddie gripped the ropes and slowly pulled his battered body up on his feet. It had never been a problem, controlling his emotions in a fight, but tonight the crowd's disloyalty and hostility made him wonder what the hell was wrong. This was his high school, his gym and his home crowd, and they were cheering for this college-prep pretty boy from Point Beach to take him out. Okay, he was an outcast during the school day—his classmates stuck him with the nickname Eddie "Time Bomb" Bonneville—but they'd always cheered him on as their boxing champion. He didn't exactly have a fan club; hell, he didn't even have any friends in his senior class at Brick Township High School. His classmates weren't the kind of kids to use a fancy word like 'aloof,' but he didn't try to fit into any crowd, and they noticed that. In the lunchroom he sat at the corner table with the One Percenters, the rock musicians, hippies, special ed kids and other misfits who couldn't sit anywhere else. He was not a bully who picked on people, just a moody, truculent loner, and a little too eager to kick ass when provoked.

Even the outcasts at his lunch table knew not to antagonize him, especially about his love for Ivy Porter, the state Senator's daughter, a reckless, promiscuous girl whose exploits regularly put Eddie in awkward situations. One wrong look from a guy who'd been with Ivy was all it took for Eddie to punch his lights out. Whether he was climbing into the ring for one of his fights, strolling through the school hallways with his arm around his girlfriend, or just getting out of bed in the morning, his whole life he'd always felt like it was Eddie Bonneville against the world.

Tonight as the crowd chanted *Time Bomb, Time Bomb* in the early rounds he'd stalked Rolly and pounded him without mercy. He'd worn Rolly down but he couldn't break his spirit, and Rolly put up a tough defense that caused Eddie the first real damage he'd ever suffered as a boxer. Then, two rounds ago, Rolly suddenly buried him under a flurry of punches he hadn't seen coming. Backing away, he tripped over his own feet but it looked like Rolly knocked him on his ass for a four count, and the crowd leaped up and adopted Rolly as their new hero. Eddie dragged himself up off the canvas as his own classmates laughed and yelled for his blood. He bobbed and weaved, he did the Ali Shuffle, he made Rolly chase him, but Rolly cornered him and threw hard punches to wild cheers before he could clinch or break free and the next round was worse yet. Now with the last round about to begin, Eddie bit down harder on his mouthpiece. Quit worrying about this shit, he told himself, or you'll lose this fight. He was the 1967 Jersey Shore Conference Middleweight Boxing Champion, and as he and Rolly came to center ring and touched gloves and the bell clanged, in one round he would either still be champion or a 17-year-old loser.

He tried to defend himself, struggling against the numbness in his arms and legs, but his battered muscles were dead. Rolly set his feet and swung at him. A hard jab stung his aching head and he stumbled and nearly fell down again, and the crowd erupted. *Rol-ly! Rol-ly!* He got his feet back under him and backpedaled, but he couldn't stay outside Rolly's reach. He blocked Rolly's punches with his forearms and elbows, then managed to pin his arms in a clinch and dance him around, hoping to run out the clock. Squirming like mad to break out of the clinch, Rolly brought his knee up into Eddie's groin protector so hard his toes almost left the canvas.

His knees buckled and he fell back on the ropes. The lights over the ring exploded in his head. Applause and laughter roared in his ears so loud they buzzed like cheap loudspeakers. The first rush of pain was unbearable, but he wound the top rope around his arms and ordered himself, *Take it!* and hung on. The ref, a short round old guy with oily gray curls, yelled in Rolly's face and pushed him back to his corner. In the bleachers the crowd stomped and chanted, *Rol-ly! Rol-ly!* Eddie's balls throbbed so painfully in their aluminum cup that his knees shook and his guts went watery. The canvas under his feet swayed and lurched like the deck of a ship in a storm and in a moment he was going to vomit. *Oh no God, not here.* The ref appeared in front of him, worried. Eddie shook his head and waved him away.

Rolly walked over and spread his gloves apologetically. *Hey, sorry man, it just happened.* Eddie heaved back and slung himself off the ropes and butted heads and almost knocked Rolly off his feet. An awful *Oh!* swept in out of the bleachers at the spray of blood and sweat. Rolly stumbled sideways across the ring, his pretty face contorted in horror as blood from a forehead cut trickled down his face. The crowd booed and cursed Eddie, who mimicked and mocked Rolly. *Hey man, I'm sorry too, but now we're even.*

The ref grabbed his shoulders and shouted in his ear, "One more foul and I'll end this right now!" Eddie sneered, yeah sure, and jerked himself free. He jeered at the crowd. *Who do you people think you're laughing at?* Down in the first row he saw his father, looking worried, and Ivy, shaking her fist and yelling her head off, a lost voice in the howling crowd. He prowled the ring trying to feel out the damage. With every step he ached and his knees shook, but he willed himself to stay on his feet and finish the fight like a man.

Wiping blood off his face, Rolly stalked over to him, took an angry wild swing, missed, and left Eddie an opening. He landed a desperate left jab to Rolly's face, the first effective punch he'd thrown in several rounds. Rolly's head rocked back. His eyes were unfocused, but his fists came up. Eddie boxed right into him. Left jab, left jab, right cross,

Rolly's head whipped back and forth to the smack of leather gloves on flesh. He refused to go down. Disappointed voices rose out of the dark bleachers: *Rolly! Take him! You can do it! C'mon Rolly!*

The next moment happened in a blur. Rolly staggered back, re-signed, and his gloves dropped to his waist. Eddie body-slammed him back into the ropes. Both of them slid chest to chest in each other's blood and sweat. He hammered uppercuts into Rolly's belly, trying to punch a hole right through him. The crowd fell into a stunned silence at the ferocity of his attack, then a woman's voice rose in a thin scream out of the dark: *For God's sake stop this! Stop it now!* Up from the bleachers a chorus of rough men's voices broke, booing and cursing Eddie, yelling to the ref to stop the fight. Finally the ref waved his hands, and the timekeeper clanged the bell. Eddie kept punching. The ref seized his shoulders. He turned and backhanded the ref to the temple, knock-ing him off his feet, and the crowd gasped like they'd been hit and everybody in the place stood up and gaped.

Eddie spun around, swung from the heels, and landed a crushing punch that nearly tore Rolly's head off. Rolly bounced off the ropes and hit the canvas face first, out cold. Eddie staggered into center ring, spit out his mouthpiece, raised his gloves and sneered at the crowd he couldn't see. He could only hear their silence.

The ref scrambled off the canvas screaming, "You little bastard!"

The ref grabbed him by the neck and Eddie let him shove him into his corner. The crowd applauded, then started cursing and booing. Eddie climbed up on his corner stool and raised his fists into a shower of paper cups and trash and a roar of outrage that swelled to the rafters. In his reverie, he shouted back, "Fuck you! Fuck *all* of you! I win!" The ref went down on his knees beside Rolly's body. He turned him over and looked into his eyes, then fell back screaming for the ring doctor.

Eddie slumped down on his stool, the rough canvas turnbuckle pads scratching his neck and back. He ignored the howling mob around him. Trash thrown from the crowd hit him on the head, back and shoulders. Ivy was yelling at the people around her. He saw his father say something to Georgie Malloy and Uncle Marcel. His father looked right at Eddie and shook his head, then got up and started walking toward the exit. Eddie shrugged it off before he could feel much of anything. He was still champion, so tonight the old man could go fuck himself, too. His corner attendants raised their sponges but he waved them away, waiting for the announcement of his victory.

The ring filled fast with people. Through a forest of legs, he saw ambulance techs in white coats frantically working over Rolly, applying an oxygen mask, the doctor's stethoscope skidding around on Rolly's chest. Rolly's corner attendants went down on their knees and screamed at him, trying to wake him up. The referee pulled them away from Rolly and a stretcher was slid into the ring. The doctor pumped Rolly's chest up and down. Eddie wanted to yell, *He kicked me in the balls, for God's sake!* He felt tears run down his cheeks and sting in the cuts around his mouth. He put his gloves over his ears and he couldn't stop cursing.

The ref ordered Eddie out of the ring. Ivy climbed up and pushed his corner attendants out of the way, wrapped him in his robe, and helped him down the steps and through the crowd. People moved aside and stared slack-jawed as she led him, dazed and blood-spattered, out of the gym and down the hall to the boy's locker room. Through the pounding in his head he heard the murmurs: *Holy Christ... fuckin' animal... coulda killed him.*

Finally they were alone, in an empty cinder block room with a cold tile floor that reeked of ammonia and a weak fluorescent light that tinged everything blue. He spat blood in a sink, groaned and gritted his teeth. He slowly straddled a bench, leaning back off his bruised groin, gasping with the pain. He hurt so bad down there he was afraid the damage would be permanent.

Ivy stripped off her black leather motorcycle jacket and tossed it on top of a row of lockers.

"Can you find out what happened to Rolly?" he said. His voice was a tired croak. "Can you find out if he's all right?"

Outside, angry voices yelled for him to come out and fists pounded on the door. A sneering man with a blonde crew cut pushed the door open. He was wearing a red team jacket from Point Pleasant Beach, Rolly's school.

"You can't hide in here!"

Ivy whirled around. She shoved the man back outside. "Get the fuck *out* of here, man!" She kicked the door closed, and snapped the lock.

Eddie held his gloves over his ears. The angry voices and pounding fists wouldn't stop. He had hoped to hide himself away in the locker room, but now he was trapped.

Ivy sank her fingers into her thick black hair and combed it behind her ears. She knelt beside him, in her usual black tee shirt and jeans and black Frye boots. Her face, pretty in a fine, delicate way, was tensed in worry.

She touched his shoulder gently. "My love?"

He took a deep breath and he shuddered. "Call me that more often, willya? I like the way it sounds."

"Usually, I just prefer—Eddie," she said, her voice soft the way he liked it. "An Eddie's like a riptide, it can pull you right out to sea if you're not careful."

That brought him to the verge of tears again but he choked it.

"How they hangin,' champ?"

He coughed and winced, and shook his head.

"Oooff! You poor thing."

"I'll live. I may not reproduce."

"Don't say that! We want everything in good working order, 'specially down there." She peeled the sweaty robe off his body. They heated the locker room during school hours only, and the damp cold made him shiver.

He rubbed his gloved hands over his crew cut and they came away with blood on them. He gasped at his reflection in the mirror, a face out of a horror movie. Well, he wasn't some pretty boy to begin with. After they iced his swollen cheeks and fixed his broken nose, twisted between deep-set worried eyes, he might come out of this still looking okay. Right now he looked awful, his cheeks and forehead streaked with blood and blood all over his gloves, shoulders and chest. God, what happened to him? What the hell did he *do*? An angry curse broke from him, and he pivoted and punched a bloody dent in a steel locker door.

"Hey *champ*!" Ivy snapped, calling a mad dog to heel. "It's *over*, all right?"

"I'm worried about what I did to Rolly." He bit the knotted laces of his gloves. "I gotta know what's happening."

"We'll deal with that later." She pulled her hair back and twisted it in a knot and pinned it behind her head. "Sit still." She wet a towel in hot water and wrung it out and straddled the bench in front of him. "This is gonna hurt." She draped the steaming towel over him and rubbed his neck and head gently, turning the towel pink. The wet heat felt good but he winced when she touched his nose and hot tears ran from his eyes.

"Oh man, your poor nose," Ivy said, washing and wringing the blood out of the towel. "All right, straighten your spine. Chin down. Breathe through your mouth, down into your belly. Nice and deep. Good, hauugghh, let it out. Right, good. Keep doing that. You're gonna be all right. It's over. You won."

"Nobody said so."

"I'm sure things were just too crazy out there. Right now, this bummer is officially over. Let's just get out of here." She wiped the blood off his chest. "Good night to put behind us."

Keys jingled. The lock snapped back and the door opened. Outside, the angry voices got louder.

"Don't let them in here!" Ivy yelled.

The boxing coach, Gary Janazewski, a popular gym teacher known as Mister Jan, shut the door and locked it. Mister Jan had taken him under his wing when Eddie was a 14 year-old sandlot brawler and helped him develop into a skilled amateur boxer. Mister Jan would tell him how to handle what happened tonight. A thirtyish redhead in a stadium coat and penny loafers, with a freckled, soft face and evasive pale blue eyes, he was clearly unhappy to find Ivy with his boxer.

"You shouldn't be in here, Ivy," he said.

"I'm not leaving."

"It's the boy's locker room."

"I'm not leaving."

"Get out of the way. Let me see him."

Ivy moved to the bench behind Eddie, toweling the blood off his shoulders. The coach sat facing him, biting his lower lip and shaking his head.

"Hello, Eddie."

"Is Rolly gonna be all right?"

"They don't know yet."

He held up his bloody gloves. "Get 'em off me, please?"

"You were fouled. Are you—"

"No. I'm hurt." His voice broke. "Get these damn things off me."

Mister Jan went to the phys ed teacher's office and came back with a small steel scissors from the first aid kit. He cut the laces and pulled off the gloves. He grimaced at the blood on his hands, and wiped his fingers on Ivy's towel.

"My God, Eddie," the coach said quietly. "What did you think you were doing out there?"

"Winning."

Mister Jan's incredulous look made Eddie shiver worse than the cold room, and it made Ivy angry. "Hey man," she said, "did you hear those animals *cheer* when he got hit below the belt?"

Ignoring her, the coach cut into the thick white tape around Eddie's fists.

"I couldn't stop hitting him," Eddy said, mystified by himself. "I wanted to kill him."

"The police are outside," Mister Jan said. "The ref filed a complaint."

"For what?"

"Assault and battery."

"Son of a *bitch* –"

"All right, take it easy. I would've never let you box tonight if I knew you couldn't handle your temper."

"I'd like to see you take a knee in the balls, to *applause*, and handle your temper."

"Okay, okay. Look, I trained you to win. I didn't train you to–" The look in Eddie's eye stopped the coach cold.

"Didn't train me to *what*? You didn't train me to beat the hell out of other guys?"

"Not like that."

"You never complained when I was winning trophies."

"That wasn't boxing out there. That was everything we've worked to get you away from."

"I got hurt!" To be criticized like this was unfair. "Things just happened! Nobody trained Rolly to kick me in the balls, either, but that's what he did. Why don't you ask him?"

"Everybody thinks that foul was an accident."

He pulled at the cut tape around his fist, working it off. "Look, I'm beat to shit, and I, I need time to think."

Tenderly, Ivy kissed the back of his neck. "Everything's gonna be all right."

"I need help figuring this out," he said to Mister Jan. A helpless plea, and he wished he hadn't said it, but there it was. He wanted to cry, he wanted Mister Jan to put his arms around him and tell him everything would be all right, but instead his coach just stared.

Ivy rubbed his shoulders. "Into the shower, champ. Clean up and let's get you to the hospital to fix that nose."

"Listen Eddie." The coach took a deep breath. "I told the police I would bring you out."

He glanced in the mirror at Ivy behind him. She heard it, too. The coach was not here to help him. He was here to cover his own ass, and to make life easy for the police by walking Eddie out to the handcuffs. Just like that, it was all over. After three years of working and training together, the coach was acting like he didn't know him. He could see it now, Mister Jan on the witness stand, his face bland and innocent. *I never trained him to kill anybody, don't blame me.* Unable to look him in the eye, like now, and selling him out.

"I'll get my father to cool this out with the police," Ivy said to the coach. "So why don't you just leave us alone, so I can help him?"

"I don't care who your father is. You're a student, I'm a teacher, and I'm telling you to shut up."

"Don't talk to her like that," Eddie said.

"Eddie needs help, *sir.*" Ivy had a way of telling people *Fuck you* without actually saying it. "You're not helping."

While his girlfriend and coach glared at each other, Eddie staggered to his feet. He leaned over, held the sides of the sink and saw stars, drank from the tap and spat bloody water.

"Don't wait for me," Eddie said. He took a towel off the shelf and wet it in the sink and finished wiping himself off. "I'll turn myself in to the police when I'm cleaned up."

"This is serious, Eddie, as serious as it gets," the coach said.

"You think I don't *know* that? I told you, something happened to me. He fouled me and I just, lost it."

"I don't believe this shit." Ivy threw the bloody towel in the corner.

"You didn't have to dump the ref on his tail feathers." Mister Jan's insulted voice made it sound like Eddie's unsportsmanlike conduct had embarrassed the whole school. "By the way, they're gonna take away your championship—"

"No—" That was a kick in a place much more sensitive than his groin. "You gotta say something to them, that isn't fair—"

"*Fair?* You beat Rolly so bad he might die. That's what you ought to be thinking about."

"*Hey* man!" Ivy was ready to punch the coach out. Eddie raised a hand to calm her. He'd already pulled back, into a lonely place inside where nothing could get to him. He opened the locker, took his Lucky Strikes from his shirt pocket, and lit one.

"You think about it too, coach. But don't worry." He savored the smoke in his lungs and the taste of his own words, bitter as the tobacco flake he spit off the tip of his tongue. "I hear you. Loud and clear. What happened tonight wasn't your fault. Your job's safe. Nobody's gonna blame *you*."

The coach stood up. He went to the door, stopped, and put his hands in his coat pockets, waiting.

"Go tell 'em I'll be out when I'm ready."

"Look at his face," Ivy said. "Why didn't you bring the doctor to see him?"

"He went with the ambulance to the hospital."

"In case you didn't notice, Rolly isn't the only one who took a beating tonight."

The coach hesitated, his eyes darted away. "Look, Eddie—"

"You were sure on my side when I was winning championships," Eddie said, unable to keep his voice steady, "and making you look good."

"Oh, come on—"

"Get the fuck out of here." He couldn't believe he had trusted this man. When would he learn?

"Hey Bonneville," Mister Jan said. "I'm the teacher, you're the student, show the proper respect."

Slowly, Eddie crossed the room until they were face to face.

"Eddie—no…" Ivy said. "He's not worth it."

Mister Jan started to speak, and obviously thought it was wiser, or safer, to shut up.

"I said, get the *fuck* out of here… *sir*."

He backed away, ripped the tape off his hand, and flipped it to Mister Jan, who never took his hands out of his coat pockets. The tape bounced off the stadium coat and fell on the concrete floor, still molded in the shape of his fist.

When he came out of the locker room the newspaper photographers took his picture as the state troopers led him away in handcuffs. At the State Police barracks on Hooper Avenue, he was booked and fingerprinted and mug shots were taken. He was released after his father, a Township Committeeman in Brick, called the municipal court judge, who called the commandant of the barracks.

Ivy drove him to Point Pleasant Hospital, where an emergency room doctor cleaned and bandaged and splinted his nose. They wouldn't tell him if Rolly was okay and he wanted to stay, but Ivy refused. "No way, man. Haven't you had enough bad karma for one night?"

The rain had stopped, and the sky had cleared, and Ivy's white '67 Corvair splashed through pools of water standing in the streets. He wasn't ready to go home and face his father, so she drove up to the Point Pleasant boardwalk where they could hang out for awhile. Once they got away from the sounds of the pinball addicts wrestling with their ringing machines in the arcades and the Friday night band in the Riptide Bar blasting out "Knock On Wood," the boardwalk overlooking Jenkinson's Beach got nice and quiet and deserted. It was a mild autumn night, but you could feel the winter cold coming. A fireplace was burning in one of the houses along the boardwalk and there was wood smoke in the air. The boards underfoot, worn from decades of walkers, were rain darkened, and you could smell salt and iodine from the heavy, foamy surf pounding the beach. Out to sea it was all black except for the lights on a fishing boat slowly making for the inlet.

She tried to talk to him, but he had nothing to say. After a few minutes, she gave up. They walked all the way to the north end of Jenkinson's beach and climbed up on the Manasquan River inlet jetty—"going to The Rocks," the local kids called it. Balancing atop the granite boulders, they kicked the sand off their shoes, then hopped from stone to stone out toward the sea. The water lapped below, smelling of motor oil and fish, and a floating empty can clunked on a rock.

At the end of the jetty was the concrete base of a rusty tower that held up a flashing green light marking the inlet for boats coming off the sea for the fishery docks or the marinas upriver. They sat on the concrete and leaned against the tower, the waves crunching against the rocks below. On one side of the jetty a cabin cruiser rode the back of a wave rolling into the inlet, while on the other side breakers made long lines of white surf down the long beach in the moonlight. Gulls soared through the mist over the swells, their cries sharp against the steady tolling of a buoy bell. The cold of the ocean was all around them, but cuddling together and smoking cigarettes made them warm.

She spit on a Dunkin' Donuts napkin and wiped dried blood from under his nose, carefully avoiding the splint and bandage in the middle of his face and the tape across his cheeks.

"What's goin' on in that crazy head of yours?" she said.

"I'm okay," he said. Actually, he felt like he'd awakened from a nightmare whose details were too shocking to remember.

"Look champ, whatever happens, it's not gonna be your whole life—"

"Oh yeah?"

"You deal with it, you move on—"

"Look. He fouled me. It was probably an accident," he said. "But I was really *trying* to kill him, y'know? And while I was doing it—" He shook his head. He couldn't even tell Ivy how good it had felt, beating Rolly senseless. He shuddered. "I gotta figure this out before it's too late—if it isn't already. That same thing gets ahold of me again—" He held out his hands and flexed them. "I could do it again to somebody. *Easily*. I almost killed a kid tonight, and for what? I didn't even get the title."

"'You're an angry guy, Eddie Bonneville'," Ivy said in his ear, quoting a poem she wrote to him when they were 16, "'and you live in an angry fog/ a bad-mouthed, big-balled, big-hearted junkyard dog.' Which is why I love you." He looked at her. She laughed at his bandaged, battered face. He moved in closer.

He nearly went out of his mind that night worrying about Rolly, but he finally fell asleep. Saturday morning he woke up late, stiff and aching all over. He laid in bed until he heard his father leave the house, then went downstairs for breakfast. Over coffee and a cigarette in the kitchen, his mother, grimacing at the sight of his injured nose, told him his father had come home last night and said nothing about the fight, but called Rolly's parents in the morning to apologize.

"And how's Rolly?"

"Not good."

On a cold sunny afternoon, bundled in his coat on the front porch, he opened the Asbury Park *Evening Press* and saw that his life would never be the same. The headline on the front page below the fold said 'Teen Boxer Hovers Near Death,' with a photo of Rolly face down on the canvas and a blood-spattered Eddie looming over him. The story said Rolly had fouled Eddie 'below the belt' but it described in detail how Eddie knocked down the referee and inflicted a 'savage' beating on his opponent even after the final bell. In a story on the jump page headlined 'High School Boxing Champ Stripped of Title' with the picture of Eddie being arrested, the chairman of the Shore Conference board said Eddie's championship was revoked due to extreme unsportsmanlike conduct. The referee was quoted saying Eddie had been out of control, and the story quoted anonymous officials at his high school who called Eddie an emotionally disturbed youth who had often been disciplined for fighting. A court date would be set for a hearing for his assault and battery on the referee.

From that day on, he was called Eddie 'Time Bomb' Bonneville in every news story that kept a death watch on Rolly. *You're an angry guy, Eddie Bonneville.* Ivy knew it, and in her own weird way she loved him, but everybody else thought he was a psycho. He even began to wonder about that himself. He had fought eleven fights as a respected student boxer; but last night, before he knew what was happening to him, he had become something else, and he'd nearly killed another kid. In one fight, his reputation fell from champion high school athlete to dangerous thug.

The pride he once took from winning fights now seemed absurd, even sick. Within a few days came a longing to make amends for more than just his last disastrous fight. He wanted to apologize to everyone he'd ever hurt. Maybe they'd never forgive him; in fact, he could scarcely forgive himself. But he wanted to try. When he pictured a different life for himself, repenting for his violent ways, seeking forgiveness and treating others and himself with compassion, he was so overcome with relief he wept, sitting on the porch of his parents house with cars passing by. A life so clear and unburdened would be like being born again. Inflicting pain on anyone again was unthinkable. When he said that at his juvenile court hearing, the judge ordered him to undergo counseling before his case came to trial.

Once a week for the next year he drove up to see a psychiatrist with an office on Deal Lake in Asbury Park. Somebody, probably his wimp probation officer or his high school guidance counselor, had told the shrink he was violent and emotionally disturbed and had a history of fighting with other kids.

"So Edward, any episodes of anger this week?" The shrink, old, gray and well fed, lived in a big house that smelled like fried fish.

"I don't know what you mean," he said.

"We've talked about this," the shrink said with an edge of impatience.

"You mean like, the hostility you asked me about last week? Or the rage from the week before? If I can't figure out what you're talking about, how can I ever get better?"

"How do you feel right now?"

He felt tricked by the doctor, that's how he fuckin' felt. This always happened. But he wanted to get better, so he groped for an honest answer. "I feel like a disease carrier, and I have to be careful not to infect anybody else."

"We'll come back to that idea. Stay with your feelings."

He endured these counseling sessions because he was hoping to find out something about himself. *Why* was he so angry? *Why* was beating the crap out of another kid in a dirty lot after school always so satisfying? *Why* did he prefer to be a loner, joining no clubs or teams or groups of friends, proud of being feared and avoided? There was something wrong with him, but he got nothing but mind games from the psychiatrist, so his own nature remained no more than a guess to him, and the counseling only worsened his confusion.

But he wanted to get better, so he tried. He told the psychiatrist that Martin Luther King's assassination in April caused a nasty argument with his father because, shocked and indignant after his father went on a tirade about the riots that followed the killing, he called his father a racist who cared more about white people's property than the murder of black people's hopes. And in June, he and his father almost had a fistfight after Robert Kennedy was killed. His father—a lifelong Republican who'd proudly introduced 5-year-old Eddie to Vice President Nixon when he campaigned in the 1956 Big Sea Day Parade in Point Pleasant—had infuriated him by saying that Kennedy had brought it on himself, going out and getting everybody all excited, promising to cut and run in Vietnam, making America look weak. When Eddie argued back, his father tossed Eddie and his typewriter out of the house, leading him to rent an efficiency apartment down at the beach in a house owned by the lawyer who was handling his assault case.

"How *do* you feel about your mother and father?" the shrink asked when he told him about being kicked out of the house. "I notice you rarely mention them."

A deep, unexpected embarrassment came over Eddie and it was impossible to say much.

"I don't know. Uh, my mother, she's a quiet, gentle soul, and my father, he's a right wing Republican, uh, reactionary."

"Those are opinions," the shrink said, "not feelings."

When Rolly came out of his coma he left the hospital with brain damage caused by oxygen starvation from the knockout. Against the wishes of both their parents Eddie helped him with his recovery. That winter, even though they went to school in different towns, he set out to become Rolly's friend and caretaker. He took him to football and basketball games at Point Beach, ignoring the stares from people shocked to see them together, and afterward he and Rolly would hit the O–B Diner or the Candy Kitchen downtown to rehash the game.

At first Rolly barely tolerated Eddie's attempts at friendship and said it was only because he felt guilty over his mad dog moment in the ring. But Eddie remained a steadfast friend, and after awhile he earned Rolly's trust. Eddie saw first-hand that the fight had changed Rolly's life for the worse. Before, Rolly had been class president and a three-letter jock. His senior year athletics were supposed to have won him a sports scholarship to a good college. But Rolly never recovered from the beating well enough to play sports again, and was often desolate because he missed it so much. Eddie listened to Rolly's despair, reckoning he had a responsibility not to avoid the pain he'd caused.

They'd go see a movie then take it apart afterward. Sometimes they'd just drive around—there was nothing to do at the Shore in the winter—and talk for hours. Rolly was getting into trouble more and more, at school, with his parents, with the police, but all he could talk about was how he was being persecuted. Once a Straight-A student, Eagle Scout and a leader in the Jaycees, he turned into a lout and a trouble-maker, a girl beater, a garbage-head who liked to show off and take more drugs than anybody else, and a car thief, until a municipal court judge gave him the choice between prison or enlisting in the military. Rolly's father began pressuring him to do his duty and join the Army, just like Eddie's father was pressuring him. But Rolly really listened to his father, so he was torn in a way that Eddie wasn't.

One time he and Ivy double dated with Rolly and Ivy's friend Carol to The Upstage in Asbury Park, but Rolly showed up late, high on speed or something, and goofed on whatever anyone said or did all night like an obnoxious brat. By then their friendship had become Eddie trying to rescue Rolly from himself. Rolly's giggling skid into delinquency, his pending assault case, these were reminders to do no further harm.

On the green and golden late summer afternoon of his 18th birthday, September 24, 1968, he drove down to Toms River to register for the Draft. Stopped by the red light at Hooper Avenue and Washington Street, the car windows open, he was momentarily distracted from thinking about what he was about to do by the beauty of the day. Stirred by a cool breeze, the leaves atop the tall oak trees dappled the sunlight across the emerald lawn and the front of the red brick white-pillared county courthouse. A lawn mower droned somewhere in the distance. From his car radio came a melody, the theme from "A Summer Place" by Percy Faith and Orchestra, a big hit record on the radio when he'd been a kid. The song made him sad, like he'd lost something, but he couldn't say exactly what.

He parked near the courthouse and tried to calm himself by meditating. On one of his last visits to Ivy up at NYU, she took him to a Zen meditation class at a place in Greenwich Village, thinking it might do him some good. He practiced the meditation each morning and evening. If it was doing him any good, he hadn't noticed it yet. But the practice wasn't like a religion, all solemn and frightening like the Catholic Church, and it did make him a little calmer, so he kept doing it. He sat in the lotus position and simply observed his breathing and thoughts. His mental turbulence was supposed to settle like sediment in a still pond, but it hardly ever did. Despite weeks of faithful practice, he still could not quiet the angry, muttering voice inside.

He entered the Draft Board office carrying his mood like a ticking bomb in a paper bag. The place was nothing but the intake valve on a huge meat grinder, the first step on the military assembly line producing soldiers for the war in Vietnam. The small office was in a rear corner of the courthouse building and still furnished in World War II era gray filing cabinets and steel desks and chairs. He was sure the only thing that ever changed in this office was the presidential portrait on the wall. Today, Lyndon B. Johnson was hanging beneath the Stars and Stripes, though not for long, since he hadn't run for reelection, and not by his neck, as Eddie felt he deserved.

He checked out the other boys in the room waiting to register. Two hippies in jeans, flannels and fatigue jackets whispered and snickered anxiously. A surly greaser with his hair slicked back, wearing a sharkskin gray suit and skinny tie, perched on the edge of his seat, a tough guy ready for action, chewing gum and talking to no one. Two buttoned-down college prep guys stared into space with their arms crossed and muttered from the sides of their mouths. A short guy with matted blonde surfer hair, in a seersucker anorak and baggy shorts and sandals, rocked in his chair, humming tunelessly to himself.

The board secretary was at least a century old, thin and dry as a stick. He could just imagine how strange he must have appeared to her. He walked up to her desk, his hands in the pockets of his scuffed leather coat. He brushed his shoulder-length dark brown hair back off his face. His slightly bent nose didn't go with the beatific smile he had assigned to his lips once he decided he was a pacifist, to signal to the world his benevolent spirit. He kept repeating to himself: *peace, serenity, good will.*

But his deep-set eyes, the sadness and intelligence concentrated there, said none of that. He didn't dress to impress, either: battered desert boots, faded jeans and a few old sweaters he bought cheap out at the Englishtown Auction, where he could throw together a whole season's clothes for less than twenty dollars.

"I'm Edward Bonneville," he said.

The quiet murmur in the room stopped. He knew why. They all recognized his name, and they knew what it meant. There was no way to escape the unwelcome attention he attracted.

"All right Edward," the board secretary said in a thin, quavering voice, "here's your paperwork. Sit right over there and fill it out, please."

He took a deep breath and said, "I'd like to register as a Conscientious Objector. Can I have the paperwork for that, please?"

Her rimless glasses enlarged her eyes and made her look startled. "You're a—what did you say?"

"I'd like to register as a Conscientious Objector."

The Secretary picked up the phone. "Mr. Mason? Can you come out here, please?" Her hand trembled as she handed Eddie his papers. "You still have to fill these out."

He sat and did as he was told. He could feel the other boys staring. That's *him*. He ignored them. The Board chairman, Aubrey Mason, a beefy, rough looking customer who owned a stationery store on Main Street in downtown Toms River, walked in, conferred in whispers with the secretary, and peered at him.

"You're a…what?" Mason demanded.

Filling in his paperwork, Eddie said, "For the third time—I'd like to register as a Conscientious Objector, sir."

The secretary looked bewildered. "I've been here since 1942. We've never had one of these." Unfriendly laughter from the other boys.

"Just show up for the bus, wise guy," Mason said as he ran a hand over his steel gray crew cut. "Six a.m. out in front of the courthouse. You get up to AFEES Newark, take your problem to the Army psychiatrist."

"That means you're coming with me, right? Because *you're* my problem."

Mason stopped short and stared. "What'd you say?"

"You want to put a gun in my hands and order me to kill people. I've got a problem with that."

The greaser sitting behind him scoffed. "What do you think we should fight the communists with, asshole? Peace and love?"

"Watch your language, there's a lady in the room," Eddie said.

"What's wrong with peace and love, asshole?" one of the hippies said from across the room.

"Guys! The *language*! C'mon!" He turned and looked the greaser in the eye. "I think you should give this a lot more thought." He had a pleasant flash of himself leaning over and smacking the greaser's face. Just a thought, but it must've registered, because the guy's eyes wavered and he started chewing his lower lip.

"You're Committeeman Bonneville's boy?" Mason said. "That was *you*?"

"What was me?"

"The boxer—"

"Yeah. That was me. Do you really want to put a gun in my hands?" Eddie got up and laid his paperwork on the secretary's desk. "I'm not a fighter anymore. I've embraced peace and nonviolence."

One of the college prep guys snickered to his buddy, and to the room. "Oh wow, the new Mahatma."

"Hey," Eddie said to the room at large, "we've got another deep thinker over there." Suppose, he thought, I break you into little pieces, jerk off? Easy boy, he told himself. This is nothing, this is nothing at all. "Can I have the C.O. paperwork, please?"

The greaser just couldn't shut up. "Y'know, other guys're risking their lives in Vietnam to keep your hippie ass free." The two hippies sitting behind him rolled their eyes. "Just 'cause you hate this country—"

"Cool it, greaseball," Eddie muttered. "Or you're gonna get your hair mussed." The guy tried to look tough, but when the others snickered at him he turned red.

Mason stared at Eddie. "Son, have you thought about the possible consequences of doing this?"

"You mean I may not get to run for President some day?" The surfer threw his head back and hooted, and defiantly rocked in his seat, chanting in a whisper, *Hey hey LBJ, how many kids didya kill to-day?*"

"No," Mason said. "It means somebody else might have to die in your place. Maybe one of these boys right in this room here."

"I don't want to see anybody die," he said. He looked around. Nobody said thank you.

"Maybe you should think about this," Mr. Mason said.

"Sir, all I'm asking is to register this way, which I have a legal right to do. I didn't come here looking for trouble."

The secretary said she would mail him the C.O. paperwork, so he left.

He weaved his way through a crowd of jurors shuffling out the courthouse door. The warm sunshine and birds singing didn't do shit for his mood. Mr. Mason had tried to make him look foolish, guilt-tripping him with that bullshit about somebody else dying in his place, with all the belligerence and confusion typical of those who still believed in that useless war. Which did they want him to do, anyway, die for his country, or make Vietnamese die for theirs? The war was also being fought over every dinner table in America and it was tearing the country apart. On television each night there was news footage of chaos and death in the jungle, of coffins rolling off planes, of flinty-eyed politicians in Washington making speeches about defending freedom, national honor and duty, about defeating a global menace. But the waste and futility of the war, escalated years ago for reasons nobody could remember anymore, had turned principles like honor and duty into obscenities. Any fool could see Vietnam was a dead end, a wrong turn, and soldiers were getting killed because politicians did nothing but talk and avoid making the hard decisions that might cost them their comfortable jobs in Washington. The greaser had it all wrong. He didn't hate his country. He hated the handful of men who stupidly got his country into this war and now stubbornly refused to end it.

Besides, no speeches by the president or anyone else could gloss over the fact that if he did his patriotic duty, somebody would die. He wasn't afraid of losing his life, it hadn't been such a great life up until then, anyway. But he wanted no part of killing or harming anybody else. Today he almost got into a fight over filling out his Draft paper-work. What would he be like with an M16 in his hands?

He slid behind the wheel of his pride and joy, a sky blue 1963 Chevy Impala Super Sport coupe parked on Washington Street outside the courthouse. He lit a Lucky Strike. He sat back and stared up the street.

On that same street, one month earlier, in a warm gray haze at dawn's early light, 18-year-old boys say goodbye to their families and climb aboard an Army drab green school bus. Family scenes: kisses, hugs, tears, manly handshakes. Parked up the block, Eddie sits behind the wheel, watching. The dashboard clock says ten minutes before six.

Rolly and his family drive past in a silver Cadillac Sedan de Ville, park across the street from the bus, and get out. Rolly looks up the street and sees Eddie's car and waves. Joe Rollins, his father, turns and also sees Eddie, and tries to herd Rolly to the bus, but Rolly brushes him off. A look passes between Rolly and his father almost audibly: Hey man, lay off!

Rolly walks up the street and gets into Eddie's car, grabs his shoul-der, shakes him roughly and laughs like Woody Woodpecker until Eddie pushes him away—their standard greeting.

With a big grin, Rolly looks out the windshield, wide-eyed, geared up, humming and squirming and fidgeting, symptoms of the brain damage Eddie inflicted in the ring. Eddie can't believe this moment has come.

"I couldn't let you leave without saying goodbye and good luck."

"I am gungho to the *max*, dude," Rolly says. "Ready for the main show. Ready to kick some serious gook ass."

Calmly, Eddie says, "I ought to knock you out again and dump you in Canada."

Rolly laughs hilariously. "Nah, I'll be back stateside before you know it, man. We'll buy ourselves a fast car, hit the road, and really live like writers."

"Two years."

"Hey, c'mon, man," Rolly groans. "After all the fights at home lately, Vietnam'll be a friggin' picnic. Fuck, over there, when I steal a car, I can probably get away with it, right? Not like this shitty little place." He punches Eddie's arm. "Fuck all the 15-year-old chicks I want. Right? Maybe I'll steal me a rickshaw for a joy ride." He falls into a giggling jag that Eddie hates because it makes Rolly sound like a lunatic.

He tries one last time to get through to him. "You don't have to do this, you know. I may never see you again. You may never see me again. Did you think of that?"

Rolly squirms, and his voice becomes a tired whine. "Well, what the fuck do you want me to do, man? The judge said, either I join the Marines or go to jail for grand theft auto. I'd go nuts if I had to sit in jail tryin' to make conversation with niggers and stupid white trash for the next two years."

"Don't talk that way, c'mon—"

"So I'm gonna make the best of this." He pumps his fist with a big grin. "Gonna go out and see *war*, man, see what the world's really made of, really get a look at the human condition in all its fucked up glory, y'know?"

"Try and make it back in one piece, okay?"

"I'll make it back." Rolly looks at him with a slow defiant smirk. "So don't sweat it. Okay?"

He shrugs. "Yeah."

It happens in seconds. Rolly leans in and kisses him, a big kiss on the lips.

"Okay, brother? You happy now?"

Eddie pushes him away, his face burning red. *Happy?*

"I love you, Edsel," Rolly says, staring out the windshield with his goofy grin again. "In spite of everything. It's not a *queer* thing, I just—love you. Okay?"

"I–" He wants to say, *Oh god, what'd I do to you? I'm gonna be worried sick until you get home.* But Rolly would probably laugh at him. Having that for his last memory would be unbearable. "I love you too, man. Be careful. And write." Rolly sits back, chuckling, babbling under his breath. One last four-handed handshake. Rolly gets out and strolls away. Before he reaches the bus, he starts skipping, turns once and flashes Eddie a 'V' with his fingers—for peace.

Another kiss goodbye—Ivy left town that same day to begin life as a freshman at college up in New York. The day after Nixon was elected president, a judge sentenced Eddie to probation already served for hitting the referee, since he'd stayed out of trouble in the year since the fight. Eddie had no money to continue his education, so he went to work and started saving for school. He showed his high school newspaper clippings to a cool editor named Frank Devlin and got himself hired by the Ocean County Daily *Independent*, a weekday tabloid with a readership of around forty thousand, working as a part time reporter covering municipal court and night meetings of local boards of this or that. By Christmas he was a full-time reporter making seventy-five dollars a week and putting a lot of mileage on the Impala.

He got his first mail from Rolly at the end of February 1969, a Polaroid and letter from a place called Cam Ranh Bay. In the picture, Rolly was in green fatigues and holding a rifle, a cigarette between his grinning lips.

"Edsel,

Been on a troop transport plane forever. Finally here. It's steam bath hot. They say it gets worse. Can't wait to get worked into the scene. Really amazing to be part of such a huge operation. Hope I can hold up my end.

Rollins."

He wrote back immediately, a diatribe on the insanity of the war. But he realized Rolly would read it and think that he was passing judgment on him, so he tore it up. He tried again, writing about his life, and got a good comical, sarcastic rant going. Then he read it over and saw it wasn't funny at all, just lonely and unhappy. How trivial his complaints would be to a guy in the middle of a war! He stuck those pages in his journal. He finally fell back on writing what everyone probably wrote: do your job, keep your head down, don't get killed and come home soon. Not very creative. But that was all he could come up with, and he wanted to reply fast and not make Rolly wait while he wrote some friggin' masterpiece. A letter from home, even a few lines, had to make a soldier feel better, even if only for a few minutes. After he finished writing, he drove over to the post office in Point Pleasant Beach and put the letter in the mail.

TWO *Christmas Eve in my hometown*

Driving to the newsroom for his four o'clock shift, the highway was a black and white movie in the silvery light from a winter sky. A few miles south of Toms River he turned off Route 9 at the Forum Diner and into the parking lot of a shopping center whose rusty, unlit neon sign read "Bargainland! Nothing BUT Discounts!"

He was already in his usual blue Christmas mood, so he was glad the winter dusk fell fast and he saw very little of Bargainland by daylight. Built in the 1950s beside a cedar creek whose waters the shopping center had long polluted, Bargainland no longer attracted attention, even from motorists who stopped into the Forum. The row of stores behind the diner started with a cut-rate grocery that had replaced an A&P, followed by a series of white-washed windows where the Bargainland department store had gone bust years ago, then a dry-cleaners, a pet store, a barber shop, a drug store, a beauty parlor, a head shop called Planet Beachwood, a carpet store, a coin laundry, the newsroom of the Ocean County Daily *Independent*, Emil's newspaper and tobacco store, and a deep narrow coffee shop called Groucho's.

At the end, an oasis of Italian American pride, Castellucci's Lounge, set itself apart from its shabby neighbors with white stucco walls, an ornate lintel over the front window and shrubs flanking the entrance. A black awning over the sidewalk proclaimed in white flowing script, *Sophisticated Dining and Entertainment* which, by local standards, was true.

Dry snowflakes blew around, suspended in the air, as Eddie hurried across the parking lot, making his daily approach to the newsroom by way of Emil's for a pack of Lucky Strike, then Groucho's for two plain donuts and a large black coffee.

In the *Independent*'s front window hung a Lucite reproduction of the newspaper's jazzy black and blue masthead. Inside at the reception desk, opposite a sun-faded vinyl sofa and dried-out potted palm, the editor-in-chief's daughter, Bailey Devlin, a 25-year-old blonde angel squeezed into a tight blue dress, poured her suffering heart out to a caller and ignored the mad buzzing of her switchboard. She put the caller on hold, waved for Eddie to stop, and handed him a thick stack of phone messages.

"When you read those, just imagine what *hell* it was to write 'em all down," she said, slapping them in his hand. "Not just the things they said. The *anger*, the *hatred*! I've been bombarded with this shit all day."

"Sorry, Bay," he said, glancing through the messages. "People shouldn't unload on you like this."

"Well—" She softened slightly. "If they were for anybody but you, I wouldn't bother." Wiggling her finger at the messages: "You better be careful, young man."

He'd like to flirt, but he was more interested in the messages. They were from *Independent* readers responding to his column this week titled "Hell No, I Won't Go." Since he'd registered for the Draft over a year ago he'd refused to comply with several orders from the county Draft Board to submit to a physical to determine his military service classification. He and his lawyer patiently answered the letters insisting it would be more appropriate for the board to hold his Conscientious Objector hearing first. After his Draft lottery number, 195, was drawn on December 1, the board scheduled the hearing for December 29, this coming Monday.

As a warning to the Draft Board, and as encouragement to himself before the hearing, Eddie wrote a column vowing that he would not allow himself to be drafted by the government and trained to kill. The government's power to draft men into uniform, he said, was a blank check that must be cancelled, because it made reckless military adventures like Vietnam virtually inevitable. War was a tragic breakdown in civilization, and violence was a curse, carried, in particular, by men. He, Eddie Bonneville, disgraced high school boxing champion, had seen the damage his own capacity for violence and brutality could cause, and had dedicated his life to nonviolence, justice and peace. He urged his readers to imagine a better world, in which people practiced mutual respect, tolerance and brotherly love.

Almost nobody agreed with him. Some of the messages mocked his pacifism, saying he'd lost his nerve after his "psycho" episode in the boxing ring, and called him a coward. Many demanded the *Independent* fire him for treason. What in the world was wrong with people, he wondered, that they preferred war to peace? He had expected people to disagree with him, but not *this*. Writing that column, he'd been a fighter again—a fighter for peace. He didn't understand why people put so much passion into contempt.

He grabbed a copy of today's *Independent* from the stack on the reception desk and pushed through the door.

The other reporters were already at work, four desks on each side of the newsroom, a deep, narrow space with dirty white walls and old, scuffed furniture. The usual fog of cigarette smoke hung under the glaring fluorescent light. He lit his first Lucky Strike, his regular defense against the vinegary stench of the chemicals from the photo offset plate room and the acrid odor of ink from the printing press that would soon be drumming away in the rear of the building.

In the middle of the newsroom the night editor, Lindy Martin, sat in the slot of the U-shaped copy desk, a Marlboro burning in one hand while she red-penciled copy with the other. Twice his age, pear-shaped in denim jeans and work shirt, and potato-faced with a fright wig of coppery hair, she offered her usual droll, affectionate greeting.

"Well, Ocean County's Number One Communist Pinko Menace has arrived." She slapped edited pages into the Out basket for the typesetters in the Composing Room, sat back grinning in her chair, and took a large gulp of coffee.

He brandished his messages. "Fan mail."

"Yeah. I read a few."

"Some of these are really gross."

"I like the one calling you a traitor who should be hung from a lamppost, preferably in Moscow."

"For refusing to do harm to others," he said. "Unbelievable."

"Hey, I suggest you read 'em, have a good laugh, and put the scariest one over your desk as a reminder: you wanna play in the free marketplace of ideas, you're gonna get hate mail." She stood up with her coffee cup to get a refill from the urn in the kitchen. "By the way, Frank was here at four o'clock, looking for you. He went out, but he wants you to stay right here until he gets back."

Uh oh. "Was he pissed off?"

She shrugged. "You know how he is."

Oh, man. What trouble was he in with Frank *now*? He headed toward his desk in the back corner of the newsroom, his anxiety growing, and stopped to say hello to Norm Crane, the senior reporter, who was gathering up his keys and cigarettes and stuffing his notebook into a jacket pocket. Tall and handsome, Crane would have fit right into a 1940s tabloid crime scene photo, as a detective or gangster, not as reporter. Silently, Eddie handed him his messages.

As he popped a Pall Mall in the corner of his tight grin, Crane took a sour glance at the fistful of messages and handed them back. "What's on tap for next week, kid? You know who you're going to piss off next?" He liked to encourage Eddie to cause trouble.

"Next week, the power of meditation to calm disorder and promote brotherly love." They laughed, as they had many nights, writing up the disorder and foolishness of the world against deadline, Eddie sneaking puffs on a reefer out back by the dumpsters and Crane sipping Fleischmann's from a pint he kept under the county phone directory in his bottom desk drawer.

"Well, Merry Christmas anyway," he said, and pulled on his overcoat. "You back here Christmas night for Friday's paper?"

"'Fraid so."

"See ya then."

"Hey Norm, was Frank out here looking for me?" Maybe Crane had heard something and could give him a warning.

Crane laughed at the back of his throat. "*Fuck* Frank Devlin. If he had half a brain, he'd be dangerous. Just keep givin' 'em all the hot foot." He punched Eddie's shoulder. "Catch you later."

He got the usual greetings from his colleagues in the other departments. Joe Scardini, the rotund sports editor, nodded as he held the phone to his ear with his shoulder and juggled a foot-long submarine sandwich in his hands, talking and eating over a sheet of waxed paper covering his desk. With a disapproving glance at this balancing act as she typed, Hildy Gotbaum, the real estate and business writer, cocked a heavily penciled eyebrow at him as he breezed past. Bobbi Ann Nelson, the police reporter, perched on the corner of her desk in a tight red shift with her matchstick legs crossed, whispering in the ear of a tall handsome State Trooper in a blue and gold uniform and making him chuckle. "From what I hear," the courthouse reporter, J. Paul Jackson, had once drawled to him, "Bobbi Ann doesn't cover the police news so much as straddle it." Mister Jackson wiggled his fingers and sat staring through his huge brown eyeglasses at the copy in his typewriter, his bald pate shining and his bow tie just-so, a Chesterfield in a black ebony holder clenched in his teeth. Eddie had once amused himself by taking one of Jackson's columns on county politics and circling the clichés, and when he was finished the only words not circled were conjunctions and prepositions. He gave each of his colleagues a quick hello and went straight to his desk to fortify himself for the expected clash with his editor.

What a way to start the day. What the hell was up with Frank now? Frank said admiring things about the writing in Eddie's high school newspaper clippings when he hired him, and Eddie had done his best to model himself after Frank, professionally if not personally. Frank was the law at the *Independent*, and Eddie worked hard for his approval. If anything was wrong between them it was agony waiting to find out about it. Sometimes his stories and columns were controversial, but didn't that help sell papers? By now, wasn't he part of the *Independent* family? Why the hell did Frank order him to stay right here? Crane had it right, *fuck* Frank Devlin. Let Frank come to him this afternoon, a man had work to do.

The top of his desk was buried under piles of back copies of the Asbury Park *Evening Press* and the Ocean County *Daily Observer*, the weekly Lakewood *Daily Times*, Tuckerton *Beacon*, Point Pleasant Beach *Leader*, and a Toms River shopper called *The Reporter*, as well as stacks of cheap beige newsprint cut into letter-sized sheets for typing copy. On a metal return at a right angle against the wall was an ancient Underwood, stripped of its top casing to make fixing its frequent ribbon jams easier. Behind him in a small closet the AP and UPI teletype machines clattered. When he talked to people on the phone, they heard the teletypes tap-tap-tapping in the background, which he thought was a cool touch.

He sighed at the pile of work waiting in his In box. Ignoring it, he opened the file of clippings labeled "Eddie Bonneville's Greatest Hits." What stories could he wave in Frank's face to show that if he fired him he'd be foolishly depriving himself of an enterprising, aggressive reporter? His first assignment at the *Independent*, given, he suspected, to see if he could really write, had been a twelve-part series called "1968: The

Year That Was," a review of the biggest stories in Ocean County that year. They included coverage of the Shore's first big drug raid, Jersey Devil sightings, septic pollution in the Metedeconk River so drastic that fumes had peeled the paint off several houses, and an interview with a carpet store owner and local John Birch Society president who had run for the Township Committee in Brick on the George Wallace ticket. Over the summer, he'd added coverage from the Atlantic City Pop Festival in July and the Woodstock festival in August and a weekend long jazz festival at the Garden State Arts Center. He'd come home glowing from Woodstock only to plunge into a sleepless, manic week covering an ugly race riot in Lakewood that ruined his rock festival-inspired optimism, but gave him another nice pile of clippings. That fall, he wrote stories about the October anti-Vietnam war moratorium in Ocean County and on-the-scene coverage of the November march on Washington D.C., including a story about what it was like to be tear gassed. Not bad for a 19-year-old reporter's first year as a professional journalist, whether Frank thought so or not.

How about his big story from a few weeks ago? *Prosecutor Admits to Secret Grand Jury, Calls Matty Esposito Shore Rackets Boss.* His story revealing the investigation of Esposito, a local hotel owner and labor leader, had scooped everybody else. Were any of the other reporters in the newsroom, love 'em though he did, getting that kind of scoop? Certainly his weekly column, which attracted youthful readers to the *Independent,* counted for something? He put the "Hell No I Won't Go" clipping in the file with the angry responses. Maybe Frank had a weed up his ass because people got so angry about that piece. Sometimes it was all too easy to fantasize scenes in which Frank unjustly and capriciously fired him, treating him as if he didn't even deserve an explanation. But would Frank really fire him over a few angry letters, even the ones that called him a traitor? One of them screamed YOU ARE NOT A REAL AMERICAN! He taped it on the bulletin board over his typewriter.

He pulled the top off his steaming coffee, grabbed a donut, and scanned today's edition. The *Independent* had positioned itself as an aggressive alternative to the sober, broadsheet Asbury Park *Evening Press* and the slapdash, tabloid *Observer.* But Christmas week was always slow for news. A man and woman who had disappeared after leaving Castellucci's Lounge one night a year ago were still missing. Troop C of the State Police in Brick Township had arrested two 18-year-old youths for intent to sell marijuana. A drug and alcohol rehab facility planned for an old hotel in Lakehurst was causing a roar of protest from the neighbors and was unlikely to go forward. Three motor vehicle accidents in one day on icy roads in Lakewood had sent three people to Paul Kimball Hospital with minor injuries. The Point Pleasant Borough Council debated whether to close the Lovelandtown Bridge, a rickety wooden structure spanning a canal that quivered beneath your wheels when you drove over it. There were good odds for a white Christmas.

Spread across most of page three was his 30 day update on the disappearance of his friend Kenny Rosenfeld, the organizer of a movement to put a stop to home building in Ocean County. After Rosenfeld went missing, he'd run down every lead and rumor no matter how flimsy, but he got nowhere. He'd haunted the county detective bureau, but they were stymied, too. Rosenfeld was simply gone. He clipped the story to an earlier piece with a picture of Rosenfeld: *Development Foe Disappears, Police Without Clues*, by Edward Bonneville, who also had no clue.

Kenny Rosenfeld's disappearance was troubling. If anything bad had happened to Rosenfeld he was afraid he was partly to blame. He was a story Eddie had broken exclusively and done some of his best writing on. Rosenfeld had formed a group that called for a moratorium on new home building to slow down the population explosion in Ocean, the fastest growing county in America. In townships overflowing with new children with North Jersey accents, the cost of building schools and providing them with an education had sent taxes skyrocketing. Giving publicity to Rosenfeld and his anti-development movement had gotten Frank a lot of complaints from local business owners and big developers, but Eddie kept writing about Rosenfeld because he'd overheard Frank say the moratorium movement was viewed as a potential threat by the county Republican machine. And Eddie liked Rosenfeld, a hyper L.A. Jew and local community college professor of history who was popular with his students. He looked like a college student himself: long curly black hair and a floppy Fu Manchu moustache, partial to Mickey Mouse T-shirts and bell-bottomed jeans and sneakers, and a gliding, slinky way of walking, like a character out of an R. Crumb cartoon. He was politically radical, energetic, and fearless, the kind of guy who would challenge the power structure no matter where he lived. They had just become friends, reporter and subject, eating together, talking on the phone, trading information, when Rosenfeld and his car vanished without a trace one night in November.

Frank's voice out by the reception desk jolted Eddie's mind back to the present.

"Oh yeah? Tell 'em thanks, but *no* thanks, know what I mean?"

"Sure thing, Daddy," he heard Bailey say.

In his trench coat and tweed golf hat, Frank Devlin swaggered into the newsroom.

"Hello, scriveners!" he said to the room. As he hung up his hat and coat, Frank's bright blue eyes, roving and mischievous, swung over to Eddie. Frank slumped into the chair beside his desk and blew out a long sigh. Eddie prepared himself for the worst.

Lean and laconic, still devilishly handsome to the ladies at fifty, Frank slicked his black hair back from a widow's peak, sharp like his long eyebrows and thin lips. He liked polka dot ties and collar pins, dressed off the rack from the local Robert Hall store in dark gray and blue two button suits that hung loose on his matchstick body, and wore the top model Florsheim wingtips. An aura of bourbon, tobacco smoke and Old Spice surrounded him. Frank had spent World War II editing copy for *Stars and Stripes* in Washington, then became the Newark Evening *News* bureau chief at the Shore until ten years ago when he launched the Ocean County *Independent* as a weekly tabloid out of his home, printing the paper on one of the local weekly's presses until he could rent office space and take out a loan to buy a photo offset press. The paper started publishing weekdays about three years ago and was rumored to be just squeaking by, financially.

Eddie thought any reporter would be lucky to have Frank for his editor. He was a tough, consummate newsman, quick to cut to the heart of any story. The look in his eye always hinted that he knew more than you did, even about yourself. He could be moody, and he was a bad drunk. Eddie had driven Frank home all but unconscious more than once.

"You were looking for me before?" he said.

"Nah, it was nothing," Frank said. *Nothing!* "I hear you got a lot of reactions to your column."

He handed him the messages. Frank glanced through them, chuckling. "This doesn't count the calls I got today from the VFW, the American Legion, and a few people who thought you should be fired."

"Did anybody agree with me?"

"Not that I heard." His eyebrows lifted and he gave a short laugh. "Jesus, a *lamppost?*" He tossed the messages on the desk. "This anti-war kick you're on is not good for my ulcer."

"The war's given the whole country an ulcer, Frank."

"Yeah, but around here, people are picking up the *Independent* to read the latest outrage from that psycho peacenik Eddie Bonneville. You're the hippie they love to hate."

"Yeah, but doesn't that sell papers?" Eddie's phone rang, he grabbed it. "Eddie Bonneville…Hey, Nicky." Nick Poliandro was his competitor at the *Press,* but he sometimes did Eddie the collegial favor, like now. "He announced this when? Hey, thanks, man. I'll be right over." He stood, hung up the phone. "County detectives just picked up Matty Esposito, they're bringing him in for arraignment."

Frank nodded. "Yeah, I know. Stay put. Jackson'll cover it. You work the Out Box." He pushed himself up from the chair and shuffled to his office, humming, having just condemned Eddie to an hour of rewriting a pile of turgid press releases, disheartening obituaries and boring photo captions.

Eddie dropped back in his seat, grabbed his Lucky Strikes and lit one. So this was the "nothing" Frank wanted earlier, to keep him away from the arraignment. He stubbed the cigarette out in the clamshell ashtray, closed his eyes, and took five long, slow breaths as he had trained himself to do. It didn't work. He got up and trailed Frank back to his office. Calmly, he told himself, let us calmly inquire just what the *fuck* was going on.

Frank slouched behind his desk in an oversize black leather chair, talking to J. Paul Jackson, who stood with his arms crossed and his cigarette holder between his fingers. The golden lamplight in Frank's large office cast a rich glow on the dark wooden walls and chairs around the conference table and on the beige carpet and sofa, but to Eddie the shadowy room felt sinister. The smoke rose lazily from the two men's cigarettes as, frozen in mid-conversation, they turned to him.

"Yeah?" Frank said.

"Why aren't I covering Esposito's arraignment?" Eddie said. The table was heaped with page proofs. He pushed a few aside and sat down.

"Jackson's the courthouse reporter. And we're on an early deadline tonight because of the Christmas party."

"But this is *my* story," he said. "I got a one-day scoop on everybody when the grand jury was formed."

"It was a *secret* grand jury, until your, uh, scoop," Jackson said in his syrupy drawl. "Thanks to you, the prosecutor's ready to tear us all a new asshole." The *all* was not-so-subtly accented—you cost me, kid. Or was he jealous Eddie got the story by poaching on his news beat?

"Heckendorfer says he talked to you off the record," Frank said, "and you quoted him anyway."

"He called you? About me?"

"Yeah. He's still pissed off."

"Is that why I'm not covering?" he said. "Because Heckendorfer doesn't want me there?"

"He says you exposed his investigation and now without secrecy it'll be hard to get people to talk."

"What happened was, after the interview, after I'd filed, after the story was in paste up, *then* he called me and demanded to go off the record. I told him 'No way.' So now, what, he thinks he can keep me out of the courthouse?"

"Sometimes a source has second thoughts. Why'd you tell him no?"

"It would have allowed him to kill my story!"

"You could have held it for a day. You could have told me there was a problem."

"I was afraid it wouldn't keep for a day. Either I had it first, or not."

Jackson smirked at Frank. *The boy doesn't know how to play ball.* He said, "It's always better to have the prosecutor owe you a favor, Edward."

"He may be prosecutor," Eddie said, "but the man's got no respect for a press card!"

"You've only *had* a press card, for what, a year?" Frank said. "So for a one-day scoop on a crime story, you bought yourself years of hostility—and from a prosecutor, no less!" He and Jackson had a prolonged chuckle. "Not smart, kid. Jackson, get going."

Which the older reporter did, leaving Eddie standing there. He'd been afraid of something like this. Lately it seemed like Frank was trying to cut him down to size, but why? A jealous snake in the high grass around the newsroom?

"I'll tackle the Out Box when I get back from dinner." He turned and stalked out.

At a few minutes before five o'clock he was up in Toms River on the top floor of the county courthouse. Most of the courts had just adjourned for the day, and the corridor was full, milling with police in uniforms from different towns, jurors wearing white tags on their lapels, and sullen defendants looking hopefully or hatefully at their lawyers.

He slouched on a long oak bench outside Judge Abraham Geifel's courtroom alongside Morris Goldhirsch, the *Independent*'s staff photographer. Goldy was a 50-year-old cynic, legendary among local journalists for his fearlessness, his flawless eye and perfect timing. He'd just won a state journalism award for a picture captured at the precise moment a Korean War veteran had jumped onstage at Ocean County College and punched a bearded professor speaking out against the Vietnam war. Goldy's large dark eyes and slick black hair made him look like a brother to Peter Lorre and he had the same sly, knowing chuckle. He spoke with a Brooklyn accent, chain-smoked Kent cigarettes, and had a rude charm that women found irresistible.

Beside him was Nick Poliandro, Eddie's friend, former colleague and now newsbeat rival, a clean cut, voluble reporter for the Asbury Park *Evening Press*. A few years older than Eddie, he dressed better than most lawyers, with short black hair and a neat moustache. The *Press* had a dress code, just like high school.

Nick reached across Goldy and poked Eddie's shoulder. "What do you mean, I'm *smug*? What're you talkin' about?"

He was easily riled, and Eddie enjoyed needling him.

"When you wrote for the *Independent*, you were hungry," Eddie said. "Now you're smug and secure, making the big bucks working for Asbury. Face it, Nicky, you're too comfortable. That's why I keep beating you to stories."

"Not to mention all the broads he's banging and you're not," Goldy told Nick with a languid chuckle.

"You know why you beat me to stories? You knock on doors at midnight. You hound people 'til they break down. You publish off the record quotes. You want more?"

" 'The purpose of journalism is to comfort the afflicted, and to afflict the comfortable'," Eddie said. He wasn't exactly sure who said that. H. L. Mencken? Mark Twain? Whoever it was, he had adopted it as his philosophy of reporting. It was like what Crane told him once: a reporter doesn't work for the signature on his paycheck, he works for the people who read the paper.

"The purpose of journalism," Nick corrected him, "is to inform the public. Without fear or favor."

"The *real* purpose of journalism," Goldy yawned, "is to come up with stuff to stick between the ads that pay our salaries. Some day, maybe you kids'll get that."

Excited voices came echoing up the corridor. *All right, all right, here we go!* Camera flashes silvered the walls and ceiling.

Goldy nudged Eddie as he rolled to his feet. "Let's go to work, Prince Valiant." He hefted his Pentax and melted into the crowd.

Nicky grabbed Eddie's sleeve. "Meet me at Castellucci's later. I gotta talk to you."

"You're not really pissed off at me, are you?"

"No, no. Something good."

Three people emerged as the crowd parted in the corridor. One of them was a man Eddie knew all too well: Ivy's father, the Republican organization powerbroker and former State Senator Thomas Porter, a handsome, barrel-chested Toms River celebrity in a black chalk-stripe suit, red tie and black overcoat, beaming his campaign smile to the folks who watched him pass. With him was a bored-looking blonde of about thirty, with black eyes and brows, full red lips and a red scarf tied around the upturned collar of her white rabbit fur jacket, wearing jeans and white high-heeled Go-Go boots.

Between them, grimacing at the camera flashes, trudged Matty 'The Mule' Esposito. He looked like an immigrant ditch digger forced to put down his shovel for a minute to deal with some legal aggravation. He wore black mailman's shoes with thick soles, gray twill work trousers, a dark red rayon shirt buttoned to the neck under a plain gray jacket, and a black porkpie hat. His teeth gritted around a huge, unlit cigar jutting from the side of his mouth, his eyebrows and the corners of his mouth hung down. He wore thick black eyeglasses, and he was clearly pissed off at all the attention.

Eddie nodded to Senator Porter, who looked right through him. The Senator had hated him from the first day Ivy brought him home, and despite his political cordiality with Eddie's father, warned his daughter that Eddie was low class. His romance with Ivy had been over for months, but if the Senator knew that he was still not willing to cut him any slack. The contempt was mutual, but the Senator could at least acknowledge him as a member of the working press.

Outside the courtroom doors, Nick grinned and yelled out, "Hey Mad-day! Are you really the Rackets Boss of the Jersey Shore?"

"Fuck you, kid." Esposito's loud gravelly voice echoed in the marble corridor. He disappeared into the courtroom.

Nick backed off, pleased with himself. "Some choice for a lawyer, huh?"

Eddie was intrigued, too. If Esposito was the gangster that the prosecutor claimed, and if the Senator was as respectable as he wanted people to think, it was an odd match.

Eddie shrugged. "Now that he's an ex-Senator, I guess he has to do a little work. Pay for that big house by the golf course."

"Matty The Mule's sportin' quite the arm piece, y'notice?" Goldy stuck a cigarette in his smirk and watched the blonde pass by. "Wouldn't mind grabbing a little of that myself."

In the courtroom, J. Paul Jackson took the *Independent*'s regular seat at the press table alongside Nick. Eddie took a seat in the first gallery row next to Buzz Thompson, the police chief of Dover Township and a high school classmate of Eddie's parents. Tall and lean, with a face of chiseled granite and short silvery hair, the chief leaned toward Eddie. "A lot of people've been waiting a long time to see this guinea bastard in front of a judge."

Earl Heckendorfer leaned forward at the prosecutor's table and scribbled on a yellow legal pad with a Bic pen, biting his lower lip like a slow-witted student frowning over a tough exam. A well-fed, curly-headed blond man of forty in a dark suit and gold tie, Heckendorfer had been plucked from obscurity as a mediocre defense attorney and made the Republican candidate for prosecutor two years ago on the assumption he could be controlled just like any other office holder. He was now considered a major mistake by the Organization. They'd had to slip thirty nine votes into the ballot box to prevent a Democrat from becoming prosecutor, which would have been a disaster, and instead of being grateful, Heckendorfer became haughty and impressed with himself.

He sat back and glanced around. When he saw that Eddie was disobeying his order to keep out of the courthouse, his gray eyes went as cold as the December sky.

"All rise," the bailiff called out.

Judge Abraham Geifel scampered in from his chambers and climbed up on his high seat behind the bench, barely able to see over the edge. "Be seated, please." A small gray man with a high voice and enormous glasses, he rapped his gavel. Senator Porter nudged Esposito and gestured with his eyes and the old man removed his hat.

"Good afternoon, Senator," the judge said merrily.

"Waive reading of the charges, Your Honor. My client pleads not guilty." Porter said. "In light of Mister Esposito's deep ties to this community as a hotel owner and labor leader, we request you kindly release him on his own recognizance."

The judge raised his gavel to swiftly and obediently end the arraignment.

"Your Honor?" Heckendorfer pushed himself onto his feet, his slow Piney drawl stressing each word. "These are serious charges, Your Honor. Loansharking. Gambling. Labor racketeering." The reporters in front of Eddie came alive like bird dogs on a scent, not at the charges, but because Senator Porter had been defied in open court by a prosecutor who presumably kissed his ring to get his job. "Mr. Esposito is a career criminal with his tentacles in many different areas. He owns a house in Florida. No question there's a risk of flight. R–O–R? I don't think so."

Judge Geifel, gavel hovering, cast his eyes helplessly toward the Senator.

"I got unions to run, Judge!" Esposito shouted. "And I'm a hotel owner!" He turned and snarled at the prosecutor: "Where the hell you think I'm gonna go?"

"It's a *nice* hotel," Judge Geifel said, as if that was the issue. "I've taken my wife to dinner and dancing there." An awkward silence. "Many times." People looked at each other and shrugged, because the Sunset Lodge had closed years ago. "Before she died, poor thing—"

Calmly, Senator Porter said, "Your Honor?"

Judge Geifel, noticing he still held the gavel, rapped it a couple times. "R–O–R." The Senator nodded and, seeing that he had done well, Judge Geifel grinned. "And if there's nothing else, I'd like to wish everyone a very Merry Christmas."

Esposito spit out, "Aggh," and dismissed the whole proceeding with a disgusted wave of the hand. He jammed his hat on, turned and pushed his way through the crowd and out of the courtroom, dragging his girlfriend behind him.

Heckendorfer sighed and tossed his pen and pad into his attache case, snapped it shut, and marched out of the courtroom in a huff.

Chief Thompson blew air out his nose, his mouth twisted. "Well, there's justice once the lawyers get ahold of it, Eddie. Of course, it doesn't help that Abe Geifel's too senile to know who's even standing in front of him."

"Can I quote you on that?"

"You do, you'll never get another story out of me."

As Eddie turned to leave, Senator Porter beckoned him over.

"Hello, Senator."

"Listen to me, Eddie." Porter talked with a slight sneer and a lisp. *Lishen da me.*

"Why is a guy like you lawyer for a guy like him?"

Ignoring him, Porter laid a hand on his shoulder, and said, close to his ear, "Ivy's coming home for Christmas. Keep away from her, or you'll be sorry."

"How about answering my question?"

With a disgusted snort, he brushed Eddie aside and walked off.

The courtroom was emptying, and nobody seemed to notice his embarrassment. He stared at the Senator's back wishing his eyes were the double barrels of a shotgun. God damn Senator Porter, not for that push or for the bad history between them, but for revealing that Ivy would be in town. He'd rather not know.

Trying to persuade himself Senator Porter wasn't worth hating, he turned a corner in the corridor and found himself face to face with his lawyer and landlord, Billy Foster, sitting on a bench outside a courtroom beside a sulking hippie in work clothes. A suave, handsome man of thirty-three, wearing a three-piece suit, Billy glanced up from scribbling on a case report.

"Merry Christmas, Bonneville. You're twenty-three days late with the rent."

"I told you. I've got to save for Canada. In case I have to go."

"I didn't hear that, as your landlord, your lawyer, or as your friend."

Don't be so quick to be honest, Eddie told himself. But if he couldn't be honest with Billy, then who?

"My C.O. hearing is next Monday, the twenty ninth."

"Great. Today they'll read your column. I'm sure Monday it'll still be fresh in their minds. Nice timing."

"That's when they ordered me to appear. Are you saying you're not available? I can't go to a hearing without my lawyer."

"I'm saying the board's going to see you as a anti-war loudmouth," Billy said, capping his pen. "You ride in there on your white horse, the System's gonna have you for lunch, and when you come out the other end, you'll either be in prison or Vietnam."

Eddie listened to Billy and trusted him. After his disastrous last boxing match, Billy arranged Eddie's guilty plea to assaulting the referee in exchange for a suspended sentence and probation. In the spring of '68 after his father kicked him out, Eddie moved into the efficiency apartment on the top floor of Billy's house on the beach in Bay Head. After he got the job reporting for the *Independent* he wrote a profile of Billy's work as the local ACLU leader and from those interviews grew their friendship.

"Y'know Bonneville, I like doing ACLU work, but it doesn't pay my mortgage."

Eddie sighed. "I'll leave it on the kitchen table."

"Groovy."

Back in the newsroom he tried to write, but he couldn't concentrate with the Christmas party underway and raucous voices singing.

> *Oh Little Town Mc Tierneyville*
> *How still we see thee lie,*
> *Above thy deep and dreamless sleep*
> *The silent stars go by*

The *Independent*'s newsroom Christmas party had to be held tonight. Tomorrow was Christmas Eve, a day off for everyone because the paper didn't publish on Christmas day. The room was jammed with *Independent* editors and reporters, advertising sales people, the girls from the composing room and the Greek press manager Kosmo and his crew, as well as publicists, lawyers, politicians and cops and the local business people who advertised in the paper and who provided the assorted pizzas, the ten foot submarine sandwiches sliced into six inch pieces, the piles of cookies, the cases of Heineken beer and Korbel champagne, a small aluminum Christmas tree and a meager string of twinkling lights.

Eddie sat behind his typewriter in the back corner of the newsroom, with more important things to do than join the Christmas party. The guest of honor was a politician who amused the local press, the mayor of Manchester Township, Joseph R. McTierney, a roly poly backslapper with tight curly hair in a beige double-knit suit with big lapels and a wide yellow floral tie. He was the second son of the legendary late political boss Col. Ted McTierney, and his older brother Roy was the heir to the Organization their old man built. Joe Mac lifted his Heineken bottle in salute to the news staff of the *Independent* and grinned, a prince feted by his loyal subjects. When Eddie had been assigned to the Manchester news beat, the mayor was the first official to walk over and shake his hand in welcome. On Township Committee meeting nights, once Eddie had written his stories, sometimes he'd have drinks with the Manchester crowd at Citta's Old Time Tavern, a political watering hole on the outskirts of Toms River. Last summer at the county Republican picnic, Joe Mac put his arm around Eddie's shoulders, treating him like an important peer, and introduced him around to various dignitaries, warning them, "He's the press, so watch out what you say."

Taking a drag on a Lucky Strike, Eddie resumed typing, undecided if he was writing a news story or a column:

```
In addition to fingering a Lakewood hotel owner and
labor official as a major crime figure at the Jersey
Shore, this indictment raises many questions.
```

Yeah, okay, like what? Like… like…

He slumped back and with one finger tapped a line of X's through the one sentence he'd managed to write. What did he really *know*? For months the city newspapers, even the New York *Times*, had published stories based on FBI wiretap transcripts of intimate conversations among members of an alleged North Jersey Mafia family run by Simone "Sam The Plumber" DeCavalcante. Last June, when the Feds filed the transcripts with the court clerk in Decavalcante's extortion trial, they became public record and privileged, which sent reporters tearing through the thousands of pages digging out stories they could publish without fear of libel—not that the Mafia ever settled its disputes in court. Eddie had begged his editor to buy the 13 volume transcripts to search for local angles, but Frank wouldn't pay the $95 court fee. "These aren't local stories," he scoffed, "just a lotta North Jersey goombah stuff."

Eager as Eddie was to write something, he really knew nothing about Esposito except the indictment and a lot of rumors. Maybe there was nothing there, maybe that lard ass prosecutor was calling him the Rackets Boss of the Jersey Shore to make himself look like a big crime buster. Esposito was probably nothing more than a loudmouth who liked to give public officials heartburn. With his grating voice, dressed in clothes that looked like they were bought at a Clifton Avenue haberdashery in the 1940s, he sure didn't resemble the courtly Don Corleone in *The Godfather* novel, or dour old Frank Nitti from *The Untouchables* on TV, or even Neville Brand playing Scarface Al. Most people knew Matty Esposito as a union boss or as a gadfly at Lakewood Township Committee meetings, griping about the waste of his tax money. Eddie wanted to write his own stories about the Mafia underworld the FBI was uncovering in New Jersey, but he was beginning to doubt that a story on Matty Esposito was going to win anybody a Pulitzer Prize.

He'd met Esposito last summer on the second night of the Lakewood riots, hanging around the police coffee wagon outside headquarters on Third Street. Eddie introduced himself and asked him for a comment on the disorder. Esposito threw up his hands: "I'm outraged! The people who run this town, they claim they were taken by surprise by this," he said. "They didn't see it coming? You'd have to be blind not to see this coming! Everybody knows with the blacks and the police there's always problems. Maybe both sides got good reasons, who knows? But first, you got all the problems the town fathers ignore, dope, poverty, lousy housing, no jobs, nothing for the kids to do. Then you got hot weather. People're on edge. One night there's a fight, maybe the police get a little rough breaking it up or arresting somebody, maybe somebody spreads a lie like they did last night, claiming somebody got beat up or killed by the cops. Then whattya got? Boom!" Esposito told it like he saw it and didn't seem to care how people felt about it. Eddie used his best quote to lead off one of his man-in-the-street stories: "This situation was like gasoline waitin' for a match!"

Before he could start writing again, Frank walked over from the party and invited him to have a drink at Castellucci's. Obediently, he grabbed his coat and went along. He expected to get yelled at for going to the arraignment against Frank's orders, but Frank seemed eager to drown any bad feeling lingering from that afternoon.

The menus at Castellucci's Lounge were subtitled "A little touch of Las Vegas," but if he closed his eyes in the cool dark and listened to the babble of rough staccato voices, he could imagine he was in Naples, or at least Bayonne. One entire wall was a highly lacquered black bar with tall mirrors behind rows of liquor bottles. With the bar at his back, Eddie gazed across three wide terraces each with fifty tables facing the bandstand. The waitresses in scanty outfits bustled in and out of the kitchen with their trays laden with steaks and lobsters and pasta, serving the State Troopers and local cops who made the lounge their off-duty recreation room, and the businessmen in silk suits and pinkie rings who greeted each other Old World style with a kiss on the cheek, holding their big cigars out to one side. The bartenders, Tino and Matthew, looked like weightlifters and Roberto, the two-fifty, six-four doorman, was their big brother.

In the midst of the chatter and clinking of glasses and the aroma of booze and beef and tobacco smoke and cosmetics, Eddie knew that with his long hair, work clothes and leather jacket he was out of place, despite the saloon's relationship with the newspaper. All the *Independent* employees had to cash their paychecks across the bar at Castellucci's every week. He'd learned the system the first time he tried to cash his check at the First National Bank of Toms River and the teller called the manager over and they looked at his paycheck, looked at him, and laughed—didn't he know the *Independent*'s bank accounts had no money in them? Back at the newsroom, the paper's accountant shrugged and sent him next door.

"'Ey, Mista Devlin, Mista Bonneville," growled a voice. Bobby Castellucci slapped them both on the back, his fingers scented with cinnamon cologne. "Merry Christmas, and a cool time at Yule time."

"Mister Castellucci," Frank said, shaking hands. Castellucci snapped his fingers to the bartender, who lined up three shots of Chivas Regal on the bar.

Castellucci, who was somewhere in his thirties, was tall, with thick shoulders and neck, and had glistening but expressionless eyes in a shiny, acne-scarred face. He wore a tuxedo with a frilly shirt front, and his long black hair was razor-cut and blow dried, with fuzzy mutton chop sideburns. Talking to Eddie and Frank, his attention constantly flickered around the room, and his tongue always seemed to be trying to free something caught in his teeth. The rumor was that his father and uncle up in Newark were the real owners of the lounge and had sent down Bobby to run the place and get him away from some trouble in the city.

Eddie wasn't sure where he stood with Castellucci, and he always watched what he said around him. These Bennies, with their city attitudes, sometimes they were hard to read. When Castellucci smiled, he grimaced, and there was no mirth in his eyes.

"Frank, whattya say we buy this kid a haircut for Christmas?" He flipped Eddie's hair off his collar. "You look like a friggin' caveman." They all laughed.

Eddie rolled his eyes. "Hey, wait a minute, man," he said, "who does *your* hair?"

"It's the new thing, it's called a shag, my girlfriend does it," he said, patting his hair in the mirror behind the bar. "Decided to change my look. I'm thinking lately the club needs an update from the Vegas look too, whattya think?"

"Nah," Frank drawled, "the place looks great, it *always* looks great, Bob." Anyplace Frank could drink for free was by definition 'great.'

"There's some rock bands around you could book," Eddie said. "There's a great band called Steel Mill. They got this guy Bruce—"

"I said *update*," Castellucci said. "I ain't about to open the doors to a bunch of hippies with no shoes."

"And no money," Frank chuckled.

Castellucci passed them their drinks and raised his glass. "To the New Year, the new decade, and uh, whatever'da fuck else comes down the pike." Eddie gulped half, then tried not to show how much it burned. Frank tossed back his whole drink and gripped the bar, blinking and shaking his head.

"You guys oughta come by tomorrow night." Castellucci brushed his jacket and tugged his tie, checking himself in the mirror. "We got the best Christmas party at the Shore. Best of everything."

"Too bad I've got the in-laws," Frank said.

"Maybe I'll swing by," Eddie offered.

"Not dressed like that you won't," Castellucci said.

"I have a suit somewhere," Eddie said. "I even have a pair of cufflinks."

Castellucci decided Eddie wasn't making fun of him and laughed.

A new round of drinks appeared. From the jukebox came a tinkling piano, and Tom Jones swore he'd never fall in love again.

"So," Castellucci said, "the law finally nailed Matty Esposito." Eddie was surprised he'd heard so quick, since the arraignment was only a couple hours ago. "Big story for you guys, eh?"

"An indictment's only an accusation," Eddie said. "Where's Kenny Rosenfeld? That's the story I want."

"Nah, Matty The Mule's a better story," Castellucci said, looking behind Eddie's back at Frank, "once you get him talking."

"Eddie," said Frank, setting his empty glass on the bar, "you've already called him, right?"

"After I got back from the arraignment. No answer."

"I want you to go after Matty Esposito for a comment on the indictment. Full court press. See what he says, and call me, okay?"

Maybe it was the Chivas Regal, or because he was paying attention to the jukebox or the waitresses jiggling as they rushed around, but Eddie didn't notice that Frank had just turned an off-hand remark from Bobby Castellucci into an assignment.

"He'll be a man of two words," Eddie said. "*Fuck you.*"

It was no joke, but Frank laughed. Well, if Frank found him so entertaining, why was he pushing him into a pen with an irritable bulldog? Screw it, he'd make the phone call, Esposito would growl and tell him to get lost, and at least he could tell Frank he tried.

"Believe me," Castellucci said. "When he's pissed off, he talks." The bartender tapped him on the shoulder and handed him the phone. Eddie saw Frank was waiting for an answer.

"I'll call him, okay?"

"Let me know how it goes."

Castellucci motioned Frank over and murmured something to him. While they had their heads together, Eddie sipped his drink and looked around the club, *The Jersey Shore's Number 1 Lounge*, according to the ads. Onstage the dinner show was beginning, and a thickset Sinatra imitator in a tuxedo and toupee snapped his fingers while he and his five musicians grooved on a swingin' medley of Christmas carols. From a nearby booth Nick waved him over. That's right, he had "something good" for him. Eddie turned to speak to Castellucci and Frank, but they were gone, their glasses standing half empty on the bar.

On the sidewalk, Nick and Eddie lingered, smoking and shivering. It had stopped snowing, leaving a light dusting on the pavement.

"Are you ever gonna quit working for Frank Devlin?" Nick said.

"I owe the guy. He gave me a job."

"Yeah, but we want to give you a better job on a better paper."

"Well, I need money for college, but I'd have to cut my hair and wear a tie."

Nick had made the job offer several drinks earlier. At first, Eddie had been flattered. But then he pictured Frank's disappointment if he went to work for the *Press*, and he lost his nerve, and avoided giving Nick an answer.

"By the way, what's your number in the Draft lottery?"

"One ninety-five. Why?"

"We don't hire guys with low numbers. Our training's wasted if we lose them to the Army."

"Or worse?"

"Ivy coming home for Christmas?"

"I hear she's coming home."

"Great." Nick started to leave. "Are you gonna be all right?"

"Yeah, so long as I don't get sucked back into her crazy life."

Nick laughed and shook his head. "I mean driving. You've had a few drinks."

"Oh. No. Yeah. I'm cool."

Eddie watched Nick drive away in an immaculate two door Pontiac. His hands were cold. He jammed them into his pockets. Passing the *Independent*'s front windows, he looked in at the noisy party still going full blast. He didn't want to go back inside. He never knew what to talk about at parties. The people in the scene before his eyes might've come from the used book of Edward Hopper paintings he'd been obsessing over since he bought it at the Englishtown Auction. Through a mist of Scotch he saw the party framed in the window as if painted by Hopper, the people frozen in the moment, the longing to connect in their bodies but their eyes focused on the distance between them. Nothing like a few drinks to inspire him to brood on the human condition—or was it his own condition that worried him? He wondered if all human beings woke up lonely in the middle of the night, lonely beyond "Eleanor Rigby," lonely without even God as the conversation of last resort. His coworkers were surely like people everywhere, huddling for warmth, hoping for meaning, while he stood on the sidewalk alone, looking in, proud of needing nobody. When he got in the Impala and started the engine, "Hey Jude" came on the radio. He turned it up loud.

Christmas Eve dawned frigid and bright and he rushed through some last-minute gift shopping. The stores on Arnold Avenue in Point Pleasant Beach were bustling and crowded, outdoor loudspeakers played Christmas songs, and despite the cold wind the sun brought out the pitch pine aroma of the trees for sale in the lot behind the hardware store. At twilight, as clouds covered the sky before an advancing snowstorm, the shoppers on the sidewalks gave a delighted "Ooooh!" as the colored lights arcing over the street came on with the streetlights.

Back in his apartment on the beach in Bay Head, he poured a drink from the bottle of Cutty Sark that Frank had given him and wrapped his presents. He was on his second drink and dressing for family dinner—his father was allowing him home at his mother's insistence—when the phone rang.

"Hello?"

"Merry Christmas, champ," said a voice that seemed to come from deep inside of him.

He froze, wishing he hadn't answered the phone.

"Is it okay to tell you I miss you?" Ivy said.

"Hi." Needlessly, he asked, "Uhhh…who is this?"

A sigh. "I told you all those punches would fuck up your head."

Calmly—somehow—he said, "Sometimes people do that, too."

"C'mon man, it's been three months. You're still pissed off at me?"

"I don't know. I really don't think about it—"

"Yeah? Well, you know what? Call me when you know, okay? Bye—"

"Hey, wait."

She waited… silently. Typical Ivy—she called him, but suddenly *he* was struggling to keep the conversation going. How had she managed to do that?

"Okay, so I'm still a little bruised." He couldn't believe what he was saying. "I'm mostly over it. How are you?"

"Who, me? I'm fine," she said, her voice hollow and unconvincing.

"Oh yeah? What's wrong?" He'd been asking that since they were 15. There was always something wrong, and he always had to drag it out of her.

"Nothing, champ. I don't want to involve you in my problems."

"Too late for that, don't you think? I saw your father in court yesterday. He told me you're coming home, and I'd better stay away from you, or else."

Ivy made the puking sound that used to make him laugh. Now it made him miss her.

"Luckily, I was in a good mood, so he got away *unscathed*."

"Yes, well, Senator and Mrs. Ruling Class have ordered me home for a Christmas of cocktails and chilly silences at the Porter Residence. And I figured, since I'm gonna be home—"

Quickly, before hesitation or fear of how she would react could stop him: "I'll be really busy. I'm up to my neck in work."

"Oh. So maybe, if you have the time, what? You'll *fit me in*? I'm coming home for Christmas, man! Are we gonna have a rockin' time or what? You don't sound very into this—"

"It's not that, it's just that I'm covering a couple big stories, my Draft hearing is coming up—"

"Are you seeing anyone?"

"No. I mean, nobody serious."

"So? Meet me when my train gets in tonight." She made it sound so simple; it would be anything but. "Eddie—I know I hurt you, but Jesus—what, do you hate me now, too? You gettin' like everybody else down there?" It was the worst thing she could say.

"You got some fuckin' balls, you know that? Saying that to *me*, of all people!"

"Look man, life in New York's kinda hairy at the moment. I could really use a little love and understanding." She waited for him to take the cue, but he refused to be jerked around by her calculated silence. "You realize this is the first Christmas we're not together since we were fifteen?"

"The thought crossed my mind." At least once an hour.

"Well, I'm not handling that too good. Okay?"

"Yeah, I'm not either." As soon as he said that he knew he'd made a mistake, but it was too late. "All right, it's a little after five. Call me when you know what train you're taking, and I'll pick you up." He hung up the phone with a long, ragged sigh.

She hung up more relieved than happy. Shivering, her breath fogging the phone booth on La Guardia Place, she wiped the glass, and there was her reflection. She made a face at herself and shrugged, tightened the red wool scarf around her neck and raised the collar of her worn black leather motorcycle jacket, and plunged back into the cold evening.

At least Eddie was willing to see her. He wasn't happy to hear from her and was undoubtedly kicking himself for agreeing to meet the train. Nothing new there. He always put himself through the most miserable trips. But this time she really needed him; by his side might be the only place in the world where she would be safe. She doubted he had a girlfriend. That *nobody serious* was a dodge if she'd ever heard one. More likely, Eddie was stuck; he wanted to avoid her, but he couldn't help himself. Well, this time, she couldn't help herself either.

NYU students, white collar office types, hippies, workmen in blue denim carrying toolboxes, all sorts of people walking home at the end of the day streamed around her as she crossed Washington Square Park. She walked around the fountain, shivering and cursing the dry cold that seeped down her jeans and made her ass cheeks itch. Her boot heels clip-clopped on the cobblestones under the Arch and up the sidewalk on Fifth Avenue, just another long-legged Village beauty in blue jeans and a leather jacket urgently going somewhere, turning heads as she passed.

Ivy went east off Fifth and walked halfway down the block, dodging black plastic garbage bags piled on old snow drifts, and climbed the stoop to a four-story brownstone. She rang the buzzer: three short, one long, three short, one long. Beethoven's Fifth.

Sylvia, vast under her denim coveralls, her basset hound face hidden deep in a nest of curly black hair, opened the door, nervously scanning the street.

"Oh. You. Yeah, c'mon in."

Ivy knew how Sylvia saw her—*political dilettante from Bumfuck New Jersey*. But like it or not, David Andrews, Ivy's lover and the dominant personality in their group, had demanded that she always be admitted to the house, even though it was owned by Sylvia's parents. Her father, a partner in a Wall Street brokerage, and her mother, a former Broadway actress, were spending Christmas in Palm Beach.

Ivy hung her coat on an intricately carved antique hall tree beside a row of leather jackets, pea coats, and green fatigues, and took a last look around at her surroundings. Having grown up in a mansion, she felt quite at home in this elegant house, built in the mid-19th century, and she kind of regretted leaving it. In a hall mirror in a gold frame she studied herself, nervously puffing out her hair, and relaxing her face into a cool mask. She would take a great mug shot, easily as pretty as Bernardine Dohrn, if the FBI ever caught up with them. Then she sighed; for once her love affair with the girl in the mirror failed to raise her spirits.

Cream, *Disraeli Gears*, was playing on the stereo inside, over a murmur of voices coming from the dining room. A cloud of tobacco and marijuana smoke hung in the softly lit foyer.

In the dining room, with its mahogany panels and crystal chandelier, marble mantelpiece over the fireplace and a Picasso and a Chagall on the walls, she walked in on exactly the kind of scene that was driving her away from here. Three men and two women sat on Hepplewhite chairs around a mahogany table for ten spread with pages of the New York *Times*, field stripping, cleaning and loading a shotgun, a hunting rifle, and several handguns. Opposite Sylvia sat the second woman in the cadre, bookish Irene, the oldest daughter of a St. Louis bank president, cleaning a revolver. Irene was small and thin, her short brown hair parted and disciplined with a few fast brushstrokes, her metal glasses perched on her long narrow nose, her thin colorless lips in a permanent sneer at wealth and privilege, starting with her own. Irene was the one who brought David into the group when they were lovers, but he dropped her when he met Ivy. She didn't know if Irene even cared any more, but at least she wasn't hostile, and she had the strongest mind and nerves in the group.

Ivy could never find anything appealing about the other men. Not sulky little Willie, from suburban Michigan by way of Brooks Brothers, in a button down shirt and tie and rumpled blue sports coat, for she never saw any sign Willie had the slightest interest in women or much else in life except sitting in his room typing vast angry socialist manifestos that everybody rolled their eyes over and pretended to read. Butch, on the other hand, came tall and blonde and lanky and cool from Massapequa, dressed like one of the Velvet Underground, and always made a habit of facing Ivy with his legs open and his crotch on display, a crotch, she had heard, that was rich in bacterial and parasitical wildlife, so no thanks. Then there was poor Harry the BUG—for Bitter Unrecognized Genius—who dressed the part of the worker intellectual in jeans and work boots and a poor boy cap but didn't quite have enough beard yet to look like Trotsky, and who now sat, sullen as always, pumping shotgun shells out onto the table and reloading, again and again, with an intense frown. He was wound so tight that she was certain seducing him would uncork an explosion with unpredictable results.

Sylvia passed her a fat, fuming joint, and without smoking any she passed it on to Butch. Expand her consciousness? No thank you, she was restless just being there, no need to amplify that. These people were cleaning and loading real guns, they had real plans to hurt real people, probably the kind of people she hated on instinct, but people just the same. *Life in New York's kinda hairy at the moment.* The FBI had arrest warrants on everyone at the table and could come through the door at any moment, but unless that happened in the next hour, she was going to walk out of here and run for her life. One last devious conversation with David was ahead of her. For the hundredth time that day she reviewed her doubts, and told herself she was making the right decision, even if her heart wasn't in it.

The front door shut hard and everyone flinched. David always slammed the door to announce his arrival and to express his working-class contempt for the townhouse and the wealth that it symbolized. He was older, in his early thirties, an actual adult among the students. He paused in the doorway, looking around, daring anyone in the room to challenge him. His small mouth in a hard, muscular face was pursed in a way that gave his pale blue eyes an odd, pleading quality. He had long straggly brown hair, and his bulging muscles came from his last state prison stretch—inciting a riot, is what he told everybody, rather than for writing bad checks and draining his ex-wife's bank account, which was the truth. He had the Black Panther wardrobe down, black beret and leather jacket and jeans, but the lingo was a work in progress, and his cheeks were white as sour milk.

Lately, Ivy had decided the story he'd impressed the cadre with was a lie, the claim that he'd been a Green Beret in Vietnam ordered to protect a CIA drug smuggling operation, who got double crossed by his officers and kicked out of the Corps on a general discharge. The horrors he witnessed in Vietnam, he'd told them solemnly, had made him a committed revolutionary. Irene had met him in Bloomington when she was a national organizer for SDS and brought him back with her to New York. Ivy met David two months ago over dinner at a classmate's apartment on the Upper West Side near Columbia and, forgetting all about Irene, he'd cleaved to her immediately and brought her into their group. For a time, she'd felt transformed, blasted out of her complacent schoolgirl's life by his intensity. But her doubts arose one night when David got drunk and confided to her that he had no real education, political or otherwise, just a hard-working class life, a couple years of high school, and a few ideas from reading some issues of *New Left Notes.* He even told her the part about spending most of his youth in Indiana behind bars for burglary and car theft. "I'm not one of these *campus activists,*" he'd sneered. He was a real revolutionary, an image he enhanced in September by inflicting minor damage to the lobby of a bank in midtown with a small pipe bomb. He was just as explosive in bed, but lately Ivy knew she'd been a fool to take his story or anything else about David at face value.

Yet she still couldn't take her eyes off him. It was like everyone in the room had been half alive, including her, until he walked in. She looked for clues as to his mood, because David was hard to read.

"We cool, Prom Queen?" he said, ignoring the others.

"Everything's just righteous, baby," Ivy said.

"Yeah? I don't think so. I mean, dig it. Marijuana and firearms. Bad combination."

"Oh, cool it, David," Irene said.

"We were having such a nice quiet afternoon," Sylvia said, polishing a pistol.

"Quiet times are over, people." David thumped a blue canvas gym bag on the tabletop.

Willie and Irene stood up, looking startled. Sylvia nodded with a grim upward look at David. Butch's mouth fell open and he seemed frozen in his chair, but Harry lit up with excitement.

"David, this stuff really shouldn't be in the house," Irene said.

"Relax," David said, grinning at Ivy. "It's safe until you stick a fuse in it." As he followed her up the stairs, he hefted the bag and said, "We need ideas, people. I don't want to keep this shit around too long, I want to use it."

Upstairs in David's room, she told him—"Oh, by the way"—that she was catching a 9:30 train for home and wouldn't be around for Christmas. "Sorry, babe."

He didn't take it well. He slammed the door so hard the room shook. When he got this way it scared her. She had to force herself to remain calm. He slowly came over and put his face in hers.

"When the fuck was you gonna tell me, baby, huh?"

"I'm telling you now. I got the call half an hour ago. My parents are demanding I come down the Shore for Christmas." To placate him she pretended to be sad, put upon by her evil parents. In fact, she was secretly relieved they were ordering her home. She had tried to leave David all on her own but couldn't. Her parents were doing her a favor.

"I've always wanted to see the Jersey Shore in the middle of winter," he said. "So what time do we leave?"

The idea of David sipping holiday cocktails with her parents and their country club friends almost made her laugh.

"Something funny?"

"You'd never pass inspection with my people."

He grabbed her arm and pulled her face close to his. "Maybe that's why you're with me, and not some sugar tit Joe College motherfucker."

"Thank you, Doctor Freud." She pulled herself away. "Look, this isn't the family visit you see on the Christmas cards, man. I gotta TCB."

"Oh, I get it. Few days of bourgeois comfort with the folks, then baby gets that big allowance check." She wished she hadn't let David know she could be guilt-tripped about her family's wealth. "Otherwise, you might have to *work* your way through school." He used that knowledge against her often, but she always shut him up by pointing out one inconvenient fact.

"Without their checks," she said, "what would *we* live on?"

David pushed her away and lapsed into a sulk. "So, go home to Mommy and Daddy for a few days, what do I care?"

"It's not a few days, it's four weeks."

"Four weeks!"

"They know I don't really have to be back to school until late January. This year they're gonna make me stay home. If I act like a good Daughter Puppet, they write me a check, and I go back to school. That's how they want it. I hate it, I feel like a friggin' monkey on a leash, but that's the way it is."

"Can't you come up with some reason why you gotta get back to school sooner?"

"One that I haven't tried already? No."

"How hard did you try?"

"I *tried*. What are you saying, David?"

"Yeah. *You tried*." He stared at her in that way, skeptical, deeply wounded, that always drove her try to make things all right again with him. Then he snickered. "Well, that's one way the rich always get over, isn't it? Using their money like a whip to make their kids behave." It was Ivy's failure that she was loyal to her parent's money and not to him; that she was a pretty, spoiled little monkey on a leash.

He tossed his beret and peeled his leather jacket off, revealing a tight tee shirt over rippling muscles. And *there* was another reason why she had to leave here tonight and never return. Just looking at him, being near him when he was psyched up, made her melt right into her panties. The vibe of danger and intrigue around him was irresistible.

His bitter class rage, contempt for authority and self-proclaimed compassion for the oppressed peoples of the world had opened her eyes, her mind, and her legs more or less simultaneously. Her problem wasn't only the guns and the dynamite and the FBI warrants. It wasn't only his jealousy and free-floating hostility, which she kinda got off on despite the danger. For the first time in her life—well, second, really—Ivy was unable to say *Caio, babe* to a man and walk away. She was afraid to, and afraid not to. So she had to force herself to take one step, then another, and this was the perfect moment, using the mandatory return to the family hearth for Christmas; but it wasn't easy, and, despite logic and what was best for her and the fact that he could be a brute, she would miss him.

"Get over here," David grabbed her wrist and swung her on her back on the bed. He straddled her, and trapped her under his weight.

"C'mon, get off me, man."

"Let's go to New Jersey and stay in your Daddy's mansion!"

"Please?"

"We'll empty the ice box and drain the bar. I'll fuck you in the bed you slept in as a little girl. When we leave, we'll burn the place down behind us."

"Hey," she said, hoping a joke might work, "maybe you *are* a boy I can take home to Mom and Dad!"

David laughed at her, helpless, pinned under him, under his control.

"I said get *off* me, man!"

"Aw, whatsa matter?"

She hauled off and smacked his face, hard.

"Bitch!" His hand flew to his face, shifting his weight just enough. She heaved David off and he fell on the floor. She bounced to her feet and sidestepped him, but David jumped up, grabbed her and spun her around, and smacked her upside the head.

"Don't! Let me go, damn it!"

"Oh yeah? Make me!"

She grabbed his wrist and the back of his head and pulled him full against her body and captured his mouth with hers.

Of course, David would ball her before she left. That would be his silly little *macho* way of reassuring himself he owned her. No need to tell him it would be their last. Nor was there any law that said she couldn't enjoy it.

Afterward, both of them drained, he lay back panting heavily, her palmprint on his cheek still bright red, but forgotten. She rolled out of bed and stretched, letting him feast his eyes on her body one last time, and got dressed. She would miss him, but not the blue gym bag of explosives sitting on the chair across the room and certainly not the gang of maladjusted so-called revolutionaries cleaning guns around the dining room table downstairs, and not the ache of guilt and desire that kept her bound to him.

"We've got plenty of time before my train," she said. "Let's go out to dinner." No need to tell him it would be their last.

When his father's appliance store went bankrupt, the beautiful split level home Eddie's parents had built was sold to pay off his creditors. Now the Bonneville family lived in an old house rented from a farmer. It stood beneath a tall oak tree on a county road on the edge of town near the Brick Township border with Lakewood, with a perpetual For Sale sign on the front lawn. But with new housing developments springing up all over, nobody wanted to buy an old wooden house with sagging porches and a drafty garage in the back, surrounded by empty, frozen fields. The summer after his father lost his store and the family's money was gone, Eddie had worked in those fields, picking vegetables for ten cents a bushel that the farmer's wife sold from a drive-in stand across the road. The farm work had paid for his school clothes that year.

Despite a couple stiff drinks, climbing the front steps from which, in June of '68, his father had tossed him and his typewriter, ordering him to get out and stay out, was hard. Since he left, he'd only gone home for visits with his mother in the daytime when his father was at work. Tonight the roast turkey aroma, and his two brothers and two sisters shouting *Eddie!* and hugging him as he put their presents under the tree, made him feel like a kid again.

He sat sipping black coffee at the kitchen table while his mother Doris, an attractive woman with a quiet, self-absorbed air, stood at the stove poking at the sweet potatoes and broccoli and carrots with a fork as they finished cooking.

"It's cold in here, Ma."

"Of course it's cold. We're surrounded by open fields and the wind blows right through this old place. I still have to finish putting plastic over the windows."

"Why you?"

"If I don't do it, who will?"

His mother's allusion was clear, and he easily fell into their old routine. "Well, I can think of somebody." No need to mention the name. "But since that won't happen," he went on, "*I'll* come by this weekend and do it. Where's the plastic and staples?"

"Your father keeps forgetting to bring them home from the store."

"So… is he coming home for dinner?"

"He said he'll try, but he'll have to go right back to work. They're keeping Sears open for the last-minute rush. Thank God he's had a good season. January first, a whole new pile of bills from the bankruptcy are due."

Just then, car tires crunched on the gravel driveway out front and an engine revved and went quiet. A door slammed and the slow, heavy footfalls he had heard so many times before trudged up the front steps. He took a deep breath.

"Pretty quiet around here lately?" he said.

"Yes, dear. But we do all miss you."

The living room door opened with a long, familiar squeak. Childish voices broke the quiet in ragged unison:

"Daddy! Daddy! Hi Dad!"

Eddie sulked in the kitchen with his mother while his father sang to his brothers and sisters:

"*It's beginning to look a lot like Christmas, everywhere I go!*"

His father took his seat at the head of the table, and Eddie sat at the other end. His father had aged, well past forty-two years old. All that was left of his store on Arnold Avenue in Point Pleasant Beach was a painful memory and a pile of debt. Now he sold appliances for Sears Roebuck during the week, worked as a watchman at a housing development on weekends, and slowly and steadily paid off his creditors. Although haggard, his father's looks were rugged and friendly, like Eddie's grandfather. Marcel Bonneville, a fisherman from the village of Honfleur, had immigrated to New Jersey from Normandy after being wounded in the battle of Verdun and losing his wife in the 1918 influenza epidemic. He started life over, worked in the Point Pleasant fishing fleet, married a local girl and had two sons, and bought a scallop boat that he lost in the Depression.

Eddie's father had the same open face, a good face for a salesman, one instinctively trusted by people like his fellow veterans of the Korean

War or those who remembered him as a handsome high school baseball hero and local wit and had voted him into three terms on the Brick Township Committee. It was a hopeful face for a beleaguered man with bills to pay, five kids, a disillusioned wife, and an errant son he had banished from the family but had reluctantly allowed to return for the holiday dinner. Eddie looked more like his mother: deep set eyes, introspective, less approachable.

He thought mentioning his job offer from the Asbury Park *Evening Press* might get them peacefully through dinner.

"The *Press* is a good paper," his father said. "Bob Jessup's the best editor in the business. I haven't spoken to Bob in a long time. I ought to give him a call for you."

"I just got the offer yesterday. I'm still thinking about it."

"Well, stop thinking and move on it. Bob won't wait forever. And you could use a break."

Beginning with you, you bastard. "I haven't decided if I want the job."

"Why not? You'll get more respect working for Bob than for that lush Frank Devlin."

He should have never opened his mouth. "They won't pay me as much as Frank."

"It's the best paper at the Shore. Why wouldn't you want to work there?"

"What is this, your way of giving me *advice*?"

"Would it help, dear," his mother interrupted, "if maybe you went to college for reporting?"

"I'm putting away every dollar I can. But right now, I am a reporter. My work is respected, whatever he says."

His father rotated his head irritably, as if he had a stuck neck bone. "The *Press* won't let you make a fool of yourself, writing crap like that thing you wrote against the draft."

"People are really talking about that piece."

"It's a piece of crap. I got people coming in the store, stopping me on the street, wondering what's wrong with my son. Of course, peo-ple've been asking me that ever since you were twelve years old and you broke all the windows in the new wing of the elementary school."

For which, he recalled, he got the beating of his life, in front of the whole family, his father's hand clamped around his arm and the belt stinging until he begged him to stop; that wasn't the last time, either, during the years after the bankruptcy. Too bad, nothing had changed since he'd moved out; the same impatience, the same scorn for his opinions, contempt for his very existence. Be careful, he told himself, but he couldn't help it:

"Instead of wondering about me, maybe they should ask what's wrong with their country. I'm just trying to save lives."

His father laughed, the usual mocking snort. "Save lives! Wait'll the Army gets you, my boy," he said with a certain expectant pleasure. "They're gonna cut off that hair, knock that smartass look off your face, and make a man out of you!" The hair thing, again. Eddie sat back, set down his knife and fork, and sneered.

"Yeah, like they did for you."

His father's face fell. His dropped fork clanged on his plate, and he rose to his feet. Eddie jumped up too, one fist ready, the other hand out in warning. He and his father hadn't come this close to blows in a year. He watched his father's hands. If they went to his buckle to pull off his belt for a whipping, he would pull the carving knife out of the turkey and plunge it straight through the old man's heart.

"*Stop!*" his mother yelled.

He and his father froze. His brothers and sisters stopped eating and stared down at their plates. The phone rang on the wall behind his mother, and she answered it.

"Hello, Billy. Merry Christmas to you too. He's right here." She handed Eddie the phone. "It's your roommate."

His father turned, shaking his head, and muttered, "*That* pinko." He sat down and went back to eating.

"He's not my roommate," Eddie corrected his mother. "I rent an apartment from him because I was kicked out of my home."

"Mom, what's a pinko?" his little sister said.

"Ssshh."

Eddie sat back down, now that it was safe to. "Billy."

"'He's not my roommate, he's my Fairy Godfather'," Billy chortled.

His father was watching so he didn't laugh, but he could have. He could picture Billy, sipping wine and cooking at the stove, probably dressed only in a bikini, a kimono, and his St. Jude medal. "Will you give those poor people a break? If it wasn't for them and a broken rubber, you wouldn't be here."

"I can always count on you to put things in perspective."

"That's because I love advising troubled youth. Speaking of whom,

Ivy called. She said her train gets in at twelve oh one. Are you insane, seeing her again?"

"I'll know at twelve oh two."

"I'm available for counseling, Bonneville, but I can't do much with self-inflicted wounds. Also, remember this house will be full of raving queens for the holidays. You *will* be discreet."

"I expect to be invited."

"Consider it so. And you'll be cool."

"Aren't I always?"

"Well, you try, I'll give you that. Oh, and there was another call. Matty Esposito. He said call him at the hotel."

He quickly got off the phone. He checked his Timex, and, pulling out his cigarettes, dialed the phone number for The Sunset Lodge.

The voice at the other end was loud and impatient. "*Whattya want?*"

"Ed Bonneville from the *Independent* calling. Is this Matty Esposito?"

His father's fork stopped halfway to his mouth, as if he'd heard *Hello, is this Satan?*

"What are you botherin' me for?" Esposito said.

"I want to get your comments about your court case and do a story."

"What story? Your paper'll never print my side of the story."

"I'll take my chances if you will."

"Yeah? Who told you to call me?"

"My editor is interested—"

"Yeah, I'll bet he is." He was silent for so long that Eddie thought he'd hung up. "What about right now? You doing anything?"

Oh shit. "Nothing I can't get out of." His mother set down her fork and stared at the wall.

"Come over." *Click!*

"I'm on my way," he said into the dead phone.

He hung up, the food on his plate untouched. He lit a Lucky Strike with a shaky match, stood up, and pulled on his coat.

"You're leaving?" his mother said in a small voice.

"Sorry Ma," he said, kissing her cheek. "Gotta go to work." As he passed his father he patted him on the shoulder. At the door he said, as cheerfully as he could: "Merry Christmas, everybody!"

Goodbye…

His mother turned to his father, her voice sharp. "Well, are you happy now?" His father sat and ate quietly and said nothing. Eddie gently closed the door.

The dark hulk of the Sunset Lodge came into view on the west side of Lakewood. The old hotel stood closed and silent beneath towering evergreens standing against a charcoal sky, its lawn a field of dead weeds. It was the first time he'd gotten a close look at the place. According to a business page story from the *Independent*'s library, the resort had stood on a whole block since the 1890s, when it had been built as an affordable retreat for city families, offering summer and winter sports and entertainment. The Lodge had been a resort popular with Jewish families for over fifty years because it was closer to the cities than the Catskills, had a menu that honored the dietary laws, and was near the synagogue and large Orthodox community west of Madison Avenue.

He'd learned the rest of the Lodge's history from Crane last week on the night his Esposito grand jury scoop broke and they were hanging around after deadline. "Matty's old man Bruno was an immigrant from Naples who owned a grocery store on First Street. Around 1915, he turned the store into Esposito's Restaurant. Since it was right off the Clifton Avenue shopping district and across the street from the Public Service and Lincoln Transit bus terminals, the place did bang up business, especially during Prohibition, when it was the best-protected speakeasy in Ocean County. Bruno didn't trust banks, and he sank his profits into local real estate. In the early '40s, he bought the Sunset Lodge from the two Jewish guys who built it. Problem was, business never recovered after the war. Who needs Lakewood when you can fly to Miami? So no sooner did Bruno buy the Lodge than it started to go downhill and stopped making money. The joint was falling apart by the time Bruno died and it passed to Matty, and he closed it. Now it's not a resort, it's only real estate."

The once-grand entrance stood above the broad lawn with its windows shuttered in weathered gray plywood. As Eddie drove slowly up the cracked concrete driveway, the Impala bounced and shimmied over potholes and large weeds. He got out and stared at the place from end to end, wondering how anyone could live there, and his enthusiasm for interviewing the Lodge's owner vanished. God only knew what ghosts rattled around in that sagging pile of stucco. Esposito had once told The Lakewood *Daily Times* that since New Jersey now had a state lottery, legalized gambling wouldn't be long in coming, and one day the Lodge would make a beautiful little casino hotel. He'd set up housekeeping for himself in a handsome apartment on the top floor and, as the place crumbled around him, he dreamed of the Lodge's future.

Eddie pulled his keys from the ignition before he climbed the front steps. The double doors rattled when he knocked.

THREE *Rackets boss of the Jersey Shore*

Tonight the ballroom was open, but nobody was dancing. Whenever the crumbling hotel creaked in the wind you heard it up in the high corners of the room. It was dark except for a round table in a pool of light under a cobwebbed chandelier. On the table, next to a porkpie hat, a Lucky Strike and a cigar smoldered in a white porcelain ashtray with an ink sketch of the Sunset Lodge on the bottom, as Matty 'The Mule' Esposito talked about his life and times.

When Eddie had first seated himself at the table, Esposito introduced the blonde from the arraignment yesterday as "Sally." She gave him a quick grin and slouched back, shivering in her rabbit fur jacket, smoking Kools, across the table from a fortyish guy the old man introduced as his son, "Tommaso." Trim and handsome, in a faded denim jacket and thick black moustache and shoulder length hair, he muttered "Tommy," and greeted Eddie with a cold glance.

He got out his cassette recorder and made sure the tape was turning. He'd begun to work with it last summer during the Lakewood riot when he couldn't take notes fast enough to keep up with the interviews. When he put it on the table and asked if that was okay, Esposito shrugged and said he didn't mind.

But Tommy shook his head. "Pop, I think you're making a mistake."

The old man was brusque. "Nah, I like the idea." Tommy shrugged, sat back, and deferred to his father with a troubled sigh that said he really had no choice.

Eddie had assumed Esposito agreed to the interview to defend his reputation. But he was sure taking his time getting there.

"I was first violin in the Lakewood High School orchestra," the old man was saying, aglow with memories. "I always had music in my heart. I was gonna be a musician. I played jazz trumpet. Nick La Rocca was my hero. I had all the Original Dixieland Jazz Band records. I even played this ballroom a few times, back in the '20s, way before my father bought the place. I could'na been older than you are now. Of course my father, he thought playing music was bullshit. He wanted his only son to take over the restaurant, so I hadta do it." He sighed. "He thought playing music was no way for a man to make a living."

Sitting in the chilly ballroom listening to the old man's stories, Eddie was getting restless. He could hear the old jazz, a solo trumpet chiming through layers of syncopated rhythm or a line of saxophones swingin' and swayin.' But those were better days. Tonight the tables were draped with dust covers, wind gusts made the walls creak, and outside bare branches on the overgrown trees scraped the high windows. The ballroom was like the parlor of an old age home, and he had to remind himself why he was here. Get the interview done and get the hell out of this haunted house, he thought. Let Matty the Mule complain about harassment and defamation of character. Maybe he'll cry anti-Italian discrimination or something newsworthy. Any story he got would scoop the other reporters, so it was worth his time to talk to the old man, but Eddie was looking forward to getting back out in the fresh air.

"We're going to have to talk about the indictment soon, Mister Esposito. I only have two hours of tape."

With a cough, Esposito lit his cigar. "Whattya wanna know?"

"Pop," Tommy said. "Please. Can we talk about this?"

"We talked enough," Esposito said. "I want to do this."

"Okay, let's get this out of the way first." Eddie consulted his notepad. "The prosecutor, Mister Heckendorfer, called you the 'Rackets Boss of the Jersey Shore.' Care to comment?"

The long silence was broken by Tommy. "Hey kid… What are you, stupid?"

Puffing his cigar, Esposito's eyes traveled to Sally. She looked at Eddie and shook her head, one eyebrow arching toward her hairline. "You don't know who you're talking to."

The wind whistled, a gust slammed something loose against a wall, and Eddie flinched.

"Hey, no offense, but here's Mister Esposito, people know him as a labor official, uh, as a hotel owner, and he's been labeled this *thing* in the headlines. I want to be fair and give him a chance—"

The look in Esposito's eyes stopped him cold.

"Don't tell me I made a mistake, inviting you here," Esposito grumbled, tapping his cigar in the ashtray. "What'd you think I called you here to talk about—the hotel business?"

Up in Asbury Park, Springwood Avenue ran eastward from Route 35 for about twelve blocks through the black neighborhoods on the West Side to the railroad tracks, beyond which were the white neighborhoods, the Cookman Avenue shopping district, and the boardwalk. The Avenue was the boulevard, the funky Broadway, of black Asbury Park, anchored at its east end by the Neptune Diner and the legendary jazz and R&B nightclub Big Bill's and at the other end, still on the wrong side of the railroad tracks, by a rougher club named the Orchid Lounge. The shops, restaurants, bars, and small stores scattered along the Avenue were all that remained of a lively district that in better days had nightclubs on every block, full of sharp-dressed people profiling and dancing on Saturday nights to swing and rhythm and blues. Now the empty storefront windows gazed with sullen indifference at the white motorists who ran the red lights on the Avenue, afraid to stop, except for those who pulled into the side streets to do furtive dope deals. Tonight, Christmas Eve, Springwood Avenue was swept by frigid winds, and deserted.

A yellow school bus stood at the curb outside the Orchid Lounge. The door to the club swung open, blasting "Ball of Confusion" by The Temptations from the jukebox out onto the sidewalk, along with a line of laughing people in a holiday mood. They were ushered to the bus by a squat, pock-marked man in a black overcoat and a priest's collar who called himself Father Anthony.

Nothing like a free party to bring out the spades, he thought. "Take your time, folks, no need to rush, plenty of room on the bus," he called out. "Free food, free drinks, free dancing, courtesy of St. Jude's Christmas Party." He watched the bus fill up, thinking, yeah, no need to rush, except for this wind, so cold he was freezing his balls off.

Eddie flipped his notebook pages until he found the quote: "So you're saying you *are* a 'career criminal with your tentacles everywhere'? The prosecutor's word, 'tentacles,' not mine."

Esposito snatched his cigar from his mouth and blew a thick plume of blue smoke over the table. He leaned forward and spoke into Eddie's microphone:

"In the '20s, my father ran the best speakeasy around, right here in Lakewood. That's how I met a couple bootleggers. I put down my trumpet and went to work for them. I didn't love it like I loved jazz, but it paid better. I started out riding shotgun on beer trucks, making deliveries from the breweries in Newark and the Bronx, all the way down Route 9 to Atlantic City. I was just a kid, but before long I was setting up my own shipments and handling protection. We did the distribution on a lot of the Canadian whiskey brought in by Longy Zwillman's boys. We'd meet the freighters out in the ocean, load the booze onto fishing boats, and bring it upriver to a marina or somebody's private dock. The cases went straight into the trucks. Nice payment to the local police chief, throw a case in his car trunk, no problems. Nobody ever got arrested on my runs. Two years is what it took, and a lot of kickin' ass, and I was the biggest bootlegger in Monmouth and Ocean counties."

"And nobody went ever thirsty," Tommy said. "Top quality Canadian, right Pop?"

The old man ignored his son and went on. "Then come the '30s, I got into the gambling and shylock. I had the biggest card games outside of New York and Philly. I had cathouses up and down the Shore, the best lookin' women you ever saw. My customers were all the top people in business and government, which is why whenever I needed a favor, I only had to ask once. Then in the '40s during the war, I sold counterfeit ration and gas stamps, I picked up some liquor licenses, I sold fireworks, untaxed cigarettes, untaxed gasoline, you name it. Made a lotta money. In '51, I set up the construction unions down here, because I knew the minute they finished the Parkway, the whole Jersey Shore was gonna go boom!"

"A man of vision and guts, my father," Tommy said.

"Obviously," Eddie said. "So you're saying—"

"I'm *saying*," Esposito's impatient voice bounced off the ceiling, "my whole god damn life I've worked with this political organization! I paid 'em enough bribes by now to open a bank! I bought and sold these fuckin' pine cone politicians like a buncha two bit Hershey Bar whores! You understand what I'm saying? I'm an established member of this community! But now, all of a sudden, these bastards, they've got me fighting for my life!?" He rose half out of his seat, livid. "What the fuck is *that*?" Sally coaxed him back down.

"Fuckin' ingratitude," Tommy muttered.

"So you're saying—"

"Forty years I ran my businesses, I paid off everybody from Colonel Ted McTierney on down! Now all of a sudden, what? They're tired of this old face? My money's no good?" His cries echoed in the corners of the empty ballroom.

I paid enough bribes to open a bank. Eddie lit a Lucky Strike off the last one with trembling fingers, realizing he had one foot in a world where he'd better not reveal his ignorance.

"That all sounds totally illegal, Mister Esposito," he blurted out. Luckily, Sally laughed, and Tommy laughed too. Not the old man, though.

"You're a reporter, right? So you *know* how things are."

"So I've heard," he lied, pretending to be casual. "I mean, I don't know many details—"

From across the table the old man's eyes burned into him. "You mean, you don't know the setup?" Was Esposito going to leave it there, stand up, interview over?

"I've been a reporter about a year, I've heard some things," he said. He had no idea there even *was* a setup. He hoped the old man would think he knew more than he did.

"How old are you?" Esposito demanded.

"Nineteen."

"You gotta know the setup. Who's who, how things work. When I was your age, I knew the setup. I made money, and I made a lotta other people rich. Now they call me a 'career criminal.' Well, tonight I'm gonna tell you about some career criminals maybe you don't know about."

"Pop—"

"*What*," he said to Tommy, turning to his son for the first time.

"What're you doin'?" Tommy said.

"I know what I'm doing."

"And after you spill your guts, what's left?" Tommy said.

"I don't worry about that."

"Did you ever once think about me, my future, the future of the business?"

"Every day," Esposito sighed. "Every day."

All the charges in the indictment were true, Eddie realized. Heckendorfer had sung the overture in court yesterday afternoon: *Loansharking, Gambling, Racketeering.* Now Esposito was about to sing the whole opera, feeling too angry and sorry for himself to give a damn whether it hurt anyone else. Too bad for Tommy. Eddie was scared of the old man, he could scarcely imagine life as his son. Calm down, he told himself, the guy across the table was still only a small town businessman with assorted interests. Keep him talking, catch your breath.

"So you're saying—"

Esposito shoved himself to his feet. He slapped on his hat, and beckoned. "You need a history lesson, sonny boy."

Giving Eddie a nervous look, Tommy stood up to come with them, and hesitated, like he was unsure if he was invited. Tommy was wearing flower-embroidered bellbottom jeans and the latest local fad in footwear, a leather bowling shoe in red, white and blue sold at a boutique on Brick Boulevard.

"I'll be down here," he said, sitting back down at the table.

"Yeah? Good," his father said, looking around the vast empty room. "Keep an eye on things."

The history lesson began on the second floor in Esposito's private quarters, once the hotel manager's apartment, whose living room resembled the lounge of an exclusive men's club. Under brass and crystal chandeliers, the intricate parquet oak floor was laid with thick Persian carpets, black and burgundy like the velvet club chairs and camel back sofas. A brass pedestal ashtray stood beside every seat, and the air held hints of tobacco and alcohol and after shave lotion. Above the oak wainscoting the herringbone wallpaper was yellow from decades of tobacco smoke. He left his tape recorder running on a long coffee table strewn with the *Press*, the *Observer*, the *Independent* and the Lakewood *Daily Times*.

In his work clothes, Esposito looked like a guy who had been sent to the elegant suite to fix the plumbing. At the other end of the room, in her white go-go boots and tight jeans and rabbit fur jacket, Sally slouched against the curve of a long bar with a brass foot rail.

"Wait for us outside, sweetheart."

After a second, Sally slid off the bar and ambled out, letting the door swing back and slam.

"Nice girl, but she oughta learn some fuckin' manners." He relit his cigar. "When the boys from Toms River had business to do in secret, this is where they did it, courtesy of my old man, and me. Colonel Ted, he had a big house by the golf course in Toms River. But he spent most of his time right here." His eyes lifted.

Over the fireplace hung an oil portrait of a husky, red-faced man with white hair and ornate whiskers, grinning large. Colonel Ted McTierney. What did Eddie know about him? Not much. Big Republican political boss, died a couple years ago.

"He sat right here in this chair, the day after I buried my father. It was the summer the war ended. We were havin' a couple drinks and listenin' to the ball game on the radio." Esposito grinned at the memory. "It was hot enough in here to melt the wax off your moustache, but he didn't sweat one drop. I think his Irish charm was the key to his success with people. Of course, he could also be so cold he could chill a glass of beer just by holding it in his hand, if you know what I mean. He said to me, 'Two per cent is what I make off everything legit that moves in this county, Matty. You pay me the same as your father did, and you'll never have to worry about the law, and you'll never have to worry about the boys down in Toms River turning against you.' And I said, 'Colonel, you are a standup guy.' We shook hands, and that was that."

"'I make two per cent,' he actually said that?"

"He said that. Of course, I knew it already."

"He trusted you with that information?"

"Of course."

"Another guy might've used that information against him."

"What for? We were businessmen. We made a deal. We made money. In those days, if you shook hands, you lived up to the deal or you weren't a real man. I used to say to him, 'Colonel, it's your Ocean, I'm just swimmin' here like everybody else.' We made each other laugh. For an Irishman and an Italian, that's something."

"He trusted that you'd really pay two percent?"

"And I did," the old man said.

"Where'd he come from?" Eddie asked.

"Originally from Philadelphia, I heard. He wasn't a real Colonel, he was the kind of Colonel who runs auctions. In the '20s, he got himself appointed to local magistrates court, which you could do in those days, you didn't even have to be a lawyer. When he died he was president of a law firm that had twenty lawyers, but I heard he himself never finished high school. From that little magistrate's job, the Colonel built the

Republican machine here. Total control over everything. A political organization richer than God. All this was possible because of one little thing. In 1933, the Freeholders passed a law. They let local companies doin' county business add two per cent to their invoices, to give 'em a little extra to help 'em keep goin', because during the Depression the county sometimes paid its bills late, since people paid their taxes late or sometimes not at all. That saved a lot of businesses and a lot of jobs. Well, that two per cent is still in every bill the county pays, but they stopped lettin' the businesses keep it a long time ago."

"That's the two per cent he told you about?"

"How it works is, whenever you do business with the county government, you overcharge them two per cent on your bill. Then twice a year, you kick back that two per cent to the McTierney Law Firm. You call the check a 'legal retainer'. It's called the Colonel Ted Tax, and it's a fuckin' river of money, straight into his law firm, and all protected by the attorney-client thing. Not that anybody would have the balls to investigate."

Eddie's scalp tingled. Was he really saying this? "So he must've been incredibly rich."

"Yeah, but he also put money back into the Organization. Every Republican campaign. They'd do mailings, buy radio time, hold rallies, things the Democrats could never afford. And once you took Organization money, you owed him forever. You wanna know how powerful he was? There was a steering committee meeting once to nominate a guy to run for something, I forget what. Half a dozen guys, Freeholders, Assemblymen, Senators, all stood up and made speeches endorsing the guy they liked. But Colonel Ted liked somebody else. All he did was stand up and say he'd consider it a personal favor if the committee members would support his guy, and sat down. It was a secret ballot and his guy was nominated unanimously. The other candidate even voted against himself, and got himself a nice county job as his reward."

Esposito stared at the chair. "My friend Colonel Ted, they don't make 'em like that anymore. This is no longer a world of standup guys. Nobody's word means shit." Esposito glared defiantly at him, his eyes shining. "Look at me! Fighting for my life! At my age! I got more knives in my back than I can pull out!"

"Maybe it's time to turn over some of it to your son."

Esposito spat disgustedly. "He can't even manage his own life." He started to say more, then shook his head. "No, the thing is, tonight I want you to listen, and I want you to get it all on tape. I got stories to tell. Nobody else can tell these stories, Eddie. You know why?"

"I guess nobody else knows them?" He seemed so dumb to himself sometimes.

"That's right. Because in my world, I'm The King. How many men can say that?"

"None that I ever met."

"You wanna hear a few stories, Eddie? You wanna hear how things really are?"

"Well, yeah, I came to get a story—"

"And that's what you're gonna get." Esposito swung his overcoat over his shoulders. "Sally!" The door opened and she poked her head in.

"Tell Tommy to warm up the car."

Esposito led them over to a black '69 Cadillac Coupe de Ville. He put Eddie and his tape recorder up front with Sally between them. Tommy climbed into the back seat.

They drove south on Route 9, the road dry and the night cold and windy.

"So, is that machine on?" he said.

"Rolling," he said. On his lap the recorder also covered the boner he got sitting pressed against Sally's warm thigh.

"So, here's what you gotta understand. This thing that looks like a racketeering indictment is really my retirement papers! What we got here is a fight over a local franchise, one it took my whole life to build. The Organization, they wanna change who runs my rackets, and who controls my unions."

"Like they should have any say at all," Tommy said.

"They wanna put me in prison, so they can give everything I built to that Castellucci punk."

"Bobby Castellucci?" Eddie said. "The bar owner?"

"He only runs that saloon because he needs an office somewhere," Tommy said.

Eddie almost blurted out that he knew Castellucci and he couldn't believe he was anything but a saloon keeper. But he remembered how wrong he'd been about Esposito and kept quiet.

"Is Castellucci mentioned in the indictment?"

"I'm telling you what the indictment *means*. Do I have to educate you about all this?"

"Educate me about how you got Tom Porter as your lawyer," he said. "He's as Organization as they come."

"That's right. And I want the Organization off my back. You think an outside lawyer can talk to those guys and get anywhere? Either the Senator works out a deal, or this ain't gonna end so good."

"So how is Castellucci involved in this?"

"Because of Roy McTierney. I guess you know who Roy McTierney is?"

"Biggest developer in the county." One night he'd been covering a Planning Board meeting someplace when Roy Mac walked in, wearing an expensive dark suit, looking freshly barbered, moving around confidently the way rich, powerful men do. The board members all stared at him until he recognized them with a wave and a smile. All he did was sit in the audience and observe the final vote approving an eight hundred unit retirement village out in the pinelands along Route 70. Apparently satisfied with the outcome, he waved and left the room right after the decision.

"Building houses, that's only his *job*. After Colonel Ted died, the sons stepped up, Roy and his little brother Joe the mayor, to take over the Organization."

"Joe Mac," he said. "Him, I know."

"Yeah. Fat little thief. He's so stupid he belongs in a fuckin' highchair, but they had to do somethin' with him, so they stuck him out in Manchester and made him mayor. Then the place exploded! The retirement village capital of America! He made enough dirty money to open a car dealership, and now all the government vehicle business gets steered to him, even the new police cars for the Law Enforcement Center, which his brother's construction company built."

"Nobody tries to stop these guys?"

"Nobody can buck the Organization. There are a million ways to buy a guy off, you just have to know his price. If he still won't bend, Roy has Castellucci and his boys for muscle." Eddie nodded. It wasn't hard to imagine the bouncers at the lounge working a little overtime. "This indictment is being done to get me out of the way, because Roy wants Castellucci controlling my unions and my other businesses. Roy ordered this indictment on me, I guarantee you."

"I thought Heckendorfer was a loose cannon."

"Not that loose. When Roy really wants something, nothing can stop him. And he hates me with a passion."

"Why?"

"We're fightin' a war, that's why. Ten years ago, when he started buildin' houses, he wouldn't recognize my unions. So we put picket lines up at his developments. The cops would come and put everybody in jail. We'd have ten more guys on the line when they got back. I tipped off the Teamsters that all Roy's supplies came by non-union truckers. They sent guys down to our lines to turn the delivery drivers around."

"How's that?"

"Talk to them. 'You drive this truck in there, you better not come out because we'll be waitin' to kick your ass.' Roy couldn't get anything delivered, lumber, cinder block, sheet rock, nothing. He sued us in court and lost. He fought us on the job site, and he lost. He had cops every day arresting and lockin' up my guys. He had cops harassin' me, harassin' my business agents. Somebody even set fire to our headquarters. But we slowed him down so much he finally had to give in and sign our contract. Plus, we signed up his Latvian and Estonian carpenters and Puerto Rican dry wallers and Polish and Hungarian house painters as fast as he could hire them." He grinned. "I had very aggressive organizers."

"Must've cost him a lot of money."

"Roy Mac *has* a lot of money. But thanks to my unions, now he has to treat workin' people decent and to pay them a fair dollar. In the next contract, we got our pension and health plans paid for by the construction companies, and that cost him even more. Now here's what I want you to understand: there's been cash pourin' in from the developers every month for years for the men's pension and health benefits. There's millions of dollars in the pension fund alone. If I go, Castellucci would have total control over that."

"That's a million reasons to get you out of the way," Eddie said, adding to himself, and a million reasons why Tommy was so intent on succeeding his father, and why he must be heartsick over him talking so much.

"So you see what this is about?"

"Starting to," he said. The known world was being erased and redrawn for him so quickly he had only a sketchy idea of what it all meant. All he could do was ask the questions. "What could he do with all that money?"

"Loan shark it," Tommy said from behind them. "Give out mortgages to phony companies who disappear and never pay back. Make silent partner deals all over the place and profit personally."

"There's a lotta ways to steal the eggs from a golden goose," Esposito said. "I guarantee you, if he gets his hands on those pension and health funds, none of those workers will see one dollar."

"We're not gonna let that happen," Tommy said.

"What Roy wants, he gets, because he controls the cash and the Organization. Don't take it from me, ask around. You'll find out I'm tellin' you the truth. When they need election workers on the street, who do you think they call? One call to me, they got all the manpower they need. And now I'm being stabbed in the back by the same bastards I been keeping in power."

"So you definitely are involved in politics as much they say?"

"Sonny boy, crime and politics are only two different ways of gettin' the same thing." Esposito ignited his cigar with a long smear of flame from his lighter. "In fact, most of the time, they *are* the same thing."

"How so?"

"Around here, you're never done payin' people off. County, local, doesn't matter, there's always somebody with his hand out. Some towns are worse than others. You want a liquor license? Fifty to a hundred grand. You need a zoning variance? Couple thousand split between the board members. Make an inspector happy? Easy, twenty five to fifty dollars."

"Did you ever buy a judge?" he asked, thinking ahead to Esposito's trial on the indictment.

Esposito looked at him like he was crazy. "Nobody *buys* a judge. Their job is a reward for party loyalty. You pay somebody else, and they tell the judge what to do."

He thought about Judge Geifel at the arraignment yesterday afternoon. Incredible, he thought, that a *judge*, of all people, would be appointed not because of his mastery of the law but for being an obedient political hack.

"But much bigger than all this, there's campaign cash. 'Quiet cash', they call it. They never shook me down, because my tribute went directly to Colonel Ted. But even *after* the Organization gets its two percent, these politicians shake down businesses like crazy for contributions. Half the time, they not only don't deliver on their promises, they forget your fuckin' name!"

"You can't exactly call the police."

"Oh, we'd never need to!" Esposito said, and Tommy snickered. "Last summer, the boys over at Troop C had a State Trooper followin' me around day and night. Each time I didn't signal a turn or missed a Stop sign, they'd pull me over, write me a ticket, frisk me on the side of the road. One time I parked legally to go into the bank in Toms River and the Dover cops fucked up and towed my car away. "

"We made them bring it back," Tommy said.

"What was that, another shakedown?"

"*Those* police? Not in Dover! They're clean as lifeguards. Buzz Thompson can't be bought, the man has done so many smart land deals he's one of the richest men around. He gets his thrills sendin' his boys to cruise the black parts of town and push people around, show 'em who's boss. He likes to kick in the front door of that sissy bar down on Merchant Street and haul everybody out in front of the news photographers."

"You always see his cops pulling long hairs over and tearing their cars apart looking for drugs," Tommy said.

Driving home late after work one night, Eddie had been stopped and searched by two Dover Township cops on a deserted county road that was pitch dark except for their headlights and revolving red and blue lights. He'd been riding and playing his eight track, Beethoven's *Eroica* symphony, and he obstinately left it on loud until they ordered him to turn it off. It was the local custom lately, police laughing at long hairs, "Stand over there, Miss," two crew cut jock types with big grins silently sharing their petty rush of power. He displayed his blue and white State Police PRESS vehicle placard openly on the dashboard. He was clean that night, but it would have been easy for them to plant dope in his car. Of all the local cops, the state police at the Troop C barracks in Brick had the worst reputation for hating hippies. Two troopers were facing charges that they took a drug suspect to their barracks, beat him up, and branded the State Police triangle onto his buttock with a red-hot coat hanger, photos of which had been printed in the *Independent*, page one exclusive story by Eddie Bonneville.

The St. Jude's school bus turned off Route 9 south into the Bargainland shopping center and stopped outside Castellucci's Lounge. As the black partygoers stepped off and into the club, Father Anthony stood outside the bus handing out tickets.

"What's this for?"

"Drink tickets, my friend," he said. "When you're ready for your refreshments, you hand in this ticket and party for free."

With dark, soulful eyes and a small gash of a mouth, the man calling himself Father Anthony might've been a school of hard knocks priest, the kind who might run an inner-city parish. But he wasn't, he was an organized crime associate with a cocktail lounge in Vailsburg and with a serious hard on for Bobby Castellucci. When Matty Esposito called and told him what he wanted, and how much he would pay for a job well done, he had to act fast, bribing a church custodian at St. Jude's to borrow a bus, paying his cousin Silvio to drive, ordering phony drink tickets printed in a hurry at a stationery store and borrowing a priest's collar from his brother-in-law's dry cleaners. And here he was, playing Father Anthony, the congenial host. Hey Bobby! Meet some friends of mine!

"Remember, you're the personal guests of the owner, Mister Bobby Castellucci!" he said. "Merry Christmas, everybody!"

Inside the lounge, a crowded noisy Christmas party of well-dressed white people was in full swing. For many of them this was the big party event of the season. They'd hired a babysitter, got the hair done, rented the upscale tux with velvet lapels and bought a new dress at Bamberger's up in Eatontown or Steinbach's in Asbury Park, and put the car through the wash and presented themselves on Castellucci's doorstep, ready to cut loose and be merry and bright and have a happy, white Christmas.

The black people off the bus walked in past an astonished Roberto at the door. The new patrons, grateful to St. Jude's for inviting them in out of the cold, were ready to party. Heads turned like a wave rippling through the crowded room. Outside, Father Anthony hopped back on the school bus. Inside, the band started a new song, the singer rendering a sappy version of "Christmas Eve in My Hometown," and nobody heard the sound of the empty bus hurrying away.

The Seaside Heights boardwalk was empty, the white garage doors pulled down over the arcades. They walked four abreast. Tommy shivered in his thin denim jacket, Sally had her ears and chin hunched down in the collar of her white fur jacket. Eddie, by now on his second cassette, ignoring his frozen fingers, held his microphone close to Esposito. The old man was boasting, and Eddie didn't want to miss a word.

"You use any machine that takes a coin in this county, it's mine. Cigarettes, pinball, wheel games, coin laundry, you name it." He pointed at the arcades, dark and silent. "All these concessions up here? You sell a fuckin' ice cream cone, I get a lick."

"And what do you give them?"

"Supervision. Anybody here has a problem, I work it out."

"So when you say Castellucci is McTierney's 'muscle,' what would a guy like that do?"

"Same things I would do from time to time when Colonel Ted was boss."

"Hurt people?"

"Sometimes."

"Like when?"

"Say a bid on a contract is rigged, the guy who loses out on the deal makes a stink about it. We'll go straighten him out. Or you fix an election, which you can't do without certain people knowing about it. We'll make sure they keep quiet."

"Which you do how?"

"Money and a word to the wise usually does the trick. Once in a while somebody gets a little bruised before they get the point."

"A little bruised?"

"Well, all I usually need to do is talk, because around here, I'm *known*," Esposito said. "Little Bobby Castellucci, he likes to hit first and talk later. You don't want him mad at you. Or his people—"

"His people. You're saying he's Mafia?"

He shrugged. "Yeah, whattya think?"

"What about you? Are you Mafia?"

"I don't like this *cosa nostra*, this 'our thing' business. I'm independent. This is *my* thing. I do business with people, in Newark, Jersey City, Bayonne, over in Philly, some of them I know since my bootleggin' days. I know they're *cosa nostra*, but down here, I'm the guy. They know me, and they respect my territory. So, I know Bobby Castellucci's story. I know who his people are. I know the guy whose wife he fooled around with and how he got himself in a jam and why he can't hang out on South Orange Avenue anymore with his *goombahs*. So he did what everybody does. He moved down the Shore. Land of opportunity!" Esposito laughed, a warm fatherly chuckle. "He made one mistake, though. He shoulda never got in my face."

The mood at Castellucci's, despite the music and Yuletide cheer, grew more uneasy by the minute. The black guests who came on the St. Jude's bus had taken a few booths off to one side of the room and were getting thirsty. At the bar and tables near the bandstand the white patrons turned and stared at the blacks as they talked, their words inaudible, the derisive snickering unmistakable. Waitresses passed their booths and brushed off their attempts to order.

Finally a tall man named Terence, in an Afro and a beige leisure suit, had had enough of being ignored. He gathered up drink tickets from the others and strolled up to the bar. Onstage the band shuffled through "Silent Night," the singer snapping his fingers and rocking his head. Terence fanned out the drink tickets on the bar and asked for nine beers. The bartender frowned *What?* and leaned closer to hear his order. He squinted at the tickets on the bar and at Terence. He backed up and grabbed a phone behind the bar.

"We got trouble here?" someone said behind him. An off-duty State Trooper, a Viking with a square jaw, showed his badge and bellied up to the bar next to Terence.

"No trouble that I know about," Terence said. Not that the trooper, his eyes glittering with malice, wouldn't love for him to start some. "Just trying to get a beer."

"Where you people from, anyway?" The trooper couldn't keep out of his voice how incredible he found their very presence.

Before he could answer the bartender came back and pushed the tickets over to the trooper with his fingers.

"Some kinda scam! Look at these!"

"Scam?" Terence said. "This ain't no scam! A priest up in Asbury gave us these tickets and brought us down here on a bus! Said it was St. Jude's Christmas Party! We're guests of a man named Castellucci!"

The bartender and the trooper looked at each other and laughed. Terence flushed from head to foot, took a deep breath, and began looking for the exit. "Okay, man, I don't want any trouble—"

The trooper examined the ticket. "Pretty good, pretty good."

"Where'd these tickets come from?" the bartender said.

"Priest with a bus who brought us here for a party," Terence said, working hard on staying polite and trying not to panic.

"Well, somebody lied to you," the trooper said. "So you and your friends get back on the bus and get out of here. Plenty of bars for your kind over in Lakewood. I'm sure you'll feel more at home."

"I think we will, even though me and *my kind* have every right to be here," Terence said, unable to hold back. His tone said, clearly, *So fuck you!* But he also backed away, acutely aware of being outnumbered, wanting no part of whatever game Whitey was playing here.

"What'd you say to me?" The trooper seized Terence's wrist and spun him around. He lost his balance, and the trooper shoved him face down on the bar, scattering glasses that fell and broke, and handcuffed him. "You're under arrest for attempting to defraud an innkeeper." Scattered applause and laughter rose from the tables, punctured by cries of protest from across the room.

Two of the black men in his party rushed up and confronted the trooper holding Terence, demanding to know what happened and why their friend was handcuffed. Two more off duty troopers and a bouncer from the front door pounced on them and they fought back. In the struggle, one of the troopers and a black guy tripped and fell over a table for four, knocking food and liquor all over some very pissed off partygoers.

This got the remaining black guests to their feet, men and women, brandishing chairs. A lady in a green satin dress marched over to Matthew the bartender, who had her boyfriend in a headlock, and crashed a heavy glass ashtray against the side of his shaved head. A scream rose from the entire crowd, black and white. Tino, the other bouncer, shoved people aside to get to her, the other black guests shoved forward to run interference, and the whole room collapsed into a fist swinging melee.

Alerted by the screaming and the crash of furniture and breaking glass while taking a stress break on the couch in his office, Castellucci pushed away the cocktail waitress giving him a blowjob, zipped up, and hurried out to see what the trouble was.

A group of wrestling, kicking, fist-swinging men fell over onto the bandstand and it was a swinging "Silent Night" no more. Out front, three police cars skidded to a stop. Half a dozen local cops rushed into the club.

"Do something!" Castellucci screamed at them. "These niggers're destroying my room!"

The police charged ahead, nightsticks swinging.

The boardwalk miles behind them now, Esposito pulled into a

shopping center in the scrub pinelands out on Route 70 near a wide lake behind the stores. He parked in a far corner of the lot and nudged Eddie.

"You know the story behind this place? The real story? Nah, you're too young, this was ten years ago, when Roy McTierney first started buildin' things. This property once was owned by a nice little guy named Jimmy somethin'. The property used to be his grandfather's cranberry farm. His father built a fishin' dock and a campground on the lake. Right where those stores are now, they had a main building with a coffee shop and a grocery store and maybe a dozen bungalows and a nice little beach along the pond. Every summer the place was jammed with families from Memorial Day to Labor Day. Well, his father got sick and died, and time came for Jimmy to run the family business and he took over with his wife and daughter.

"Then one day Roy Mac decided he wanted this property. It was close to Route 9 and the Parkway, and the right size for the shoppin' center he wanted to build. He offered Jimmy big bucks, serious money, even offered to build him a new house on the beach or anywhere else, and help put Jimmy's daughter through college. Jimmy said no, he'd promised his father this land would be in the family forever. He got threatening phone calls. And he kept saying no. A small fire started in one of the cabins, they said from a leaky propane tank. People came around to lean on him, and that's when one of my guys brought Jimmy over to see me.

"Fifty thousand bucks, take it or else somethin' really bad was gonna happen. That was their last offer. And Jimmy's really hurtin', it's been his family's property for like a hundred years, he ain't givin' it up for any price. He told me what was up. I said, 'Tell 'em I'm your partner, tell 'em to come talk to me.' Well, he decided not do that. He didn't wanna be publicly associated with me, with my reputation. Long story short, him and his wife went to run some errands one day, and they never came back. They never found them or the car. The daughter, nicest girl you'd ever want to meet, she took the deal and moved away. I hear she lives in Arizona."

Esposito pulled back onto the highway and for a long time he drove and nobody spoke. Eddie had never heard of a nice little guy named Jimmy, but now he wanted to tell the world his story, along with all the other shockers he'd heard. Jimmy's story would make a perfect stand-alone episode in the series he was plotting in his head. He was sure he was onto the biggest, most incredible news story he'd ever *heard*, much less written. He'd track down the daughter in Arizona, get photos of the old fishing camp to go with the story. Maybe it would restart the investigation into the disappearance of Jimmy and his wife. He'd have a chance to do something good, and more important, to do something bad to people who really had it coming.

They stopped at a diner on a traffic circle in the pines out by the air base in Lakehurst. The old man was embraced by the owner, a short exuberant Greek with slicked-back gray hair and a flashing smile who seated them in a large corner booth and refused to let them pay for their pie and coffee.

"I don't know what to do about this prosecutor, this *Heckendorfer*," Esposito groused. "Even if he does have an attitude, he's the Organization's boy. This indictment is supposed to put me away legally, no muss no fuss. You know that during the last campaign, the Organization put a muzzle on him because he was turnin' voters *off* on the whole ticket? They still had to spot him an extra thirty-nine votes even though the Organization made sure the mother of the Democrat's abandoned bastard popped up in the newspapers a week before the election!" Esposito hooted. "Oh, the sex stuff I could tell you!"

One hour later, the Cadillac bumped slowly along a dirt road through oak and pine forest near Cassville. Peering into the vast darkness around them, Eddie wondered how far they had driven off the county two lane and into the woods. They went over a rise and down into a dirt yard behind a dilapidated clapboard farmhouse. Esposito swung the Cadillac around, so the headlights lit up a weedy field ending in a row of gray, empty chicken coops, the first two fallen in on themselves.

Esposito turned and looked at Eddie, their faces inches apart. A hard gust of wind rocked the car.

"Last stop. I bought this place in '55." He pointed to the field in the headlights. "Over there is Benny Nails. The Terranova Brothers. Pussy DeFasio. Sick Nick Gugliocello." His voice was heavy with regret—the things a man had to do in this world. "I'm tellin' you things people would pay a lot of money to know. Things that could put me in jail. Ain't that right, Tommaso?"

"That's right, Pop." *So why are you doing this?*

"They all tried to take me on. And there they are. The thing I'm tellin' ya is, compared to men like these, Bobby Castellucci is a *girl*."

Eddie lit a Lucky Strike with a steady hand. Ignoring his feelings, he was trying to understand why Esposito would give him all this dirt and even put it on tape for others to hear. He was giving him a story which, if true, could destroy careers and reputations, send people to prison, or… worse.

"Another thing: I got a special patch in that coop on the end, a little job I took on for one of our fine upstanding public officials. So you see, if they keep coming down on me—"

The nearness of death gave Eddie a certain clarity and courage.

"Is Kenny Rosenfeld out here?"

Esposito seemed surprised by the question. "No."

"Are you saying, 'No, I don't know,' or 'No, because I know where he really is'?"

"Why would I wanna hurt Rosenfeld?"

"Rosenfeld's movement wants to stop home building 'til the school taxes level off. That'd put a lot of your union boys out of work."

"True, but I wouldna let it get that far. Everybody has their price, even a Rosenfeld."

"Do you think he's dead?"

"Probably. But I didn't kill him."

"Then who did?"

"Somebody with more to lose than me."

"Rosenfeld's moratorium threatened Roy McTierney's business."

"More than anybody else's."

"You're saying Castellucci got rid of him?"

"Do I have proof? Of course not. But that's what makes sense, doesn't it?"

"*Maron*!" Tommy groaned in the back seat. "Why are you telling this kid all this? You know how many people you named on those tapes?"

"I have my reasons," Esposito sighed.

Eddie barely listened. If Esposito believed that Castellucci killed Kenny Rosenfeld, how many other people did that make sense to? The obvious answer was anybody who knew the real setup, which had to mean a helluva lot of people. Yet his disappearance remained officially a mystery, the investigation going nowhere. Like, on purpose? It made him sick at heart to hear that Rosenfeld was probably dead and remember that only yesterday he'd been toasting the holiday season with the man who probably killed him. And another thing—how could Frank be so comfortable with a two-bit gangster like Castellucci?

"So Eddie, you got your story?"

"In more ways than one."

"Got more than you bargained for, eh? So now what?"

"Well, first I talk this over with my editor."

"No. No talk. Play him the tapes. You got that? I gave you an interview, now you do somethin' for me. Play him the tapes."

"It's a deal." They shook hands. Esposito thought he was a standup guy he could do business with. A deal between men. He couldn't wait to play the tapes for Frank anyway, so he saw no harm in making such a promise.

Esposito nodded, satisfied. He started the engine.

"Can we go home now?" Sally yawned.

"Sure. Hey Eddie, you know I lost my cherry in a graveyard? It's a cute story." Esposito started the car rolling. "Turn that thing off first."

Esposito never stopped talking on the drive back to Lakewood. The story of the loss of his virginity to a waitress at his father's café was scatological and hilarious, especially as he described the sexual positions possible in his father's Model T. Eddie nodded and laughed like he was paying attention, but his mind was really on Kenny Rosenfeld.

He'd covered the first Building Moratorium Now meeting back in March. In a lecture hall at Ocean County College in front of a couple dozen homeowners and a few reporters, Rosenfeld laid out his radical solution to halt the rising tax bills for school expansion: stop populating the county so fast. Ban building residences for two years, which would increase the value of the homes already built and shift the labor force to public works like new sewerage systems and recreation areas. It was a long meeting with a lot of discussion, and afterward, Eddie complimented Rosenfeld on how well he had connected with the audience.

"Tomorrow night you'll get a better story," he said, twirling his moustache between two fingers and wiggling his eyebrows. "I'm speaking to the Chamber of Commerce."

The next night he gave the same speech and was booed and cursed as Eddie watched from the back of the room. Rosenfeld's public relations fiasco at the chamber dinner was the first news story Eddie wrote about him and his movement, and the next day Rosenfeld called him to say he liked it. That spring his movement opened chapters in Dover,

Lakewood, Jackson, Brick and Berkeley Townships, the fastest growing towns in the fastest growing county in America. "We'll be taxed out of our homes before we've had a chance to live in them," is all Rosenfeld usually had to say. "Who should control a community's growth, the developers who take their profits and go away, or the residents who have to live with the results?" The chamber members denounced his proposal as socialism and said worse things behind his back.

Rosenfeld, a competitive poker player, admitted to Eddie that he enjoyed the battle. What Eddie liked most was how Rosenfeld's story took him to worlds far beyond the Jersey Shore. Rosenfeld grew up in Long Beach, south of Los Angeles. He graduated from UCLA in 1955 and joined the Army and spent three years in France and Germany doing soft duty in a transport company, learning the back roads and the cultures of those countries by heart. A placid Army life of regular hours, wine and fine cuisine, and the company of women with "European morals" was possible when he did his service in the late '50s. That all changed, Rosenfeld explained, after President Kennedy hurt his back planting a tree on Arbor Day, 1961, and met shortly thereafter, heavily sedated, with Khrushchev, who lectured and humiliated Kennedy all through their Vienna summit, sending Kennedy home determined to stand up to the Communists, somehow, somewhere. The place he chose was a former French colony in Indochina known as Vietnam.

"The French raped Vietnam for a hundred years," Rosenfeld once said. "I doubt most Americans know that Ho Chi Mihn was at the Versailles peace talks *fifty years ago*, arguing for independence. This is a post-colonial war of national unification and we're getting in the way, propping up the stooge government left by the colonial oppressors. If the people running America really had any morals or brains, they'd help the Vietnamese unite their country, then undermine communism with foreign aid and consumerism, not bomb it into oblivion. But we have a military-industrial complex to feed, so…"

By day, Rosenfeld taught history at Ocean County College. His worldview, delivered over a bottle of zinfandel one night at his house, a cheap one floor ranch and carport affair in Point Pleasant, was that the human being was a flawed animal who could always be relied upon to screw up under the best of circumstances. "But see, I'm a Jew," he'd say. "Germany, the most culturally enlightened, technically advanced, *rationalist* society in Europe, built factories to exterminate Jews, including my grandparents, with maximum efficiency. So you'll pardon me if I don't trust any society to do what's right, and if I believe there's no order in the universe we can grab onto for solace or balance. We just make it up the best we can."

He was out of place at the Shore. He admitted he'd never be here except that his wife, a Lakewood girl he met at UCLA, had to help her widower father run the family chicken and vegetable farm off County Line Road. He'd prefer to make his living at the card tables in European casinos, to drift with the summer weather from the Edinburgh Arts Festival in the north to the big jazz festival in San Remo to the south, and to follow his desires and interests as they arose. But for now, educating young minds in New Jersey had to suffice for excitement.

During the October moratorium against the war, Rosenfeld led an all-day teach-in at the college. Eddie wrote the story and shot all the pictures. By then they were talking on the phone at least once a day to trade information, gossip and speculation. For the march on Washington in November, they drove down to the capitol the night before in the Impala, talking the whole way, and slept on air mattresses on the parlor floor of a college friend of Rosenfeld's who had a house in Georgetown. The next day they marched peacefully with a half million demonstrators to the Mall and listened to speeches on a crystal-clear freezing afternoon. Eddie wore the white dove on a blue button from that march on his jacket collar for months afterward.

That night they were standing on the outskirts of an SDS protest rally at Dupont Circle when it turned violent. Bricks from a nearby construction site got thrown and windows were broken. The police arrived as Eddie and Rosenfeld tried to get through the dense, milling crowd. Trotting down Connecticut Avenue, Rosenfeld had gotten ahead of him because Eddie couldn't resist staying behind to observe the action. Then a tear gas shell exploded a few steps in front of Eddie and a stinging burning cloud knocked him against a building. He closed his eyes against the heat, and his face and hands and nose burned so badly he was sure his skin was peeling off. He sank to the sidewalk, terrified he'd been blinded, leaning against the wall, the cold air burning his nostrils when he breathed. Running feet stampeded around him, blurred in his streaming eyesight. He felt two hands grasp his coat cuffs and heard Rosenfeld say, "It's me, it's me, you're okay, just don't rub your face or your hands, you'll make it worse. Get up. Can you see okay?"

"I can't see, I can't see…"

He put an arm around Eddie's shoulders and walked him several blocks to the headquarters of the protest march in an old Abyssinian Baptist church. Leaning on a wall in the entrance, through his blurred, streaming eyes Eddie saw bedlam inside the church, people rushing around in every direction. Rosenfeld yelled for help and a guy wearing an armband helped carry him downstairs to the basement. The whole way, half blind and gasping, Eddie gave up all control and trusted them with his life. They put his head and hands under the faucet of the janitor's slop sink and turned on freezing cold water. "The longer you can stay in the water the more of this shit will wash off," the volunteer said, "but whatever you do, don't rub it."

Rosenfeld held him by his jacket collar and Eddie put his face and hands under the spigot for fifteen minutes, his eyes burning and his head throbbing from the cold water and half drowning in the process, washing his hair with numb fingers. It took a little of the burn out of his skin, but his stinging face and hands were swollen and red. The volunteer put Eddie's jacket in a shopping bag and told him to have it dry cleaned to get the chemical out. Rosenfeld called a cab for them and they went back to the friend's house where Eddie lay awake all night ensconced on the couch with his hands and face throbbing. Rosenfeld laughed and said with his red swollen face he looked like Charles Laughton in the movie *The Hunchback of Notre Dame*. Next day, Rosenfeld drove them back up to New Jersey, six hours of talking about everything under the sun, Rosenfeld calling him "Quasimodo" the whole way, "Quoz" for short. Two days later, Rosenfeld vanished.

They got back to the Sunset Lodge around nine o'clock, veering off the driveway and into a small parking area behind a screen of hemlocks. Tommy and Sally said good night, glad to be rid of him, and walked toward the hotel.

"Snow's comin'," Esposito said to nobody in particular, looking at the sky. He turned to Eddie. "So?"

Eddie managed a casual shrug. "Gotta go to work." He was still blue from thinking about Kenny Rosenfeld, but he had a story to write, the first of several.

"You'll play the tapes for Frankie Devlin. That's our deal, right?"

"That's our deal." He swelled, saying that.

"You see why I'm so fuckin' mad?" Esposito said. "It's against everything I believe in to talk about people this way. But look what they're trying to do to me. We had a deal, they broke it. And for years, these people did business with me and kept their reputations clean."

"Not for long." Don't get so cocky, he told himself, not just yet. There was one more thing he'd been aching to ask all night. "Mister Esposito—do you know my father?"

"Who's your father?"

"Ed Bonneville."

"Ed Bonneville. Right. Brick Town Committee."

"Right. Where does he fit in all of this?"

"Well, I won't bullshit ya."

Eddie nodded.

"He ain't *okay*, is how people see him."

"You mean—"

"Nobody trusts him, because he's, like, a fuckin' Boy Scout. He's a good Organization man like the rest, but he won't take a nickel. He's a big vote getter so he's good for the ticket, and they'll never run against him in the primary, but when they talk money—you know, I mean *money*—they don't talk about it around him."

"He's not crooked enough to be trusted."

Esposito shrugged. "That's your old man."

"You're telling me the truth?"

"I'm telling you what I know. If he's in on the setup, I don't know about it."

"And if anybody would know, you'd know, right?"

Esposito shrugged.

"Okay," Eddie said. "Thanks a lot."

They shook hands and said goodbye. The old man's hand closed around his hand so hard he thought bones would break. He got in the Impala and left.

Esposito watched the kid drive away. He lit his cigar again, hawked and spat noisily, muttered, "Merry Christmas, boys," and headed inside the Sunset Lodge.

Driving south on Route 9 out of Lakewood, he could barely keep the Impala under the speed limit. Eddie kept his hand on his cassette recorder, as if to prevent the stories captured there from escaping. Instead of turning east on Route 88 and going to his apartment at the beach he decided to head south on Route 9 and go to the newsroom, which would be deserted on Christmas Eve. He needed a cool, quiet place where he could sit and play back the confessions of Matty Esposito.

Christ Almighty, what a story! Not the image you got from those "Greetings From The Jersey Shore" postcards. How dare those so-called respectable citizens indict Esposito? Were the men who took his bribes for decades any better? The men he said he'd been the muscle for, even committed murder for? The men that Eddie, as a young reporter, had interviewed so tremulously, impressed by their fancy government titles, and felt so lucky to rub shoulders with? How proud he'd been of himself, walking among the big shots! Well, look at what the backstabbing weasels were doing to Matty Esposito. They even stuck him with a label in the press, branding him the boss of the dark and criminal side of a supposedly clean, upstanding community. But to hear Esposito tell it, the darkness was everywhere.

Esposito trudged into his suite at Sunset Lodge and found himself alone.

"Sally?" No reply. He tossed his overcoat over the sofa. The phone jingled. Esposito checked his watch before he answered.

"Seven four two four."

"You fuckin' old bastard!" a man snarled, so loud the earpiece buzzed.

"Bobby Castellucci. I'm honored," the old man said, without a trace of feeling. "Merry—"

"You couldn't just fuckin' retire, right?! You had your chance! Now I'm gonna fuckin' kill you!"

"Speak up Bob. I wanna make sure the FBI gets all this on the wiretap."

"You're dead! You are fuckin' *dead*!"

"Sorry I missed the party, Bob. Did you have fun? I hope so."

"You're dead! You hear me old man? You're fuckin' *dead*!"

"Merry Christmas, Bobby. Ho. Ho. Ho."

Around eleven o'clock the train stopped. The lights in the passenger coaches dimmed to a weak yellow as the Shore train changed its electric locomotive to diesel on a ten-minute stop in South Amboy. A few passengers got off and trooped across a cinder back yard to the rear door of a tavern and came back out with six packs and white cardboard containers of beer. Cold beer on a freezing winter night, Ivy thought, I'm back in New Jersey. She was dying, in fact, for a cup of tea, for anything warm. She fidgeted in the corner of her seat, unable to fit her shoulder to the windowsill, unable to relax.

Her escape from the townhouse and from David had required more lies to cool him out, over dinner at his favorite Indian place in the East Village. Of course, she had to say those things—*I love you, I'll call you, I'll hurry back, I promise*—because otherwise he wouldn't have let her leave. But those things were also partly true. She wanted to say to hell with her parents and Christmas and just stay in the city with David, a bad urge that fortunately was impossible to indulge on a southbound train. One day she might be glad to be free of him. For now, she had to force herself to ignore her feelings, do what her mind told her was best, and carry out her plan: separation for a few weeks, then a phone call to David quickly breaking it off. Just keep moving, she told herself, and give yourself time. Right now you're better off anywhere but New York, even back home down the Shore.

The train lurched as a diesel locomotive backed in and coupled. The coach lights came on, and the passengers outside climbed aboard and hurried to their seats.

She lit a Marlboro as the train picked up speed on the journey south. With every mile she left David behind and traveled deeper into her past, and both moves made her nervous. She tried to console herself with the thought that after an oppressive visit home with Mister and Mrs. Ruling Class and some sweet days and nights with Eddie Bonneville, her future would be as open as the dark sky over the vast Aberdeen estuary that the train rattled across before plunging back into the woods of upper Monmouth County. There were fourteen stops before the tedious journey ended, fourteen stations whose names she could recite like a poem whose metrics needed work: Matawan, Hazlet, Middletown, Red Bank, Little Silver, Long Branch, Elberon, Allenhurst, Asbury Park, Bradley Beach, Belmar, Spring Lake, Manasquan, and finally Point Pleasant Beach and Bay Head.

Once home, the farce of a family life at the Porter mansion would play out for a couple more acts, starring the blinkered busy mother, the father who has turned into a monument to his career, and the daughter who hates them both. For her, it would be four weeks of inventing ways to avoid being alone with her father and concocting cover stories as to why. This time, they wouldn't allow her to lie and claim that school work required a quick return to New York, or to throw a fit and walk out and still have her allowance check show up in the mailbox at her apartment in the city. In her last phone call, her mother, still pretending she didn't understand why Ivy dreaded coming home for the holidays, said her parents would no longer tolerate any more "dramatics." Ivy would be required to celebrate Christmas with her family, and not leave until her classes resumed in late January. Her mother had said if she refused or failed to comply, she and her father agreed they would reevaluate paying for her schooling and life in New York, based on what they're *not* getting in return.

If that meant enduring excruciating boredom at the country club Christmas party just so the Porters could pretend to be a happy family in public, suffering small talk with people she'd like to put in front of a firing squad, then these hypocrisies were the price she had to pay to keep her parents happy and their generosity flowing. So she would play her part in the farce. She would not inform them just yet that she had taken a leave of absence and was not going back to school. Before she left they would write her a check, but instead of life at NYU it would finance a future she hadn't quite figured out yet. Meanwhile, tough and tender Eddie was always there, dear screwed up, fierce, confused, well meaning angel of mercy Eddie, and girls, all that's before you rip his clothes off. She settled back in the seat corner with her coat wrapped around her. She had found something warm to focus on, something that called her imagination out to play.

Sweating, chain smoking, knees pumping, Eddie hammered at the Underwood, piling up pages of copy beside the typewriter.

Two hours ago, he'd pulled into Bargainland, hurrying to the newsroom to write the confessions of Matty Esposito, only to come upon ambulances and police cars and a crowd of angry, dazed people outside Castellucci's Lounge. He showed his press card and the police let him look around the crime scene. Bloody bandages littered the sidewalk. People in party clothes sat in the back doors of ambulances being treated by paramedics. The glass front doors were starred and smashed. Inside, broken furniture was strewn around at weird angles. Down by the bandstand Bobby Castellucci was in a huddle with two local detectives, waving his hands around and hissing like a broken steam pipe. The burgundy shag carpet sparkled with broken glass and the place reeked of booze from broken bottles. Back outside, as he watched the ambulances pull away from the shattered club, a police sergeant told him a busload of black agitators down from Asbury invaded the place and started a riot. He said something about seven arrests. Eddie just nodded, trying not to let his astonishment show, remembering Matty Esposito chuckling, *He shoulda never got in my face.*

He let himself into the empty *Independent* offices with his key. Behind his desk, he lit a cigarette and sat there in the dark, thinking like mad. Christ Almighty. Of course. This whole night had been Esposito's revenge for the indictment. And who better to hit than the Organization's muscle, the guy they're trying to brush him aside for? So he'd hired a busload of street types to bust up Castellucci's Christmas party. Telling Eddie all those stories betraying the Organization had been another kind of attack, a warning Eddie would deliver by publishing a story and playing the tapes for Frank. He was uneasy with the trade-off, letting Esposito use him like that, but at least he'd get stories out of the deal. People needed to know about this shit.

He turned on his desk lamp and plugged his earphone into the cassette player. For an hour and a half he worked his way through the whole Esposito interview, making notes and deciding what to write.

Now the first installment, an advance announcing the series, was almost finished. His own suggested headline, in capital letters at the top, read GOP ORGANIZATION ALLEGED TO BE TOTALLY CORRUPT. As he put the pages in order and read what he'd written he could barely contain his excitement:

LAKEWOOD — "Crime and politics are only two different ways of getting the same thing," said Matty Esposito, the "Rackets Boss of the Jersey Shore," re-lighting his perpetual cigar. "In fact, most of the time, they are the same thing."

In a far-ranging interview with this Independent reporter, while leading a tour of his criminal enterprises from behind the wheel of his '69 Coupe de Ville, Esposito tore the cheerful, family resort facade off Ocean County and revealed a shadowy world of official corruption, organized crime and even murder, with himself often the man at the center.

Indicted on Tuesday for racketeering-related crimes, and labeled the area rackets boss by prosecutor Earl Heckendorfer, Esposito struck back at a variety of well-known political and business figures and the county Republican machine, claiming a corrupt relationship for decades with the organization.

Esposito's indictment and subsequent accusations are the latest in a series of revelations about organized

crime and political corruption in New Jersey, many of
them gleaned from wiretap transcripts of conversations
by Mafia members used by the FBI as evidence in a
federal extortion prosecution in Newark.

Esposito charged that the political machine was
trying to imprison him to allow Robert J. Castellucci,
a local cocktail lounge owner that Esposito described
as a rival organized crime figure new to the Shore area,
to take over his labor unions and his various illicit
businesses. He claimed Castellucci had close ties to
the powerful development and commercial interests
driving the county's phenomenal housing growth, the
fastest in America.

Reveling in his public image as rackets boss,
Esposito was candid about his role for forty years
as the central figure in local political corruption
and vice activity, detailing a self-proclaimed resume
that included bootlegging, gambling, prostitution,
counterfeiting, election fraud, loan sharking, as well
as his role in organizing the labor unions for workers
in the burgeoning construction industry.

He portrayed a political machine that has siphoned
two percent of all county business into its own coffers
since the Depression and maintains total control of all
patronage and budget priorities.

"This indictment, these are my retirement papers,"
he said. "They want somebody new to run the rackets,
somebody who'll pay off more."

Four more pages followed, dense with names, dates, crimes, and
dollar amounts, the words always coming out of Matty Esposito's
mouth, since he could quote him verbatim, precisely, with the tapes to
back him up. As he made notes for his next stories, he was disappointed that Esposito never connected Senator Thomas Porter to anything
illegal. Eddie was willing to bet Esposito never told the Senator he'd decided to rat out the Organization to a reporter. He wondered how long
the Senator would be the old hoodlum's lawyer once this story broke.

Finished, he stood and stretched and walked through the shadowy
newsroom to the front windows. The police cars and ambulances were
gone. The front doors to Castellucci's were covered in plywood and one
of the poles supporting the awning was bent. The weather had begun
to change, and the wind blew snowflakes, paper litter and bloody bandages around the parking lot.

He went back to his desk, checked the time, and called Frank Devlin.

"I talked to Matty Esposito tonight," he said. "There's a phenomenal story I just finished writing, and more to come. I'm bringing it right over. My Christmas present to you."

Frank yawned, loud. "It's after eleven o'clock, what's your hurry?"

"You're gonna wanna read this right away."

"Kid," Frank said in that dry slow *Do you get it stupid?* voice he used on people who irritated him, "I'm gonna do the Horizontal Mambo with Mrs. Devlin, and then I'm going to sleep. Call me tomorrow."

"Frank, wait!" His editor was treating him like a pest. "It'll take you ten minutes to read. You gotta read it and give me your reaction—"

"I'll read it Friday—"

He stood up to pace, his nerves and the phone cord stretched to the limit. "*You* put me on special assignment! Pursue the guy 'til he talks! Well, he talked! Believe me—"

"What are you so shook up about?" Frank said. "Did he say anything that can't wait until after the holiday?"

"Forty years of organized crime and political corruption at the Jersey Shore. A total history, told by the guy in the middle of it all." He lit a Lucky Strike and inhaled deep.

"Kid, he has a tendency to rant and rave as you know —"

"That's not what this is. He gave me names, dates, places, dollar amounts. We took a nice long ride. He *showed* me where the bodies are buried, for Chrissakes. Let me bring the copy to you tonight. You gotta read this thing."

"Listen, kid. You got the story. Good work. Another Eddie Bonneville Exclusive. Put the copy in an envelope, swing by and *quietly* put it in my mailbox. I'll read it in the morning."

"You'll call me, right?"

"Right."

Eddie, separating the carbon copies of the story, asked, "You want me do the Castellucci story, too?"

"What Castellucci story?"

"They had a riot in the middle of their big party tonight. They're claiming a busload of blacks came in and busted the place up."

There was silence for a moment, then: "What? N–n–no kidding." He'd never heard Frank so flustered before.

"Yeah. I'm gonna make some calls—"

"Don't bother people about it tonight, kid."

"Yeah, but Frank—" He wanted to tell his editor it was all one story, that Esposito engineered the mayhem at Castellucci's, but Frank cut him off.

"Jackson'll get it tomorrow for Friday's paper." That stung. Worse, somehow Eddie knew that Frank's next call would be to Bobby Castellucci. He found himself wondering what Frank's real relationship was with Bobby. "Eddie, it's Christmas Eve, what're you doing working?"

"Didn't you *hear* the story I got tonight?"

"Don't take that fuckin' tone with me, Eddie," Frank snapped. "*Ever.*"

"Sorry."

"I see and hear a lot more than you could possibly know."

"That's why I'm working for you, Frank. I know I still have a lot to learn."

"Leave the copy in my mailbox and go home," Frank said. "Better yet, go get laid. It sounds like you need it."

He hung up. He wanted hurl the phone through a wall. Sometimes his editor was impossible to understand. He lands a story that lays bare forty years of organized crime and political corruption, and Frank isn't impressed. But when the saloon where Frank drinks for free gets busted up, that gets his attention?

Well, when he read the Esposito story, he'd better give it the respect it deserved. Having written it in one mad streak of concentration, Eddie was drained, wise and disillusioned, powerful and sad, all at once. He grabbed his jacket and pulled it on and tied his scarf too tight around his neck.

FOUR *Rama Lama Ding Dong*

He parked the car in front of the bank near the Point Pleasant Beach railroad station. Nervous about what to expect—not from Ivy, from himself—he got out and started pacing. On his Timex, it was a few minutes before midnight. He lit a cigarette as feathery snowflakes floated down to the black street and died.

For the hundredth time that night, he told himself it would be simple. Just greet Ivy like a former lover who was now a friend. Drive her to the Porter mansion and wish her a Merry Christmas. Go home and forget that she's in town. He kept telling himself he could do it… even as his resolve evaporated in the heat of his longing for her. He was still angry with her for dumping him last fall, and disappointed with himself for betraying his decision not to see her, but then he remembered her touch, her low quiet voice, how breathtaking she looked naked, how excited they got making love. Maybe things could be different, this time around. Maybe—

The whistle of an approaching train shook him back to reality, and he became annoyed with himself. What did he mean, 'this time around?' They broke up months ago in the city, when she hurriedly flipped him off and walked away. He knew it was better if he didn't see her now. So what the hell was he doing here?

He turned his collar up against the cold. Snow fell heavily now through the yellow cone made by the headlight of the approaching train. The snow caught in the angles of the station's tiled roof and coated the long green copper canopy on black iron columns that sheltered the platform. The train, a blue steel locomotive and four rusty coaches, came to a stop in a cacophony of screeching metal and hissing brakes. Point Beach was the next to last station, and only a few passengers were left to get off, greet their rides with a handshake or a hug and a kiss, or wave to one of the yellow Checker cabs idling outside the taxi office across the street.

Ivy stepped down into the lights of the platform, dressed in jeans and a black leather motorcycle jacket with a canvas rucksack over one shoulder. Her hair was loose and longer than he remembered. He tossed his cigarette and crossed the street toward the station as the train moved away. She saw him coming, and, with a huge smile, she waved. His heart sank; loping toward him, she was more beautiful than ever.

"Hello, champ." She gave him a quick hug, no kiss. Her hair smelled like Clairol Herbal Essence, the hip new shampoo. "Typical me, right? Getting you out on a cold night like this?"

He stood there dumbstruck, looking at her with a sudden, intense interest in the snowflakes collecting in her hair.

"I guess it's not fair, is it," she said, "popping up out of the blue a couple months after we broke up and all?"

"Is that what we did?"

"Well—" she said— "whatever we did—"

"Well, I said I'd be here, and I'm here."

"And in such a good *mood*. So uh, do you want to go to the O–B and eat, and we could talk and catch up, and all that rot?"

He shrugged.

"Are you hungry?"

"No, I don't think so," he said, forgetting he'd missed dinner. On the edge of an abyss, who thinks about his stomach?

"Champ, if this whole thing is too much for you, why don't you just drop me off at my parent's place?" He puzzled her, he could see that. Hell, he was puzzled with himself. Sure, he had a plan, but what did he really *want*?

He gave her a little shrug, paralyzed, and shook his head.

"No good either," she said. "Well, what do you wanna do? Or are you gonna make me guess?"

Well, he'd forced this choice on himself, and now it was time to decide. He could do the right thing, the wise and healthy thing, and drop her off with her parents. Or he could do the risky, wrong thing, and take her to his room. The right thing would be good for him and feel terrible, the wrong thing would feel wonderful at first, but after that…

"Well, there's always the boardwalk," she said, meaning if something was wrong they could walk and talk it out, like always. A sly grin. "Too bad it's too cold to go underneath."

She alluded to one of their favorite memories, a hot summer afternoon lying on a blanket on the cool sun-striped sand under the boardwalk with people strolling overhead. With her hand down her bathing suit, she'd crowed, *Women don't need men to have orgasms*, then demonstrated, moaning softly as he watched in amazement, to which he replied, *Well, we don't need girls to get off either*, and with a few tugs on his cock came all over her bare belly, after which they laughed themselves silly.

For once in your life, for all the right reasons, drive the girl to her parent's house and be done with it. But that was a pretty weak sermon compared to his memories.

"I think this snow may turn into something," he said, sounding stupid even to himself.

"So maybe we better get going," she said, shivering. "*Somewhere.*"

Like—his apartment under the roof of the beach house, the surf crunching outside, in bed tangled with her warm body and long legs under the blankets, while snow collected on the windowsills and the radio played low...

"Okay," he said. "Can we start over?"

"Whatever."

He walked a few steps away. He shrugged, turned, and sauntered back, grinning slowly. He leaned in, his hand in her hair getting wet from melted snowflakes, and kissed her on the mouth, and she eagerly pulled him against her. Her lips were warm, her mouth tasted of cigarettes and chewing gum.

"Your *ride* is here, m'lady."

"*Veddy good*, driver," she said, in her parody of the hated rich girl she happened to be. "Anywhere around this sleepy little town I can get a little Rama Lama Ding Dong?" Borrowed from the old rock n' roll song—by The Edsels, of course—it was their private nickname for fucking.

"Oh—" How could it be so easy for him to throw away a decision that had been so torturous to make? "I'm sure something can be arranged."

She stepped close to him and put her lips next to his ear. "Then quit acting weird and take me to your love shack in the sky."

He drove down to the boardwalk and turned south. Ocean Avenue was empty, everything was coated in snow. He concentrated on keeping the car from skidding, but the whole way to his place in Bay Head the scolding voice in his mind wouldn't leave him alone. You're in for it now, dude. He'd thought he could take Ivy to her parent's house, but here he was, driving in the other direction. He'd really thought he could resist her. So much for will power. He had decided that to keep her at arm's length was necessary to his mental health. So much for mental health.

He turned off Osborne Avenue into a one block street ending at the beach. The lights were off in Billy Foster's house, a rambling old three-story Cape Cod facing the street with its side to the ocean, with weathered brown shingles and white trimmed windows and white porches at every floor. They climbed the long white stairway on the ocean side of the house up to the top floor.

The best thing about Eddie's apartment was the view from outside his door. From here the rolling Atlantic was endless. Shafts of moonlight broke through the black clouds and made silvery trails down the backs of the waves breaking along the beach. Up the coast, a string of blue lights glowed along the Point Pleasant boardwalk.

"Ah." She leaned on the railing, gazing out over the ocean. "This is one of the places I go to in my head, whenever I want to feel better." She hugged him closer and sighed contentedly. Snow began to swirl thicker around them.

The apartment, smelling faintly of the sun-baked mildew of summer, occupied the whole top of the house with large window gables north and south. In the north gable was a double bed and a small table holding a lamp and clock radio. A battered old desk and chair and shelves of books and records were crammed into the south gable. At the far end of the flat was the bathroom and a kitchenette, with a cafe table and two chairs beside a window looking west over the rooftops and highway to the head of Barnegat Bay. It was a peaceful place to live for seventy-five dollars a month, echoing with the surf breaking on the beach, the cries of gulls, and the wind under the eaves, and it had been the first place where they could really be alone together.

"So... still a pacifist?" she said, hanging up her coat and folding down the collar of a black and white checked flannel shirt.

"Some days more than others."

From a center rafter a punching bag hung from a battered plywood circle, above which were stuffed his speed bag gloves and a jump rope. Ivy reached up and slapped the punching bag. "Penny for your thoughts when you're hitting this thing."

He laughed. "If that bag could talk—"

"What would it say?"

"It's good exercise, that's all," he shrugged. "Sometimes I need to blow off steam."

"Don't I know."

Ivy went into the bathroom and water began running in the sink. He turned off the ceiling light and switched on his desk lamp. It gave the room a shadowy, romantic atmosphere and hid the fact that he hadn't cleaned up the papers, stacks of books, and album covers strewn around. Tacked to the wall over a beat up black Royal portable on the desk were posters of Allen Ginsberg, Jean Paul Belmondo, Bogart, Bob Dylan gone electric, the Beatles, and Muhummad Ali. In the corner stood a Yamaha acoustic guitar, and an old Zenith television with rabbit ear antennae sat on the bookcase. He turned on the radio, and despite the snowstorm WNEW-FM came in strong from New York, Allison Steele "The Nightbird" playing Marvin Gaye, telling his girl he'd heard some talk, he knew she planned to make him blue. The song got on his nerves and he turned the dial to the jazz station in Long Branch.

"I like the Gladys Knight version better anyway," Ivy said.

"Me too."

"She's so *sassy*."

Ivy draped her arms over his shoulders and lifted her face. Even while kissing her, he heard Billy asking, Are you insane, seeing her again? He really didn't know. His heart was pulling him along, his mind could only watch and wonder what the hell he was doing. How many nights this fall had he sat outside on the porch, smoking, watching the sea, willing the phone to ring and her voice to be there, then telling himself to stop it, but picking up the telephone to call her in New York, then somehow finding the strength to put the phone down before dialing that last number? After all that work detaching himself, why the hell did he bring her here? Why was he doing this to himself? Because he'd lost her once and the loneliness had been unendurable? Did he want her so much he didn't care if he got in over his head again? Why the hell did Ivy always get her way?

She giggled, nipped his ear, loosened his belt and unzipped his trousers. Kissing her neck, half dressed, he sighed. "I must be crazy."

"I know exactly what'll restore your sanity."

"Slow down, okay?"

"Sure. I found what I'm looking for."

"I'm not even sure I'm into this."

"I have a handful of evidence that says you're wrong."

He pushed her away. Her feelings were hurt. Too bad. She knew she pissed him off, but as usual she didn't care as long as she got what she wanted.

He zipped up his pants. "Remember what you said to me in New York, the last time I saw you? Before you jumped in a cab with your friends? 'I can't have some guy from my hometown in *New Jersey* hanging around Manhattan, complicating my life'." He let her hear how bad that hurt. "So what are you doing here now? Complicating *mine*?" He realized that he was still stuck in that moment she dismissed him on that New York street corner.

"Y'know, let's just forget this, man," she said, sliding off him. She grabbed her coat off the peg near the door. "Just take me home."

"Answer my question."

"Take me home!" She wrestled her way into her coat.

"Answer my question! Why'd you call me? What do you want from me?" He lit a Lucky Strike; a condemned man's last smoke? He'd dragged them into uncharted territory. She was offended, and unaccustomed to explaining herself. "Why are we even together tonight?" he said. He wished he hadn't asked, but it was too late to stop now.

"You're really asking me that? After three years?"

"I promised myself I'd never see you again," he said, weakly, like he needed her help to keep that promise.

She looked stricken. "Okay, well, that settles that. Let's go."

But he couldn't. He had tried to convince himself that he was finished with her, that he was, theoretically at least, used to life without her. So why was he unable to just put on his coat and take her home?

Oh man, why not just tell Ivy she held all the power? Because she knew that already, didn't she? And she was so sure of her power over him that she decided to let him off the hook.

"On the other hand," she said, dropping her coat over a chair, "promises to yourself are the most fun to break." She was never one to call it a night if there might be something more interesting to do.

She slid her arms around him. He gently disentangled himself. She chuckled, took his cigarette and dragged, and watched him pace miserably around the room.

"How the hell," he said, "could you even *ask* if I'm getting like everybody else around here?"

"When did I say *that*?"

"This afternoon on the phone."

"Oh, yeah. I guess I did," she said, popping her shirt buttons. "Sorry."

"Was I like everybody else when the story got out about you and Mister Angelo, and everybody in school hated your guts? Who told you, 'Hold your head high?' Even after he hung himself?"

Her eyes lowered, she handed him his cigarette, slipped off her work shirt, and dropped it. "You were the only one that didn't want me burned at the stake."

"What about springtime, '68? I was ready to quit school and get a job! I was ready to marry you and be a 17-year-old father!"

Popping open her Levi buttons, pulling out her tee shirt, she shook her head, hurt. "That's not fair. You know my father dragged me to that doctor."

"Yeah. I also know why."

Her eyes grew large, her voice, very small. "Can we not talk about that? Please?"

"I'm trying to get you to notice something," he said.

She peeled her tee shirt off and dropped it. Bare breasted, she took off a long string of ebony love beads and piled them atop the bureau. She sidled toward him. "Notice what?" she said. She laid her wrists on his shoulders. He noticed something new, tufts of black hair sprouting from her armpits. He smelled the men's cologne from Spain she always wore. Spelled *Canoe*, she pronounced it *kan oh ay*. He gazed into her eyes, those violet jewels with the mischievous gleam.

"When all the others bite the dust," he said, "I'll be here. Any other guy—"

She put a finger to his lips. "You're not just any other guy. You're the only person on this entire planet who understands me. Who accepts me the way I am. Nothing means more to me than that. Nobody means more to me than you."

Her arms tightened around his neck. They kissed long and deep, and it all rushed back to him: the chewing gum and tobacco taste of her mouth and how she liked to hunt for his tongue with hers, the clean smell of her thick black hair that was always slightly damp at the roots, her aroma, the curve of her hip beneath his hand, the easy way her body fit against his as if they were old dance partners, the way her hands always knew what to do, beginning with his clothes. He closed his eyes, feeling her fingers getting reacquainted with his body. He eased her back on the bed and pulled her blue jeans off, dragging her panties off too in one smooth stripping.

After so long, making love with her was a return to familiar wonders. Every thrill she made him feel and every thrill he gave—and they gave each other all they had, as always—reminded him how terrifying it was to experience such beauty, to plunge into such pleasure with a girl who might be gone again tomorrow. The longer they fucked, the further he traveled down the road to ruin. It ended with an explosion of sheer joy that erased all doubt, all irony, all thought, except one: he'd just made a date with heartbreak again. But he'd worry about that tomorrow.

He woke up a little while later. The room was cold, and he was shivering. His desk lamp cast a golden glow and the radio was softly playing Sinatra singing on a record from the '40s, "These Foolish Things." Ivy lay asleep, curled on top of the sheet where they'd passed out, the blankets kicked down to her feet. He got off the bed, pulled the blankets up and tucked them gently around her shoulders.

He pulled on a sweatshirt and pants and a pair of thick socks, turned off the radio and the light, and sat down at his desk in the dark. The storm gusted against the house like it was trying to blow it out to sea, and the windows rattled slightly and glowed with a blue, milky light. Out the window, the beach was a stark white curve where it met the black ocean. The wind was white and nearly blotted out the rooftops and telephone poles, and the swaying cables strung between the blue streetlights were thick with snow.

Across the room Ivy murmured something, stirred under the blankets, and rolled on her back. Streetlight entering though a crack in the curtains shone over her face and her tranquil grin. Soon her breathing became soft and deep. Being within the sight and sound and smell of her did strange things to him inside, aroused feelings he thought he'd put away. How could she lie in bed so peacefully while he sat there unable to sleep, a riot going on in his heart?

There was no going back to his life of only a few hours ago, so admirably disciplined and hard working—and so predictable and joyless. He was still in love with her, and tonight the world and all things in it were blessed, even his suffering was sweet. Gazing at Ivy, sleeping blissfully in his bed, undid whatever had held him together in the months since he saw her last.

He went quickly and quietly into the bathroom and closed the door. He caught a glimpse of himself in the mirror, his face crumpled and flushed and bewildered. Oh man, he wasn't really gonna do this, was he? He sat on the edge of the tub and held a plush towel across his face and began to cry for the first time in weeks. It was difficult at first, then he was overwhelmed by sobbing that seemed like it would never end. Was he crying with relief because she was back in his life again, or was this a purge of still more sadness at having lost her, or was it both? Were these tears of thankfulness at the rebirth of his soul, or was he sad realizing how long he'd buried it under the numbness of routine? When he looked in the mirror there was no explanation, just a boy, haggard and tired.

Quietly, he padded back to the chair at his desk and settled down, gazing at her sleeping in his bed an arm's length away, still not quite able to believe what had happened tonight and that she was really there. She was the only lover he'd ever had, hers the only body he'd ever coupled with so ecstatically. Drained for the moment of desire and resolve, he was defenseless against the memories that flooded his mind.

It is a green and fragrant morning in the spring of 1965. The Bonneville family, hurting for money, has moved to a rented old farmhouse on the edge of town, a world away from the split-level his parents had built then lost. It is Eddie's first day on a new school bus route, and the bus stops at a rustic shelter by a split rail fence. Behind it, up a hill of rolling green lawn, is a distant white mansion. The girl from the house gets on, and the kids on the bus hush and stare as she walks to the rear.

He has never seen or met Ivy Porter and knows about her only by reputation: straight A student, incorrigible, rich, opinionated, lusted after and loathed. Her 15-year-old body is the legendary reef on which many boys claim to have been shipwrecked, losing their virginity, their hearts and sometimes their minds. The other kids in the freshman class, scornful of her rich and powerful father and the big house by the golf course, and feeling morally superior to her notorious promiscuity, have labeled her poison, and made her the object of smutty fascination and vicious gossip.

For two weeks, Brick Township High School has been wracked with grief because a popular math teacher has killed himself, leaving a distraught suicide note. The female student said to be involved is too young to be named in the newspapers, but everyone's been blaming Ivy Porter. According to rumor, his note didn't say he hung himself because he'd ruined his marriage, or because he'd destroyed his career, or because he was in trouble with the law, but because he was heartbroken that he couldn't have her all to himself. Curious about what kind of girl could drive a grown man to do such a thing, Eddie had pictured a young Sophia Loren, or Ursula Andress, a female animal oozing sex who left men shattered in her wake.

But the girl who gets on the school bus that morning is tall and lean and subtly curved, wide-shouldered and high-hipped, with fine pretty features, thick black hair with bangs like the silent screen actress Louise Brooks, and penetrating violet eyes. It is the *way* she walks that gets to him. Chin up, hips gently swaying, ignoring the stares and looking slightly bored with an ironic smirk as she makes her way down the aisle. *Oh my God*, he thinks, *what class.*

He sees how much the other kids love to hate her. Eddie, a loner himself in school society, stands up without even knowing what he's doing. He follows her to the back of the bus, tells the kid sitting next to Ivy to get lost, and sits down.

She has her nose deep in *The Catcher in the Rye.*

"My name's Eddie Bonneville."

Without looking up she says, "And I should care about this—*why?*" Her voice is low for a girl, and unafraid to sound intelligent.

"Uh well, I've never met you before—"

"But you know who I am."

"Well, sort of."

A crooked little grin. "And you just had to mosey on back and see for yourself, right?"

"Well, yeah, but—"

"So, go ahead. *See.*" She looks up from her book at him with eyes deeply hurt and angry, and brimming with tears. He falls in love on the spot. "Okay?" She moves her eyes back to her book. "Now, *fuck off.*"

"Hey, all I know is what people say."

"Right," she muttered. "The tramp who drove her teacher to suicide."

"Oh yeah? I didn't hear that one," he says. "I only heard the *really*
bad stuff."

She turns and peers at him. He doesn't look away. She hauls off and
punches him in the shoulder, hard.

He grins. "What's the matter," he says, "you wondering if I can take
it?"

She leans back, takes a long second look, and closes her book.

"What is this, your half-assed idea of how to meet a girl?"

"I saw you, and I had to say something—"

"Who are you, again?"

In time, they make a notorious couple in high school society, the
surly boxer and the rich tramp, but for awhile no one knows they're
together. It is their best period, before he learns that loving Ivy comes
with two major hassles, her talent for drama and her insatiable appetite
for sex.

His turn comes on a warm spring night when they sneak onto the
beach in Point Pleasant and spread a blanket under one of the over-
turned lifeguard boats. It is his first time to experience the wondrous
female orgasm, a series of demanding, thigh-gripping, fingernail-goug-
ing, hip-thrusting explosions from a woman holding him in her grip
with all she's got. Just when it seems her seizure has passed and her
hold on him relaxes, her rhythm increases and her hands grab his hair
and seize his ass and she demands pleasure all over again, and again,
and again. So awestruck is he to discover his power to unleash such
wildness in a girl that he totally forgets to come, until she gets on top
and wraps her arms and legs around him and, slowly rolling her hips,
teases the ecstasy out of him, whispering the filthiest language he's ever
heard, breathlessly and lovingly, in his ear. He passes out, and when he
wakes up later with his arms around her neck, half her body and one
leg are lying on top of him, her cheek hot and his shoulder wet with
her tears. "Hey," she says, giggling, "is that you tapping on my thigh?"
They fuck for hours under that boat until she finally pushes him away,
complaining of "windburn." Just before midnight they run down to
the surf nude and dive in. The water is so cold he thinks his heart will
stop. He comes out of the water a very different boy.

She teaches him all about love making. He proves to be an enthusi-
astic student. But his ardor soon turns to anguish when he realizes he

is not the first boy to whom she's given lessons, nor will he be the last. Her nonchalant promiscuity becomes his torturous preoccupation, his ticket to ecstasy and misery. Once his love for her becomes public, his fellow students—some puzzled, some as a warning, some with malicious helpfulness—make sure he hears all the notorious Ivy stories, like the guy with a stack of nude Polaroids of her he shows around, like the stories about the boyfriends she's stolen from nicer girls then tossed back, as well as the rumors that she's a Communist, uses drugs, has sex with black men. To him, Ivy is the most beautiful living being he has ever known, and the wilder the stories get about her, most of them sheer fantasy or spiteful lies, the more fiercely he defends her. He punches out more than one kid at the mere mention of her name in the wrong tone of voice.

Their sophomore spring, she performs in the high school talent show, in a black bikini even smaller than the one she rehearsed in, to "The Girl From Ipanema," dancing and miming as the earthy girl who makes all the men sigh. Her flirtation with an imaginary male admirer is so sexy the principal orders the curtain brought down halfway through the song. The audience groans and protests. Ivy dances right back out in front of the curtain. The audience applauds wildly. The principal stops the music. She finishes the dance anyway, singing the song acapella, takes three bows and leaves the stage. The performance is a fresh scandal, one Ivy coolly pretends not to notice. The principal and the faculty advisor to the show reprimand her backstage in front of the other performers. She listens intently, and rolls her eyes and says, "Oh, you are so pa–*thetic*!" and walks away, into a three-day suspension. She writes erotic poetry, first for the school paper until she is banned, and later, to him.

When she gets pregnant and she swears he is the father he never questions it, though any sane man would have. He convinces himself her pregnancy is a blessing that will end her screwing around and strengthen the love between them. In fact, the experience nearly wrecks them for good. After two weeks the whole crisis—the doctor's confirmation, the fight with his parents to become legally emancipated, the plans with Ivy for a life as husband and wife and as parents—ends when her father drags her on a plane to an abortionist in Puerto Rico and she vanishes from Eddie's life for two weeks. When she reappears, and tells him what happened—and everything else, more than he ever would have suspected or wanted to know about Ivy and her father—he is so shocked and angry that he can't stand to be near her. But then, in remorse and sadness for Ivy, he comes back, more determined than ever to stand by her side. He cannot forgive her father, nor dismiss the idea that if the Senator hadn't been involved, he and Ivy would have had a son or a daughter. He thinks about how the mingling of their genes might have worked in a new little human being, if her father hadn't insisted on killing it, getting rid of the evidence of his evil. He obsesses over this until he has to stop making himself so sick and sad, and he never stops believing the child had been his, the other possibility being too unspeakable to consider.

After he almost beats Rolly to death, she approves of his embrace of nonviolence as heroic and encourages him to stay on the forgiving, loving path in life. Of course, during their senior year at school, behind his back she still goes with any guy who appeals to her. He hears about some of these infidelities, but instead of losing it and giving the guy a beating, he controls himself. He keeps his dignity, he stares them all down, never again throws a punch or makes a threat, and keeps loving her for all he is worth.

Then after a year of long-distance romance, near her off-campus apartment on one of his weekends with her in New York, she dumps him without warning and leaves him standing on Broadway and Eighth Street, shattered. She makes him feel like a hick, and for days afterward he can only think of her with passionate hatred. In time, his rage burns down to just waking up heartbroken every day. Reluctantly, he comes to accept that a new life must begin. In this new life, he decides, he will not lose himself to love or anything else, he will know what is best for himself and be strong enough to live by that.

That vision of a new, better life *After Ivy* ended tonight, some time between the railroad station and his last orgasm. He had never wanted to be so vulnerable again, but in the deep heart of the night it was impossible not to love the beautiful, inscrutable girl lying before him, and this was the only way he knew how.

He got undressed and slipped back into bed. Murmuring a question he didn't hear, she slid up beside him, stretched a warm arm and leg over him, and laid her head on his shoulder. He closed his eyes and listened to her breathing.

They woke to a clear cold Christmas morning. He slipped out of bed, barefoot on the icy linoleum. Out the windows the snow lay thick on the sills, the sky was pure blue, and the sun gleamed brilliant white along the beachfront and on the whitecaps of a restless, gray green sea. He turned up the electric radiators under the windows and crawled back under the blankets.

She yawned, stretched and grinned, and rolled full length on top of him, her hair a tent over their faces. The rusty smell of the red hot coils rose, the heater going pling pling pling, as they made languorous morning love. Afterward they showered together, taking turns using the soap and sponge on each other in the narrow tub, and dressed so he could drive her home to the Porter mansion.

"Time for me to go play Daughter Puppet," she said, draping her ebony love beads around her neck. "Hey champ, what's the matter?"

He decided to risk the truth. "I'm *involved* again, and in a few days, you're gonna leave."

"Actually, I'm not going back to NYU." She pulled up her jeans and buttoned them. "Or New York," she said, tucking in her tee shirt. "But don't tell anybody."

"You're flunking out of NYU?"

"Not with a 3.9 average, I'm not." She'd always gotten good grades without even trying hard. "I took a leave of absence. I haven't told my parents yet."

"What's wrong?"

"Nothing," she said, hopping on one foot and pulling her boot on. "Just taking time off."

He wound his scarf around his neck and draped Ivy's leather jacket over her shoulders. "The day you were accepted at NYU, you did a back flip off a bench on the boardwalk."

"I need a break, man. I've been running like a hamster on a wheel."

He sighed. "Why won't you ever be honest with me? Just tell me what's wrong."

The problem, he knew, would be a breakup with some other guy. But why did he want to hear about that, since it was guaranteed to hurt? For the first time, he realized that he often tried to get her to pick that particular scab. It seemed he actually wanted to feel angry and betrayed by her. But why, especially after last night?

"Certain situations, okay?"

"Like for instance."

Ivy pulled on her backpack. "Things are a little hairy in New York, that's all. It doesn't matter why, I'm out of there." She stepped up to him, slipped her arms around him under his coat, and pulled him tight against her. "I'm *here*, champ. I love you, and I'm not going anywhere. Isn't that enough?"

FIVE *This is how things are*

After driving Ivy home, Eddie ate breakfast downstairs with Billy at the kitchen table and told him all about his interview with Esposito last night.

"The part I'll never forget," Eddie said, "was the chicken farm. I mean, he was showing me where he buried people that he murdered."

He knew Billy loved gossip and scandal, especially involving the high and mighty. But Billy was clearly not at his best that morning, hung over and pale, the house a mess and holiday guests arriving on the train before lunch. Eddie was disappointed all his story got from Billy was a bloodshot stare.

"Does what he told me surprise you?"

"No, not really," Billy said.

"I always thought public service could make people better. You know, *Ask not what your country can do for you—*"

Billy rolled his eyes and shook his head. "Yeah, Kennedy was my hero, too. But I grew up in Jersey City."

"What's that mean?"

"Never trust politicians. They steal your money, and they steal your hope."

"If corruption around here is really that big—"

"It's a big story for you."

"A story people have a right to know."

"But what if it's nothing but the ravings of an angry old man?"

"Then I guess, no story."

"Are you going to be able to tell the difference?"

"Yeah, of course."

"I don't know…" Billy sighed a toxic gust of dragon breath. "I think you're looking for a fight."

"No—"

"Yes you are."

"No I'm not."

"You're trying to prove something to people."

"I don't give a fuck what people think of me."

Billy's look said, Oh, really?

"I'm a professional. I think I know what I'm doing."

"Yeah. That's what worries me." Billy swirled the coffee in his cup and drained it.

Billy went off to get the house and himself ready for his holiday guests, leaving Eddie to ponder what he'd said. Although he wasn't deterred, he always took Billy's advice seriously. Billy encouraged his efforts toward peace, love and understanding, but he also never hesitated to be blunt when he thought Eddie needed it.

His introduction to that honesty had begun the night his father threw him out of the house. He went to talk about the situation with Billy, who thought it over for a moment, then invited him to take the efficiency apartment on the third floor of his house on the beach, which he hadn't rented yet for the summer. Before he moved in, Billy sat Eddie down, poured them both a whiskey, and told him that renting him the apartment meant he had to know if he could trust Eddie with the fact that he and all his friends were gay. Would Eddie be comfortable with that? More importantly, none of them were out of the closet, a secret Eddie had to be sure he could keep.

It was the first time Eddie had heard the word gay, instead of "homo" or "queer," "sissy" or "fairy." Everything he knew about such people came from a major story he read when he was thirteen in LIFE Magazine headlined "Homosexuality in America" (*A secret world grows open and bolder*). He didn't know why but he was fascinated by the story, although he'd freaked out when he saw in the magazine photos that his favorite style of dress—tennis shoes, tight black slacks and angora sweater—was a kind of gay uniform. He immediately changed his look to boots, jeans, and a leather jacket, just so people wouldn't get the wrong idea. He assured Billy he would be comfortable with the situation and that the secret would be safe with him. Besides, he couldn't keep sleeping in the back seat of his car.

He really liked Billy's friends. They were worldly, cultured men with a festive, insouciant attitude toward life, who came down the Shore to party on the weekends away from their jobs in the city in the exotic worlds of film, advertising and publishing. Soon, because Billy told his friends Eddie was hip and could be trusted, they were Eddie's friends as well. For the past two summers, they'd even brought him along on nights when he had nothing else to do. They smuggled him into the M&K Bar on Cookman Avenue for long nights of drinking and hilarious repartee in Asbury Park, and took him along to say hello to the rugged, profane-talking women on the sidewalk in front of Maggie and Marilyn's *Chez L*, or to observe the cruising men on the boardwalk north of Convention Hall. Feeling like a spy in a foreign country, Eddie danced and got drunk with Billy and his friends, hung out on the gay beach at Avon-by-the-Sea, and enjoyed their gossip, laced with acid wit, without matching their prodigious alcohol consumption.

Sex, however, was another matter. "If anyone tries to seduce you, and you're not interested," Billy said one night, mindful that Eddie was still 17 and a minor, "just say 'No.' My friends are faggots, not child molesters." Most of the men did want to take him to bed, and their advances disturbed him in a way he didn't understand, but he was consumed with love and passion for Ivy Porter, and he always declined. Even when he laid in bed trying to fantasize what it would be like, it seemed too strange, and he couldn't imagine going through with it. Eddie loved hanging out with Billy and his friends, they were hip and smart and they knew things about life that Eddie could scarcely imagine, but he'd decided sex wasn't part of it. He played it cool and friendly whenever one of the men made a pass at him, but he kept his door locked at night.

He also kept the secret about Billy and his friends, even from Ivy, who was around Eddie's apartment a lot the summer of '68 before she headed to school in New York. If she noticed that only men hung out at Billy's, or that on the beach the men fussed over their bodies even more than women, she never said anything, and they liked her tart language and cynical sense of humor and ballsy attitude. Rolly, however, caught onto the vibe immediately one day when he was waiting for Eddie in the car. From then on, he razzed Eddie about being queer, but Eddie never told him the truth, and for all Eddie knew Rolly never told anyone.

None of this was the growth process, if any, that his father intended when he kicked him out of the house, though he probably would have approved of the outcome. The boys at Billy's house shook their heads, sighed "Queer for girls," and accepted Eddie even though he was different. Eddie amused Billy and his friends, and Billy watched out for him like an older brother. Whenever Billy took him aside to give him advice Eddie listened, because Billy knew how the world worked.

None of the local newspapers ran any kind of story about the riot at Castellucci's last Wednesday. On Monday morning, Eddie went down to the county courthouse and when the doors opened, he found out at the clerk's office when the people who got arrested would get a hearing.

In the courtroom, he took a seat among the motley group of regulars who hung out in the courthouse all day, gossiping and knitting and entertaining themselves watching the trials. J. Paul Jackson came in at the last moment, taking the *Independent*'s chair at the press table. The defendants were brought in and the assistant prosecutor tried to make short work of it: five men and two women were charged with attempting to defraud an innkeeper, assault and battery, and malicious destruction to property.

That usually would have been that, except the public defender, Chris Bonelli, a young short-haired guy in a cheap suit, insisted to the judge that his clients were the victims of a cruel hoax. He displayed the phony drink tickets given to the defendants by somebody who called himself Father Anthony of St. Jude's parish in Newark, a priest who apparently didn't exist. He said the church had denied knowing the priest or allowing one of their school busses to be used the night of the riot. Obviously, this phony Father Anthony deceived the defendants into going to a party in a place where racial conflict was all but guaranteed, to damage the club and cause personal injury to its patrons.

While Bonelli and the assistant prosecutor argued, Eddie realized he'd seen the riot all wrong and so had the police. These weren't professional thugs or agitators hired by Esposito to bust up Castellucci's Lounge. Esposito had one of his hoodlums deceive these people into thinking they were going to a party and dump them in a hostile situation to inflict mayhem and injury on Bobby Castellucci. He felt infuriated for the seven black defendants, whose clothes were matted and wrinkled and who were depressed and angry. They'd been cruelly manipulated and injured, then jailed since Christmas Eve, and now were being treated like criminals when all they'd been expecting was a party. They were probably the only innocent people in the whole Castellucci incident.

Bonelli asked the judge to drop the charges, release the defendants, and empanel a grand jury to investigate who had deceived them. If a grand jury was assembled, Eddie thought, wasn't he a witness they should hear from? He could play them the tape of Esposito saying he ordered the hit because Castellucci was being installed by the Organization as the new rackets boss. He could tell them Esposito alluded to attacking Castellucci the night it happened. Then, despite his compassion for the defendants and his anger at how they'd been used, he realized he couldn't do any such thing. It wasn't his job to help the investigation. If he got the old man arrested again Esposito would be furious, and for Eddie there would be unpredictable and undoubtedly painful consequences, and his tapes would be impounded as evidence before he could write anything more. So he sat there and watched as the five men and two women were sent back to jail on bail too high for any of them to pay.

Downtown Toms River stood still in the fog. He went over and picked up Billy at his law office. They walked down Washington Street under the bare branches of the trees to the courthouse for his appearance before the Draft Board. While Eddie walked, he ranted about the smalltown totalitarian pinhead redneck militarists he intended to confront at the hearing. When he paused to catch his breath, Billy held up his hand.

"Get this all out of your system now," Billy said, "'cause if you let that attitude show to the Board, you'll be putting the noose around your own neck."

"You know what I'm saying is true."

"Listen to me," Billy said, stopping in front of the courthouse. "You have to be absolutely clear about this. We're *not* doing this to champion truth, justice, peace, love and understanding. We're trying to keep you out of the Army because you have psychological problems that military service will only make worse."

"So you think I'm a psycho, too."

Billy sidestepped the question. "If you had taken my advice, seen your old shrink and gotten a letter to the Draft Board, we'd have a much stronger case."

Eddie scoffed. "He wasn't much help before."

"Well, he might've been this time, but now we'll never know, will we?"

"What psychological problems?"

"Number one, rage, and a tendency to attack people physically and verbally." Billy glanced at his watch. "Number two, disconnection from reality. For the last three blocks you've been walking beside me, but you've been hallucinating yourself at war with all sorts of enemies. You're not *here*, man. You're fighting ghosts in your own brain."

He stared at Billy a moment, and then the worst thing happened. A soft wave of sadness and shame overcame him, like he'd been caught doing something he thought he'd kept hidden.

Seeing tears in his eyes, Billy gripped his shoulder. "Just stay in the real world until we get through this, please. That's all you have to do."

He nodded and followed him into the courthouse, baffled by what had just occurred. He had those angry hallucinations all the time. *Disconnection from reality?* Was that what he was doing? *Stay in the real world?* Where was that? His grip on things suddenly felt dangerously weak.

They reported to Room 201, a high-ceilinged conference room that smelled like steamed paint and stale cigarette smoke. Eddie sat at one end of a long wooden table facing the members of the county Draft Board, his notes in front of him and his attorney beside him. He took a deep breath and tried to relax. He told himself to remain calm and reasonable, but inside he was doing the Ali Shuffle on the edge of a razor.

"If I may," he said, "I have a brief statement I would like to read." Nobody spoke, so he began.

He knew Billy would watch the five members of the Draft Board as carefully as he would a jury in court. Mister Mason, the board chairman, stared at Eddie with thick disdain. He'd told Billy he resented the need to schedule this hearing at all. Chief Thompson, in a suit and tie and appearing to be reasonably sober, shook his head sadly. The lawyer on the board, Red Clayton, a droll beanpole in a three piece, looked grave and bored. Jim Gibson the building contractor in his VFW cap with the ribbons, folded his hands over his belly and glared. Lloyd Washington, the county director of the federal antipoverty and jobs creation programs and the only black guy on the board, worked himself into a visible fury, making faces so the others would see his patriotism, too.

"In closing," Eddie read, "let me repeat: I have a serious psychological problem with personal violence I am struggling with. I have come to believe that inflicting violence is immoral. I totally reject the idea that it is the soldier's duty to inflict destruction and death on human beings designated by others as the 'enemy.' These are the reasons for my application to be classified as a conscientious objector and a non-combatant. Otherwise, I stand ready to serve my country in any way it needs me."

"Well, ain't that *big* of you," Washington sneered. "You want us to find you a nice safe job someplace where you won't have to risk your neck."

"No," Eddie said. "Where others will be safe from me." Washington scoff-laughed at him.

"This is not about Mister Bonneville's courage or patriotism," Billy said.

"Or the lack," Washington said. Scoring red, white and blue Brownie points with Whitey, Eddie thought with a sneer.

"Mister Chairman," Billy said, "I had hoped we could keep the hearing on a professional level, and not stray into personal attacks."

"You don't wanna face a personal attack?" Jim Gibson sputtered. "There're boys from this county in Vietnam who face worse'n that every day."

They shouldn't be there, he wanted to scream, but he held back. The inference of cowardice was unmistakable, yet he was sure he could whip any man at this table. Easy, boy. He tightened down the lid on his rising anger. If only he could take a couple of these men by the throat, and explain things to them.

"Mister Bonneville," Clayton intoned, poking with a pencil through his copy of Eddie's application, "do you base your objections to violence and war on any religious or spiritual beliefs?"

"Yes. The sacredness of all life."

"Go to church regularly?"

"No."

"Are you a member of any congregation?"

"No. But I don't need a priest to tell me I should love and value life for its own sake. I believe attacking another person is wrong, especially if they're no threat to you."

"You believe in self defense?"

"No, it just perpetuates the violence, and when you resort to violence you not only lose the moral high ground, you make this a more violent world."

"*Apart* from Mister Bonneville's beliefs about violence and war," Billy said, "he is a very angry, disturbed young man, with one assault and battery conviction on his record already. Putting a rifle in his hands would be an irresponsible act."

"Hm… I see." Suspiciously complicated, Clayton's droll tone said, while the board members exchanged smug glances, which drove Eddie finally over the edge.

"Do you?" Eddie said, shrugging off Billy's restraining grip on his arm. "No, I don't think you do. So here's the way it is. I've got a problem. I get angry, I lose control, and I not only hurt people, I enjoy it. If that ain't sick in the head, what is? If I take that into the Army and into the war, I might make a good soldier but it'll destroy me as a human being. Not that you care. You need an Army of killers to justify your propaganda about the so-called threat to our freedom. But that's bullshit and everybody knows it. Nothing happening in Vietnam, halfway around the world, is a threat to my freedom. *You* are, right here in this room." He slapped together his paperwork. "The government has all this firepower. All I have is the power to say 'No.' I'm not going to let you draft me and turn me into a killer. I'm fucked up enough as it is."

Billy was speechless for a long time after they left. Standing next to the Impala, he sighed. "Why didn't you just tell them *fuck you*? You could have saved us a lot of time."

"Sorry. I couldn't keep it under control."

"Which actually proves the point we were making," Billy said. "Though I doubt they'll see it that way."

Eddie drove home, made a cup of coffee and sat at his typewriter, and wrote about the hearing in his journal, trying to calmly analyze what happened. He'd expected a cold but polite reception from the Draft Board members. Their undisguised contempt took him by surprise. He decided he had been naive and should have expected it.

That afternoon the Board Secretary had a letter hand-delivered to Billy's office. The phone rang in Eddie's apartment as he was leaving to go to the newsroom.

"Unanimous?" he said.

"Don't tell me you're surprised."

"Denied, why?"

Billy read from the letter. "'Applicant's request for conscientious objector classification is denied because his objection to war is not based on any recognized system of religious belief.'"

"Well, what *do* they recognize?"

"Whatever it is, you don't have it."

"You know, Muhummad Ali refused to join the Army because war is against the teachings of the Muslims," he said. "That's a major religion and look what they did to him." Convicted of Draft evasion, Ali was on bail appealing a five-year prison sentence. The boxing commission had stripped him of his heavyweight championship, he was considered a traitor by much of the public and by the sports press, and as the world of boxing moved on without him many believed his boxing career was over.

"Don't worry," Billy said. "This decision blatantly establishes religious belief as the only basis for a valid objection to war. That's where we got 'em."

"I think they've got me."

"No, this clearly violates the Constitutional separation of church and state. It discriminates against the nonreligious person of conscience. I'll write the brief immediately. Meanwhile, they'll send you a notice for a pre-classification physical. This time make sure you go. Maybe the doctors'll turn up a heart murmur or a tumor or something and you'll be exempt."

"Hey. Something to hope for."

Eddie walked into the newsroom at four o'clock. Bailey followed him to his desk.

"He wants to see you right away," she said, breathless and urgent, her eyes indicating Frank's office. He tossed his coat and scarf over his chair and hurried in.

A thin cloud of smoke clung to the ceiling light over Frank, who stood behind his desk, staring at Eddie's story. He dropped the copy on his desk like a letter bringing bad news. He stared at Eddie in a way he never had before. *I thought I knew you, and now this.*

"What do you think, Frank?"

Frank chuckled dryly at the question. "A fight over a local franchise? That's what Matty called it? Hey, I know! We'll run it on the Business Page as a joke!" His voice trembled with scorn. "Didn't I tell you this guy was fuckin' crazy?"

Unprepared for this reaction, Eddie closed the door. "It's no joke.

It's a series. Wait'll you hear some of the other stories he told me! Forty years of crime and corruption at the Jersey Shore. Unbelievable stuff—"

"I'm sure it is," Frank said.

"You know what I mean. You told me to get him to talk, didn't you?"

"Yeah, but *this*? How can we run a story like this, when Bobby Castellucci's our friend?"

What the hell—"Since when does that matter?"

"It matters to me. I guarantee you it matters to Bobby."

Okay, the story would put Frank in a sticky social position. So what? Wouldn't a real editor applaud an assignment well done? What mattered more, the story, or a saloon keeper's tender feelings?

"Eddie, you're nineteen years old. You can't say these kind of things in a story."

"I don't say them, Matty Esposito does. With permission to quote him verbatim. Who knows better than the man in the middle of all this corruption?"

"What have you got to back all this up?"

"Well, as a matter of fact—" Suddenly, despite his promise to play the tapes for Frank, he knew that if he did, he would lose them. "I'm still writing up my notes."

"*Notes*? Notes are nothing! How about proof? There's a dozen libel suits in this story. And anyway" —he shook his head slowly— "you *believe* all this stuff he told you?"

"Should I?"

Frank gave him an insulting look, surprised and sorry for him.

"Is he lying? Or is it true?"

"Matty Esposito wants revenge for being indicted. He's out to ruin the reputation of everybody he thinks is out to get him."

"That doesn't change the fact that this is news." Frank was purposely confusing the issue and it burned him up. "Why do you mock the whole idea of this story? Why do you care so much about Bobby Castellucci's feelings? Do you know he probably had Kenny Rosenfeld killed?"

Frank's face fell. "You don't know what you're talking about."

"And what about the public's right to know?"

"You kids these days, with your self-righteous fuckin' morality! You think the world can somehow be made right... as if it ever was!"

"The world can take care of itself. I'm talking about this place, right here, right now. Where we can make a difference. We can blow this whole corrupt setup sky high."

Frank slumped in his chair, lit a Pall Mall, and sighed. He looked up at him through pouched, clouded eyes, and murmured, "We can end up in the ocean in a barrel of cement."

"Is that where Kenny Rosenfeld is?"

"Eddie– Eddie–"

"So it's all true."

Frank stared at him that way again, like, oh you poor fool. "*True?* Who the hell knows what's *true?*" He scoffed and shook his head. "Look, this may be news to you, Eddie, but this is how things are. *Everywhere.* People in power are crooked. They're out for themselves. They abuse their power, lie to the public, steal whatever isn't nailed down, and then they bullshit the voters into reelecting them. Forget about what you learned in civics class."

He was stunned. "Frank—I thought that's where *we* came in." He meant the work of journalists everywhere, the fraternity of diggers for the truth.

"Hey kid, I don't need a fuckin' journalism lesson from you, okay?" Frank jerked to his feet and leaned his whole body into jabbing out his cigarette, spilling an overfilled ashtray on his desk. "You're so wrapped up in right and wrong, you can't see that you're being used."

"This is *news*, Frank," he said. "And anyway, is there something better to be wrapped up in besides right and wrong?"

"Yeah, reality!" Frank came around the desk and put a finger in Eddie's chest. "You keep your fuckin' mouth shut about all of this. I'm not kissing everything I got goodbye because you wanna get a scoop."

"I want to do my job." That he had to say this to his editor blew his mind. Frank's *everything I got* obviously meant more to him than the integrity of his own newspaper or the best story Eddie had ever written.

"Stay off this."

"That sounds like a threat."

"No! No! Don't you see? You pompous little asshole! *You're* the threat!"

"To who? A bunch of corrupt old men?"

Frank was astonished. "Do you know any other kind?"

He grabbed his coat and walked out of the newsroom and into a cold drizzle he didn't even feel. Fog was drifting in off the creek through the cedars and the traffic was heavy on the slick highway. He needed to take a long walk or a drive in the rain.

Instead, he walked up to the Forum diner. The tables and booths were empty, it was after lunch and before the dinner rush. He took a corner booth, grabbed a glass ashtray, lit a Lucky Strike. All he could stomach was coffee. He took out his pad and pen and tried to make notes but his mind was moving faster than his pen could follow.

He'd always thought Frank was a great newspaper editor, aggressive about getting the news first, unimpressed by politicians, businessmen, cops, bureaucrats, judges, anyone. He'd even saved a few of Frank's editorials over the past year. In one of them, he reassured parents outraged by the loose sex and drug taking at Woodstock that those kids would turn conservative once they had their own children. In another piece, he accused the October and November moratorium marchers against the Vietnam war of abandoning the troops, but also blasted the government for having no strategy for either victory or withdrawal. When the story on the My Lai massacre rolled out of the AP teletype last month—a story which made Eddie shudder because he understood how easily brutality and violence could get out of control—Frank wrote the longest editorial ever in the *Independent*, a cry of frustration over the war and the conditions the troops had to endure, balanced with sorrow for the civilian dead and a plea to give the soldiers the presumption of innocence until the investigation was over. Eddie clipped and saved those editorials because he thought he could respect the man who wrote them.

Not after today. That same man had just told him that government was a rigged game, played by politicians and businessmen, routinely violating the trust of the people and picking money from their pockets, and that he, a reporter, had better not mess around with that.

As Eddie got back to his desk, Crane was on the phone. He turned with his hand cupped over it. "Tommy Esposito on 3."

He picked up. "Ed Bonneville speaking."

"It's Tommy Esposito," he said, his voice hushed. "Can you talk?"

"Sure."

"I mean can you *talk* talk, you know?"

"We're fine. What can I do for you?"

"Those tapes you made with my father. You do anything with them yet?"

"Anything like what?"

"Play 'em for anybody, tell anybody about 'em. How many people know about the things my father said that night?"

"Only my editor, and only in general, because he hasn't listened to them yet."

"So you haven't played 'em for him yet?"

"No. Tell your old man I'm sorry, I'm trying."

"Don't be sorry. It ain't the worst thing if this story don't get around too much."

Carefully. "I see. Well, nothing's happening yet."

"Okay. And if you talk to my father again, obviously you and I didn't have this conversation. *Capisce?*"

"What conversation?"

"This – right, okay. Thanks. Happy New Year. Whatever."

The next day, faced with a job he wanted to do more urgently than ever, he began work early with coffee at the OB Diner and the morning newspapers. He was disgusted with J. Paul Jackson's story on the hearing for the Castellucci defendants, the people Jackson had snidely described out of the corner of his mouth as he and Eddie left the hearing as the "Orchid Lounge 7." Cynical and wise though Jackson could be, this time he didn't see the real story that had dropped right in his lap. He made Bonelli's charge—that a sinister person sent the defendants to a white cocktail lounge knowing a violent reaction was likely—sound like far-out speculation from a desperate public defender. He described the lounge owner, Robert J. Castellucci, as an amiable local businessman involved in a wide range of local charities. In the story, Castellucci said his patrons were not prejudiced. He insisted the riot was caused by troublemakers from out of town, and said he was mystified why anyone might wish to harm him or his business.

Common sense told Eddie if every company doing county business kicked back two percent, somebody who paid the bills must check the ledgers and know how much each company owed. Tuesday morning he pushed through the pebbled glass door with gold letters reading Department of Finance. Very imposing, but he warned himself not to be deceived by appearances.

Walter O'Neill was the mild-mannered king of a filing cabinet empire. In his late sixties, bald and shaped like a gourd from forty years of desk work, he welcomed Eddie with a merry, high pitched voice and a handshake and waved him to a seat facing his massive desk.

"Hello Eddie, how's your Dad?"

"Doing fine, Mister O'Neill. I'll say hello for you."

"And how do you like newspapering?"

"It gets more interesting every day."

"I'm sure it does." He leaned back on his leather throne. "So what can I do for you?"

Eddie tapped his pen on the notebook on his lap. "You've been comptroller for how many years?"

"Thirty three years. Since 1936."

"All the county business, all the bills for it, they go through you?"

"Through this office, yes."

"So, when you took this office, the two per cent markup on county business was an established system."

O'Neill was puzzled. "I don't know what markup you mean."

"The 1933 law allowing businesses to charge an extra two per cent because the county was slow paying its bills during the Depression."

"Oh, that law was here when I came in, yes. Kept many a business from going under, and the jobs with it. I'll tell you, those were terrible, terrible times for folks."

"I'm sure they were." Eddie, with *one* of Esposito's facts finally confirmed, sighed and relaxed. "To your knowledge, has that law ever been repealed?"

Half of O'Neill's smile vanished. "I honestly don't know, Eddie."

"So, as far as you know, the practice continues even to this day."

"The practice of what?"

"Overcharging the county two per cent."

"Well, I'd have no way of knowing, it never appears on anyone's invoices." O'Neill's voice shrank on the last word, and Eddie was certain he winced.

"So it's possible businesses are still overcharging the county two per cent on everything?"

"Like I said, there's no way to know. What's your interest in this?"

Later, he would realize this was the moment he should have shrugged, closed his notebook, made up an innocuous story, and quickly left. But he wasn't interviewing an accountant, he was a brave reporter battling a corrupt system.

"I'm doing a story about the Colonel Ted Tax," he said.

O'Neill sat stock still. The ornate chandeliers overhead reflected in his eyeglasses. Chuckling, O'Neill leaned forward. "Somebody send you here as a joke?" He was caught, Eddie heard the nervousness in his voice. "Phew! You're good at this, you know! You had me going for a minute there!"

"Sir, I'm not joking." The merry old bastard, lying and laughing at him.

"Then somebody's playing a joke on you, Eddie." He laughed, but when Eddie didn't join him, he cleared his throat. "Is there anything else?"

He pretended to look over his notebook for a few moments. "Ever heard of this Colonel Ted Tax?"

"Not until you mentioned it." Eddie noticed he didn't ask what it was, or how it worked, obviously because he already knew.

"So you don't know anything about a kickback system?"

"No, of course not."

"You're not the person who tallies what each business should pay McTierney?"

"Certainly not."

"These tallies, are they told to the business owners verbally, or is this all written down somewhere—"

"I don't tally up kickbacks, Eddie," O'Neill said, turning red. "I already told you that."

He nodded, looked over his notes, flipped his notebook closed and pocketed his pen and stood up. "Thank you, Mister O'Neill. I'm sorry if this got uncomfortable."

"No, no, no problem at all," the old man said, ushering him out. "I'm just concerned that you've been misinformed. Where did you get your information?"

"Well, it's a pretty widespread system, sir. Things're coming to light. I really could've heard it from anyone." Eddie stood and shook his hand. "Thank you for seeing me, Mister O'Neill."

O'Neill patted his shoulder. "If I think I can be helpful, I'll be sure to call."

"I'm over at the *Independent*, you've got the number, right?"

It was as though he'd had two conversations with O'Neill: the words they said to each other, and a second exchange in the language of facial expressions in which he thought O'Neill seemed to say, *This is the system, what do you care?* while Eddie just grinned and persisted. Now maybe the word would spread that the *Independent* was investigating the setup. Maybe people would come forward with information.

When he walked into the newsroom Frank pounced on him and ordered him into his office, slamming the door shut. Frank thrust his face so close that he was slightly out of focus. Eddie jammed his hands into his pockets to keep from grabbing Frank by the neck.

"Walter O'Neill just called me," Frank said. "He was so outraged he was sick. And what he told me made me sick, too."

"Yeah? What's so contagious?"

"This is a hardworking public servant. This is a gentle, kindly man. This is also a man who can make one phone call about what newspapers the county runs their legal ads in, and the *Independent* will forever lose advertising revenue that is very fuckin' important to this newspaper."

"Maybe the *Independent* shouldn't be so dependent."

"So when he calls me and he's *furious*, and tells me the *Independent* has insulted him, that one of our reporters has accused him of being the fuckin' linchpin of a vast system of corruption, well—" Frank seemed ready to lunge forward and sink his teeth into him, he was so mad—"naturally my thoughts turned to you."

"He doesn't sound so gentle and kindly to me, trying to bully a newspaper."

Looking at Eddie from deep beneath his brow, Frank went back behind his desk and sank into his chair.

"You told me I needed more backup for the story. I had information. It had to be checked out," Eddie said, knowing what he'd done was right, even if he didn't get what he was after. "I never accused him of anything. I only asked what was true and what wasn't."

"Drop this story," Frank said.

"He's a public official, Frank," he said. "Answering questions is part of his job, like it's my job to ask them."

"I told you—"

"Yeah yeah, stay off this."

"So?"

"So why aren't you backing me up on all this?"

"I'll tell you why. Because this has nothing to do with reporting. This has nothing to do with the public's right to know. You want to score. You want to get a scoop. You want to be a *star*. That's all you care about."

"No it isn't." But so what if it was true? Better to be too ambitious than compromised and intimidated like Frank. "Either the Organization is corrupt, or it's not."

"I told you: even if it's true, it ain't news. It's the way of the world. You don't seem to get that."

"I get it, I don't accept it. People have a right to know—"

"Stay off this."

"If you're so unhappy with what I'm doing, fire me."

"No," Frank said, "I'm keeping you on a tight leash. Left on your own you're liable to—"

He didn't finish. He didn't need to.

That afternoon Frank sent him out to cover the ribbon cutting and official opening of the new Manchester Township Law Enforcement Center. He'd already toured the building and written a feature a couple weeks ago, so today all there was to cover were remarks by local dignitaries. The compound was off Route 70, set deep in a thick pine forest surrounded by a ten-foot chain link fence topped with razor wire, with guard booths at the front and rear entrances. In the planning stages, he'd heard, the police chief had demanded that the building be set back far from the fence, too far for a radical to throw a bomb.

He showed his press card to security twice, left the car in the designated lot, and went over and mingled with the crowd. Cold drizzle had not dampened the enthusiasm of the applauding platoons of uniformed cops, firefighters, ambulance crews, and their families. A stage had been erected in front of the brand new, windowless fortress, built of red brick like the township hall and several local banks. When boredom and the cold finally overcame him, he wandered inside out of the drizzle to the press office, got a cup of coffee, and picked up mimeographed copies of the prepared remarks that were laid out on a table.

When he returned to the back of the crowd, Mayor Joseph R. McTierney Jr. was just finishing his speech:

"We go forward into a new decade, with this new Law Enforcement Center designed to meet the needs of our rapidly expanding community, enabling our police to protect our citizens from any threat, foreign or domestic, armed with the latest equipment. I think this shows our township is right in step with the times. With the Nixon Administration setting a new moral tone, this country has new priorities, and is back on the path to traditional American values in our schools and homes, and law and order in our streets."

He was determined to get more out of this event than a rewrite of the press release. He wore his tape recorder like a pistol in a shoulder holster under his jacket. The cable ran down his arm to a microphone taped to his right wrist under his cuff. He could take notes on his pad during an interview, but the microphone would pick up every word that was said, so he'd have the kind of proof that was so important to Frank.

Once the ribbon was cut and pictures taken onstage, Joe Mac, in a Mod suit and wide yellow tie and his forehead glistening with drizzle and perspiration, came off the stage and gave Eddie a wave and a pre-occupied frown.

"Mister Mayor."

"Hey buddy! C'mon, let's get out of the rain," the mayor said, walking toward his car.

Eddie fell in step with him as they crossed the parking lot. He surreptitiously switched on the recorder.

"Mister Mayor, quite a speech!"

"Yeah, it was pretty good, wasn't it?"

"Mister Mayor, your brother's construction company was the general contractor for this building. Your own company sold them the entire new fleet of police cars. People are calling this a conflict of interest. Care to comment?"

The mayor stopped in the middle of the parking lot, and took a second look at him, almost like asking, Are you serious or is this a gag between friends? Eddie waited, pen over pad.

"Well, in both cases, these were the lowest bids," he said. "That's the law. And I abstained from voting, when it was proper to do so." He scribbled, and the mayor, not so cheerful now, looked around at the crowd dispersing to their cars. "What people?"

"Sir?"

He put a gentle hand on Eddie's wrist, nearly touching the microphone. "What people say it's a conflict of interest?"

"Oh, that's just a figure of speech—"

"*Your* figure of speech," the mayor said, his voice lowering.

"Well, yeah."

"Oh, I see." Joe Mac was getting restless. "In fact," the mayor said, "the only person that cares about this is you, right?"

"Well, people do have a right to know—"

"Okay, then." The mayor gripped Eddie's shoulder. "Listen Eddie. You're a good kid, I like you, everybody likes your dad." He looked left, and right, then at Eddie with eyes dead as nickels, his voice high and shaky through gritted teeth. "But if you ever ask me a question like that again—"

"Mayor, these are legitimate questions—"

"You *ever* ask me a question like that again, I'm gonna have somebody rip your fuckin' balls off and shove 'em down your throat." He pushed his shoulder away. "Understand?" The mayor was trembling from his voice box down to his knees.

Eddie stopped taking notes and stared at him. Fear sweat had beaded in a thin moustache along the mayor's upper lip.

"Would you mind repeating that?"

"You heard me."

"You can't talk to the press like that."

"Then how about this?" The mayor laughed heartily, and patted Eddie's cheek. Then, hand on his chest, he shoved Eddie backwards and he fell on his ass and hands on the cinder parking lot. His clipboard clattered away somewhere but his jacket was buttoned, and the tape recorder stayed hidden. "Mind your own fuckin' business."

It took every ounce of strength Eddie had to stay there on the wet ground.

"This is my business," he said. "I'm *making* this my business!"

"That's a bad idea, son."

"You know, Matty Esposito gave me quite an earful about you—"

"An earful of bullshit," the mayor said, with sudden vehemence. "What'd that old bastard say about me?"

Eddie stood, reasonably sure his homicidal moment had passed, and brushed himself off.

"We'll see how much of it I can use."

"That two-bit guinea thief, talking about *me*?"

"Did a lot of business with your father, from what I hear."

"You've been warned." The mayor waddled over to his car, a gray Lincoln with a fake leather brougham. He unlocked the door, and fixed Eddie with one last angry stare, before he got in and drove away. When Eddie got to the Impala, he played back the conversation, happy to discover he had recorded it all, loud and clear.

Back in the newsroom, attacking his typewriter with skinned and bleeding fingers, he wrote the ceremony story from copies of the speeches handed out to the press. He wrote automatically, but another part of his mind seethed over Mayor Joseph R. McTierney Jr., a guy he'd been dumb enough to think was his friend. That fat, brazen little bastard, pushing him around like that. Still angry from the mayor sneering in his face, and knowing he shouldn't indulge it, a note of contempt crept anyway into the story:

```
Companies owned by Mayor McTierney's brother, GOP
political boss Roy McTierney, built the police complex
at a cost of 5 million taxpayer dollars. The mayor's
own automobile dealership sold the township its new
fleet of police cars, price tag nearly $200,000. Both
were the lowest bids as required by law, the mayor
said, and he denied any conflict of interest.
   Mayor McTierney pointed out that he abstained from
voting on these parts of the contracts and threatened
an Independent reporter with castration if he asked
further questions.
```

He read the line again and laughed himself silly. He added two paragraphs of background about the building design and features, tossed the copy in the news desk basket, and headed out to his meeting assignment whistling, certain when he returned that Lindy or the copy editor on the news desk would call him over and bawl him out.

Wednesday morning he woke up to rain pattering on the roof and streaming down the windows. He stretched under the blankets, warm and comfortable in the cold room, looking forward to a day off because the *Independent* didn't publish tomorrow, New Year's Day. The phone rang and he jumped up and grabbed it, expecting Ivy.

"The only reason I don't fire you," Frank said, "is because I may want to *kill* you first."

Shivering, standing nude on the cold floor, he got scared. "What's wrong?"

"Joe McTierney threatening a reporter with castration?"

"Oh," he said, realizing he'd become so busy last night he'd forgotten his little prank. "Who told you about that, the Desk?"

"No. I read it at breakfast in my morning paper. Along with maybe forty thousand other people."

"It got *in?*"

"Joe McTierney has already called and screamed at me. He says you ambushed him asking all sorts of insulting questions, and if we don't retract the castration bit, he's going to sue."

"That's stupid, it'll only call more attention to it," he said. "The Desk, they missed it, it was supposed to be a joke."

"This isn't the Desk's fault. I already had it out with Lindy for missing this, but she's furious it was in there at all. What the hell's happened to you? You found out this place ain't Mayberry USA and, what are you, the new fuckin' sheriff in town?"

"He *said* it."

"Can you prove it?"

"You need more than just my word?"

"You're God damn right I do! Any witnesses?"

"You want proof?" He'd been insulted enough. "Hold on." He put his tape recorder by the phone and put in the tape. "Okay?"

"What?"

"Listen." He played back the interview with Joe McTierney, up to *You've been warned.*

"Jesus," Frank said, in almost a whisper, "did he know you were taping him?"

"No."

"What was that noise near the end?"

"He pushed me and knocked me down."

"Jesus. Did you tape Walter O'Neill?"

"No, I didn't have the holster figured out yet."

"God dammit, just because a politician says something stupid that doesn't mean we have to print it. First you accuse this newspaper's best friend in county government of being corrupt, then you insult the mayor of a major township."

Eddie said, in absolute certainty he was right, "Just going where the story takes me."

"There *is* no story. I told you that. Leave it alone," Frank said.

"There is a story here, only for some reason you're afraid of it."

"I told you—"

"Yeah. You told me. I heard you."

"Everything you file goes in my In box only," Frank said, "You got that?"

"Yeah, sure."

Why wouldn't Frank fire him? That's what *he'd* do, if he were Frank. Was somebody telling him not to?

"Happy New Year, Frank."
Frank cursed and slammed the phone down.

SIX *New Year's Eve, Asbury Park*

The cold rain fell all day, a dismal end to the year. He stayed in his warm dry apartment at the beach, exercised with free weights, meditated longer than usual, cooked himself ratatouille and brown rice for lunch, played Beatles records, and flirted with Ivy on the phone, inventing erotic fantasies of how they could spend tonight. After they hung up, he wondered if he could persuade her to move into his apartment. What a time they could have: cozy mornings under the blankets, mid-day phone calls to plan their evenings, wine-soaked late-night dinners and smoky, erotic wee hours. For weeks he'd trudged through his days, loveless and bored. Now the future seemed to promise a much better life, a life he burned for, no longer afraid to hope.

When afternoon became dense misty evening, the rain weakened to a foggy drizzle. He dressed in tight black corduroy jeans and black engineer boots, a black sweatshirt, and his old trench coat.

The roads were slippery, and visibility was low. Ivy was waiting in the school bus shelter outside the gate of the Porter mansion. She climbed in the car and leaned over the console, wrapped her arms around his neck and kissed him long and lovingly. No, he realized, Christmas Eve had not been a dream; they were in love again.

He proposed dinner someplace nice, followed by an evening by candlelight at his apartment. But Ivy, unpredictable as always, wanted a big night out. "I'll drive if you don't want to," she offered eagerly.

In this weather, that was a death sentence, because she drove like she made love, pedal to the metal. So after eating at the unromantic

Laurelton Diner on the traffic circle—she had a cheeseburger deluxe and two cups of coffee, he had iced tea and a chef's salad without the meat—they ventured out around ten o'clock, Eddie peering into the murk and praying a drunk merrymaker wouldn't come skidding out of nowhere and turn the Impala into their coffin. Driving slow and careful, it took nearly an hour to make the trip to Asbury Park, the buildings tall and the avenues blue in the fog-softened street light.

Alongside Wesley Lake they found a parking spot. Ocean Grove was across the lake and reflections of a row of golden-lit Victorian houses shimmered on the dark water. Holding hands in the chill, they hurried up the sidewalk on Bond Street. At Cookman Avenue, they took a left and went through the first, unmarked doorway into The Upstage.

The club occupied two windowless lofts over a shoe store. They climbed up a long flight of stairs, the black walls hand-painted with bright psychedelic shapes, the music getting louder and louder. A big guy with a beard and a wide belt around his belly collected the price of admission at the first landing and stamped the date on the back of their hands in invisible ink that showed up blue under a black light next to the cash register.

Eddie led her into the mayhem on the rock n' roll floor. It was hot inside and they had to work their way to the back of a crowd of wall-to-wall people. The rock n' roll floor was a black room with a low plywood stage, lit by a motley collection of colored lights and two black light fluorescents. The whole wall behind the musicians was perforated with rows of speakers. There were very few chairs, most people sat on the floor or stood and stared and a few of them danced. All he could see of the musicians were haircuts over the heads of the crowd. The music was deafening, electric blues, it went straight to Eddie's pelvis and he couldn't stand still.

Ivy pried herself away from him when he tried to get her to dance, shy about calling attention to herself. He tried not to let it bother him but after awhile it was a little weird dancing alone. They'd walked in on a long jam on a twelve bar blues, including multiple guitar solos, a long saxophone cry, somebody playing Booker T. style on the Hammond organ, a drummer who hammered out a long solo, and a bass player who rode a simple blues riff into outer space then landed precisely on the beat and restarted the song. Somebody blowing a blues harp put it all to bed.

He was rocking with it, he was ready to stay all night, but after a few songs Ivy rolled her eyes and dragged him downstairs to the cafe on the folk music floor. There it was quiet, they sold herbal tea and banana bread. Two long-haired girls in long tie-dyed dresses, one orange-haired and the other black-haired and finger picking a Yamaha acoustic guitar, gently sang "Helplessly Hoping" from the Crosby Stills and Nash record in perfect harmony. Empty tables were plentiful. She ordered them cups of tea.

"Better?"

"Quieter," she said. "I couldn't hear myself think."

"What's there to think about?"

"Oh, you know me."

At their tiny table with a red and white checked cloth and a candle in a green vase, she posed for him without seeming to, lovely in her long gray skirt, black velvet tunic with gold piping and buttons, and her hair loose over her shoulders.

"New Jersey," she sighed, looking around. "Is this really where I'm from?"

Not this again, he thought. "Not like anybody had a choice."

"Well, I'm sorry, but this scene is just so low rent."

She was getting dangerously close to reopening an old wound—*I can't have some guy from my hometown in New Jersey hanging around Manhattan, complicating my life*—but he held it closed, for now. "Is there someplace else you'd rather go?'

She laughed. "Like where?"

He clinked his teacup against hers and drank.

"I tell people up at school where I'm from," she said. "Places like South Dakota or Arkansas get more respect."

"From people who've never been here, right?"

"Their idea of New Jersey is a junkyard in the middle of a swamp."

She was starting to piss him off. "So tell them all to go to Arkansas."

She scoffed. "My ex-roommate calls people from New Jersey 'The Australians of the Middle Atlantic States'."

"And you let her get away with that? Where's she from?"

"Delaware."

Eddie laughed. "There's nowhere, and then there's Delaware." He was tired of this. But Ivy was never very considerate of other people's feelings. It's New Year's Eve, and she still drags out her old routine?

"This place, it's just so... or just *not* so... something, I dunno."

"It's not *hip*. Thank God."

"Hip? Are you kidding? New Jersey's a national joke."

"I wondered what was wrong with this country." If Ivy kept it up, it was gonna sour the whole night. Before she could continue, he mock-begged, "Hey. Not on New Year's Eve, okay?" It was true, cultural experience at the Jersey Shore was what you made of it. Sometimes there was a great house party, but otherwise, unless you were queer for pep rallies and sports and cruising in cars and CYO dances chaperoned by nuns, you and your friends got some drums and guitars and you formed a band and if you were any good you might get to jam some night at The Upstage.

"Well, it's a shock," she said, "after life in New York, coming back here."

"Shocked you made it out of New York *alive*, you mean."

"Shocked at how much I want to leave all this behind," she said, then gripped his hand. "Most of this, anyway."

"I'm glad you think we have a future."

"What future does anybody have?" she shrugged. "I'm just glad we've got tonight."

That should not have bothered him, but it did. The tea was making him sleepy and the night was still young.

"C'mon," he said, "let's get some fresh air."

Back in the Impala, they cruised in the fog along the lake to the boardwalk, passing a block-long green building with a painted sign that read Palace Amusements. Out of the middle of the building, higher than the roof, rose the outline of a Ferris wheel stripped of its seats. The light turned red next to the Empress Motel and brought them to a stop.

Across the intersection sat the carousel house, dark and silent, whose roof of green copper sections was like a large crown. On each window was a medallion with the head of a long-haired spirit. For a moment, he was a kid again in the back seat of his father's car on a summer night, looking forward to eating Kohr's frozen custard up on the boardwalk and riding the carousel ablaze with color and swirling screaming children and pumping calliope music. But tonight the fog off Wesley Lake rolled in around the carousel, and the only lights visible changed from red to green, and the only screams came from the tires of a guy careening around in a Nova Super Sport challenging others to a race up

Ocean Avenue. Eddie parked beside the miniature golf course across the street from Mrs. Jay's, the beer garden whose curb was always lined in the summer with Harleys, and they walked up onto the boardwalk.

Each streetlight had softened to a big blue glow. Fog off the ocean, salty and wet, blew in their faces, and the damp cold seeped into their coats. The boardwalk was nearly deserted from the Casino all the way up to the Convention Hall, and only a few hardy, foolish or just plain drunk strollers were out braving the bad weather. Then from somewhere he smelled marijuana.

"Here!" She was holding her breath and offering him a burning joint.

If he stopped to think about whether he wanted any, it would paralyze him with indecision. So he smoked, toke for toke with her, until the joint was burned down. With a twist of her wrist she flipped the roach out over the beach.

"Oop—*sy*." She giggled. "I uh, forgot this stuff is pretty strong."

A large bubble swelled inside his head and when it popped he started laughing. Her voice was hollow, as if coming down a long tube, like a cartoon character's.

"We probably shouldn't have smoked the whole thing, now that I think of it."

This, they both found insanely funny, and they sat down on a bench until they stopped laughing and were sure they could walk.

For a moment Eddie was high, then he was *too* high, and in a fascinated, transcendent state. He was dissolving into the dark. He waved his hand and the fog seemed to swirl in the air in front of his face in slow motion. The herringbone pattern of the Asbury boardwalk vibrated under his boots and before his eyes. The waves hitting the beach sounded like millions of steel shovels tossing gravel into steel buckets.

Then, without warning, he was too high. He started sweating and breathing hard and got so depressed and anxious he was dizzy and slightly nauseous. A wave of deep hopelessness washed through him, drowning his high spirits. He cursed his own carelessness for smoking too much. He concentrated on putting one foot in front of the other, telling himself he was okay, he had just unwisely put too much of a chemical in his brain and it would scramble his feelings for awhile until it wore off.

"Are you all right?" she said, apparently unaffected.

"Feeling paranoid."

"It's just your ego feeling overwhelmed by the dope."

"I just have to wait it out."

"Yeah. Deep breaths. Think positive thoughts."

She linked arms with him. She ducked her chin and ears into the scarf wound around her neck under the collar of her motorcycle jacket. Her black hair fell down over her shoulders. She gazed around, big-eyed in wonder. Oh, but you are beautiful, he thought.

"Too bad the rides aren't open," she giggled. Behind them the steel curves of a tall roller coaster stood etched in black against the blue glow of the city.

"How about a little miniature golf?" he said. "Did you bring your clubs? I'm sure the *Senator* has a spare set he could lend you." She jerked his arm and gave him a warning look, then laughed.

Arm in arm, they strolled past Madame Marie's tiny Temple of Knowledge and the Howard Johnson's building with all its shops closed for the winter, until they reached the Convention Hall, on pilings towering out over the beach. High above the doors, sculptures of giant seashells and flying sea horses chased by fierce serpents were mounted along the brick and cement parapets and lit by replicas of lighthouse lamps. Usually you could pass through the huge arcade between the auditorium and the Paramount Theater, so vast that pigeons flew around overhead, and filled with souvenir shops and candy stands and snack bars and games and fun machines that dated back at least to the '40s. But tonight the doors were locked.

Walking back to the car, Ivy went off on a vivid recollection of a night the summer of '68 when they'd been outside Convention Hall with hundreds of other kids waiting to get into a concert by The Doors. The band's long black limousine sped up onto the roadway alongside the auditorium and parked there overlooking the beach. The three musicians got out of the car, Densmore and Kreiger and Manzarek, stretching, rubbing their eyes, waving to the crowd of cheering whistling people cordoned off by the police on the boardwalk. The fans weren't kept off the beach, however, and a mass of kids flooded onto the sand below where the Doors stood. After awhile, Morrison got out of the car, in black leather and dark sunglasses, and the fans on the beach below whooped and hollered and went wild. He toasted them with a bottle of Jack Daniels, polished it off, leaned back, and hurled it out into the surf. A stampede of kids swarmed into the water in their clothes, wrestling each other and diving for Morrison's empty whiskey bottle.

Laughing with Ivy at the memory, his highly amplified brain gradually calmed down and the terror receded, the foggy, cold New Year's Eve began to feel peaceful and beautiful, with his woman holding his arm. A year ago, home from college, Ivy had brought along two thick joints in wheat straw paper. It was the first time he got high. They'd smoked one, on the landing outside so that his room wouldn't smell illegal, put on a Frank Zappa record called *Hot Rats*, and wrestled each other onto the bed and made intense, highly audacious love until dawn, torturing each other with pleasures made epic by the marijuana. Then they'd gone to the O-B Diner and eaten a perfectly delicious breakfast, goofing on the people they saw. Because he liked marijuana a little too much, he was ordinarily much more careful than tonight with how he used it, but at least high on pot he didn't want to kill anybody.

Fireworks popped a few times in the distance. She stopped, grabbed his wrist and looked at his watch. Through the Casino's high windows, fireworks blossomed above the next boardwalk over in Ocean Grove.

"Happy 1970, my love," she said, and kissed him long and deep.

He settled down behind the wheel of their space cruiser. Ahead lay Ocean Avenue, one hundred miles long, disappearing into the fog. Time to resume the adventure, a long perilous journey through the galaxy that lay ahead before they could return to their home planet, assuming he could recall the coordinates and get them there without spinning off into deep space.

"Okay, ignition." He started the car. "Exterior illumination." He turned the headlights on. "Restraints lifted. Prepare for locomotion." He let the emergency brake off. "What sort of signals from beyond are we picking up?" Ivy curled up on the seat, laughing at him.

Every radio station was counting down the end of the decade by playing the best songs of the 1960s, so it didn't matter that his car only had an AM radio. She punched a button and turned up the volume on The Rolling Stones playing "Honky Tonk Women."

He launched them at breakneck speed into the traffic moving up Ocean Avenue. Buildings to the left, boardwalk to the right, cars swooping down on his rear bumper and screeching around them. He was on The Circuit, where restless drivers orbited the blocks up Ocean and back down Kingsley Avenue, looking for a race, a friend, a girl, some music, any kind of action worth getting into. It was not the best place to be stoned behind the wheel, and it was all a bit too much, with Mick Jagger on the radio bragging about laying a divorcee in New York and Ivy squirming rhythmically on the seat next to him. Plus, at any red light some guy might pull alongside and challenge him to a race, even in the fog. That made him nervous, it might become a matter of honor, after all, why drive a 409 Impala if—

She turned the radio down. "Hey champ," she said, "you know we're only going ten miles an hour?"

"Feels like a hundred."

She laughed.

"Seriously. It's too foggy for me to go any faster."

"Champ! Speed up before we get busted for going too slow!"

They crept past the Convention Hall. From the street it was a mountain of red brick in Moorish patterns, a thousand feet tall and a half mile long.

"Maybe we better pull over," she said.

"Maybe I'm okay."

"Good," she hooted, "cause no way can I drive!"

But on the narrow strip of land between Deal Lake and the ocean the fog thickened and forced him to slow to a walk. He could see nothing in front of the car but a gray wall. He should have never smoked that stuff! Here he was, lost in the fog, rolling head on into the unknown at the wheel of a ton of steel!

"Wow, where *are* we?" she said, gazing into the murk.

"Good question," he said, trying not to sound scared.

"Are you okay?"

"Yeah, until we hit something." That got her laughing again.

He dimmed his headlights and gained a foot of visibility. Not enough! Then out of the murk off to his right came a strip of sidewalk and a parking meter, sliding slowly past, and that restored his bearings. On the speedometer the needle rested barely above zero.

A driveway opened in the sidewalk. "I'm pulling over for a minute to get my head together."

He turned off into an empty gravel parking lot between two lines of dunes. He inched ahead until his bumper hit a telephone pole laid on its side, and the car bounced backward, a bit of slapstick that caused another burst of hysterics. He doused the lights, left the engine and the heater running low, and turned the radio down.

Then the fog was no longer dangerous and became their best friend. It hid them deep in their own little cloud. Ivy locked the doors. Eddie climbed into the back seat. Ivy pulled off her jacket and scarf and boots and crawled back on top of him, her lips hunting for his.

At two o'clock in the morning, moist and peaceful and their clothes still askew, they got a table in a corner of the front room at The Inkwell. A few years ago, somebody had turned an old white clapboard house about a block from the beach at Second and Brighton in Long Branch into a coffee house. The outside was ringed by porches and on the first floor was the cafe. Inside the crowded front room a perfectly trimmed Christmas tree hung upside down from the ceiling.

Poking the lemon peel in her espresso with a tiny spoon, she frowned. "You ever wonder," Ivy said, "why they call this part of Long Branch 'West End?' We're a block from the ocean."

He shrugged. "I never thought about that." He scooped the nutmeg-dusted whipped cream off his cappuccino and licked the spoon.

"We're about as far east as you can go without getting your feet wet." Her eyebrows did their little dance of scorn—typical half-assed New Jersey. He could feel her slipping toward the negative again. He'd brought her here because it was the only place at the Shore you could get espresso and cappuccino, and because The Inkwell had the best jukebox in the world, which at the moment was playing Bob Dylan singing "Just Like a Woman." If she wasn't happy now—after wild rock n' roll at the Upstage, after sharing a powerful reefer and a back seat orgasm so intense that he changed positions without her even noticing—well, would she ever be happy?

As he pondered this, she put her chin in her hands and asked, her brows knitting together:

"Eddie?"

"Yeah?"

"I get my allowance check in a couple weeks," she said. "We could live on that a long time, if we're careful."

He wasn't sure what she was saying at first, then he thought he knew. "Live on it? You mean like, me and you?" Was it possible she was having the same fantasies of cohabitation as he was?

She squeezed his hand in her cold fingers. "Let's get the hell out of here."

"Don't you want to finish your coffee?"

"I don't mean *here*, I mean New Jersey."

They once had dreamed about taking to the highway and zooming around America like the characters in *On The Road*. But he got the feeling she wasn't proposing a romantic quest.

"Are you in some kind of trouble?"

"No," she said.

"But you said things in New York—"

"Well, yeah. The life I had in New York, I can't have anymore. And I don't want to stay down here. I'm just restless. I'm young. I want to go places, see things. Don't you?"

"What are you running away from?"

"That's not it, it's just that, when I think of me and you, out there traveling around America—" Now he was sure she wasn't being honest with him.

"I can't just up and hit the road, just like that."

"That's exactly what we're *meant* to do, champ" she said. "We're not meant to get stuck in nowhere New fuckin' Jersey the rest of our lives. Who cares what happens around here?"

"I do."

"Since when?"

"Since I found out the politicians are ripping off the taxpayers."

"Of *course* they are," she said. "That's news to you?"

"I'm onto a story people have a right to know."

"You used to *hate* those people. Remember? We used to call them the Proles, like in Orwell."

"Yeah, well," he said, embarrassed to be reminded of that. "I wouldn't use that word now." He hadn't seen much of the world, but it stood to reason New Jersey was no better or worse than anywhere else.

"So what happened?"

You're still stuck in high school, my love, and I'm not. He didn't dare say it. High school was when he'd hated anyone who looked down on her, but that was then, this was now. He spoke softly and carefully to her, because he didn't want to spoil what so far had been a pretty good night.

"You know those straight people we used to goof on?" he said. "Well, those are the people who work hard, pay taxes, try and raise their kids, and put their trust in public officials to serve them, and in a lot of ways, those people are getting screwed. That ain't fair. Do I care about that? Yeah."

"I see."

"This story can also make my career as a reporter."

"Yeah but, as a reporter, don't you want to go places where things are happening?"

"Right now, that's here. I'm on this story, and I'm trying to write it."

"So after you write this story, you might leave?"

Highly unlikely, but he leaned toward her anyway and said, as though confidentially, "I might *have* to."

"Well, don't take too long."

"I'm working as hard as I can."

"I don't know how long I can wait."

"Well, don't run off without me. Promise?"

She shrugged, unhappily. "Okay, I guess."

SEVEN *Home the hard way*

On New Year's Day he raced from town hall to town hall as almost every municipality in Ocean County held its reorganization meeting. In each town the ceremony to swear in newly elected members of its governing body was the same. The men, fresh-shaved and quietly hung over from the revels of the night before, all wore white carnations in the lapels of their suit jackets. Their wives and children, dressed as if for church, sat in the audience as the men raised their hands and took the oath of office from the town clerk. In years past, Eddie had gone along to watch his father sworn in, Ed Sr. in a stiff gray suit and red tie and swelling with pride and good will. The first time, 1961, he was just a kid, and he was proud of his father; four years later, as a sullen teenager, he was restive and bored, and got irritated when someone made a wisecrack about his Beatle haircut. As his father read the short speech Eddie had typed for him, his brothers and sisters were in awe of the occasion while their mother watched, droll and unimpressed. He skipped the ceremony last year, in which the re-elected committeeman had to read his remarks from handwritten notes, because he'd thrown his typist and his typewriter out of the house.

Writing the pile of reorganization stories went quickly and according to form—omit the congratulations, welcoming speeches, and pledges of cooperation as meaningless bullshit, and just write about who got sworn in, appointed, or confirmed.

With his stories written, and now forced to cool his heels in the newsroom until the 11 p.m. deadline, a gnawing anxiety returned he thought he'd dismissed. Making love with Ivy last night had confirmed his earlier impression. She'd always made love with a girlish sense of play followed by intense submission. In the months that they were apart, however, she had learned something new about her sexuality. In bed, he found himself challenged by a woman intent on getting off, who demanded that he be more aggressive than ever. He was sure it was the influence of another man, someone he knew nothing about except that he'd fucked Ivy and now she had a rougher, more demanding way with sex. At moments it was like they were in one of the porn films he occasionally slipped in to watch at the old Strand Theater in Lakewood. It made Ivy kind of impersonal, and somehow, more exciting.

He buried himself in another round of work just to keep busy, writing nine obituaries from the preprinted forms the reporters filled out when a funeral director called in. He put the copy in the In Box, and walked over to the news desk to flip through the rest of the Out box stuff before he went to dinner.

On an Asbury Park *Evening Press* story stapled to a sheet of copy paper, in Frank's block capital handwriting was scrawled, "Where's our story on this kid?" He started reading the clipping with the headline "Wounded Marine Comes Home." His eyes jumped to the picture of a clean cut youth, in U.S. Marine dress uniform.

POINT PLEASANT BEACH — The Defense Department has confirmed that Lance Cpl. Brian A. Rollins, who joined the Marines in August 1968 and saw combat duty in Vietnam, has returned home after being gravely wounded.

His parents confirmed that their son arrived home just after Christmas. They declined to provide details of Cpl. Rollins's injuries, only that he faced a period of intensive physical therapy, beginning with a series of tests that will keep him hospitalized for as long as two weeks.

He stared at the picture. He could not look away. Oh God, this can't be happening. He dropped into the chair behind his desk. He'd been hit on the head, the room spun around him. He could not take his eyes off the picture of the young Marine.

He called Point Pleasant Hospital and they confirmed that Rolly was a patient. After telling Lindy he was off in pursuit of a story that Frank wanted, he was on the road five minutes later. For the whole drive, he battled with himself, one minute tempted to turn around, put this chapter behind him, simply rewrite the *Press* clipping and get on with his life, the next minute telling himself to grow up, that what he did to Rolly and everything that followed was his responsibility, and he had no right to spare himself.

Visiting hours had just begun on the second floor. The ward was overheated and crowded. Patients on cots lined the corridors for lack of rooms. Nurses in white, and girls in their candy stripe uniforms, hustled around.

"Are you family?" the nurse asked at the reception desk.

"He's my brother," he said. She gave him the room number. He found it at the end of the corridor.

Rolly was sitting up in bed staring into space. When he saw Eddie he broke into a huge, lopsided smile.

"Hey-y-y-y!" Rolly said in a hoarse voice he'd never heard before. "Edsel!"

He was horror-struck for the second time in an hour. The once-beautiful young man lay in a hospital bed emaciated, nothing but flesh and bones. His face was so gaunt it made his eyes and teeth look huge. Eddie pulled up a chair and sat next to the bed and gripped Rolly's hand. There was no way to hug him. He had tubes running into his arm and nose and under his sheet. The room reeked of a medicinal smell that made Eddie want to gag.

"I just found out you were back," he said, as cheerfully as he could manage. "Welcome home."

"Yeah." When Rolly wasn't speaking his mouth hung slack. "Home the hard way." He shook his head. "Yecch."

"So, you look good."

"Don't." Rolly's head lolled back and grief crumpled his face. "I got shot." Rolly was unwilling to look at him. He kept his face turned. "I don't wanna talk about it."

"So we won't," Eddie said. "Is it good to be home?"

"You fuckin' kiddin' me?"

"It's good to see you, brother," Eddie persevered.

"Yeah?" A small sneer twisted his shriveled lips. "Come by to give me a kiss?"

He stood up and leaned over and planted a kiss on Rolly's forehead. His skin was clammy and cold and tasted sour. "I'm glad you're home.

I'm glad you're alive."

"Yeah. Thank God for that, huh?" He cleared his throat, which was congested. "So the news is, I can't walk anymore, man."

"What happened?"

"A bullet hit my spine. Pfft!" He mimed breaking something in half. "Below the waist, I'm dead meat. Including the kielbasa." His lips quivered. "That's what I mean."

Eddie's mind searched frantically for something to say. All that came out was, "I'm so sorry, man."

"What're you so sorry for?" Rolly scoffed. "*You* didn't shoot me, did you?"

"I don't mean that," Eddie said. "Never mind what I said. You're home, you're my friend, and we'll pick up things right where we left off. We've got a lot to do, once you're able."

"Once I'm *able*? What'm I gonna do it *with*? I can't walk, can't drive, can't dance, can't fuck, can't do nothin'.'"

"That's not all there is to life," Eddie said.

"Don't do that, man," Rolly said, his voice breaking. "Please."

Eddie was losing control. The words caught in his throat. "I'm going to the men's room," he said. "Uh, don't go anywhere."

"Yeah." It was half a laugh, at least.

Down the corridor in the men's room he locked himself in a stall. People came in, did their business and left, and if anyone noticed his quiet sobbing nobody interfered. In a hospital a crying man in the toilet was probably not so rare. After a few minutes he was back under control. He wiped his eyes and blew his nose.

In the mirror over the sink his eyes were bright and reddened and his face flushed. It took several splashes of cold water on his face to clear things up. He rubbed a paper towel over his face and tossed it. He told himself in the mirror that no matter what Rolly's condition, he would be the best friend he could. He could do at least that much.

In the hall outside the room he stopped short. Rolly's father Joe sat in the chair where Eddie had been, with his back to the door. His voice was low and soothing. Rolly's head was turned away from his father, a blank look on his face. Eddie once had been angry with Joe Rollins for pressuring Rolly to enlist, but now all he could see was a terribly distraught father. Eddie stepped back from the doorway before he intruded. Down the corridor were a few empty chairs facing each other across the hall. He slumped into one, unsure whether to stay or go.

Up the corridor came Rolly's mother, Grace, her blonde hair down around her face and wearing no makeup. She walked past with their minister, gray, slim, soft spoken Reverend Carver. Reverend Carver acknowledged Eddie's presence with a curt nod. Rolly's mother seemed not to see him.

"Leave everything to me, Grace," he was saying. "Anything you need, call."

"Joe's taking this so hard. Would you—"

"Of course. You look after the kids. They need your strength." Reverend Carver went in and laid a hand on Joe Rollins' shoulder. Grace Rollins took one of the chairs across the corridor, looking lost in more than just thought.

Joseph Jr., a pimply 16 year-old wearing a soccer team sweatshirt, came up the corridor from the vending machines and handed a paper cup of coffee to his mother. Slouched against the wall, he stood by his mother, his head hung, glowering at his father.

"Look at him," Joe Jr. glared at his father's back. "He better know we ain't never gonna forget the way he—"

"Joseph!" his mother said, glaring. "I told you I won't stand for talk like that. What's done is done. With the Lord's help, we'll live with it. Go find your sisters. They were looking for the chapel."

Joe Jr. leaned down and hissed, "He starts that 'patriotic duty' shit with me, I'll put him on the floor!"

"Don't talk that way," she said. "Please? Now, go."

Grace watched her second son stalk down the corridor. She put her cup of coffee on the floor, stood up and crossed over and took the chair beside Eddie. She took ahold of his hand, startling him, and regarded him with the kindliest eyes. "I'm surprised to see you here, Eddie."

"I had to come. Mrs. Rollins, I'm so sorry. About everything."

"We know that." Grace looked Eddie in the eye, patting his hand tenderly, as if it was he who was suffering. "Brian told me what a comfort your letters were to him. Hearing from you meant a lot to him. He calls you his best friend." She sighed. "I never wanted him to be a boxer. That was his father's idea. I never wanted him to be a soldier either, but…" She squeezed and released his hand. "My husband hates you, Eddie. He blames you and that last fight for everything that's happened to Brian. If he finds you here, I don't know what he'll do."

"I don't want to cause any more trouble," he said. "I'll go, I just wanted to say how sorry I am."

"We know that, Eddie."

"You do?"

She said it, either because she meant it, or because she felt that Eddie needed to hear it and she was a kind soul. "Don't blame yourself for this, Eddie. What's happened with Brian is not your fault, not any of it."

He couldn't believe her, but he was grateful anyway. "Thank you," he said, getting to his feet. "I want to be his friend, I really do. Would that be okay?"

"Of course," she said. "We're not gonna let this beat us. Brian is going to know he is loved, no matter what."

"I'd better go." He turned and headed for the stairs.

Joe stood and he and Rev. Carver embraced. Joe came out of the room. Grace rose to comfort him.

"Joe, you're cold as ice. Let's get this hot coffee into you." She handed him her cup, but he didn't notice it. Joe saw Eddie leaving.

"Was that him?" Joe began to weep, a high keening that Eddie heard as he passed the reception desk. "Was that *him*?"

Eddie hurried downstairs. He hustled for the shelter of his car, crashing emotionally. He'd better do his crying on the ride back to the newsroom, because once he got back to his desk, he had a story to write. The one phrase he couldn't say in the story he could barely speak to himself. *What a waste.*

As he was digging in his pocket for his car keys, quick footfalls behind him on the pavement gave him one second's warning, then Joe Rollins was all over him, grabbing his jacket lapel and hitting him with his fist. Eddie blocked the punches, but Joe had a grip on his jacket. They stumbled around in circles.

"You fuckin' psycho!" Joe screamed. "Fuckin' psycho! You killed my son! You killed my *son*!"

Wrong thing to say, Joe. Eddie got his feet under him, grabbed Joe's arm and swung him around. He tore his jacket free and pulled back. Joe fell belly first onto the fender of the Impala and staggered back, the wind knocked out of him, gasping.

"After the beating you gave him, he was never right in the head!"

Eddie bent over and screamed in his face. "He listened to you, and he went to war! That *proves* it!" Over Joe's shoulder he saw Grace Rollins and Joe Jr. hurrying over.

Joe gathered himself, hands on his gut. "He was a sweet, well meaning, good kid. He was an *Eagle Scout*. He was never the same after you—"

"I'm trying to make up for it! I'm trying to be the best friend to him I can!" He was screaming and he didn't care who heard him. "Better than you making him feel guilty with your patriotic duty shit!" In two seconds he was going to start punching Rolly's father for emphasis.

Grace put her arm around Joe's shoulders, and Joe Jr. stood by looking fearfully at his father.

"Where else was he gonna get discipline?" Joe said. "The judge said join the military or go to prison! My son! *Prison*! He was supposed to go to Princeton, Yale!"

"He can still do that!"

"My son died the night you beat his brains in."

"Don't you give up on him, God dammit!" Pull it back, he ordered himself, there's been enough damage done. "Look, I told you I'm sorry for everything that happened. I'm trying to make up for it." He found his car keys. He walked around, putting the car between himself and Rolly's father. Grace was talking quietly in Joe's ear, her hand on his shoulder. He was shaking his head.

Eddie didn't want to leave without saying something more than just an apology. "Well," he said, "at least he got wounded fighting for his country."

Grace turned her face away. Rolly's father huffed, began to cry. His voice warbled, incredulous at the words he spoke. "He wasn't fighting for his country. He got shot by a prostitute in a whorehouse in Saigon. She told the MP's he beat her up. I'm pretty sure they don't give medals for that." Joe leaned toward him, his hands on the hood of Eddie's car. "I ever see you around my family again, I'll kill you."

He was tempted to take the easy way out right, using Joe's threat as an excuse. But he couldn't hide, couldn't excuse himself, it would be wrong.

"I will see him," he said, "whether you like it or not. He's my friend."

With Grace and Joe Jr. hugging him, Joe turned and staggered slowly back into the hospital.

Eddie woke on Friday, his day off, the queasy, desolate memory of last night still pressing on his nerves. He pulled the blankets around himself, curled up on his side. Brilliant sunlight through the south dormer window fell on him, warm as a golden blanket. He closed his eyes, they were red behind the lids.

He heard footsteps on the staircase outside. The door to his apartment opened across the room, he heard a large surf rolling and crunching onto the shoreline, and smelled *Canoe* and cigarette smoke when the door closed.

"Hey champ," he heard Ivy say, tenderly. "You awake?"

"Yeah."

He rolled on his back. He was not ready to start a day even bright sunshine wouldn't cure.

"I just read your story in the paper." She hung her jacket and scarf over his desk chair, and sat down to pull off her boots. "How bad is he?"

"He was shot. He's paralyzed from the waist down."

"Oh my God," she said. "Did he talk about how it happened?"

"Not really. He said, 'Below the waist I'm dead meat, including the kielbasa.'"

"He joked about it."

"No, not really." He shielded his eyes with his hand. "Pull the shade, will you?"

She slid her boots under his desk and lowered the shade. The room went dim. She lit one of his cigarettes. A shaft of light from the edge of the shade cut through the spirals of blue smoke like light projected through the smoky air of a movie theater. The cigarette in her lips, she started unbuttoning her shirt.

"Going to the hospital took nerve," she said. "Didn't they want to kill you?"

"His mother was okay. The old man threw a few punches at me. He's gonna hate me the rest of his life. I may as well accept it."

"And what about you? Are you going to beat yourself up over this for the rest of your life?"

"Kinda hard to avoid right now." He hated when his voice shook like that.

"You can't do it over, man. It is what it is. All you can do is keep on being good." She pushed her jeans down to her ankles and stepped out of them.

"His mother told me not to blame myself," Eddie said.

"If she feels that way, why don't you?" She draped her clothes over the chair. Naked, wearing only crew socks, she brushed out her hair, backlit by the smoky sunlight.

"She was just being nice about it," he said. "They know everything bad in Rolly's life started the night of the fight."

"Champ, whatever you may think, you didn't turn Rolly into the obnoxious asshole he became."

"There's a straight line from there to Vietnam. A line I put him on."

"No you didn't."

"Yes I did."

"Even so, what can you do about it now?" she said.

"Accept it. That night ain't never going away, it's gonna be in my life forever."

"You sound like that's how you want it." Ivy's tactless realism was unwelcome. "Haven't you punished yourself enough over this?"

"I guess not."

She tossed the brush in her bag, staring at him. "You're not gonna do something stupid, like enlist, are you?"

"Give me a puff."

She handed him the cigarette and he inhaled, and handed it back.

"Me enlisting won't help Rolly walk again," he said. "That's not the answer. I'm not sure there is one."

"Here's something, 'til you find one." She licked her lips, and leaned over and kissed him. He let her, but it didn't distract him from his misery.

"I'll just keep going over to see him," Eddie said. "He's my friend. We have a friendship to continue."

"Good, but don't overdo it on the guilt and responsibility shit. Be kind to yourself, champ."

He moved over and she got under the bed linens and slid her body against him, her skin silky and warm, her knee pushing between his thighs. She leaned down and sucked his nipples. He didn't laugh so much as gasp, then he forgot about his sorrow for awhile.

Afterward, he lay sprawled under the covers. Ivy strolled naked out of the bathroom, bent over and peered out the window with a view of the highway and the bay. As she walked slowly down the middle of his apartment, tucking her hair behind her ears, he got excited all over again. She noticed, and cocked a hip.

"What are you looking at?" she sneered, posing beside the bed.

"I'm looking at you."

"It's not polite to stare."

"It's impossible not to. You're the most beautiful thing I've ever seen."

Silence. "I am not a *thing*." He knew that flat voice well.

"What's the matter? What'd I say?"

She put her hands on her hips. "I'm not a thing. I've got a problem with that word, *thing*."

She wasn't joking. A chill crept between them. "You know what I mean."

"I'll bet I know better than *you* what you mean."

"You're not a *thing*, you're a woman, very much alive."

He reached for her hand. She swiveled out of reach.

"Yeah, right. To most men a woman is a body and if they like your pretty face and laugh at your jokes, that's a bonus. Try to get any man to see you as a person. It's like trying to bring eyesight to the blind."

"And you're putting me in with that bunch?"

"Well, I don't know, after what you just said."

"You *know* what I meant. I was paying you a compliment, for Chrissakes."

What was this, a lesson of some kind? Ivy had a new dogma, and she was taking it out for a walk? Laughing at his own wisecrack helped cool him down. If he had to start apologizing for ogling her body, they were in trouble.

"Being seen as a sexual object isn't a compliment," she said. "One thing I learned in the Movement is that leftist men are just as piggish as men everywhere."

That made him laugh out loud. "Are you calling me a pig? Because if I am, look at you, rootin' around down in the mud with a pig like me."

She shrugged. "It isn't your fault you were born male."

"Spare me your pity!" Eddie fell back and laughed. "Okay, that's it," he said. "No more opening doors for you, you're on your own. No more standing up when you enter the room, and that goes for every part of my body."

"Ha! You *know* you don't have that kind of control, but okay! We'll see!" She got back in bed beside him, on her side with one thigh across his, and one hand free to roam.

"Also, from now on, just to reassure my fragile male ego, you will assume whatever sex positions I desire," he said, "especially all the female submissive—"

"You'll be scheduling a hard on for me? Wow, I'm honored."

"And, of course, I'll be open to suggestions."

Her fingernails combed lightly through the hair at the base of his belly. An eyebrow raised, usually a bad sign. "Really? How open?"

Uh oh. "Within reason."

"Well, that's no fun," she said. "Ever been to bed with one of the boys downstairs?"

He didn't see that coming. He laughed. "Why would you ask that?"

"C'mon champ, I figured *that* scene out the first time I came over here. But you were obviously sworn to secrecy, so I didn't say anything. And you seemed to fit into that scene so well." She squeezed his bicep. "Look at you, champ, between the long hair and the rockin' bod, you're serious queer bait."

"Even if somebody was interested," he said, mindful he had secrets to keep, "the answer would be 'no.'"

"Why not?"

"I like women."

"Me too," she said. "Once in awhile."

He got up on one elbow. "You're kidding."

"Who knows a woman's body better than another woman? Does that gross you out?"

"No, not really," he said.

"I've had a few flings here and there. One girl who was a really great person, but decided to get engaged to her high school sweetheart back home in *Nebraska*, for Christ sakes, and another who was totally queer and an absolute fox… but nuts. That one ended bad. I thought we had a casual thing, but she developed, like, this obsession with me, and started following me around with this insane jealousy. They finally removed her from school."

"Why didn't you just stop seeing her?"

"I tried, but it was hard." With a smirk: "She was the most beautiful *thing* I ever saw." She laughed, but Eddie couldn't tell if she'd been putting him on, or if this was some new kind of game women cooked up to torment men. She rolled over him and lay on top. "Look, I've always told you, women don't need men to have orgasms."

He slid his hands from her thighs slowly up her back until his thumbs stopped in the moist hair under her arms. "Doesn't stop you from coming back for the real thing, though, does it?" he said.

EIGHT *Digging in frozen ground*

Monday morning as he cleaned the apartment he heard the brakes on the mailman's truck squeak downstairs. In the mailbox was a letter from the U.S. Selective Service System, ordering Edward Bonneville to get on a bus to Newark this Thursday, January 8, 1970, and undergo a pre-classification physical for military service. He wasn't being drafted, but he would undoubtedly pass the physical, and that would place him one step closer to a showdown with the government.

When he got to work that afternoon, Esposito's Coupe de Ville was sitting in the Bargainland parking lot, its jet-black skin and chrome trim gleaming in the fading daylight. The driver's window slid down, and Tommy beckoned him over.

Inside the car it was hot. Esposito sat beside him in the back seat, his hands in his coat pockets and his hat pushed back on his head. In the front seat Sally had her fur jacket open and blouse off her neck and shoulders. She had the radio on softly, humming tunelessly.

"Hello Eddie," Esposito said. "What happened to our story? There's nothing in the paper."

"Yeah, I know."

"You play them tapes for anybody yet?"

He caught a fearful look from Tommy in the rear view mirror. "I wrote the story, I gave it to my editor. Getting him to print the story is what I'm working on now."

"Did you play Frank the tapes?"

"He hasn't given me the time yet—"

"It's been two weeks," Esposito said. "It's only a couple hours of tape. You haven't played it for anybody yet?"

"Right."

"Why not? That's what I asked you to do, isn't it?"

"Well, you gave me a story—"

Esposito nodded. "That's right. And we made a deal. I give you the interview, you play the tapes for your boss."

"I've been trying to get him to listen. He won't make the time"

"You gotta get him to listen to 'em."

"Everything you said on the tape is in my story," Eddie said. "I guarantee you, he heard you loud and clear."

"I want 'em to hear the tapes. That's the deal we made."

"It's a story that'll get told, I promise. I still have a lot more digging to do."

Esposito's voice hardened. "You're not living up to our deal, kid. And you're wasting your time, writing a story. Frankie Devlin'll never let one word of this into that newspaper. I know Frankie very well. He's been cheating on his wife since their wedding day. I always had a room at the Lodge for him and a bottle on the dresser whenever he wanted to shack up with one of his chippies. Frankie's a good kid, except he drinks too much, he's weak, and he sold his ass for Hershey Bars to Bobby Castellucci and Roy McTierney."

"Frank and Bobby are friends, I know that."

"You bet. Bobby got Frankie his real job, bein' McTierney's bagman." At the look on Eddie's face, Esposito laughed. "Look kid, Frankie used to sell *me* political information. For years, he handled cash payoffs for *me*, until he switched sides. He's perfect for it. He's a newsman, so he goes around talking to everybody, and he doesn't steal as much as a lawyer would."

He didn't want to believe it. Frank as a compromised, cynical editor was still better than a pathetic Frank delivering bribes for his whiskey money.

Esposito scowled and demanded, "What the hell kinda reporter are you? Everybody knows Frankie Devlin's crooked right up to his fuckin' eyeballs! Everybody but you, his fair-haired boy! I stuck my neck out, telling you all this! Play him the tapes! I want those bastards to hear what I have to say! And I want them to hear it from *me*!"

Sure, for Esposito it was simple. Eddie plays the tapes, and Frank freaks out and warns everybody else: Back off, he's already started spilling his guts! The cruel deception of a busload of black people, the mayhem and injury to them and to Castellucci's guests and property, that too had been part of the warning.

"I swear to you, I'm gonna get this story out—" But he could barely get those words out.

"You're gonna, you're gonna. Yeah, right." Esposito laughed at him, a series of short barks. "I'll bet you don't even know Frankie and that newspaper are owned by Roy McTierney!"

That took him a moment or two… "What the hell are you talking about?"

"About a year ago. Frankie needed money. He came to me but I said 'No.' He went begging to Roy, and Roy bailed him out by buying him out. The whole thing was kept hush-hush. Roy McTierney owns the *Independent*, not to mention your boss. Not to mention you too, I guess. Okay, Tommaso, let's go. We're done."

"I swear to you," Eddie said, stumbling from the car. "I really didn't know."

"From you," Esposito said with some disgust, "I can believe that."

Please let this be the final absurdity, he thought.

Esposito shook his head, livid, leaned over and pulled the door shut. The Cadillac surged away, leaving him standing there, a jerk off in a world of savvy people.

It was 4 o'clock. He was due in the newsroom. *Fuck that.* He detoured down to Groucho's where nobody was likely to happen upon him. He ordered a coffee, lit a cigarette, and hid out at a back table. He wondered if any other *Independent* reporters knew that Roy Mac owned their newspaper and, if they did, how they felt about it. He didn't know if he was angry or heartbroken or what was happening inside him. He kept picturing Frank stopping by offices, dropping by bars and making small talk, passing information and envelopes of cash. Then, quite unexpectedly, he was struck by a thought that hollowed the pit of his stomach. He'd agreed to play the tapes and deliver Esposito's warning. Hadn't he been just as unprofessional as Frank? What would it take for *him* to go from messenger boy to bagman? If everybody had their price, what was his? Maybe it wasn't a matter of dollars and cents but getting a good story by doing a favor for an evil man.

He walked into the newsroom and hung his coat on the hook over his desk. "Hey." Frank was at the door of his office. "Inside, you." Eddie shrugged and went in, expecting a lecture about getting to work on time.

Instead, he found Frank slumped down on the sofa, his elbows on his knees, and Bobby Castellucci in a gray suit and dark overcoat perched on the corner of Frank's desk. The door was closed behind him and blocked by a guy he recognized as a bouncer from Castellucci's saloon.

Once upon a time, in a fair fight, he could wipe the floor with Bobby and his goon. Eddie gave Castellucci, a big, defiant grin. "Hello Bob, how you doing?"

"You got some balls, calling me the new rackets boss of the Jersey Shore," Castellucci said, waving Eddie's copy in his hand. "You want my wife and kids to read this in the paper?"

In disbelief, Eddie turned to Frank to ask why his copy was in the hands of a saloon owner and Mafiosi. But Frank wouldn't look him in the eye.

"I oughta kick your ass for this alone," Castellucci said.

"Well, don't kick anything just yet," Eddie said. "Remember, Matty Esposito said all that, not me."

"You know he busted up my club?"

"Really? Why you?" Eddie said.

"He's fuckin' bananas, that's why, he don't need a reason." He waved his copy in his face. "You have any idea how mentally fuckin' deranged that ole Wop is?"

"I was getting a news story," Eddie said. "It was assigned to me. You were there, in fact, I think I remember you suggesting it."

"But if somebody says stuff that's totally bananas, you don't write it, do you?"

"Unless it's true. Then, it's news."

"The good news, Eddie," Frank interjected quickly, "is that I'm making you assistant managing editor." But he wasn't listening. He and Castellucci stared at each other, like two tough opponents in the ring. "No more writing news," Frank said with a hopeful note in his voice, trying to make the offer sound better than the obvious bribe it was, "and you'll help me develop story ideas for other reporters. Your salary doubles."

"I'm a reporter. I'm not a desk guy."

"Okay, let me put it another way." Frank stood and hitched up his trousers. "You either work in the office as an editor or—"

"Or what?"

"I don't have time for this bullshit," Castellucci snapped.

"I don't think you understand," Eddie said. He spoke with exaggerated simplicity, as if to a child. "This is a newspaper, Bob. We've got a responsibility to the public to tell the truth about how things are around here. That's very different from running a saloon, Bob. I'm surprised you don't understand that."

Castellucci turned to Frank, who facially disowned any such idea and jabbered: "Take the desk job, Eddie. Move up to the big time."

"The big time's looking smaller by the minute."

"Aw, c'mon, kid." Frank stood there almost begging. How could any real editor do this? In the privacy of his office, a hoodlum threatens one of his reporters and he stands there watching like a whipped dog. Giving Frank his story so fast had been a bad mistake. Frank had given his story to Castellucci and he undoubtedly showed it to the McTierneys. Self-debased with booze and ass kissing, his editor was less a journalist than the Organization's congenial whore.

"I hear you're a boxer," Castellucci said.

Give me a reason, the killer in him begged, sensing that Castellucci was just as eager for a fight.

"I used to be a boxer, yeah."

"Yeah? How many rounds you think you could last with me?"

He couldn't resist. "That's a joke, right?"

Castellucci looked like he was about to hit him. "No joke."

He nodded toward the bouncer behind him. "You alone?"

"Yeah." Castellucci's red eyes burned with the pain of all the insults he'd ever endured. "Just me and you."

"I don't box anymore. I've embraced nonviolence."

"Didn't work too good for Martin Luther King, did it?"

Frank emitted a smarmy, ingratiating chuckle that Eddie found intolerable.

"C'mon Bob," Eddie said with exaggerated patience. "What would a guy like *you* know about Martin Luther King?"

Castellucci got on his feet, eye-to-eye with Eddie. With some difficulty, Eddie kept his hands down.

"Just me and you."

"Why would I want that?" Eddie said.

"I want it. I'm gonna kick your hippie ass."

"You're letting your fantasies run away with you."

"I don't like you."

"You don't know me," he said, "and the last guy I fought almost died."

"I heard about that. See, that's the difference between me and you."

"What?"

"I'm a professional." Castellucci's lips parted in an ugly grimace meant to be a smile. "And you're an *almost*."

Wondering if Castellucci would dare to attack him, he also wondered how many years of his young life *he* had walked around brimming with the pain of all the injustices ever done to him. Despite their superficial differences, it occurred to him that he and Castellucci were very much alike.

"I'll try to remember that." What he'd like to do was shed Castellucci's blood, make him squirm with pain and beg to surrender.

Castellucci flicked his hand dismissively to the bouncer. The door opened behind him and the bouncer stepped aside. As he left, Eddie glanced back at Frank but said nothing.

The door closed. Castellucci whirled on Frank. "He's gonna go around digging into shit, Frank!"

"Whose idea was it to send him after Matty Esposito in the first place?"

Castellucci slapped Frank across the face with Eddie's copy, knocking him over on the sofa with the pages scattered around him, his arms up.

"When Roy finds out about this, what're you gonna tell him?" Castellucci said.

"C'mon Bob," Frank whined, "he's no threat, he's just a kid—"

"Make him grow up. *Fast*."

That night after deadline, instead of going home, he drove around the two-lane county roads through the pine and oak forests on the west edge of Jackson Township, searching for Esposito's abandoned chicken farm.

He remembered that on Christmas Eve they'd passed Rova Farms, the big Russian resort beside a lake in Cassville. When he came upon it, he pulled over and parked on the shoulder. The buildings were dark and silent, the tips of the bare weeping willow whips were frozen to the surface of Cassville Lake, and the moonlight glowed on the gold onion dome of St. Vladimir's Memorial Church up the road. He sat there trying to remember the night they taped the interview. He thought they had traveled about a minute farther, to somewhere west of Perrineville Road where there were only farm lanes. He pulled back on the road, went too far, doubled back and found it. He pulled into the thick woods deep enough to be hidden from the road, turned off his lights and engine, and got out.

It was dead quiet. A light wind made the cold sharper and he shivered. Old snow lay on the dirt road and he saw no tire tracks or footprints. He got back in the car and drove slowly with the lights off, alongside a large field, over a rise and down into the yard between a crumbling barn and a dark house. He parked and got out and stood a long time, listening. By his odometer he was a half mile in from the road, far enough to go about his business unheard and unseen.

He walked slowly around the house. There was plywood nailed over the windows. A crust of snow covered the front steps and there were no footprints. The barn was chained and padlocked on the outside. None of the patches of leftover snow were disturbed. From his trunk he took a short-handled spade borrowed from Billy's garage, and stuck a flashlight into his coat pocket. He made his way in the moonlight down the dirt road that circled the field and ran along the chicken coops. He was determined to bring back evidence from the gangster's graveyard. He could interview people and get the runaround until he drowned in bullshit, but if he dug up one body, that would move things quicker and save him a lot of shoe leather.

The door was long gone. He ducked under the broken, sagging lintel. He flicked the flashlight on. The coop was about twenty feet long and ten feet wide, with stacks of empty wire cages down the sides and a dirt floor corridor down the middle. Chicken manure and feathers were stuck everywhere, on the grayed wood, in clots on the wire and in piles below the bottom cages, and in the cold there was a dank, musty odor. Up in the angle of the roof was a mass of spider webs and a wasp nest as big as a man's head. At the other end the door was open. Weeds and grass had grown from seeds blown inside the doorway.

He squatted and peered at the dirt floor between the cages. Unless they'd gone to the trouble to move the cages to dig beneath them, they must have buried the bodies here. He laid the flashlight down near his ankles so it shone across the floor. He picked up the shovel, then noticed something. He played the flashlight low across the packed dirt. The outlines of two sunken patches showed, faint but unmistakable. He ran his fingers over the impressions and felt a definite ridge. The soil had settled slightly in two patches, each about thirty inches wide and six feet long, roughly the size of a grave. He swore excitedly. He stood and put the point of the shovel on the ground and stomped it deep into the dirt.

Or so he wished. The shovel bent against the frozen ground, popped right out of his hands, and clattered away. He picked it up, knelt, and rammed the point of the shovel into the dirt, again and again, sending tiny chips of frozen earth scattering. After a solid minute of grunting and chipping, he had dug more of a dent in the frozen ground than a hole. He sat back, boiling with frustration.

Furious with himself, he seized the shovel and stabbed madly at the frozen hard packed dirt. It was pointless, it was futile, but it felt good to slam something. January! Why hadn't he thought of this? At this rate he'd be here for a month! He chipped at the earth until he was sweating and gasping, then threw the shovel down and gave up. He sat back and cursed and lit a cigarette. So much for letting the buried bodies speak for him. That would have to wait until spring, at least. He knelt over the mess he'd made in the dirt, and brushed the chips out of the three-inch deep hole. His fingertips brushed against something. He shined the flashlight on it, leaned over and blew the dust out of the hole. He put the shovel point in the ground and chipped a few more times and bent over and blew the dust away and brought the light in close, so he could see what he'd touched. It was a black button, on the cuff of a blue jacket.

At five o'clock the next day he slouched behind his desk, smoking, as Frank stood over him reading the next story in his Esposito series. He'd written it at home last night after brushing the dirt and chicken shit off his trousers and shoes. He'd slept badly, dreaming of spring and digging up the corpses rotting in the ground at Esposito's chicken farm.

Frank had no excuse to spike this story. It libeled nobody, he thought, because almost everybody in it was dead. He was especially proud of the lead:

JACKSON TOWNSHIP - Matthew Esposito gazed over the
weedy field of a deserted chicken farm and pointed to

where the bodies were buried, reciting name after name.

He thought he saw Frank stagger slightly. Frank folded the copy and tucked it in his shirt pocket. "You must be kidding."

Frank walked toward his office through the crowded newsroom. It was the evening hour when the day and night shifts overlapped. Insulted, Eddie jumped to his feet slamming his chair back.

"Where you going with my story, *Bagman*?" he yelled at Frank. The other reporters turned and stared at him with expressions ranging from puzzled to astonished. Frank's office door slammed, loud. He stubbed out his cigarette and went after him.

In his office Frank slumped, brooding over his desk, flicking his lighter at a cigarette.

"Listen Frank—"

"What'd you call me?"

"I called you what Matty Esposito said you *are*. Is it true?"

"He's a liar, and you're a fool to believe him." Frank tossed a few pages of copy to the edge of his desk. "Your column for next week? Out! I'm sick of your God damn unpatriotic bullshit and so is everybody else!"

This is the end, he thought, even if Frank had been told to keep him working for the *Independent* where they could keep an eye on him.

"Okay," he said, taking his column back. "But keep the space open. I've got a better column to write: 'When the press fails to do its job, who suffers?'"

Frank seemed not to have heard him. "And for the last time, drop this story. You know, you keep digging into this, you may end up embarrassing somebody near and dear."

"What are you talking about?" He thought for one bizarre moment Frank was referring to himself.

"How do you know your own father isn't just as crooked as the rest?"

"Because I asked, and Esposito told me he wasn't."

Frank laughed. "Well, what'd you expect him to say?"

There was no answer to that. He knew how square and severely ethical his father was, but how could he be sure about anything anymore?

"All you're doing is pissing people off and making everybody nervous."

"Yeah, I got a little taste of that yesterday. Thanks for watching my back."

"What did you expect me to do?" Frank said. "Look who I was dealing with."

He was so disappointed in Frank it made him ill. He shook his head. "Esposito also called you a Hershey Bar Whore. Now I know why." He stalked out of Frank's office ready to smash anyone or anything in his way.

He had just reached his desk when two hands seized his shoulders. "Self righteous little cocksucker!" Frank screamed, shoving him face first at the wall, "If you're so unhappy here, *quit*!"

He broke the fall with his hands. He pushed off the wall and spun around. Neither meditation, nor taking five slow breaths, even occurred to him. He punched Frank with a hard right hook that landed between his cheekbone and nose. Frank, looking startled, rocked back on his heels, arms flailing, took two steps backward, and fell heavily to the dirty linoleum. The newsroom went dead silent, and Bobbi Ann let out something between a sigh and a scream.

Frank got up slowly, helped by Joe, the sports editor and Hildy, the society page reporter.

Eddie slowly uncoiled his stinging fist. "Shouldna done that, Frank."

"What about you?" Hildy muttered.

"I defended myself," he said, and shook his head. "Look, I'm sorry."

Frank touched the side of his face with his fingertips and winced from the pain. "Go on!" he croaked. "Tell everybody why you can't stand working for me anymore! See if they care!" Eddie could see clearly in the faces around him that they didn't. They were scared of him, and worried about Frank.

Frank coughed and his nose spurted blood over the back of his hand and stained his white shirt and gold tie. "Shit!" He mumbled a couple things, said, "Aw, God damn it," and his face crumpled. "My favorite tie—"

"I'm sorry I hit you, Frank, it's just that, I've had two bad days in a row, now, and nobody knows why better than you." He stepped up and plucked his copy, spattered lightly with blood, from Frank's shirt pocket. "I'll go back to work."

"The hell you will!" Frank's swollen bloody nose made him honk, like he had a cold. "You're fired! Get out of here!"

Frank shook free of his helpers, squared his shoulders and lurched toward the men's room, his hand cupped under his nose. Eddie watched him, hating himself for losing control and letting himself be pulled down to Frank's level. He should have deflected Frank's assault and treated him with peace, love and understanding. Yeah right... maybe next time.

Eddie lifted his coat from the hook and headed for the door. Mister Jackson sat bolt upright behind his typewriter as his eyes followed Eddie. In the silence, he drawled softly, "Edward, I thought you were a pacifist."

"Some days are easier than others."

Crane shook his head at Eddie. This time he wasn't amused. "Jesus Christ, kid, what's wrong with you?"

"I don't like being pushed around, do you?"

Bobbi Ann was behind her desk, arms indignantly crossed, eyes shining and downcast as if he'd smacked *her*.

Beside her, Bailey Devlin stared at him in disbelief.

"I'm sorry, Bay." Was there a way to explain, so she wouldn't think badly of him? He had no idea what to say.

"Just *go*," she said, loud and hard, like she was speaking for all present. He felt his face turn red.

At the entrance to the newsroom, Nick Poliandro stood with his mouth agape. At first Eddie was shocked to see him, then he remembered tonight was their weekly dinner night.

"What the hell was that?" Nick said out on the sidewalk, following Eddie to the Impala.

"Something I wish I didn't do," he said.

In the parking lot he stopped and asked Nick, "Do you know if Roy McTierney owns the *Independent*?"

Nick shrugged. "I hear rumors. That's all."

Not everybody knew, so maybe he wasn't an idiot.

In the car, Nick stared at him, obviously expecting him to explain what just happened. As if he could! As soon as he hit the highway, he wanted to turn the car around, go back and beg Frank's forgiveness, and ask for his job back. But he couldn't trust himself not to punch Frank out again. So he kept driving north on Route 9, getting himself out of the moment, slowly calming down.

"I don't believe I did that," he said. "Of all the stupid things to do. It's like two years of nonviolence haven't taught me a damn thing."

"What happened?"

"Me and Frank aren't getting along too good."

"Yeah, I noticed."

"He killed a story of mine. I called him a name and he shoved me and I just lost it." He groped for his cigarettes. He'd left them on his desk. "God, I hope he's all right."

Nick held out his pack of Marlboros and lit them both up. "What's this story he killed, can you tell me?"

"Get my tape recorder out of the glove compartment." When Nick put it on the console between their seats, Eddie slipped the first Esposito cassette into the player. "Listen to this. Then tell me if I should take it seriously or not."

"What is it?"

"An interview I did with Matty Esposito, the day after the arraignment."

"Great," Nick said. "He didn't return my calls, but he gives you an interview. Did he say anything newsworthy?"

By seven o'clock they had finished dinner in Eddie's car, parked behind Mc Donald's on Route 37, and were having coffee and cigarettes.

"Hey, you know I lost my cherry in a graveyard? It's a cute story. Turn that thing off first."

Eddie turned the machine off and pocketed the cassettes. For the moment he forgot about his hunger for the big story that would raise him above his fellow reporters. He just wanted another reporter to agree there was a story and get some advice on how to do it. But Nick was hard to read, he stared pensively out the windshield.

"We all have fights over stories," Nick said, "but that's the first time I ever saw a reporter slug his editor."

"This story's got Frank scared shitless," Eddie said.

"Yeah. I can see why."

"*He* sent me to get Esposito's reaction to the indictment. I wrote two stories. He spiked them both."

"That sucks," Nick said.

So did so much else. His editor was a weakling who was the Organization's bagman. The newspaper he wrote for was owned by the Organization. The new gangster in town was begging him for a fight, and the Rackets Boss of the Jersey Shore was pissed off with him because he wasn't a standup guy. But Eddie kept those problems to himself. All he wanted to know was how to cover this story.

"He knew Esposito'd be pissed about getting indicted," Eddie said. "Maybe he figured he'd say something newsworthy. I doubt he expected *this*. I sure didn't."

"And Frank is freaked out that you take it so seriously."

"Don't you?"

"Some of it, I guess."

"Does this jibe with things you know about?"

"I don't know." He shrugged. "You're always hearing things. Usually, somebody's trying to use you and your newspaper to ruin somebody else. It's all part of the political game, if you want to play it. Me, I don't have the time."

Nick's nonchalance made him doubt himself. Maybe this story wasn't worth a reporter's time and sweat. Maybe he was naive, maybe people really didn't care if their government was corrupt. Maybe he'd just bloodied his editor by mistake, because he held a childish view of his profession, and for that matter, of life.

On the other hand, Nick's dismissal of Esposito's revelations was like an automatic reflex, a quick swerve around a pothole.

"What I'm saying is, Esposito's not a total crank," Nick said. "I wouldn't be surprised if some of what he says is true, but who really knows?"

"Who would know better than the crook at the center of it all?" Eddie said. "If even half of this is true—" He shrugged, and Nick snickered.

"Sometimes on that tape you sound like you're in over your head."

"It got scary a couple times, like the chicken farm." He almost told Nick he went back to the farm last night and believed he'd found at least one buried body. But he kept quiet, noticing for the first time how much he wanted to impress Nick. "Would the *Press* run a story on this? If I came to work for you?"

Nick's reply was cautious. "You'd have to work on it a lot more. You'd have to back up everything Esposito says. Then after you write it, the lawyers have to go over every word. Stories like this take time and money to do. But that's the only way you can do it and not lose a libel suit."

"But it's all on tape. He said I could quote him—"

"Jesus," Nick said, looking at him in disbelief. "If you worked for any editor but Frank Devlin, you'd know about the libel and slander laws."

"Of course, I know the tapes alone aren't enough."

"You have one source, and no proof or privilege, so no story. The tapes are notes, that's all."

"What do you mean?"

"Journalism 101, man." Nick fired up a new cigarette off the last one. "In a story like this, for each thing that Esposito claims, you need at least two more unrelated sources to corroborate it. Witnesses, documents, physical evidence. You need proof that'll hold up in court if somebody sues the paper for libel. The only other way would be if something happens like the De Cavalcante papers. Once all those conversations were filed with the court clerk, they became public record. Then under the law the press has access *and* is protected by privilege. A reporter can *carefully* describe what's in there and be libel proof."

"Sounds like an incredible amount of work," Eddie said, realizing both stories he'd written were inadequate and a long way from being ready for print, and he hadn't even known it.

"It's tedious, it's expensive, and it's risky," Nick said. "Then once it's published it's a headache, because you're under attack by people with real power to fuck you up. That's one reason why so little of it gets done."

"And in the end, is anybody really listening?"

"I guess so," Nick said, "or we ought to be in another line of work."

"I thought I'd come to work for the *Press* and we could work on this."

Nick shrugged. "Well, we can talk about that. But right now, I've got to cover a planning board meeting at eight, so I've got to get back to my car. Let's shove off."

As he drove, Eddie muttered to himself. The enormity of the real job of reporting, a job he hadn't even started yet, made a mockery of his fantasy that he would write an expose, corrupt politicians would crash, mighty reputations would be brought down, and at the end of it all, government reforms would ensue for the betterment of all. Behind the wheel, he cringed at his foolishness.

Nick appeared to be deep in his own thoughts. Listening to Esposito's accusations about the Organization had clearly made him uncomfortable. Well, when a reporter hears a story like this he should do something about it, but Nick either couldn't, or wouldn't. So there was another reaction Eddie hadn't anticipated, like the way Frank got insulted when he reminded him of a newspaper's mission.

He dropped Nick off at his car and watched him pull away from Bargainland.

Eddie gazed across the lot into the windows of the newsroom. He wondered if he should walk into Frank's office, apologize, and beg for his job back. For two years he had disciplined his anger and impulsive brutality and harmed nobody, even though many times he'd been tempted. Why did the fight tonight with Frank go differently? Why did he react so quick and so violent? It couldn't be just because Frank gave him a little shove. What the hell was wrong with him?

Only one way to find out. He started to get out of the car, but just then he saw Frank leave the newsroom with Bailey, the two of them laughing and talking animatedly, walking toward Castellucci's. It figures, Eddie thought, Frank was probably over it by now, while he felt worse than ever. He sat back for a moment, then changed his mind, started the engine and drove away.

From Toms River he could drive east at 50 mph on Route 37 and cross Barnegat Bay to the coast highway. But then he would have to crawl up Route 35 to Bay Head through lots of empty beachfront towns whose cops had nothing better to do on dead winter nights than ticket speeders who couldn't drive under 25 miles per hour. Or he could drive north on Hooper Avenue and Brick Boulevard at 45 mph, bypass the old villages of Breton Woods and Adamston, and pick up the county road taking him to the Mantoloking Bridge over the bay. From there he'd only be a couple miles from home. He was in no mood for driving slow so rather than risk a speeding ticket, he took the inland route.

Part of his mind wondered how to keep pursuing the Esposito story, while another part drove the car. In no time, he came out of Adamston Road and onto Mantoloking Road, a concrete two lane built during the Depression. It ran for a mile and a half through pine woods and marsh and cedar swamps, with dangerous shoulders of soft, deep sand, over the bay bridge to the coast highway.

Something caught his eye in the rearview mirror. Nothing there— no, wait, there was a large sedan with a huge chrome grille and its headlights off. The car rushed his rear bumper, and backed off. Stupid ass, put your lights on before you run into me, he thought. Now the guy was trying to pass on his left, lurching to and fro like a drunk. He slowed down and edged as close to the sandy shoulder as he dared. He flicked on his high beams to help the other driver see, hoping the jerk wouldn't sideswipe him. A Cadillac sedan pulled up beside him and the passenger's window slid down. Sure, we can talk, you fuckin' idiot. He rolled his window down, cold wind hit his face.

A man with a hard face and ball bearings for eyes leaned out of the other car pointing a gun. Eddie hit the brakes. The Cadillac leapt past him and the shot boomed over his hood. He jerked his car left behind the Cadillac. The gunman twisted around trying to aim at him. The Cadillac lurched into the right lane and Eddie floored the gas pedal and tore past on the Cadillac's left with gunfire cracking behind him.

The Cadillac's blinding high beams flared in his rearview mirror. He swung back to the right lane. He put the pedal down and the Cadillac chased him, his speed rising fast. The Cadillac swung back and forth behind him trying to pass him, and he kept blocking him, careening back and forth. He tightened his grip on the wheel. If his tire caught one of the sandy shoulders he was done for. Gunshots cracked behind him, and something hit the rear of the car. Who the hell was this?

The pine and cedar woods opened up to the low, grassy wetlands at the edges of the bay. The lights of the bridge, a two lane concrete span, rushed toward him.

He hit the bridge going fast and raced to the peak. Behind him he heard a gunshot. His driver's side mirror shattered. Cursing, Eddie floored it and the big V-8 engine put an Apollo mission rocket boost under his ass. Topping the bridge, the Impala sailed above the pavement for a second, and slammed down. He almost lost control, then the Impala whipped back into line. He pumped his brakes and downshifted, thanking God there was not a line of traffic in front of him at the light, and he fishtailed to a stop in the middle of the intersection with Ocean Avenue.

Behind him the Cadillac made the same leap but its heavy chrome nose dropped and its rear end lifted. At the foot of the bridge it landed on its front bumper, sending off a roar of grinding metal and a shower of sparks. The back wheels dropped hard and uneven on the road and flung the heavy car sideways and it crashed through a utility pole. The tires screamed as it spun the opposite way, ripped through a section of guardrail and rolled down an embankment of scrub pine and dune grass at the base of the bridge.

Sparks sputtered and dropped from the wires holding the top of the broken utility pole suspended in the air. The Cadillac lay on its roof, wheels spinning, in an empty lot of dune grass and beach plum bushes. Porch lights flashed on and doors began to open in nearby houses. Eddie turned around and drove away, staying under the speed limit.

He pulled his father away from the television in the middle of *The Honeymooners* and sat him down at the kitchen table. He played him parts of the Esposito tapes, and let him read the copy for his first two stories. His mother had already gone to bed, luckily, because he didn't know how he would have included her in this particular conversation. When he was done, Ed Sr., picking at Frank's dried blood on the second story with his thumbnail, sighed and shook his head.

"This is what you lost your job over?" his father said in his *What the hell have you done now?* voice.

"No. He fired me because we argued, and he shoved me into a wall, and I decked him."

His father shrugged, since he detested Frank. "This isn't worth the trouble you're making for yourself."

"I think it is."

"And now you say you were shot at tonight?" he said, disbelieving. Nothing new there.

"Hey, don't take my word for it. C'mon."

They pulled on their coats. He took a flashlight from the shelf beside the door and they went out to where the Impala was parked in the driveway. He showed his father the broken mirror. They found the bullet hole in his trunk lid. His father poked at it with his finger.

"Open the trunk." He did and his father flashed the light around. "Good thing they missed your gas tank, or you'd be charcoal right now." He peered deeper, probed around, and nodded. "The bullet's probably in your back seat." Eddie found the bullet hole in the back wall of the trunk. He closed the lid.

"Look," his father said. "I was planning to call you anyway. I was spoken to about you."

"By who?"

"Who do you think?"

"Roy Mac."

His father looked at him as if nothing more need be said.

"What'd he want?"

"He wanted me to talk to you about what you're doing."

"You mean talk me out of it."

"Yeah."

"Do you owe him anything?"

"I do, and I don't. I never took Organization money for my campaigns. I was too smart for that. But I took their endorsement, because without it I would've been invisible."

"So that means you owe him – what?"

"I have to listen to him. That's all."

"And what'd you tell him?"

"I said I'd talk to you, that's all."

"Good. Now that you've talked to me, how about talking to him for me? How about telling him I don't like him sending guys to run me off the road and shoot up my car?"

"Did you hear me when I said this isn't worth it? "

"You just don't like me pissing off your political cronies."

"No, I mean this story isn't worth the trouble you'll cause for yourself."

"There you go again," he said. "I'm getting all excited over nothing, right? I got my head up my ass again, right?"

"Take it easy," his father said.

"People want to know if their public officials are corrupt."

"Says you," his father said. "What are you, smarter than everybody else now?" Eddie wondered what he was listening to, a father trying to protect his son, or bluffing from a crooked politician? Or was this just the same exhausting negativity he'd gotten from this man his whole life?

"This is my job."

"Your job," his father scoffed. *Your work in this world is meaningless, my boy, and besides…* "People don't care."

"Maybe if they know more, they will."

"You're giving 'em too much credit."

"Maybe you ought to have a little faith."

"You've got a lot to learn about people." His father paced restlessly beside the car, shaking his head.

"Well, I sure didn't learn much from you." He put his tape recorder back in the glove compartment and pocketed the two tapes.

"Oh, it's all my fault, now? Look, why'd you bring this to me?" His father didn't want to be bothered with his problems, and that hurt, even though he expected it.

"I wanted your advice. I guess I got it." Eddie leaned on the fender and stuck his hands deep in his jacket pockets. "Now—what about you?"

"What do you mean?"

"You've been a Committeeman for eight years. Are you as crooked as the rest?"

His father stared at him and it was impossible to read his expression. "What the hell do you think?"

He knew better than to take that bait; or was there something his father needed from him? Too bad, if there was. "I really don't know."

His father's face darkened. "What do you mean you don't know? I'm your father, for Chrissakes."

"After hearing all this," he said, "I don't know who to trust."

"Including *me*?"

"Like I said, I don't know," he said, managing to keep his voice even. He was astonished that this man, short-tempered, fast with the whipping belt, who often seemed repulsed by Eddie's very presence, had the audacity to expect his trust. What the hell else did he feel entitled to—love? "Right now, I'm not sure what to think about a lot of stuff."

His father stared off into the dark for a long moment. Then he shook his head, and said in a soft voice Eddie'd rarely heard: "So you didn't learn much from me?"

Eddie thought, *Asked and answered*, and just shrugged. *Sorry.*

"Come on," his father said.

They entered the garage by the side door. It was cold inside and they could see their breath on the musty air. His father turned on the light over his work bench. On the far side of the garage was the family's 1958 Plymouth wagon. On the near side was a pile of cartons stenciled BONNEVILLE APPLIANCES. He really didn't like being in the garage with the remains of his father's bankrupt business. Too bad his family's heartache couldn't be as easily packed away and forgotten as the files stored in those dusty boxes.

His father knelt beside the cartons and peered at the end labels until he found what he was looking for. He pulled out a gray metal lockbox, set it on his workbench and opened it.

He lifted out a .45 caliber Army automatic pistol, and polished it with its wrapping cloth. He put the magazine in the grip and shoved it home with the heel of his hand. Eddie watched him, speechless.

"I fired it last summer at the range in Sea Girt. It's in good condition. It's loaded, the safety is on." His father held the pistol out to him. The handgrips were walnut on a weapon of dull steel.

"What the hell are you trying to do?" Incredulous, it was all he could think to say.

"People mean to do you harm, my boy."

"I just told the Draft Board I wouldn't pick up a gun." He waited to hear his father's disapproval but all he got was a stare. "I can't take that from you."

"You believe in self defense?"

"No. It only keeps the violence going."

His father shook his head in disbelief. "You want to stay healthy long enough to write your big story?"

"What the hell are you saying?"

His father held the pistol out to him. "The only thing worse than you hurting somebody again would be you getting hurt. Or killed. I couldn't take that, Eddie." He stared at the .45, realizing what his father was saying. "Protect yourself. You're the only one who can."

"You never answered my question."

His father laid the .45 on the bench between them.

"I love being a Committeeman. Working with people, serving the public. I love the game of politics, all of it. And I'm good at it. You don't believe me, ask around." He sighed and stared at the space between them for a long time, finally saying, "I'm a man with five kids and a failed business. Every day, I have to face a choice. I could get out of politics, but that would be like admitting I'm not strong enough to resist temptation. Or stay in politics, where I know there is definitely money to be made. Not part time job money, either. Money that might turn our life around as a family. But what kind of life?"

"It's good to know my old man stands on principle."

"Principle?" His father shrugged. "I just hope nobody ever makes me an offer I can't turn down. Because then it'll be time to get out."

"I guess Matty Esposito was right, everybody has their price."

"A smart man knows that."

Thus, the wisdom his father was offering him: know the ways of the world, know your weaknesses, and when necessary carry a gun. "But now you're telling me don't bother doing this story, even though it might be true, even though exposing this is the right thing to do."

"It isn't worth you getting hurt over."

"I think it's worth the risk."

"I know you do," his father said. He picked up the pistol and held it out to him. "So here."

Eddie slowly shook his head.

"Look… Eddie… You're scaring the hell out of me," his father said. He'd never heard that waver in his voice before. Although he was the one in danger, he felt a strange pity for his father. "You're playing with political dynamite, and then you say you don't know what to *think* about a lot of things?" His father was dead serious. "What you're into here, you have to know what you're doing. This is not for somebody who's *confused*. Do you understand that? You gotta be able to handle yourself."

"And what—a gun will do that for me?" His father stood there holding out the gun, his only answer. "This is a sad commentary, isn't it?"

"No," his father said. "It's just life. It's what *is*." He reached out and took him by the shoulder. His father was embarrassed, eyes glistened, his voice was tight. "Believe me, I don't like doing this, especially with your attitude. But maybe this will give you a better chance. You're a tough kid, but suppose that isn't enough? Imagine how your mother would feel if you got hurt, or worse."

He took the .45 from his father, and closed his hand around the grip. It was heavier than he expected. Although it had an attractive balance in his hand, it would be like carrying a small sledge hammer strapped to his body. And, like a hammer, it was a tool—a tool for killing people. In his hand, the gun gave him an almost erotic sensation of power, the power to destroy, and it was strangely exciting. At that, he shuddered.

"Let me show you how this works," his father said.

"No," Eddie said, handing the gun back. "I know you're worried, Pop, but this will only make things worse."

The next day he went out and got the morning newspapers from the machines in the entrance foyer of the O–B Diner. He had coffee at the counter and scanned them. The *Independent* had no story about a car crash. The *Observer* had a small page 2 story: a Cadillac flipped over at a high rate of speed last night near the Mantoloking Bridge. When the Mantoloking police reached the scene there was no driver or passengers and none turned up during a search of area hospitals. There was no mention of another driver being involved. The Cadillac had been reported stolen in East Orange, fifty miles to the north, earlier that day.

NINE *Useful lies*

Ivy cooked herself scrambled eggs and ham for breakfast, and was halfway through eating it, gloomily facing another boring day in New Jersey, when the phone rang.

"Hello, Porter residence."

"Hey, Prom Queen."

"Hey, *que pasa*, baby," she said, startled to hear from him. How did he get their unlisted number?

"Holidays are over. What're you doin', still hangin' around down there?" He sounded lonely. He was in a phone booth, she recognized New York street noise behind him. None of them used the townhouse phone for fear the FBI had it wiretapped.

"Slowly goin' nuts. I told you they'd keep me here."

"Doing what?"

"Playing the daughter game, what else?" she said. "I've got a couple more weeks to go."

A weary groan. "D'fuck is there to do down there in winter any-way?"

She neatly sidestepped that trap. "Make myself available for inane social activity when Mister or Mrs. Ruling Class need me to. I take long walks on the beach, lay around the house and read. Some cousins came to visit and it was cool to catch up with them. Mostly I get in the car and ride around. It's pretty boring, but here I am."

"And you're doing all this like, with who?"

"All by my lonesome."

"Oh really."

It hadn't taken long for the conversation to become irritating. "Do you remember me telling you I was unpopular in high school?"

"So?"

"So I'm down here for a reason. It ain't to see old friends. I'm only waiting for one old friend, man, the one I can take to the bank. And I can't push the situation."

"I know that, but the others have been hassling me over where you are and when you'll be back."

Right—like they missed her. *Why is that any of their fucking business?* She caught herself, and said instead, breathlessly, "Wow, I am so sorry to be causing a problem, I'm so embarrassed."

After a long pause, in which she wondered if she'd said the wrong thing, he said, "We're all in this together, don't forget."

"I won't forget. I miss all of them." *They always treated me like a virus that somebody sneezed up.* "And you."

"Well, you know, you're seen as, kind of aloof."

"I had to go home for Christmas, that's all."

"Well, they don't know that."

"Explain it to them. It's my parents, that's all. It's what they want, and for me to get what *I* want, I have to give them what *they* want." Did they really need this explained to them? "They have parents, too, don't they?"

"They'd just feel better having you back here, that's all." Under their control, he meant. Suddenly she realized she was hurting his stature in the cadre, being out of his control.

"Well, I can't come back with empty pockets, can I?"

"That money's nothing but a leash around your neck."

"Maybe, but it pays the rent and puts food on the table. *Our* table. Unless you've found a job somewhere."

"Hey, I *have* a job."

Full-time revolutionary. No salary, no benefits. "I haven't forgotten," she said.

Cling cling, the phone swallowed his money. "Shit, I'm out."

"Oh damn," she said, relieved. "I love you! Call any time!"

When he hung up, Ivy sat back, her heart pounding and her throat dry. She stared out the back window at the lawn sloping down to the canvas-covered swimming pool. Three dark starlings swaggered around the yard pecking at the snow. Beyond the brown dead flowerbeds at the edge of the pool, a dense woods of oak, evergreen and maple trees stood against the deep blue sky. The spacious quiet and beauty of the yard could not calm her down.

She might still have him under control. She wasn't so sure about herself. It was a good thing she was forbidden to call the townhouse under any circumstances. The urge was almost irresistible to call David back, especially after guilt-tripping him like that about not having a job, to reassure *herself* that everything was okay—and she was the one who was supposed to be running away.

She got up and poured a cup of coffee and breathed in the aroma. She lit a cigarette and put herself in an armchair in the sunroom. She drank coffee and smoked and let her mind sink into the *Today* show, vacuous and comforting, and after a few minutes she was more or less back to normal.

At six o'clock on Thursday morning in the frigid dark outside the courthouse in Toms River, a yellow school bus full of 18 year-old boys lurched forward with a loud grinding of gears to begin the journey up to the Newark military induction center. Eddie shared a seat with a black kid named Clarence from South Toms River who said he'd just finished the night shift stocking shelves at an A&P. He said a shy hello, yawned, and dozed the whole trip. A few guys on the bus were solitary and brooding, but most made fast friends with anybody they could, too scared to face the military machine alone. Eddie didn't want to talk to anyone. He read "Animal Farm" and stared out the window and seethed, telling himself this was life under totalitarianism. The stream of traffic north on the Parkway grew thicker as the day dawned blue. As they topped the Victory Bridges over the Raritan River, golden sunlight broke through the sky of soft low clouds and glinted off the choppy waters of the bay between the dirty shorelines of South and Perth Amboy.

In Newark, they parked in a long line of school busses from all over New Jersey out in front of the massive beige slab of the Federal Building. People passed by in a blur, marching to work up Broad Street, their breath steaming in the cold sunlight. He stepped off the bus and came face to face with two barking MPs rushing the boys into large elevators and upstairs to an installation called AFEES, the Armed Forces Entrance and Examination Station.

Two hundred boys were herded into a huge open room. Eddie sat in a chair with a little fold-down desk. It was like sitting in a study hall in high school, except the subject was war, and he wasn't here to study, he was here to submit. He sat back, knowing they could arrest him, they could order him to take the oath, and they could pack him off to jail if he refused.

The door opened and in walked a Drill Instructor with a shaved head, a chest full of insignia, and a locked jaw and neck. He slammed the door loud enough to quiet the buzz in the room. He stood at attention at the front of everybody, and bellowed in a high west Texas voice:

"Welcome to the U.S. Army, *ginnul–mun* ! Today you will undergo a series of tests to determine your fitness for military duty!"

A loud, jive voice echoed from the back of the room: "Stick your military duty up your ass, Cracker," slow and languid with contempt.

Heads turned. Against the rear wall, two glowering Black Panthers slouched insolently in their chairs, in full regalia: berets, Ray Bans, leather jackets. Eddie exchanged thrilled glances with the white boys around him. Baaaad…

The D.I. ignored the Panthers and the chuckles rippling through the room.

"Here at AFEES Newark you are under Army command! You will obey any and all orders! You will complete all the forms properly! Any deviation from acceptable behavior will result in your being taken downstairs, and given a choice between jail or immediate induction into the United States Army!"

"Shee–it," the other Panther laughed. "No *Vietnamese* never called me nigger. But I know where *you* come from, Cracker!" The D.I. paused for a moment, then pivoted and marched out of the room.

Giggles and chuckles, derisive and bold, rose and filled the room with a pattering of applause, everybody getting off on the defiance. The Panthers had won a psychological victory, and for a minute order broke down and every boy in the room was a rebel.

The door slammed open. Four burly white M.P.s burst in and sped like defensive linemen down the aisles, knocking desks and boys aside, and the laughter died on a weak collective "Whoa!" The M.P.s seized the Panthers so forcefully that their chairs rose with them, and fell away. They hurled the Panthers, kicking and swinging, into the back wall. When they bounced back, they kicked their feet out from under them and flung them on their faces on the floor, stomped their boots in the middle of their backs, wrenched their arms behind them, and cuffed their hands. The M.P.s lifted the Panthers by their elbows and dragged them, kicking and cursing, through the crowd of shocked boys toward the door.

"I'd rather rot in a white man's prison than shoot a Vietnamese!" the first dude shouted.

"Don't be a fool, don't be the white man's tool!" the other screamed.

The D.I. checked out the boys who'd been knocked aside and got them seated upright again. He picked up a pair of fallen Ray Bans, opened them, and laid them on the front desk so they stared blankly out at the room. The boys began to laugh at that but the D.I. spun around.

"*Shut up!*"

They did, fast. When the D.I. resumed bellowing, Eddie barely listened. His adrenaline accelerator was stuck to the floor. His heart was pounding out of control. He tried counting his breaths. He wanted to kill the M.P.s with his bare hands. But the Ray Bans gazed blank and cool at him from the desk, reminding him that resistance was futile.

Thus frightened and subdued, he and hundreds of boys would spend the next several hours trudging in an endless line through twenty four doctor's stations, wearing only their underwear and shoes and socks, each carrying his valuables in a green cloth drawstring bag. At each stop a specific health factor would be checked, including the dreaded "greasy finger" prostate exam. The process began in that huge room with a health questionnaire, a densely printed government form with dozens of questions about his health and his family's. It took over thirty minutes to answer. At the bottom was a long list of maladies to check if they applied to him. He checked Frequent Terrifying Nightmares, Insomnia, Chronic Anxiety, Depression, Migraine Headaches. He tried to portray himself as a head case even though he'd heard rumors all that would be ignored—hell, the military routinely inducted real criminals. He could claim every neurosis on the list and it would not get him to his goal, an interview with the Army psychiatrist at Station 25. To get that, he had to claim he suffered either from Drug Abuse or Homosexual Tendencies. Neither was strictly true, but thanks to hanging out with Billy's friends, and a few rock musician friends in high school, he figured he knew enough about being queer and taking dope to put on a convincing performance for the psychiatrist.

And he had absolutely no qualms about lying to the military. Look at the way the Draft Board brushed his C.O. application aside! Being honest with these people was suicide, because their might would always make right! Most frightening of all, the government obviously didn't know what to do about Vietnam. The American people were now solidly against the war, and *still* nobody in Washington had the courage to withdraw the troops. As the politicians fumbled around, afraid to risk their pampered positions as petty celebrities, soldiers were coming home with their bodies maimed, their minds broken, or in coffins. If treason meant refusing to be a passive victim of that kind of decadence, so be it. The three paths open to him were expatriation, or to refuse induction and go to prison, or to lie and claim he was a gay dope addict and brazen it out. Canada was too cold; as alluring as Paris was in his fantasies, he didn't speak the language. And he wasn't ready for martyrdom and jail.

So he lied. Twice.

That afternoon when he got off the bus back in Toms River and returned to his car parked near the courthouse, he found a handwritten note under the windshield wiper. It was an urgent request to meet with Matty Esposito at a housing development down in Lacey Township where he could be found all day. Well, so much for a peaceful afternoon writing at home.

He ate a chef's salad at Tommy's Restaurant on Main Street. He really wanted to go home, but it was better to go find out what the old man wanted than to have him appear suddenly, maybe at the worst moment. Three days ago, Esposito had been livid and disgusted with him. It was doubtful that had changed, and there was a chance he'd go see Esposito only to get his ass kicked. He had failed to live up to their deal, and was wondering how to face the old hoodlum's rage again when the perfect solution occurred to him. Giving Frank Devlin the story had more than delivered Esposito's message. He nearly came to blows with Castellucci over it, so Frank had obviously told the right people. So, done deal, and he would lie and tell Esposito he'd played the tapes for Frank. He should have just lied in the first place, but he was still too much of a friggin' Boy Scout.

It was late afternoon, golden sun and cool blue shadows, by the time he turned off Route 9 at a large sign reading "Roman Estates." A ten foot tall square-jawed centurion in silver helmet and armor painted on plywood pointed his sword west toward the 300 houses nestled in the pine and oak forest. He drove carefully on the bumpy, unpaved gravel of Roman Boulevard. Side streets were lined with half-built houses on one acre wooded lots, bi-level and split level, sheathed in plywood rather than chipboard, faced with real stone and not veneer, most with bay windows and gables, all these features well above the usual tract house quality.

Outside a construction trailer, he found Esposito talking to a small group of workers. Eddie parked across the street. Esposito shook a few hands, and the workers dispersed.

As they stood outside the trailer Esposito waved his hand expansively. "Well, what do you think?"

"Think of what?"

"All this. Roman Estates. This is mine."

"You're the developer?"

"I own the biggest piece."

"Wow."

"I wanna show you something." Esposito wrapped a possessive arm around his shoulders and he found himself being walked across the dirt street to the Cadillac.

"I want you to know, Mister Esposito, I played the tapes for Frank."

"Okay, thanks."

"I'm still trying to write about what you told me."

"Okay, thanks."

"Listen, I need to talk to more people before I can publish anything. Can you steer me to anybody who can confirm what you told me?"

"That's just where we're going."

"Oh good."

He got in beside Esposito and the old man drove them deeper into Roman Estates, passing workers headed for home. The development was still, the work frozen with the men gone. The place had a kind of dignity, even beauty, at that hour. Real work happened here, hard work done by teams of men with tools in their hands in every kind of weather, work very different from the thievery, dishonesty and manipulation of the men he was investigating.

They turned into a side street, four houses on a *cul de sac* cut into a thick grove of evergreens. The curbs and sidewalks, storm drains and fire hydrants were all in place, but the gravel road was four inches too low and the lawns were still bare topsoil.

Esposito stopped the car in the middle of the street and cut the engine. The dim twilight hardly penetrated the tall firs at the edge of the yard. The street was dead quiet. They were a long way from anywhere.

"I want to show you something," Esposito said.

"Really?" He suddenly realized there were a long way from any witnesses, too.

"Yeah, really. C'mon."

He got out and followed Esposito across the dirt lawn of a house under construction. Eddie decided he was not going inside the dark house no matter what, even if he had to turn and run like hell.

The cinder block base of the front steps hadn't gotten its flagstone finish yet. Esposito put his foot on the bottom step, and lit the cigar in the corner of his mouth.

"Write down this address. Twenty-two Twenty Mockingbird Lane."

Eddie, writing: "Why?"

"You dig under these steps, you'll dig up your friend Kenny Rosenfeld."

He stopped writing. He kept his head bowed over his notebook, staring at Esposito's scuffed, unpolished black shoe resting on the ugly gray block. "How do you know that?"

"You got your little tape recorder with you?"

"In my car."

"Good. C'mon."

Esposito drove them back to the office trailer, saying nothing, which was just as well, because Eddie wouldn't have known what to say. He grabbed his tape recorder from his car, quietly praying that Esposito was wrong.

Inside the office trailer it was dark. He could smell the muddy carpet. He reached out to guide himself between long plywood drafting tables strewn with blueprints and paperwork. They passed the lavatory, which smelled overdue for a cleaning. Esposito pulled out a ring of keys and unlocked the back office.

Inside, under a glaring fluorescent light, was a metal desk and two metal chairs. Cardboard had been taped over the windows. Behind the desk a swarthy, chubby young man in a dark suit sat up stiff and straight because his chest and arms were tied to the chair with thick extension cords. His eyes were blackened, and his lips were puffy and cut and his tieless white shirtfront was stained with blood. In the small office he was sweating heavily, and his body odor was strong. A red tie wound around his head held a black sock stuffed in his mouth. Eddie glanced under the desk. The young man wore cordovan alligator shoes, and one foot was bare. Eddie recognized the look in his eyes, the look of someone almost blacking out from pain.

"Okay, get yourself set up," Esposito told him.

Eddie put the tape recorder on the desk and the microphone near the man. Esposito released the tie and pulled the sock from the young man's mouth, allowing him to gasp through bloody teeth.

"Turn it on," Esposito said.

Eddie did what he was told. Esposito stood over the young man and barked in his ear.

"What's your name?"

The young man's eyes lifted to Esposito, full of cold hatred. "Tony Notti."

"Who do you work for?"

"You know—"

"Say it!"

Notti winced. "Bobby Castellucci."

"What do you do for him?"

"Security."

"Where does your paycheck come from?"

"What—"

Esposito slapped him in the face, hard enough to rock his head back. "Where does your paycheck come from?" he yelled in Notti's ear.

"Castellucci's! Castellucci's! You know, the bar!"

"All right," Esposito stepped back, and motioned to Eddie. "Go ahead."

He didn't know what to do. Was he supposed to introduce himself? Yell at Notti? Slap him around? How can you believe an interview if the subject is being tortured? But Esposito was raging, and he was afraid to refuse him. Tony Notti had obviously crossed him and look what was happening to him.

"Go on, go ahead!" Esposito said.

"What happened to Kenny Rosenfeld?" Eddie finally said.

"Who's this fuckin' kid?" Notti sputtered.

"He's the press," Esposito said. "He's your priest and this is your confession. Don't worry about who he is. Tell him what you told me about Rosenfeld."

"Put it on *tape*?"

Esposito put his hat on the desk and began to remove his overcoat. "Kid, step outside for a couple minutes—"

"No! No! All right! All right!" Notti turned desperately to Eddie. He'd already had enough time alone with Esposito. "Okay, so, we pulled Rosenfeld over on Route 88 one night. Back in November, I think it was. Bobby said to scare him, bust his balls, smack him around, you know, tell him to lay off the building boycott thing. But the guy got pissed off. He started runnin' his smartass Jew mouth, givin' us attitude. And then he threw a punch. So he got shot."

"Then what?" Esposito said. "Tell him everything."

Notti began to sob miserably, and to whine. "His car went to a junkyard out in Pennsylvania. We took the body down to the woods, cut it up, burned the parts in a barrel. We brought it here and buried it."

Eddie was shaking, staring at Notti. He forced himself to think of a question, forced his voice to stay even. "You were out in the woods. So why bury him here?"

"Very good question," Esposito said over his shoulder.

Notti shrugged. "Somebody knew a hole that was already dug."

"Yeah," Esposito snarled. "On my property."

Esposito pushed Eddie aside, leaned in close to Notti, and grabbed a handful of the man's crotch. Notti squirmed and kicked in agony.

"You work for Bobby Castellucci?" he roared in Notti's ear.

"I said I do!"

"Castellucci ordered Kenny Rosenfeld killed?"

"Yeah, yeah, I told ya!"

"He tell you leave the body here?"

"Yeah!"

"To pin the murder on me?"

"Oh my God! Yeah!"

"Are you a lying mother*fucker*, or are you telling the truth?"

"The truth, the truth, I swear!"

Esposito released him and Notti collapsed against his bonds, his head hung, whimpering. Esposito put his hat back on and turned to Eddie. "Well?"

Notti had obviously said what the old man wanted to hear, true or not. Eddie shook his head, saying, "You're trying to get me killed." But wasn't the truth exactly the opposite? Esposito had been trying to use him to keep himself from getting jailed or killed.

"Play *that* for that prosecutor, too. Then if you do get killed, he'll know who did it. Maybe he'll get the hell off *my* back."

"Prosecutor," Notti whined under his breath, "Jesus Christ."

"One more question," Eddie said, even though he felt more like Esposito's accomplice than a reporter.

"You heard enough." Notti spit blood on his tape recorder. "Get the fuck out of here—"

Esposito lunged in and slapped him again, a stinging backhand. Notti pulled himself upright defiantly, gasping through teeth gritted in pain. Eddie was too shocked to continue, but Esposito barked at him so loud he was afraid he'd get hit next.

"Go ahead, ask!"

"Why'd Castellucci tell you to beat up Rosenfeld?"

"How much of this do I gotta say?" Notti cried, shaking with rage and indignation.

"It's a simple question," Esposito said. "Why did Bobby want the guy beat up?"

"Money," Notti blubbered. "What else?"

"I don't understand," Eddie said. "Somebody *else* paid you guys to beat him up?"

"No, no," Notti said. "Bobby said Rosenfeld shook down Roy Mac. Bobby said he demanded a payoff to quit organizing people against the developers. Bobby said he took the money, but he kept right on busting their balls. We were supposed to give him a beating, remind him to live up to the deal. But things got out of hand."

"He demanded money," Eddie said. "How much?"

"I don't know. But he must've got it. That I do know."

"How?"

Notti was offended. "We don't pull people over and give them a beatin' for nothin'."

"He shook 'em down, is what he's saying," Esposito said. "Rosenfeld took Roy McTierney's cash, and he wasn't a standup guy."

"Right," Notti said. "He was not a standup guy."

"What'd I tell ya?" Esposito said. "Everybody's got their price. Even a Rosenfeld."

Notti hung his head and whimpered, his nose bleeding onto his shirt.

"What about him?" Eddie said.

"Him?" Esposito grinned. He pinched Notti's earlobe and twisted it, making Notti cry out. "He works for me now."

Esposito whirled and seized Eddie by the lapel of his coat. He was barely able to grab his tape recorder before the old man pushed him backward through the office trailer. Esposito's knuckles against Eddie's chest were hard as stone. He stumbled, barely keeping his feet under him.

"Go play *that* for your editor," Esposito said. "And I better see county detectives out here tomorrow morning with shovels. Now get goin'!"

Esposito shoved him off the steps of the trailer. He landed on his feet, took a step backward and caught his heel on something and fell on his ass in the dirt, cutting his palm on a rock. The trailer door slammed. He gathered up his tape recorder and hurried across the street to his car. He leaned on the fender and it was a minute or so before he could even organize lighting a cigarette. Darkness had fallen, they were deep in the woods. It was pitch black and dead silent, a long way from anywhere.

From inside the dark trailer he heard Notti scream, a long, despairing cry of pain. Shuddering, Eddie put one hand on the fender and leaned over and puked up the chef's salad and coffee he'd had for lunch.

He pulled off Route 9 north and into a 7-11 store and stopped at the far end of the parking lot. He bought a bottle of club soda and washed out the throbbing cut on his hand and dried it with a bunch of napkins. He washed the taste of vomit out of his mouth and drank a fresh black coffee. He sat in the car for a long time, smoking and trying to steady his nerves, as a darkness deeper than the cold evening settled over him.

He rewound the tape and listened to Tony Notti's confession again, and the sound of Esposito slapping and degrading him almost made Eddie sick again, even though Notti had murdered Kenny. When the playback ended, he kept picturing Kenny's last moments, like a black and white movie. A gunshot cracks, in shock Kenny falls, the shot echoes and fades into the empty sky. A lonely place in the woods, gangsters grunting as they chop up Kenny's body, jamming the pieces into a barrel, the odor of blood, of kerosene and charring flesh, flames engulfing his head.

He came close to throwing up again and he couldn't quiet Notti's voice, echoing, ugly, from a world where murder is just another fact of life: *Kenny Rosenfeld shook down Roy Mac... He was not a standup guy.*

He couldn't breathe. He felt trapped in the car. He felt trapped in this story. He got out, dizzy, and walked to the trash can and threw away his coffee cup. The walk back to the car felt like it lasted forever. He got back behind the wheel and got back on Route 9 north again.

He hurried toward the solitude of his apartment where there would be time to think. He had definitely fumbled this investigation, but now he could locate two corpses, one in a chicken coop and one in a housing development, both allegedly connecting organized crime to political corruption. The corpses might give him *some* advantage, once there was something to trade them for and he'd figured out his next move. In a way, having no newspaper to write for was lucky. He could stay on the story like he should have in the first place, patiently assembling facts with no need to rush to the typewriter. He silently apologized to Rosenfeld if he had to use his corpse as a bargaining chip before reporting its whereabouts to the police. Since Kenny had already been in the ground over a month, a few days more wouldn't matter.

Just below Toms River a red light began pulsing in his rearview mirror. His heart hammering, he pulled off Route 9 into the parking lot of a coin laundry. An unmarked sedan parked behind him, and two county detectives he recognized, Gillis and Pyle, came forward. Pyle rapped on his window and he rolled it down.

"Bonneville. Follow us."

"What for?"

"Earl wants to talk to you, that's what for."

He tailed them up to Toms River. Now what? He didn't like how the detectives bracketed him front and rear as they walked into the dark, echoing courthouse. The night security guard, a middle-aged black man, glanced up from his newspaper and cheerfully waved them past his desk in the lobby.

"Howdy Hollis."

"Batman and Robin," the guard chuckled, "back to the cave!"

Upstairs in Heckendorfer's office, paneled in dark wood and lit by chandeliers, the prosecutor paced behind his desk talking on the phone, in shirtsleeves and suspenders, clutching a large fuming cigar. He waved Eddie to an armchair. Pyle and Gillis took chairs against the wall. Heckendorfer hung up and settled back down into his chair.

"Eddie," Heckendorfer said, grinning through the smoke cloud, "what's new?"

"Nothing."

"No?"

"Nothing."

"That's not what I hear. I hear you got fired." Heckendorfer spoke to him but was playing to the detectives. "I hear you cold-cocked your boss and got tossed out on your ear."

Gillis yuck-yucked behind him.

"I was told you wanted to talk to me."

"Isn't that what we're doing?" Heckendorfer said. "I thought I'd give you a chance to get back on my good side."

"Oh yeah? When does that start?" Eddie said, lighting a cigarette and snapping his Zippo shut.

Heckendorfer's fat lips twisted distastefully. "You're supposed to co-operate with me, you know. You refuse to cooperate with me, you'll never get another story out of me."

"Okay," Eddie said, wondering what kind of cooperation the pros-ecutor was after. "I'd like to be back on good terms." Not as much as he'd like to smack his cow-eyed, blubbery face. Easy, boy.

"What do you know about a riot at Castellucci's Lounge a couple weeks ago?" he said.

"The place was busted up pretty bad," Eddie said.

"By who?"

"I don't know."

"I'll tell you who. By somebody who knew that dumping a busload of spooks into Castellucci's would cause a riot."

"Well, that sure narrows down the list of suspects," Eddie said. Behind him the detectives chuckled.

"You were with Esposito that night," Heckendorfer said.

Careful. "Interviewing him—"

"At his invitation, I'll bet, right?"

"Actually, I was assigned by my editor to get his reaction to the indictment."

"And now you're his alibi for the hit on Castellucci's."

"I have no idea what you're talking about."

"You talk about Bobby Castellucci?"

"He talked. I listened."

"What'd he say?"

"Not much," Eddie said.

"You're telling me Esposito didn't say anything about what was happening at Castellucci's that night?"

"Nothing I could connect to causing a riot."

"When you interviewed Esposito, did you talk about Kenny Rosenfeld?"

"He said he didn't know anything about Rosenfeld," Eddie said, proud of himself for lying so smoothly, so soon after standing over what was probably Rosenfeld's grave and interviewing one of his killers. Impatient, he pulled out his notebook. "If you're done, how about answering a few of my questions?"

"I'm not done," Heckendorfer said. "Riding around talking with Esposito, what *did* you talk about?"

"Small talk, really. Nothing newsworthy."

"I know for a fact that's not true." Was Heckendorfer bluffing? He had to be, unless Frank had shown him his first story, and why would he?

Eddie was wondering how to reply when the phone rang, and the prosecutor grabbed it.

"Yeah." As he listened, his eyes rose to his two detectives. "What?" He stood slowly, cursed softly and hung up. "That was Sammy. He's up in Lakewood. Sunset Lodge is on fire."

Eddie was the first out the door.

The night sky to the north glowed orange as he crossed the Route 9 bridge at the end of Lake Carasaljo. He parked the Impala, flipped down the press placard on the visor, and sprinted past the fine homes and hotels along Madison Avenue, running around and between fire trucks and hopping over hoses crisscrossing the street.

As he rounded the corner the dark hulk of Sunset Lodge came into view. High flames rose out of swirling clouds of gray smoke from the rear of the building, crackling and blazing madly against the dark evergreens. Two pumper trucks sent long arcs of water onto the flames and the runoff was freezing in pools on the lawn.

He held up his press card and a Lakewood cop let him duck under the police rope. His eye was caught by a flash off to his right where Goldy was stalking around, photographing the firefighting. He waved to him and came over. His shoes and the trouser cuffs of his gray suit were soaked.

"How 'bout this shit?" Goldy said, stamping out a Kent and lighting another.

"Anybody hurt?"

"Nobody said nothin' yet. They were pouring water on it when I got here. They think it was set, somebody smelled gasoline. No sign of The Mule or any of his people."

Eddie counted the windows until he reached Matty Esposito's apartment, in the path of the flames. The windows were dark. Eddie trotted down the driveway. Behind a row of hemlocks the Coupe de Ville was parked in its usual spot. He waved and yelled, "Goldy! C'mon!"

"Hey, I heard you got fired."

"Fired from the paper? Yeah. Fired from the job? No fucking way."

He walked around to the east side veranda and peered into the windows at the front of the hotel. He pulled one of the French doors open and smelled no smoke.

"This way." He slipped inside and tugged Goldy in with him. They crossed the ballroom where his Esposito story had begun a couple weeks ago. "C'mon, it's okay, the fire's at the other end of the building."

"Are you serious?" Goldy said. "You know where you're going?"

"Yeah." Retracing the steps he'd taken the night Esposito began his history lesson, he led Goldy up to the second floor. He hurried down the eerie and silent main corridor, toward the back of the hotel, closer and closer to the fire.

"This place could go up any minute. This better be worth it," Goldy said.

The lights blinked in the wall sconces and a layer of thick smoke hung in the air. Goldy held a handkerchief to his face, Eddie breathed through a piece of his shirt tail.

They rounded the corner outside Esposito's suite. The door was ajar, stuck open on a man's foot, toe up, in a leather bowling shoe in red, white and blue. The foot led to a denim trouser leg, bell-bottomed with flower embroidery.

The lights in the corridor flickered out, leaving them in darkness. He pushed the door wide open. There were only dark shapes inside. Goldy reached in and felt around and flicked the light switch. Nothing.

"Get back."

Goldy raised his Pentax and flash gun.

FLASH!

Tommy Esposito lay on his back in the entrance, his shirtfront a bloody mess, his eyes wide open and his mouth silently yelling. Eddie crossed to the windows and pulled back the curtains, letting in streetlight and flashes from the fire trucks. Deeper in the dark room a foul odor hung in the air that made Eddie retch. FLASH! The suite had been thoroughly ransacked. FLASH! On a sofa down by the bar, still in his coat, Matty Esposito leaned back, wide-eyed and bareheaded, a bullet hole in the middle of his forehead and blood running in his eyes and down either side of his nose. His glasses lay upside down in his lap. FLASH! A .38 revolver was clutched in his hand. FLASH! Tony Notti sprawled on the brass foot rail of the bar, hands tied behind his back and still missing a sock, his lifeless eyes staring into space and both sides of his head bloody.

"God, it stinks in here," Goldy said. "One of these guys soiled his diaper."

Whether it was death or shock or horror that made his head suddenly clear, Eddie didn't know. But he could see how this must have happened. Esposito had come home from Roman Estates and brought Notti up here with his hands still tied. The killers must have been waiting for them. Esposito's hat hung on the rack by the bar, but he didn't have time to take off his coat before the killers came through the door. They shot down Tommy immediately. The killers stepped right over him and caught the old man empty-handed. They sat him down on the couch, Notti standing behind him. Probably the killers were Castellucci's people, which meant Notti, after a long painful day, must've thought he was being rescued. At some point Esposito pulled a gun, but before he could use it, he was shot, almost between the eyes, and turned instantly to stone, his eyeglasses popping off and landing neatly in his lap. He could imagine Notti, full of brotherly spirits, shocked when the guns turned on him, groveling down on the floor, shitting himself in fright, then shot through the head. Why would they kill him? One look at his battered condition and they probably assumed he'd spilled whatever secrets he had. Why let him do it again some day in front of a jury? When the killers left to start the fire they didn't notice or care that the door got stuck open on Tommy's foot.

Goldy squeezed Eddie's shoulder. "You all right?"

He was all right, but his pulse was hammering so hard he thought the top of his head would come off. "I've never seen a dead body before."

"Yeah, the first time's always rough."

"Two hours ago I was down in Lacey Township with these guys."

Goldy just stared. "These guys?"

He was just about to tell Goldy a lot more, about Rosenfeld's body and Notti being tortured by the old man, when a sudden thought occurred to him. He crossed the suite to the bedroom. Even in the dark he could see it was disheveled and torn apart and empty. He checked the galley kitchen and the bathroom, but there was no-one else there. He came out and said, as much to himself as Goldy, "So where's the girl?" Several possibilities occurred to him—she'd been kidnapped and killed elsewhere, or she escaped somehow. Or, maybe *she* shot all three men, since she could catch Esposito off-guard. It was getting harder to know the truth, yet at the same time, the worst possibilities seemed the most likely.

The rank odor, composed of shit and blood and the firecracker smell of gunpowder, hung heavy in the room, making Eddie's stomach spasm. "Shoot the hell out of this place," he told Goldy. "I want a lot of pictures to remember this by." FLASH! Esposito's cigar still smoldered beside his body leaving a black burn in the sofa cushion. *That's twice today you made me want to puke, Mister Esposito.* From his oil portrait on the wall over the fireplace, Colonel Ted McTierney grinned down upon the carnage.

"Fuckin' Pulitzer material," Goldy muttered, the filter of his cigarette between his teeth.

In the corridor near a window where there was dim light and better air Eddie pulled out his notebook and began making notes. Within minutes, Goldy's flashes in the tall windows brought the firemen and the police up to the suite to investigate. Eddie and Goldy showed their press cards and moved out of the way. Somebody opened more windows in the suite to clear out the smoke and the stink. A staticky voice on a walkie talkie declared the fire under control.

Twenty minutes later the Medical Examiner arrived with an assistant and they went to work on the bodies. One of the county detectives, Pyle, came up the stairs followed by Heckendorfer, who stopped to stare into the crime scene where work lights brought out every ghastly detail. He showed no emotion, but when he saw Eddie in the corridor outside the crime scene, he swaggered over.

"I hear it was you and your photographer who found them," Heckendorfer said. It was an accusation.

"They were like that when we got here," Eddie said.

"Did you touch anything?"

"Of course not."

"How'd you know to come up to this room?"

"I've been here before."

"I'll bet."

"Doing my job."

"Oh, of course." Did this guy ever let up? Down the corridor behind the prosecutor he saw Frank coming, his trench coat open and his hat on the back of his head, coughing into his hand while the other held a cigarette.

Frank nodded to them both and stood there listening, wide-eyed and mute. No visible evidence of the punch in the mouth remained.

Eddie turned to Heckendorfer. "This should make *your* job easier."

"Listen kid—" said Heckendorfer.

"No need for a trial." He'd had enough of Heckendorfer putting him down. "With Esposito gone, you guys got your big job opening. Wasn't that the point of indicting him? Isn't that the job you were *told* to do?"

Frank scoffed quietly and shook his head. Heckendorfer raised his bulk to full height, stiff and offended. "That smart mouth is going to get you in real trouble some day."

"The Organization was tired of Esposito. You were the delivery boy with his retirement papers." From the prosecutor Eddie got a look of pure dead-eyed hatred.

A trio of firemen came clattering up the stairs in their heavy waterproof gear and boots, pulling their helmets off their sweat-matted hair.

"So Eddie," Heckendorfer said, steaming with every word, and playing to everybody within earshot, "this interview Esposito gave you back around Christmas? Guess you got quite an earful, right?"

"Nah." He raised his voice for the onlookers. "We had a pizza and we waited for Santa Claus, but he didn't show." Two of the firemen heard him, turned to each other, and laughed.

"Hey comedian," the prosecutor said. "We got three people brutally murdered here."

"That's right, and Esposito's girlfriend is missing. You know who to talk to, why're you bothering me?" That got everybody's attention, Frank, county detectives, assistant medical examiner, cops and fire fighters, watching the longhair kid sass the county prosecutor.

"You still refuse to talk about Esposito?"

More to Frank: "I was here doing my job. Just like you seem to be doing yours."

That got a laugh and Heckendorfer didn't like it. "You better quit hiding behind your press card and cooperate with me."

"What good would that do? Your suspect is dead in there on the couch."

"You never know where information is gonna lead."

"Go dig up your own."

He was sure that any information he gave Heckendorfer would either be used for his political advantage or buried, and along with it, his story and any chance for the public to learn the truth. He knew everyone's eyes followed him as he got out of there.

Eddie said to his former editor, trailing a couple steps behind, "I got nothing to say to you." Frank squirmed, but he followed him downstairs.

"I told you to back off," he said. "Now you're in deep shit."

"I know that. Okay? *I know that.* Maybe if you'd taken me seriously—"

"Yeah sure. *My* mistake."

"How's your jaw?"

"I can chew soft food. I'm fine."

"Good. See you around."

"Walking away from a good story? Why don't you come back and write it?"

Had Frank been told to hire him back, get him back under control?

"It's a good story," Eddie said. "It ain't good news."

Frank stayed on his heels as they walked out the front door, stepping over fire hoses on the driveway. Firemen were pouring water on the roof from pumper trucks. The flames were out, only smoke and steam billowed into the sky. The cold night air burned his smoke-irritated nostrils. He was sweating and his clothes stank of burnt wood and plaster. The stench in Esposito's suite clung to his memory and he could taste it in the back of his throat.

"Goldy says he got great pictures," Frank said, in step with him. "There's plenty of time before deadline."

He stepped out of the way of two firemen carrying an extension ladder. "Write it yourself. You were there."

"Come back to the newsroom, write the story." For a guy who'd fired him two days ago, Frank was becoming a pest.

"In depth?"

"What *depth?* The fire and the killings."

"Castellucci kills Esposito and takes over his rackets," he said. "Political power structure approves. Business outlook upbeat."

"Listen to you, you sound like your pinko lawyer friend."

"That's what's happening, isn't it?"

"Depends on how you look at it."

"I think I know how you look at it, Frank."

Eddie kept walking. Police with flashlights detoured the traffic away from Madison Avenue. Fire hoses ran to every available hydrant. Frank stayed at his elbow as they crossed the street and walked in the shadows down the sidewalk along Madison Avenue.

"C'mon, write the fire and the killings," Frank said. "Put in a graph about the history of the place. 'Death of a landmark'."

"The *building* isn't the story, Frank."

"I'll call the AP, they'll put it over the wire with your byline."

That got Eddie's attention. "It's the first story in a series."

"We take it one story at a time. You're back on the payroll, but you're on probation."

"Yeah? So are you."

Frank stepped in front of him. "You better wise up—"

"How's this for wise? You never wanted a story. You guys knew Esposito would take the indictment as a stab in the back from people he did business with. You sent me to talk to him and take his temperature. See if he was angry enough to retaliate."

"Right." Frank shrugged, hands in pockets. "And he used you and a busload of niggers to do exactly that."

He almost smacked Frank for that, and for being a lackey and a bagman masquerading as a journalist. Instead, he stepped closer and got right in Frank's face.

"The night I talked with Esposito? I didn't just take notes. Every word he said is on tape. The whole thing, every detail. So don't fuck with me, or I'll get in the car and drive the tapes straight to Trenton and hand 'em to the Attorney General. Tell that to Bobby. Tell that to the *real* owner of your newspaper, and anybody else who needs to hear it."

Was it him, or did Frank get a tick more serious? "What's this? 'Back off or I'll talk?' Bad tactics, kid. Look where it got Matty Esposito."

Eddie was stunned. Frank was directly implicating his stories about

Esposito as the cause of the hoodlum's death. "That's what got him killed?"

"How do I know?"

So Esposito's plan had almost worked: Frank had warned the Organization the old hoodlum had talked about "the setup" to a reporter. But instead of backing off, they killed him. Well, Frank was to blame for that, not him.

"You just said that's what got him killed."

"No, no, I'm just *saying*—it's something maybe you ought to think about."

"I can't figure out whether you're hiring me or threatening me."

"Who? Me?"

Eddie unlocked his car. "Esposito's dead. But his memories aren't. There's even a short but very detailed chapter about you."

"Okay, so let's hear the tapes."

"Not yet." Sorry, Matty.

"You wanna be careful."

"I wanna do my job."

Eddie got in his car and fired up the engine. He pulled across traffic, and headed south for the newsroom.

He sat down behind the Underwood. He rolled paper into the machine. Before he'd finished one Lucky Strike, the story was written.

LAKEWOOD — Matthew Esposito, recently labeled "The Rackets Boss of the Jersey Shore" by the Ocean County prosecutor, died last night and a fire severely damaged his hotel, in what police are calling a case of arson and triple murder.

Esposito, his son Tommaso, and an associate named Anthony Notti were discovered shot to death in the fiery ruins of The Sunset Lodge, Madison Avenue.

Firefighters were called shortly after 6 p.m. when a neighbor to the west of the mammoth hotel, which had been closed for several years, spotted flames in the main kitchen area. Fire quickly engulfed the rear of the aged wooden structure, pushed by a 10 mph wind and helped by a liquid accelerant believed to be gasoline which the fire department is analyzing.

An Independent reporter and photographer team discovered the victims in a second floor suite that

Esposito used as living quarters. All three victims
were dead from gunshot wounds. Tommy Esposito lay on
the floor at the entrance to the room. Notti's hands
were tied behind his back. Esposito died sitting on a
sofa with a revolver in his hand.

The room was ransacked and bloodstained. Police
speculated that the fire, which was brought under
control before it reached the murder scene, was
supposed to cover up the killings.

Esposito's companion, a blonde woman named Sally,
was missing at the time of the fire and is wanted for
questioning.

Esposito, a controversial Lakewood political gadfly,
hotel owner and labor leader, was labeled "Rackets
Boss of the Jersey Shore" by county prosecutor Earl
Heckendorfer and was indicted on Dec. 23 by a grand
jury for a variety of alleged crimes.

In a freewheeling and wide-ranging interview on Dec.
24 with this Independent reporter, Esposito, whose
nickname among law enforcement was "Matty the Mule",
talked about his life and times with astonishing candor
and revealed, if he was to be believed, that he more
than qualified for the prosecutor's sensational label.

Matthew Esposito was a Lakewood native who inherited
the Sunset Lodge from his father, Bruno Esposito, a
Neapolitan immigrant who opened Esposito's Restaurant
on First Street in 1915. From his father, Matthew
inherited the hotel, a local landmark and relic of a
gentler era, built in the 1890s.

When he was a boy, Esposito graduated from local
schools, and played violin in the school orchestra.
He gave up his aspiration to become a jazz musician
during Prohibition because bootlegging was more
lucrative. Over the years he engaged in a variety of
business enterprises, presumably including the illegal
activities alleged in the indictment.

Esposito was the founder of two local unions
representing workers in the Shore area's burgeoning
home building industry. He ruled those unions with an
iron hand and was known as a fierce fighter for worker's
rights. As boss of the union workers crucial to the
construction industry, he was an influential figure in
the area's economy.

His son Tommaso, an only child, attended local
schools but dropped out as a high school sophomore. He
managed Esposito's Restaurant and was a business agent

in the construction worker's union. Little is known
about the third victim, Notti, except that he had been
selling his services as a security consultant in the
area.
   Next of kin for the alleged racketeer were unclear.

There was so much more to write, and he still had thirty minutes before deadline. But so much had happened in so short a time
that he couldn't organize it in his head, much less in a news story.
He wanted to show the police where Rosenfeld's body was supposedly
buried, and to do right by his friend. He wanted to write Notti's account of Rosenfeld's murder, even though he already had plenty to fear
from Castellucci. And Notti's claim that Rosenfeld shook down Roy
McTierney, promising to sell out his own movement for cash, wouldn't
go away. He couldn't believe Rosenfeld dreamed up the building moratorium just to extort money from the developers. However, he could
definitely imagine Rosenfeld tricking them into unwittingly financing
his movement. He preferred to believe that, and not the possibility
Rosenfeld may have thrown the money away across a poker table somewhere.

   Pushing himself away from the typewriter, he became aware of the
bustling newsroom around him as everyone worked against deadline.
Lindy was in the slot editing copy, composing room girls carried past-
ed-up pages from Frank's office to the composing tables, and in the rear
of the building the early press run rumbled and out streamed the inner
pages. He dropped his copy in the basket on the news desk. Nobody
looked his way or spoke to him. The other reporters pounded their
typewriters. The last time they'd seen him, he'd bloodied their editor
and got himself fired. What must they think of him now? He hadn't a
clue. In the middle of the newsroom, it was like he was invisible.

   When he got home, he was tired. His clothes smelled like smoke,
the sharp odor of his own sweat seeped through. He scrubbed himself
with soap under scalding water and put on fresh clothes, but the grisly
memories and the taste of fire and death remained, even after he chased
it with a slug of cold vodka from the bottle in his freezer.

   He rolled a sheet of paper into his typewriter and wrote the date at
the top. In his journal, he tried to be as honest as he could about himself
as a reporter. Whether Esposito had told him the truth or not remained

to be proven. What bothered him is that he'd believed Esposito's tales of corruption without even a second thought, because they confirmed his belief that older men could not be trusted. He'd agreed to deliver Esposito's warning, which was wrong for a reporter to do. His next mistake, immediately giving Frank the story, happened because he'd been naive and didn't *really* know the kind of man Frank was, and worse, because he craved Frank's approval. No danger of repeating that one. Next mistake, he showed his hand too quickly, confronting Walter O'Neill and Joe Mac, clumsily revealing the focus of his investigation. He cringed, remembering how impressed with himself he had been, how childishly eager to show people what he knew. And what did he ultimately want from this story? A better-informed public? The real answer made him disgusted and ashamed, but he forced himself to confess it, in black type on the white page of his journal. Frank had been right. He needed the world to sit up and embrace him, applaud him as a bearer of the truth, to call him a hero.

Now what? He had his job at the *Independent* back, but he'd made that job much harder. Bad enough that his newspaper was owned by the political boss whose organization he was investigating. Word was surely out by now that Eddie Bonneville was poking around in matters best left undisturbed. Getting anyone to talk would be a miracle. He'd made it hard for even a more experienced reporter to cover the story.

He went to bed that night telling himself he'd been stupid. He woke up the next morning determined to do at least one thing right.

The black people arrested for the Castellucci riot were still in the county jail. He made an appointment and drove down to Toms River to see their public defender. Bonelli was eager to talk to him. Eddie said since Matty Esposito was dead, there was no longer any need to keep his confessions confidential. The lawyer sat down with him at a conference table in the dining room of the old house that was now the county legal aid offices. Eddie told Bonelli about the interview on Christmas Eve in which Esposito hinted strongly that he'd struck out at Bobby Castellucci. But when Bonelli, impatient and drumming with his pen on his thigh, pressed him for details, Eddie could come up with very few. He realized, embarrassed, that his contribution really wasn't helpful. Bonelli needed somebody who could testify that Esposito set up the fracas at Castellucci's Lounge. But Matty was dead, so was Tommy, Sally the girlfriend was missing, and this Father Anthony, he could be anywhere. As for Eddie, all he'd done was arrive at Bargainland in the aftermath of the riot, heard what happened, remembered what the old gangster had hinted, and put two-and-two together. The conversation was frustrating for Bonelli, because it implicated Esposito, but anyone who could confirm it was either dead or missing, so he was no closer to finding evidence that would get his clients out of jail. The judge was unlikely to set them free based on some hint Esposito may have given to Eddie.

"Unfortunately," Bonelli said, after thanking Eddie for trying to help, "the best deal my clients can hope for is to plead guilty to lesser charges and get released with credit for time served. Maybe they'll get a nice warm *Happy New Year* when they let them out of jail."

TEN *Don't ask, don't tell*

At the breakfast table with Billy's friends Angus and Ralph, Eddie could no longer avoid thinking about his appointment today in Newark with the U.S. Army psychiatrist. So, hoping they'd approve or offer some advice, he told the guys that he'd declared to the Army that he was gay.

"If you're asking me to agree with that, forget it," Billy said, as he stood at the stove whisking a frying pan full of scrambled eggs.

"I tried playing by the rules," Eddie said. "I applied for a C.O. They swatted me like a fly."

"At the Draft Board hearing, at least you were honest, even though it was counter productive. But now, you're going to lie?" Billy shrugged. "Maybe it'll work. After all, in the Army, like everywhere else, No Fags Need Apply, right?"

"That's not fair. You know I'm not like that."

"But you're not above taking advantage of it."

"Whoa man," Angus said. He was tall and lanky with blonde hair and worked as a model. "The kid's got, like, a serious problem here."

"By doing this, you help to keep the world a hostile place for men like us," Billy said.

Ralph's face crumpled in agony. "Oh, give him a break, Billy, please. It's not like *you* never told a lie." Ralph painted scenery, and was round and bespectacled, with wispy long brown hair.

"I don't agree with Billy at all," Angus said to Eddie. "Do whatever you have to do. Claim you're gay if that works. Lots of guys are doing it."

"We'll write you a letter of reference," Ralph said, and Angus laughed. "Yes! From the boys at the M&K!"

Billy muttered, "You don't have to join the Army. But you do have to be ready to pay the price for saying 'No'. Unless you're happy being a liar."

"What?" Angus said.

Ralph put down his fork. "Wait a minute. Every day, when we sally forth into the straight world, we flirt with the secretaries, we make up stories about all the pussy we get to tell the guys at the water cooler—"

"You don't!" Angus gasped.

"When he needs an alibi he's shameless," Billy said.

"—and we lie to everybody, including our families, about who we are. Then we go out at night and live our real lives."

"Right," Angus said, "because it's either be real and get beat up, or lie and be safe."

"*Disgruntled* but safe," said Ralph. "Unfortunately, some lies are necessary."

"Now *that's* not fair," Billy said. "That comparison."

"We lie, to get along in a world that doesn't accept us," Angus said. "But Eddie's lie is about *war*, which is, like, life and death."

"Just don't be so quick with that word *liar*, Wilhelmina," Ralph said.

"Why should I fight fair when the government won't?" Eddie said.

"'Cause it'll make you a better person," Billy sighed. His two friends collapsed in laughter. Billy shook his head, looking around the table. "Don't listen to these two." His eyes met Eddie's. "If you go through life only doing whatever works, you'll never make much of a man. But that's up to you. Take the easy way if you want."

Ralph and Angus shook their heads in sympathy with Eddie. He shrugged and went back to eating his oatmeal. He had a long train ride ahead of him when he could think about all of this.

He was upstairs about to leave to catch the train to Newark when he heard footsteps climbing the stairway. A heavy hand pounded on the door.

Gillis the county detective stood on the landing. He thrust a folded paper into Eddie's hand. He opened it and saw the words *You are hereby ordered…*

"What's this?"

"Subpoena," Gillis said. "You've been served." He gave him a snide little wave and went back down the stairs, whistling. Back inside Eddie grabbed the phone, and called the prosecutor's office. Heckendorfer took the call.

"Morning, Eddie my boy," he said.

"Subpoena for what?"

"You are hereby required to immediately turn over to this office all evidence or information you have related to organized crime and political corruption."

"You can't do this."

"You will be required to answer questions under oath in front of a grand jury. If you refuse to produce your notes, or answer questions, I'll put you in jail for contempt of court until you comply."

"There's no way this is legal."

"It's legal, until somebody says it's not, and they won't."

Somebody surely would. The whole idea was crazy. This wasn't a police state.

"Bring it all down to my office right now. I'll be here until four o'clock. "

"I know my rights, my notes are mine—"

"Last chance, kid. Four o'clock today or I'll send my detectives after you with a search warrant, and you go to jail for contempt."

Eddie slammed down the phone. He'd have to talk to Billy about this later, if Billy was still talking to him.

Station 25 was a small windowless office in a far corner of AFEES Newark. Dry-mouthed and his hands trembling, well aware this might be his last chance to avoid going to prison or to war, Eddie squeezed into a chair across from the Army psychiatrist.

He took stock of the doctor: blonde crew cut, neck widening from the ears down. The doctor wore a long white smock and COBB, DR. L. was stitched over his shirt pocket. His lips moved as he silently read Eddie's health questionnaire. His eyebrows rose, and crunched together at something he read. He set the file on his desk, which almost filled the tiny office, sat back and stared at him.

The phone rang on the desk. The doctor answered it. "Yessuh? Yessuh, I've got room for one mo'. Y'all send me whatcha got, that's what I'm here faw. You betcha. Layduh."

Eddie's internal redneck alarm went off full blast. So *this* is who he pleads his case to, *this*—then a voice inside snapped *Stop it!* Stop reacting to these people! Stop deciding what you'll do based on them! When you do that, they own you! What's in your heart?

"You are Edward Bonneville, is that correct?" said Doctor Cobb, in a deep bass voice as thick as congealed grits.

"Yes sir."

"Your number in the Draft lottery?"

"One ninety-five."

"According to your health questionnaire, you suffer from a variety of ailments, Mister Bonneville," the doctor said, "including drug abuse and homosexual tendencies." It was not a question, he didn't attempt a response.

He was ready to explode. He pictured himself pulling one of the pens from the holder on the desk and shoving it into the doctor's eye and straight into his U.S. Army regulation brain. At the same time, he wondered *Why do you give these people the power to anger you, to upset you, to turn you into a violent nut?*

"All these other things you checked," the doctor said, "Frequent Terrifying Nightmares, Insomnia, Anxiety Disorder, Bed Wetting, they don't amount to a thing as far as the U.S. Army is concerned. And your drug abuse? Two weeks into boot camp at Fort Dix, you'll be so physically fit you won't remember what drugs felt like. But this homosexual thing." He folded his hands on top of the file. "We're gonna have to go into that in detail, y'understand?" He said it with just enough leer to tip Eddie's decision. Fuck these people, I am who I am.

"I lied," he said, unable to look the doctor in the eye. He stared at the linoleum floor.

"What do you mean?"

"I'm not homosexual. I don't take drugs. I heard that checking those things was the only way I could get in to see you. I didn't really know how to deal with my specific problem, but sitting here, talking to you, now I think I do."

"Uh huh. How's that?"

"I used to be a high school boxing champion. I enjoyed it, beating up somebody else. Inflicting pain. One night a kid in a match fouled me. I lost my temper. I beat him so bad I gave him brain damage. He turned into a nightmare for his parents and the cops. To straighten him out, to give him some *discipline*, he was ordered by the court to either join the Marines or go to jail for car theft. Last month he got wounded and came home paralyzed from Vietnam."

"That's a very tragic story."

"I never want to hurt another person again."

Doctor Cobb cleared his throat. He was making notes on his paper-work. He was listening. Maybe he was getting through to him.

"I have this anger. I have these impulses, homicidal, destructive, crazy urges," Eddie said. "Ever since that boxing match I've been afraid I'll lose control and hurt somebody again. Last week I punched out my boss and got fired." Unexpectedly, saying that caused a surge of sadness that he had to choke down. "I've committed myself to a life of nonviolence."

"I don't mean to minimize what you're saying, Mister Bonneville," the doctor said. "I don't question your sincerity. But guilt is not an allowable exemption under Army regulations."

"It's not that. Putting a gun in my hands, giving me people to kill, that would encourage a sick side of me, something I'm trying to fix. You want me in the service, I'll work non-combat, even in Vietnam, I'll drive a truck, I'll be a cook, I'll do laundry, I'll deliver the mail. I'll do anything, except kill other people."

"Son, that's what soldiers do."

"Well, it's not what I do," Eddie said. "I don't know the solution for the war, any more than I know why I like beating the shit out of people. But I know for me the answer's not the Army—"

The doctor sat back. "You think prison will be any better?"

"Not much of a fuckin' choice," Eddie said, "here in the land of the free."

"At least in the Army you won't live in a cage," the doctor said, an-noyed Eddie didn't get this. "You'll be among brothers in arms, you'll receive specialized training, you'll be part of a patriotic effort to serve your country." Or, his tone of voice said, you could remain an unpatri-otic and selfish coward.

Bit by bit, Eddie lost control. "You haven't listened to a word I said. What you're saying is, the Army'll teach me to kill people and give me a legal way to do it. I'm not scared of the Army, I'm scared of myself! What's *your* prescription? 'Join the Army, kill Vietnamese, and get this rage out of your system?' Go ahead, put a gun in my hands, send me over there! I'll give you a My Lai massacre every day of the fuckin' week! You call yourself a fuckin' *doctor*? What shithole hillbilly college gave *you* a fuckin' degree?!" He was half standing, he forced himself to sit back down.

He'd turned the doctor pink. "One phone call from me, and the MPs'll bring you downstairs. You will be instructed to take the oath. Then it's up to you where you sleep tonight: Fort Dix, or Federal prison."

"*That's* up to you," he said. "Just remember what I told you. I'll never hurt another human being again, for as long as I live."

The doctor looked Eddie, then at the phone, and scribbled on his paperwork.

"I'm classifying you 1-A, fit and eligible for military service, Mister Bonneville," the doctor said. "When your lottery number comes up, your local Draft Board will send you an induction notice."

Eddie shook his head, coming to his senses and embarrassed by his outburst.

"By the way, Mister Bonneville," the doctor said, writing and not looking at him. "I graduated from Yale."

"Doctor, I'm sorry about that. I told you, I have this temper—"

"Next!" the doctor shouted toward the door.

Eddie trudged out, thinking, hip fuckin' hooray, he told the truth. Hopefully, Billy would be proud, and ready to defend him when the FBI came knocking with the handcuffs.

By six o'clock he was back down the Shore and late getting to work. Bitter cold weather had blown in on blustery winds out of the northwest. Stars became visible as the clouds blew out to sea, the clear night sky sprinkled with cold and distant diamonds around a platinum crescent of moon. He hurried across the Bargainland parking lot in the frigid wind, his eyes streaming in the deep freeze.

The newsroom was quiet. The other reporters were out to dinner or driving to cover meetings or municipal court. Lindy was back in the composing room laying out the back pages with the paste up girls. His first night back to work, he had no meeting assignment, and his In box was depressingly full. Off the top he grabbed a manila envelope. It was full of Goldy's photos from the Esposito murder scene. He closed it quickly; his nightmares of the past few nights needed no more encouragement. There was also a message from Ivy: *Call when you get in.* He called the number Ivy'd left, but it rang without an answer. He put her message reluctantly aside to get some work done. He plowed through the stuff in his In box, hoping Ivy would call again.

She didn't, and at eight thirty he dropped his copy into the editor's basket on the news desk. He pulled on his coat and cap and yelled back to Lindy that he was going over to the Forum for dinner. He planned to grab a quick meal, staff the newsroom until the eleven o'clock deadline, and split. With any luck he'd be quickly home in bed, riding Ivy to Heaven and beyond.

Five steps down the sidewalk he found himself standing between Tino and Matthew, the bartenders from Castellucci's. Tino sidled behind Eddie and cut him off from the newsroom door. Matthew had a vivid red scar on the side of his bald head.

"What happened to your head, man," Eddie said, "you cut yourself shaving?"

"Black bitch smacked him in the head with an ashtray," Tino said.

"You must've really pissed her off," Eddie said. He tried side-stepping but Matthew held up a hand. "Hey, what's the matter?"

"Man wants to talk to you," Matthew said.

"I'll be back in an hour." He side-stepped again and was again blocked by Matthew.

"The office. In the club."

"No thanks."

"Don't give us a problem, okay?" Matthew's hand slid half out of his coat pocket, gripping a pistol. "I already got a headache."

Around them, the shopping center was deserted. Most of the stores were closed for the evening, and there was nobody around to call to for help. He shrugged and held up his empty hands, and walked with them to Castellucci's, telling himself he'd foolishly let his time run out.

As they passed through the lounge, crowded for dinner, he considered breaking into a run for the exit. But he didn't think it would work, and innocent people might get hurt. He looked for somebody to say hello to, who might help or at least remember he'd been here tonight in case he was never seen again, but he saw no one. Life went on all around him, laughs and chatter, knives and forks working over beef and lobsters, the smoky air scented with perfume and alcohol and tobacco. But nobody even looked up as he passed by.

They took him past the kitchen and down a corridor ending in a heavy wooden door. Matthew pushed a button and the door buzzed open. He stepped into Bobby Castellucci's office. Tino and Matthew withdrew and shut the door.

The man behind the desk wasn't Bobby Castellucci, he was Roy McTierney. He was muscular through the chest and arms, and wore a white polo shirt under a black suit. Cocky, Irish, and movie star handsome, with bright blue eyes and a ruddy tan and an irrepressible smile, the gray streaks in the thick black hair over his ears gave Eddie the impression of a pampered and well-dressed skunk.

McTierney pushed himself to his feet and came around the desk. He peered at Eddie with a curious look on his face. For a moment he thought the guy was about to lean in and sniff him up and down.

"You know who I am, right?" The voice was hearty, the eyes suspicious.

"I guess I do, yeah."

"Nah, you don't," he said. He pulled a handful of press clippings from his jacket pocket, glanced at each, and tossed them one by one on the desk with a dismissive smirk. "Chamber of Commerce Man of the Year, Roy McTierney. Rotary Honors Roy McTierney. Roy McTierney gets Businessmen's Council honor third year running, as the man who does the most for this county's economy."

"Wow," Eddie said, pretending to be impressed. "Sounds like you're pretty hot shit."

"It does, doesn't it?" He laughed, a rich belly laugh. "Sit down. Be comfortable."

"I'm comfortable," he said, staying on his feet. McTierney was crowding him, purposely, but he'd been in worse clinches. "What do you want?"

"You're Eddie Bonneville," McTierney said.

"That's right."

"I don't need you to confirm it. I checked you out with a few people. Your old man's a Korean War veteran. Sits on the Brick Township Committee. Fucked up his business and had to go to work for Sears. Calls himself an honest politician, and he doesn't have two nickels to rub together. You used to be a boxer, until you nearly killed a kid. People think you've got a screw loose. You run with Tommy Porter's daughter, the one with the dirty mouth and the loose knees. Now you're a reporter for the *Independent*. My newspaper."

He found it difficult to remain unprovoked. "So I hear."

"That you work for me?"

"I don't work for you."

Chuckling, McTierney backed up and sat on the corner of the desk.

He had small feet in black alligator slip-ons. "You wrote that anti-war thing—what's your Draft classification?"

"1-A."

"I can make that go away, if you want."

"I'm handling it."

"Hey. Semper Fi. Myself, I'm a proud graduate of Admiral Farragut Academy." McTierney dropped down on his fancy footwear and strolled around the office. "That anti-war stuff you write in the paper? I agree with you one hundred per cent. Vietnam's the biggest mistake we ever made. America won't be the same when it's over. If it's *ever* over."

"So write a letter to the editor," Eddie said. "Why did you have me brought here?"

"To find out what *you* want."

"To tell the truth to people."

"Truth about what?"

"About how government works around here, and to whose benefit."

"And who's that?"

"Everybody but the people, it seems."

"The People, capital P, those people?"

"Yeah."

"Well, aren't *I* one of The People, too?" McTierney answered his own question, loving it. "Obviously not." He fingered the lapel of his suit jacket. "Let me ask you something. Are The People, as you call them, going without anything they should expect from government?"

"Yeah," Eddie said. "Honesty."

"Okay, but is crime up because there's not enough cops? Do houses burn down because there's no firemen? Do people live with garbage because nobody picks it up? Do the roads get fixed, do schools get built, do towns grow in a planned sensible way or chaotically—?"

"Your Republican machine siphons two per cent off all county business—"

"That's the oldest myth in Ocean County politics."

"—to maintain one party rule."

"Totally untrue," McTierney said. "Who would know better than me? I *am* the Republican machine, now that my Dad's gone."

"Who would have a better reason to lie? And more to lose if the truth got out?"

McTierney paused and seemed to decide that being called a liar didn't bother him—yet. "Let's say you're right. To the average person, that still doesn't stink as bad as their day-old garbage." McTierney gazed down on his buffed fingernails and smiled, as if he'd seen himself reflected in them. "You get my point? There's no market for Matty Esposito's fairy tales about corruption. People don't care."

Eddie found a cigarette in his shirt pocket and lit it. "Let me ask *you* something. What was your relationship with Kenny Rosenfeld?"

"None. Never met the man. Which never stopped him from attacking me and trying to put me out of business."

"Is that how you see it?"

"How else? People want to live at the Jersey Shore. I build houses for them. Yeah, it's a problem that these towns can't build schools fast enough for all the new kids, and taxes are going through the roof. It could even be a problem for my business one day if the taxes are so high that people can't afford to live here. But a moratorium on all new home building? Fastest way I know to throw this county into a depression."

"What do you know about Rosenfeld's disappearance?"

"Only what I read in the papers. Less than you, I'll bet. Why? Should I know something?"

"A gangster named Tony Notti told me that he and another man killed Rosenfeld on orders from Bobby Castellucci," Eddie said, glancing around the office, "your, uh, security consultant."

"There's the phone. Call the prosecutor."

"Castellucci's going around telling people Rosenfeld shook you down for a lot of money and kept right on busting your balls."

McTierney blinked slowly and laughed. "Good story, but it's not true."

"They were supposed to rough up Rosenfeld for you, but they wound up killing him by mistake."

"That's terrible. His poor family." McTierney shook his head gravely. "Tell Earl Heckendorfer. Or better yet, play him your tapes. I hear they make interesting listening."

Heard from *where*? Would Frank put him in that kind of danger? "They're only good if I get more information."

"Well, I sure don't have it." McTierney settled back down in the big chair behind the desk. "Y'know, I once had my eye on you. You're a smart kid. The stories you wrote last summer about the Lakewood riots, I thought you had all sides in there fairly. I should've offered you a job. I just had a PR job, but I filled it with the guy from the Asbury paper, Nick Poliandro. Friend of yours, right?"

"I know him." Could he have told McTierney about the tapes? My God, Nicky, Eddie thought. No, it must've been Frank. Or it might have been Nicky, unwittingly.

"So what do you want? What's it going to take for you to quit digging into this story and spreading it around town, and for you to turn those tapes over to me?"

"If it's all a myth, what do you care?"

"A lie can wreck somebody's reputation just as easily as the truth. You reporters, you smear a guy on Page One, and you bury the correction in the back pages." He stood up and strolled over until he and Eddie were close. "What's it going to take?"

"How about you testify under oath before a grand jury?" Eddie said.

McTierney exploded in laughter, a whoop then rapidly descending barks, trailing off to a giggle, while Eddie stood there and burned.

"Anything else?" McTierney recovered from mirth, caught his breath. "Okay. Now: give up the story, hand over the tapes. I'm your employer, I've got every right to demand this."

"Sorry."

"You *do* know I'm the reason you didn't get fired, at least not until you punched out your boss?" McTierney didn't seem to disapprove. "I figured we better keep a close eye on you. All along I've been doing what's best for you, you just didn't know it."

"Once upon a time, I might have been stupid enough to believe that."

McTierney's grin melted. He shrugged, and his voice turned somber. "All right, for the last time: give up the story, hand over the tapes. Otherwise, you force me to show a side of myself that I'm, well, I'm not proud of, frankly. So what do you say? With a nice big cash bonus on delivery."

"How big?"

McTierney didn't pause for an instant. "Name your price."

He shook his head. "You don't have enough make me stop."

"There are ways."

A thought struck. "You wouldn't dare touch Ivy."

"What?!" A look of horror. "The Senator and I are the *closest* of friends." McTierney shrugged. "No." He checked the time on a slim gold wristwatch and picked up the phone. "Let's just keep this between me and you."

The dark end of the rear storage room at Castellucci's Lounge stank of old cheese, and the yeasty odor of spilled beer, and the concrete floor was cold and wet. Eddie, his head and blackened eyes throbbing, his lips split and his knees trembling, slowly pulled himself up, his arms around a vertical pipe, his wrists bound with gray duct tape. A bright overhead bulb cast a painful glare. A foot swung out of the dark and kicked him in the ribs. He spun and tumbled to the concrete floor, landing on his torn and bleeding knees. Again, he struggled to his feet.

Like an exhausted swimmer treading water, he tried to keep his damaged body upright, when he really wanted to sink down into the black sea of unconsciousness. A deep breath made his belly flutter. He hurt so much his whole body trembled uncontrollably. But he fought against the longing for painless oblivion, his mind yelling, *Get up, get up*! If he gave them what they wanted, or he lost consciousness, they would kill him and get rid of his body and car. He had to stay awake and get through this, so he did it the only way he knew how. He kept getting up off the canvas, and he kept the hate in his heart alive.

Around him unseen voices muttered. "You believe this fuckin' kid?"

"Hey kid, stay down, take the eight count at least!" Laughter all around.

Not yet.

Hands seized his ankles and yanked his feet out from under him. He flopped to the wet concrete on his sore belly, and it knocked the wind out of him and jerked his neck painfully. His raw knees and skinned elbows burned. All the laughing men around him groaned, as if they were taking a beating, not him.

He struggled to his feet, soaked with floor slop, panting. A fist whistled out of the dark and punched him in the face, dropping him again to his skinned, bloody knees. Again he forced himself back onto his feet. His shirtfront was soaked in blood. He peered into the dark outside the circle of harsh light, where the voices came from.

Then he giggled, half out of his head, and croaked: "How many rounds you think you could last with *me*, greaseball?"

Castellucci stepped into the light, towering over him. He was stripped to an undershirt. His fists were bloody. He grabbed him by the throat.

"We can keep this up all night if that's what you want."

Eddie whipped his head back and pulled free of the hand on his throat, and coughed, his shoulder on the cold pipe keeping him vertical.

Castellucci put his face inches from his. "I'm gonna get every copy of this story, every tape, every note you made, and I'm gonna burn 'em. Then your story has no backup."

He laughed through his split, bloody lips, spraying Castellucci, who grimaced and stepped back wiping his face. "Only my memory," he said.

Castellucci grabbed a handful of his hair and banged his head against the pipe. "Dead men have no memory."

"That's not true. Matty the Mule's gonna speak from the grave."

"Give me the fuckin' tapes."

"You don't need the tapes. You're gonna read all about yourself in the newspaper. Trust me."

The unseen chorus of men outside the light laughed, but not because they thought he was funny.

"Last chance, faggot," Castellucci hissed.

"Fuck you."

Castellucci lunged in and punched him in the solar plexus. The impact paralyzed his midsection. He gasped for breath, but he couldn't breathe at all, and the rough voices around him yelling *Aw!* and *Oh!* and *Ma-ron!* faded to a whisper as he sank down into nothingness.

"Don't worry," he heard Castellucci say, as he blacked out, as he passed beyond caring and let go. "I got people for this."

One of the bouncers found Eddie's car keys in his jacket pocket and drove the Impala around to the service road behind the club. He blew the horn twice. The light over the rear entrance went dark. Two men carried Eddie out the back door to the Impala, his taped hands hanging in front of him and his toes dragging. They dumped him face down on the back seat, bent his knees, and shut the door. They put a couple of things in the trunk, and got in the Impala, the older man driving, and took off.

The driver, Michael "Dee Dee" Denardo, smoothed his long sideburns and patted his graying pompadour over his bald spot, looking at himself in the rearview mirror with the sour pout of the chronic loser. He was dressed like he was going to play golf, in a lime green shirt and matching slacks and Hush Puppies and a brown overcoat. His young partner, a chubby little weasel named John "Puggy" Pugliese, had seen too many Rat Pack movies: big cuff links, skinny tie and dark alpaca suit and dark overcoat, and a black fedora with thick white band, very Sinatra, post-Ava.

The wind gusted against the Impala's grille, rocking the car gently. About ten miles south of the club, they made a right turn off Route 9 and onto a two-lane blacktop that would take them west, out into the middle of nowhere.

ELEVEN *The Barrens*

The hopelessness and panic that overwhelm the nervous system just before vomiting forced Eddie awake. His mouth was sticky and his swollen lips tasted like blood. His head throbbed with each heartbeat, his whole body trembled. His bruised stomach cramped painfully, but he clenched his teeth, kept his gorge down, and concentrated on breathing. He became aware that he was lying on the back seat of his own car, face down on his taped-up hands, and the car was moving.

"Phew!" a young guy's voice exclaimed from the passenger seat. "Fuckin' Bobby."

"He really lost it," said an older, deeper voice, the driver.

"For a fuckin' hippie, the guy took a beating like a man, I'll say that. He never gave it up."

"Yeah. He's so brave, he's dead."

"You think he's dead?"

"Dead enough for what we gotta do."

Cold fear overcame him and he nearly moaned. He lifted his face off his taped wrists. Desperately, he gnawed at the tape with his teeth.

The car slowed. They turned off the blacktop onto what felt and sounded like a bumpy gravel road. Jostled painfully with every rut and dip the car made, he chewed away at the tape, trying not to groan.

"*Maron!*" the young guy said. "Where we takin' this guy to, fuckin' Dogpatch or what?"

The older man laughed, which turned into a phlegmy cough.

"You know where we're going?"

"I was out here a couple months ago," the older man said. "The night me and Tony Notti clipped that Jew from the building boycott thing. Hey! That's right! Tonight you bust your cherry!" As they drove deep into the pine barrens, Eddie realized that if he died tonight, nobody would ever find Rosenfeld's body, or know how and why he died, because he'd kept all that to himself until he could use it to his advantage.

The road ran perfectly straight for several minutes. At the end of that road he knew what waited for him: death, dismemberment, burnt remains in a barrel, which would be buried someplace and forgotten. Unless he did something violent and ugly and against everything he believed in, he was living his last moments on earth, beaten like a dog and trussed up waiting to be slaughtered.

The car slowed, braked and stopped, and he almost slid off the back seat. The two men got out and slammed the doors and he was alone.

I'm not going to die tonight he kept telling himself, while he chewed and pulled frantically at the thick tape wound around his wrists, trying to control his rising panic. No way he could get out of this peacefully. To save his own life he would have to fight like an animal. If he didn't, if he remained a true pacifist to the end, he would have a short brutal journey from the moral high ground to a hole in the ground. Angrily, he scolded himself: pacifism was a way of peaceful life, not a peaceful way of submitting to murder. *I'm not going to die tonight*, he kept insisting, with no idea how he would save his own life.

The Impala's high beams lit up a wide clearing of gray sand in the middle of the road. Icy winds hissed through the pine boughs overhead. The undergrowth, a dense web of common greenbrier with sharp thorns, shook in the frigid gusts, as if agitated, disturbed.

Dee Dee and Puggy whooped and cursed at the cold, pulling their overcoats tight and rubbing their hands. Puggy pushed his fedora down tighter on his head. From the trunk they lifted a 55-gallon steel barrel and placed it in front of the car in the glow of the headlights. Dee Dee pulled the spring fastener off the barrel and removed the top. Puggy brought out a five gallon can labeled Kerosene. Dee Dee brought out a long-handled, double-bladed axe and leaned it against the barrel.

"You gonna let me cut?" Puggy said.

"I'll cut. You'll take too long and it's fuckin' cold out. You *zotz* the guy, then you do the barrel and the kerosene."

"Great," Puggy said. "I gotta cook?"

"Too bad, kid. You're the rookie, that's your job. C'mon, let's do this and get out of here."

They came around and opened the Impala's door. Eddie felt their hands around his ankles. His bent legs were pulled painfully straight. They dragged him out of the car. He flopped face down on the sandy ground with a thud that nearly knocked the wind out of him. They hauled him by his heels, coating his bloody clothes with sand. He pulled like mad at his hands but couldn't break the tape binding his wrists.

"So, watch my axe work and learn something," the older man was saying to the young guy. "When I was your age, I could cut and pack a body in like five minutes. The secret is the right cuts in the right places."

"Sure. You gotta know where everything connects. Like everything else in life."

No, he thought, raging against the enveloping numbness that promised to take away his pain if he would just surrender. No! Not like this! He was too beat and sore to fight back, to get up and run. They dragged Eddie next to the barrel, and turned him over on his back, pulling ineffectually at his bound wrists.

"Hey, he's movin'," Puggy said, putting a cigarette between his lips. "This guy ain't dead."

Dee Dee peered down at Eddie. "He ain't far from it. Okay kid. You're on. Pop this guy in the head and get it over with. I don't want him floppin' around when I chop him up."

"No floppin' with the choppin'," you got it." Puggy turned his back and hunched down against the wind to light a cigarette, repeatedly flicking his lighter. "My wife gave me this lighter for Christmas, and already the goddam thing don't work."

Eddie threw himself onto his side and with his bound hands he grabbed the axe leaning against the barrel. He rolled back swinging the axe and chopped down hard. Dee Dee couldn't move quick enough. Eddie cut his foot off, halfway down the arch, with a wet crunch. Dee Dee screamed at the top of his lungs, jumped away on one foot and crashed on his back in the dirt, his severed foot spraying blood, connected to the rest of him only by a floppy sliver of the sole of his lime green Hush Puppies.

Puggy jumped at his partner's scream. He spun around, and clawed at his coat buttons, digging for his gun, his mouth wide open. His cigarette stuck to his lower lip, burning his chin. He frantically brushed it away, showering sparks on his overcoat. Eddie swung the axe backward and buried the blade in the side of Puggy's knee. Puggy howled and pulled his leg back. The axe ripped out of Eddie's hands, bounced off the barrel and fell into the sand.

Hopping on one foot, Puggy got his gun out, but his wounded leg collapsed under his weight and he fell on top of Eddie. He swung his bound fists together at Puggy's face but only knocked his hat off into the dust. He battered him with his elbows and knees and hammered with both hands on his face. As he tore the gun out of Puggy's hand the pistol fired and the shot jerked his arm and slammed in his ears. The slug hit the ground and sprayed dirt on Dee Dee, laying on his back howling in pain and disbelief and trying to hold his foot together.

Eddie got a two-handed grip on the gun, a heavy automatic, and brought the butt down hard on Puggy's nose. Puggy, stunned and desperate to get away, rolled his weight off Eddie's legs and curled up on his side in the sand, holding his broken knee and his bloody nose. Beside him, Dee Dee lay whimpering and bleeding.

He got his finger on the trigger of Puggy's gun. He sat up and swung the gun back and forth between them. "Hands out! Hands out where I can see 'em!" he said. His voice shook hard, suddenly he was an alto.

Gasping and cursing in disbelief, Dee Dee and Puggy showed their bloody hands. Eddie kicked and slid in the dirt backwards towards his car until he sat back against the front bumper between the headlights. Holding the gun on them, he pulled the axe towards him with his foot.

"You move and I'll kill you!"

He let them hold their wounds and moan in the dirt. He positioned the axe blade between his knees with the edge up. Pointing Puggy's gun at them, he sawed his taped wrists on the edge of the blade. His bonds split, the tape ripped the hair from his wrists and his hands came free. He could have burst into song, or prayer, but he cried instead.

"Don't move!" He didn't care that he was blubbering in front of two killers.

He propped one hand on the car bumper, the other hand holding the gun, and pushed himself to his feet. Bloody and filthy, on numb legs, he was nearly too dizzy to stand up.

Dee Dee lay on the dirt gasping, his eyes squeezed shut. Eddie staggered over and put the gun to his head and tore off his overcoat, popping off all the buttons. He found a small automatic in his coat pocket. He put it in his waistband and made sure Dee Dee didn't have a second gun. He put the gun to Puggy's head and grabbed him by the collar and kicked him out of his overcoat. By accident, his suit jacket came with it, leaving him in his shirtsleeves. He frisked him, and he was clean. He stuffed their coats into the barrel.

"Kid… kid…" they begged, shivering in the bitter cold.

He ignored them. He sat back on the warm hood of his car, the engine idling under him. He dug out a bent Lucky Strike, lit it with his Zippo, took a deep drag, and let out a long plume of delicious smoke on a grateful sigh, snatched away by the wind. Dust, exhaust from the idling car, and bits of dry leaves blew through the headlight beams and in the faces of the shivering, terrified men. His hands burned from the cold but he ignored it. His vision kept blurring and clearing, the cold wind made his eyes run. He used a clean tail of his shirt to wipe them. He coughed and spit in his palm and held it in the headlight. Clear, no blood.

Now what?

Kill these muthafuckers. Shoot each one in the head and leave the remains for the foxes and birds. Shoot them in the guts, run the car over them. Soak them in their own kerosene and burn them to death. Horrible, yes, but better than what they did to Kenny, what they would've done to you. Use the axe and cut one of them to pieces while he's still alive. Make the other one watch, make him see what he's got coming…

He aimed Puggy's gun, a heavy automatic, at the dirt between the two gangsters and pulled the trigger. The shot jerked his arm painfully, the boom was loud, echoing in the woods, dirt sprayed all over them. They flinched, their babbling and whining—"Kid, kid"— such music to his ears he almost laughed.

"Shut up! Take off your shoes!"

Puggy tossed one shoe over. Dee Dee pulled off his one good shoe and kicked it over. He let him keep the shoe holding his foot together.

"Kid, you can't leave us out here—" the old man said, his elaborate pompadour fallen down in his eyes. Eddie stood over Dee Dee.

"Maybe I won't leave you. Maybe I'll show you *my* axe work. I'll practice on your friend here and you can grade my performance, how's that?" He kicked Dee Dee hard in the ribs, felt something crack, and the hood doubled up on the ground, wailing and cursing. God damn, it felt good, doing that.

He dropped the shoes into the barrel on top of the coats. He stood over Puggy. "Give me the other one!"

His wounded leg wouldn't move and he was too fat to reach his other foot. He howled with pain as Eddie trapped his wounded leg under his heel and tore his other shoe off. He kicked Puggy's face in the sand and threw his shoe in the barrel. He unscrewed the cap off the kerosene can with his free hand. He emptied it on the coats and shoes in the barrel and tossed it aside. The wind blew Puggy's fedora against his leg, and Eddie scooped it up and dropped it in the barrel.

On the ground, Dee Dee cried uncontrollably and Puggy was blubbering in panic. The men's bodies quivered involuntarily from the freezing cold wind and from pain.

"Dee! Dee! He broke my fuckin' nose!"

"Your nose! I'm bleeding to death over here! I'll never fuckin' *walk* right again! Kid! Don't leave us here! Put us in the trunk if you want! Don't leave us out here to bleed to death!"

"We're gonna fuckin' *freeze*!" Puggy wailed.

"I got nine hundred bucks in my coat pocket—"

"Shut up!"

He fired again at the dirt near the two men. They screamed as if they were hit. It was hilarious.

"Shut up!" He fired again, they screamed again, he laughed again.

The slug kicked up a geyser of dirt that spattered on them as they cowered and begged. He fired again, close to their heads. The two gangsters screamed and scratched frantically at the dirt, trying to dig holes to hide in. He limped around them, studying them from full height, as they writhed and suffered on the sand in the stark pool of light. Making them suffer was deeply satisfying, yet he felt oddly detached from his actions.

He bent over Puggy, grabbed his shirt front, and jammed the muzzle of the gun to his temple. Puggy's nose bled into the dirt and his face froze in a grimace as he waited to be shot.

"You were gonna shoot me in the head," he said. "Give me one good reason why I shouldn't blow your fuckin' brains out right now."

"I'm sorry, I'm sorry. I was just obeying orders." Blood bubbles blew from his nose.

"Beg, fuckface." He ground the muzzle of the gun harder against his head.

"Please, please don't shoot me," Puggy sobbed.

He pushed Puggy's face in the bloody, snotty sand. "You look up at me again, I'll kill you."

He grabbed Dee Dee by the hair and threw him over on his back. The older man was sobbing out of control, one hand clutching his bleeding foot and an elbow clutched to his ribs. "This is my job, kid! I'm just doing my job!"

He put the gun in his face so it was all Dee Dee could see. "Was it just your job when you murdered Kenny Rosenfeld?"

"Yeah! Bobby ordered it, Bobby ordered it!"

"You and Tony Notti."

"Yeah!"

"Anybody else?"

"Nah." *Of course not.* "It was a two man job." In Dee Dee's line of work, murder was a craft you learned like in trade school, with lessons on how to crew up a killing, how to chop and dispose of a corpse, how to hijack a truck, the psychology of loan shark collections.

"He meant nothing to you, right?"

"Never met him!"

"That makes it ten times worse."

"It was my *job*, for Chrissakes, I was just doing my *job*—"

"Kenny Rosenfeld was a friend of mine." He bent over and hit Dee Dee with a jawbreaker to the side of his face that almost knocked him out. But as he stood up, the man's pitiful weeping began to get to him, and his hand throbbed.

With a sudden gasp, his euphoria and strength were gone. He staggered back to the car, unsteadily, and fell back on the hood. His vision was blurred, his head pounding. The damage from the beating was overtaking him, weakening him. His stomach began doing flip flops. He was afraid he might faint before he could get out of here. Only one last thing to do.

Despite the shooting pain in his ribs, he screamed at them. "I'm gonna kill you both!"

Make them wear their kerosene soaked overcoats and shoes, light them up, let 'em run for home.

"Please kid, please please—"

"Please *what*? You came out here to kill me! Right?" When Puggy whimpered he got a kick in the side. "Right?"

"We were just doing our job!" Puggy wailed.

"Who the fuck are you to ask me for anything?"

"Kid—" Dee Dee groaned, his mouth bloody, spitting out teeth.

"The world'll be a better place without you!"

"Please kid, please please—"

He prodded Dee Dee with his foot. "I'm gonna shoot you both in the belly. Then I'm gonna run you over with the car."

They both moaned.

He wanted to do it. One look at his battered condition and any cop, any judge, any jury, would understand why he had to kill two gangsters to save his own life. He was going to do it. If anyone in this world deserved to be put to death by him, it was these two, especially the older one. The *casual* way he'd mentioned it: "The time me and Tony Notti clipped that Jew…"

But on the verge of taking these two lives, something made him stop and think. Kill these killers, and would the world be a better place? Definitely, but would that make him a better man? How would he live? These were two killings the world was allowing him and would shrug off, two more vermin crushed and flicked away. He looked forward to killing these two criminals as ardently and as sweetly as he might look forward to making love.

And yet, he wondered: What if taking a life meant exactly that? You took all that was good and evil in your victim into your own soul? He took a long look at Dee Dee and Puggy. He was certain if he took these killers' lives, they would never die, they would become evil companions to the killer inside of him.

Once over *that* line, then what? He might as well enlist.

"I'll give you one chance, right now. Get up and run. *That* way." Further on up the road, deeper into the barrens. "Get up and run! Go!"

Sobbing and whimpering in the cold, Puggy and Dee Dee crawled on their hands, dragging their wounded legs and limping up the road deeper into the woods. He fired a shot at them and the dirt kicked up at their feet. They both staggered off the road and into the undergrowth for cover, scrambling into the woody shrubs. He raised the gun and fired into the air over their heads. They screamed and tore deeper into the shrubs, then stumbled and fell into the dense greenbrier where they were trapped by the thorns like flies in a spider's web. They'd be stuck there until morning if they didn't freeze or bleed to death.

He dropped his cigarette butt into the barrel. A flame slowly crawled out from under Dee Dee and Puggy's coats and shoes and soon was blazing tall and hot. The heat licking his face felt very good.

He lowered himself, wincing and cursing, into the Impala, and turned the heat on full blast. He placed the gun on the seat beside him. A careful K turn in the small clearing and he was headed out of there. Soon there was nothing but a flaming barrel that became a red dot in his rearview mirror.

The gravel fire road was a straight white line that ran like a tunnel through the thick pine forest. Here and there, hand-painted signs on scraps of wood nailed to trees marked dirt roads that led away into the forest. Suddenly, coming up on a rise, his headlights showed the windshield and grille of a old Ford truck, fifty yards ahead, blocking the road. A pale face behind the steering wheel stared back at him. A man stepped out of the trees in front of the truck with a shotgun in his hands. Eddie tucked Puggy's gun in his belt under his jacket and braked to a stop. He turned on the dome light and showed his empty hands to the man standing in front of him. The man wore greasy blue coveralls and an old sheepskin jacket and wool cap. He raised the shotgun and aimed it right at him.

A hand slapped on the roof of the car and the noise made him jump. Outside the driver's window was an old woman's face, as round and white as the moon, wearing a black kerchief over her head. He rolled down the window, but not too far. When she spoke, her voice resembled a scratchy old record.

"What's all the shootin' about, honey?"

Pineys, he thought. From high school geography he knew the Pine Barrens covered one thousand square miles, but he knew nothing about these families of the Jersey pine forest who'd lived deep in the Barrens for generations.

The old woman had a wide smile, which faded when she saw he was a man with long hair.

"Two men back in the clearing," he said. "They beat me up, bad, look at me." Her eyes looked over his face and bloody clothes and she nodded. "They brought me out here in my own car. They were gonna kill me and burn my body up, but I got away."

"What's all the shootin'?"

"I took their guns away. I didn't shoot anybody. I fired a few shots to scare them."

"They still out there?"

"Yeah. They're hurt, but they're alive."

"They still got guns?"

"I don't think so. I threw them in the bushes."

She looked him over for a moment, then turned and yelled, "All right!" to the man with the shotgun. He nodded, his eyes staring at Eddie, and lowered the gun.

"They brought you out here?"

"They were gonna kill me and burn up my body."

She just stared at him through the window. "Je–sus Christ."

"I'm sorry if I disturbed you folks, m'am, but I got to get to a hospital. I'm hurt real bad."

"What kinda men?"

"Mafia."

Her face changed. "Oh." She waved the man with the shotgun aside and the truck backed up into a side lane. She peered back where Eddie had come from. "We'll take care of them, all right." She slapped the roof again. "Go on, *git*."

The emergency room at Community Memorial Hospital in Toms River was quiet at one o'clock in the morning when he limped in. He showed his press card and gave Goldy's phone number to one of the nurses who helped him to an examination room.

Lying on a gurney in a gown, his clothes in a filthy heap on the floor, he surrendered to exhaustion. He shifted his body around, testing the damage, and winced at the pain radiating from his ribs and head. His arms and legs were numb in places where there would be pain later. But he could live with it. To raise his spirits, he told himself this beating was no worse than his last bout in the boxing ring, but he knew that wasn't true.

The ER doctor, a young guy who looked Arabic and spoke English like a Brit, told him he had two cracked ribs, a split lip and loose molar, contusions all over his upper body and legs, and a possible concussion. His belly muscles and internal organs were bruised. The skin on his elbows and knees was torn and dirty, and his legs and arms were massed with purple bruises. The doctor insisted that Eddie tell him, in confidence, how he got hurt. He had no desire to relive the experience and no idea what the doctor would do if he told the truth. So he said he'd gotten his ass kicked in a nasty bar fight with two men who objected to his long hair. He would talk to the police in the morning.

He was still in Emergency when Goldy arrived. "Holy shit, Prince

Valiant, what happened to you?" Against the doctor's wishes, he stood and posed so Goldy could photograph his cuts and bruises and battered face. Goldy stood by while the doctor finished working on him. Medicated and patched up, he told them his vision was blurring and his ears hissed loudly. They admitted him for overnight observation, put him in a quiet corner of the corridor on a cot, gave him a pill for pain and another one to make him sleep, and told him to rest.

When they were alone, Goldy pulled up a chair, and Eddie told him what had happened. Hearing that he had been beaten up by their neighborhood saloon keeper, on orders from the owner of their newspaper, Goldy said, deadpan, "I always figured Bobby was connected. Good guy to avoid." When Goldy started to show more interest in one of the nurses than him, Eddie asked him to leave so he could sleep.

But once he was alone his mind wouldn't leave him in peace. For years he had tried so hard to rid himself of anger and violence, yet tonight that's what saved his life. Clearly, the killer inside him was his guardian, one he'd been mistaken to renounce. There was no need to fear the killer, because tonight he had learned he was its master.

Tonight on the brink of two killings, he had not given in to anger, and had spared two lives. The two gangsters he might've killed would heal and no doubt resume their lives as degenerate criminals. He had no control over that. He hadn't spared their lives because they were worth much, but out of concern for the worth of his own life. Those two small mercies probably meant very little in what Kenny Rosenfeld had liked to call "the absurd slaughterhouse that is this world," but tonight maybe he'd improved his odds of seeing Heaven, and not the other place.

He tried to sleep. But he lapsed into terror, not awake and not unconscious. He felt himself being struck again, and again. As he tossed and turned, the ripped skin on his knees and elbows burned, and he felt like he couldn't breathe into his bruised chest and broken ribs. He felt like he was floating in space, spinning, head over feet and sideways and around and around. Dizziness forced him to nausea and over the edge, but his stomach was empty, and he could only dry heave, squeezing his broken ribs painfully, his whole body pulsing with heat and shivering, bathed in cold sweat. At one moment, he woke and pulled the sheets tighter around himself to get warm, but that only wrapped him in a freezing shroud. He curled up and began crying softly to himself. He heard his voice saying things he didn't comprehend.

A warm hand that smelled like soap touched his forehead. His eyes suddenly jerked open and in the dark all he could see was a young nurse with a worried look on her face, her hand stroking his hair. All he could do was look at her and cry.

"It's all right," he heard her say, "it's all right."

Her words, in that soft voice, echoed right through him and the tension gripping his whole body let go. After a few moments he slipped into unconsciousness.

He woke up some time later, it was impossible to say how long. His eyes jerked open to bright morning and the sight of nurses and doctors and patients in gowns moving around.

His body was eerily at rest, his breathing deep and easy, and he no longer had any sensation of pain, or even of his physical existence. This must be what it was like to be paralyzed, he thought, this sensation of being only a mind floating in space. Then he had a scary thought—what if he *was* paralyzed, what if something broke while he was suffering through the night, what if this was death—but he wiggled his toes, and his whole body arched beneath the sheet in a full body-stretching yawn, reawakening the pain in every scrape, cut and bruise.

He limped over to the reception desk and called Billy at seven o'clock. He started to tell him what happened, but Billy stopped him. "I'm coming over right now. You can tell me about this later."

By eight o'clock Billy was at his bedside. He waited as a morning shift doctor examined Eddie and decided to discharge him. Eddie got dressed in the khakis, tee shirt and sweater Billy brought him, gingerly, because pulling them on made his cuts and bruises hurt worse. When he bent a knee, or an elbow or his back, it felt like he could never straighten out. His legs were so bruised he was afraid they might not support him, but he pulled on his dirty coat and walked out of the hospital to the car on his own two feet, his vision clear. His head still ached, and he carried it carefully atop his shoulders, feeling like it would fall off if he leaned too far off-center.

Outside, the morning was cold as a grave, the sky a sheet of gray lead with a pale smear of sun. He drove the Impala, carefully following Billy down to the beach.

He climbed slowly up to his apartment. In the bathtub, Eddie sponged the last traces of dirt and blood off himself, careful to avoid wetting his bandages, got dressed again, and stuck a fresh pack of

Lucky Strike in his pocket. He took the Esposito tapes from his desk drawer, put them in a buff envelope addressed to himself and sealed it, and limped downstairs.

He was ravenously hungry. Billy lit the fireplace and fixed oatmeal with milk and honey, toast and strong coffee. Over breakfast, Billy listened intently as he described what happened last night.

"Roy McTierney," Billy said when he finished.

Eddie nodded.

"Any witnesses?"

"The two bouncers from the lounge who brought me to him."

"Why did you let it go so far?" Billy said. "Why the hell didn't you give him the tapes?"

"I just couldn't bring myself to say 'yes' to Bobby Castellucci while he was beating the crap out of me. I couldn't sink that low. Same reason I won't give them to Heckendorfer." He told Billy about the subpoena he got yesterday morning.

"We'll deal with that," Billy said. "You may have to let go of this story, at least temporarily. The more you know, the more he's going to try to pry out of you."

"I've been threatened, fired from my job, shot at, and had my ass kicked for trying to report this story. But I'm going to see it in print, somehow," Eddie said. "If I lose these tapes, I can't prove that he even *made* his accusations. So you'd better hold on to them." He handed Billy the envelope with the tapes inside.

"I'll put them in my office safe." Billy sighed and shook his head, and glanced at his wristwatch. "As soon as you're able," Billy said, "we have to get over to the prosecutor with all this."

"What the hell for?"

"You're the victim of a crime, that's what for. Look who's involved."

"He's the last person I want to see right now."

TWELVE *Exhibits A and B*

When they were shown into the prosecutor's office, Heckendorfer's scowl toward Eddie turned into a wince. "What the hell happened to you?"

"I got all banged up," Eddie said, easing himself into a chair, "rushing down here to tell you where to shove that subpoena."

"Don't—" Billy quieted him. "Just tell him what happened last night."

He told the prosecutor everything, from the meeting with Roy McTierney to escaping death down in the pines. Heckendorfer took notes on a yellow legal pad. He gave a description of the two gangsters he left in the woods. Billy handed over a paper bag with the pistols Eddie took away from them. Heckendorfer didn't say anything when Eddie implicated the county political boss in his torture and attempted murder. Coffee was ordered, and Heckendorfer called in a county detective. He gave him the guns and told him to get the State Police involved and to canvass local hospitals for men with leg wounds and arrest Dee Dee and Puggy when they turned up.

He tossed his pen atop his notes and stretched back in his throne. He said to Billy, "Does this kid not get it yet?" and smirked at Eddie. "You're in over your head, Eddie Bonneville."

"Stop calling me a 'kid'." He pulled out the subpoena papers and tossed them on Heckendorfer's desk. "You're not getting my notes."

Billy said, "Let's stick to your kidnapping and attempted murder, shall we?" speaking to them both.

"I'll give you two more days to comply," Heckendorfer said, and turned to Billy. "Maybe you and your client should talk."

"Two days from now my answer will be the same," Eddie said. "Let's get this over with right now."

"Wait a minute—" Billy said off Heckendorfer's antagonized squirm in his chair.

"It wouldn't be right to throw you into county jail in your condition. But I will."

"This is pointless, Earl," Billy said. "Esposito is dead, and your case is over."

Eddie said, unable to keep the mockery out of his voice, "You gave the Organization the job vacancy they wanted. Too bad Bobby Castellucci won't be able to fill it for maybe 25-to-life."

Bristling, Heckendorfer fell back with his arms spread wide. "Our indictment of Esposito was based on solid evidence. We investigated his rackets for months. We *had* him. If anything else was involved, I don't know about it."

"Well then, you're the only one—"

Billy raised a hand to squelch Eddie's reply. "Why are you trying to force Eddie to give you his notes?"

"I need to know what Esposito said to your client *because* he's dead, and I can't question him."

"This is no way to treat a guy who just handed you an attempted murder case on a silver platter," Billy said.

"Along with my *ass*. He's claiming *Roy McTierney* had him beaten and nearly killed. Gee, thanks."

"It is what it is," Eddie said.

Heckendorfer pushed himself, irritably, to his feet. "Look, I'm busy, and your client's refusing to cooperate with my investigation."

"He has a right to refuse. It's called the First Amendment. And under the New Jersey press shield law I'll have that subpoena thrown out—"

"And I don't like his attitude."

"C'mon, Earl. Last night he got his brains beat in, this morning you're threatening him with jail. What would *your* attitude be?"

"Matty Esposito did not become the racketeer he was all on his own," Heckendorfer said. "Shield law or no law, this kid's got knowledge of God knows how many crimes, and he can't just sit on it. I'm sure what's in his notes will point to new people, new areas of investigation—"

"Oh, dozens," Eddie said.

"Too bad you got yourself into this condition, Eddie," Heckendorfer said, rolling to his feet and strolling around his desk. "I can see you're in a lot of pain, even for a tough kid like you. But you know what? I don't care. You're under arrest for failure to comply with my subpoena."

"What the hell—" Billy said. "We came here to report a crime and you're arresting him?"

"He asked for it. Right Eddie?"

"All I did was say 'No'."

Heckendorfer went to the door, said something into the next room, and came back, while Eddie, angry and ready for a fight, waited for the first round to begin. He didn't want to go to jail, but he wasn't going to take any crap from Heckendorfer.

Billy held Eddie by the shoulder. "My client just got out of the hospital this morning. Get us a hearing before a judge immediately, please."

"I'll find a judge. The sooner he's behind bars, the sooner he'll get that I'm not fuckin' around."

A quick laugh from Eddie, dry and mocking, was all it took. Heckendorfer snatched up the phone.

When he was told they had been added to Judge Bertrand Gordon's calendar for that afternoon, Billy shrugged. "Hmm, we'll see. Wasn't much of a lawyer, ain't much of a judge."

Eddie and Billy sat at the defense table in Gordon's courtroom. The press table filled up fast, reporters were even there from the weeklies, the Newark *Evening News* and *Star Ledger*, plus J. Paul Jackson, the *Press* Toms River bureau chief and courthouse reporter, and Bobbi Ann Nelson, who leaned over the gallery rail and told Eddie that word went around like lightning about his subpoena hearing. The reporters kept staring at Eddie's battered face, shaking their heads, and looked expectantly at the judge when he swept in from chambers.

"All rise."

Judge Gordon was large and jowly, his brown hair Brylcreem'd, with glittering blue eyes and a certain lift to his chin, his rosy cheeks aglow from two Scotch and waters before lunch at Citta's Old Time Tavern. The judge had a brisk, impatient style. Billy said Gordon liked to take charge and settle matters quick before they got too complicated. Eddie disliked him on sight, and from the judge's stare from the bench down at him, the feeling was mutual.

Judge Gordon gaveled the hearing open. Heckendorfer stood up at the prosecution table and told the judge Eddie was withholding evidence of multiple crimes. He asked the court to declare Eddie in contempt for defying the subpoena, and to put him in jail until he changed his mind.

"Mister Bonneville," Judge Gordon said, "is it true you have evidence pertinent to ongoing investigations by the prosecutor's office?"

"I don't know, Your Honor," Eddie said. "Since he won't tell me what he's investigating, I can't honestly answer that question."

"Is it *likely* your materials are pertinent to the prosecutor's work?"

"I guess we have to take his word for it, Your Honor." That brought laughter from the press table, and a rap of the gavel from the judge.

"Your Honor," Billy cut in. "This subpoena violates Mister Bonneville's First Amendment right to freedom of the press. The government just can't swoop down and confiscate a reporter's notes, whatever the reason. Under the New Jersey press shield law, Mr. Bonneville's subpoena and arrest are improper, and I move—"

"Your Honor, the defendant is concealing evidence of multiple felonies, and the shield law should not apply," Heckendorfer said.

"The suspect in those alleged felonies is dead, Your Honor. Why this investigation at all?"

"Others involved may not be dead," Heckendorfer said. "And as for the First Amendment, that's for a higher court to decide. Noncompliance with the subpoena is the issue in this hearing."

The reporters in the room stared holes into Heckendorfer but he ignored them.

"I'm not surrendering anything to anybody," Eddie declared, loud. "Look at what some goons did to me last night, and they didn't get my notes either. You think jail scares me?"

The judge gaveled him quiet.

Billy grabbed Eddie's shoulder. "Do you *want* to go to jail?" he said.

"No, but—"

"Shut up and let me handle this."

The judge was clearly uneasy with this case. "Mister Bonneville, you received the subpoena, and you refuse to comply with it, is that correct?"

"Yes, Your Honor."

"If the prosecution allowed you more time, perhaps to confer with counsel—"

"My answer would be the same."

"Your Honor, Mister Bonneville has the right, like every report-er—" Billy began.

Heckendorfer spoke right over him. "Your Honor, this court is not the place to argue broad Constitutional questions."

"Your Honor," Billy said, half laughing at the preposterous situa-tion. "The prosecutor is trying to force a reporter to work for him. I think *somebody* ought to mention the First Amendment."

The reporters at the press table growled their support and Judge Gordon cut them off with a hard, petulant crack of the gavel.

"Your Honor, I ask the court to incarcerate Mister Bonneville on the simple, straightforward issue of noncompliance," Heckendorfer said. "Tomorrow, if he still refuses to comply, I will ask the court for harsher sanctions."

Eddie knew the decision before it came from the judge's mouth:

"The issue before the court today is clear and uncomplicated. The defendant received a subpoena, he refuses to comply. Mister Bonneville, I remand you to the county jail until you do."

The reporters at the press table erupted in a loud disgusted *No!* A bailiff moved behind Eddie and cuffed his hands behind his back. Reporters jumped up yelling at the judge, "Oh come *on*, Bert, what are you doing?" and he glowered at them and banged his gavel for order, then gave up. Judge Gordon stood to exit the bench. The bailiff yelled, "All rise!" but it was hardly necessary.

Two corrections guards each took an arm, avoiding his bandaged elbows, and led him out of the courtroom and down the back hallway to the county jail. They let him limp at his own pace. Billy stood by and fumed as Eddie was stripped and thoroughly searched, photographed and fingerprinted, his shoelaces and belt and personal effects dropped into a brown paper bag. Eddie was courteous to the jail staff, and qui-etly endured the processing indignities without showing one second of his fury.

Being locked up, however, was harder than he expected. His con-crete cell was barely larger than a toilet stall and smelled like one. When the cell door clanged shut and was locked and the jail guards walked away, he reached out and grabbed the door of steel bars. Immovable steel, embedded in cement. That was hard to take. He sat on the cot that hung from the wall, in a shirt, belt-less trousers and shoes with no laces. He wanted to meditate. Instead, he lit a cigarette to escape from the stink. The closest other inmates were around the corner and down the corridor.

Occasionally he heard someone mumble or cough. Despite his bold outburst in court he began to wonder how long he really could sit here and do nothing. Before he had too much time to think, Heckendorfer and Billy entered the cell block muttering insults at each other.

"This'll make an impressive line on your next campaign brochure, Earl," Billy said. "Locking up a reporter."

"Obstruction of justice is a crime. Withholding evidence is a crime."

"What you're doing to this boy is a crime."

Eddie sat up on the cot. "Don't promise him a thing Billy! I'll stay in here as long as I have to." Brave words, since he was already getting anxious about rotting in a jail cell.

Heckendorfer shrugged at Eddie. "Well, that's up to you."

"The longer I'm locked up, the more you're hated by every reporter in town."

"Got their attention though, didn't I?" He laughed, waved a hand dismissively, and turned around to leave. "Enjoy the accommodations."

"Hey Earl?" Eddie said. "No hard feelings. Okay?"

"Wait 'til you sit in jail for awhile," his voice came back down the hall. "There will be." A prisoner in a nearby cell muffled a laugh.

"Just to prove there's no hard feelings, I'll take you to Kenny Rosenfeld."

Billy stared at him, like, what the hell he was up to?

Heckendorfer sauntered back. "Don't play games with me."

Eddie took out a Lucky Strike and lit it. It gave him one last moment to reassure himself it was time to trade Rosenfeld's remains for the advantage he needed.

"Esposito showed me Rosenfeld's grave," he said. "He said it was, anyway. And I got corroboration—"

"Esposito killed Rosenfeld?"

"No. That was Tony Notti, the guy who died with Esposito and his son. I interviewed Notti a couple hours before they all got killed." Billy's jaw dropped. "Notti told me Bobby Castellucci ordered him and Dee Dee, the older guy I left in the woods last night, to grab Rosenfeld and lean on him, scare him off the building moratorium. He says Rosenfeld got angry and mouthed off with them, there was a fight, and they wound up killing him. I have Notti saying all this on tape, but I don't know what it's worth legally, because he was being tortured by Esposito—"

Billy, stunned: "While you were *talking* to him?"

"Yeah." He couldn't bring himself to mention Notti's claim that Rosenfeld shook down Roy McTierney for a bribe.

Heckendorfer turned and called for the corrections guard with the key. He muttered to Billy: "This better be for real." The guard unlocked the cell, and went back to his post outside. Heckendorfer turned to Eddie. "Okay, let's go."

Billy held the door closed to Eddie's cell. "Not 'til we hear what you'll do for us."

"Wait a minute," Heckendorfer said. "You complained in court I was trying to force him to work for me. Now he's *offering* to."

"He's offering to be a good citizen," Billy said. "And a witness. But not for free."

"Okay. Take me to Rosenfeld's body, tell me what you know about his killing. Let me hear Notti on tape. I'll give you another week to produce your Esposito notes."

"Not even close." Billy shook his head. "Why don't you try working with us instead of being such a hard ass? This morning he gave you Roy McTierney. Now he's giving you Bobby Castellucci and a cast of scumbags, for *murder*."

"If you're telling the truth—"

"Don't you believe me?"

"—at best, it's political poison. Gee, thanks."

"Your political problem," Billy said, "is not our concern. For all he's done for you, a show of gratitude would be appreciated."

"Okay, I'll drop the subpoena."

Billy turned to Eddie. *Okay?*

He nodded, numbly, to a victory that seemed pretty small. His mind was on Twenty Two Twenty Mockingbird Lane.

Eddie was exhausted. Riding through Roman Estates at dusk, in the back seat of a county detective sedan with his attorney, he wished this night was over. When they parked across from the house on Mockingbird Lane, he stayed in the car. Heckendorfer and his detectives walked up the dirt lawn of the house.

"I better keep a close eye on these clowns," Billy said, getting out of the car. "Are you all right?"

"I'm okay." He sat in a corner of the back seat, watching.

An excavator and his helper arrived in a rack-sided truck, towing a backhoe on a flatbed, and set up work lights. They swung sledge hammers and broke away the concrete block base for the front steps. The excavator drove the backhoe into position and dug down a few feet into the sandy earth with the toothed bucket. Other people began arriving, photographers, reporters that he knew, and two local policemen in their cruisers. Where did these people come from, he wondered, and how had they heard?

The backhoe's bucket pulled back. The excavator and his helper used long-handled spades to dig the hole out wider. They ran a chain down into the hole and attached the ends of it to the teeth of the backhoe's bucket.

With a series of small jerks, a steel barrel, rusty red and blackened around the top rim, was lifted by the backhoe out of the ground. The news camera flashes kept strobing a frozen silent crowd, staring at the backhoe rolling in reverse down the driveway. The jointed arm swung around and lowered the barrel on the truck. The helper jumped up, freed the bucket, and chained the barrel tight into one corner of the truck bed.

Shuddering, Eddie watched all this from the back seat of the car, trying not to imagine the contents of the barrel. But for the grace of God and the killer in him, *his* charred remains might have been buried tonight somewhere in the Jersey earth.

Then the reporters discovered him and hustled over to the car. Reluctantly, he rolled down the window and flashbulbs went off in his face for a few seconds. The backhoe motor made a racket driving back up on the flatbed behind them and they all had to raise their voices.

"Eddie, how did you get out of jail?"

"We made a deal. They let me out so I could bring Heckendorfer here. I told him where the body was buried."

"The body?" "Who are they digging up?"

"Kenny Rosenfeld. Supposedly."

Nobody said anything. Then somebody asked, "How did you know?"

"Last Thursday, Matty Esposito brought me down here. He told me Kenny Rosenfeld was buried under those steps."

"Did he kill him?"

"He said no. He said he was being framed for the murder by who-ever buried the barrel in his development."

"Who's that?"

"He didn't say," he lied. *You never know where information is gonna lead*, as the prosecutor had once said. Information had nearly gotten Eddie killed last night, an experience, he noticed, that had cured him of his boyish desire to impress people with what he knew.

The backhoe motor shut down. It became very quiet. The excavator and his helper chained the backhoe down to the flatbed trailer.

"What happened to your face, man?" another reporter asked.

"I got beat up by people who want the same information the pros-ecutor wants."

"Who?" "What people?" "What's in these notes?" They were getting noisy.

"They didn't get it—and neither will *he*."

Heckendorfer heard him talking to the reporters and hurried over. "No, no, you don't talk to these guys until we're done." He called Billy and his driver over, and they all got back in the car and took off.

Up in Toms River, wisps of wood smoke from fireplaces hung in the air. From a gray impenetrable night sky, large feathery snowflakes drifted down. In the parking lot behind the courthouse, Heckendorfer released Eddie to his lawyer's supervision for one hour so they could go eat dinner.

They walked downhill to a restaurant on the riverbank. In the bar an elderly woman with carmine lipstick and a neck scarf played Rogers and Hart songs on the piano, ignored by the drinkers. A smiling young woman cradling menus in her arms brought them into the half empty dining room and seated them beside a window. The place smelled like boiled lobster and soft bread rolls. Billy ordered two iced vodkas, and nobody asked Eddie for I.D. Cold on the taste buds, warm down the middle of him, it was the most delicious drink Eddie ever tasted. He asked the waiter for a hamburger, suspending his diet for one meal, and settled in to wait for the food.

He stared out the window at the snow falling, slow and hypnotic through the dock lights, onto the canvas covered boats and the black water of the river. The restaurant was a little too warm, it was making him sleepy. He could have just returned to jail, gotten some sleep, and heard the M.E.'s report in the morning. But he needed to hear some-body confirm that Rosenfeld's remains were in that barrel. He needed to know he'd done at least one thing right in this whole mess. "I was totally not ready for any of this—"

"Nobody's ever ready for anything," Billy said. "Life just *hits* us, and we make the best of it. And in the end, it all comes out in the wash." Billy ordered two more drinks and when they came he raised his glass. "To Kenny."

"Kenny." Eddie drank half. "I was just starting to learn a lot from him," he said.

"Oh yeah? Like what?"

"Mainly, constructive ways to channel anger into political idealism and protest."

Billy looked dubious. "I thought you said Kenny got angry, got into a fight, and got killed?"

"Yeah. I can imagine Kenny getting pissed off at these gangsters with their fifth-grade educations, daring to boss him around."

"Would you consider *that* a constructive use of anger?"

Stung, he said, "Unfair question."

"You think so? Look where it led." Clearly feeling the vodka, Billy peered at Eddie. "Look, I liked Kenny. I'm not surprised you liked him, you're both angry guys. And I agree we need idealists and fighters for a better world, now more than ever. Government being the cruel joke that it is, there's always reasons for anger, and for marching and chanting and protesting against all the things that are wrong. But on one point I disagree with Kenny totally. Mixing anger with politics is a bad combination."

"But you have to put your energy where it will do the most good."

"*Exactly*. And channeling anger to drive idealism doesn't work. Look at the protests in Chicago before the '68 election."

Puzzled and little hurt, still taking it as a repudiation of Rosenfeld, Eddie said, "I think they did what had to be done."

"I think they helped elect Nixon."

"What? Are you kidding me?"

"Those protestors were *not* Southern blacks, facing police dogs and fire hoses. Those were *not* the Freedom Riders, sitting at lunch counters getting punched and spit on and not fighting back, or refusing to move to the back of the bus and getting hauled off to jail. Those people had *dignity*. People respected them because they would not lower themselves to respond to violence with violence. But in '68, the hormonal Left brought their anger and idealism to Chicago to confront the Democrats on the war. They had themselves a tantrum on TV, the police kicked their ass as the country looked on horrified, the Democratic Party split into factions and lost the socially conservative working class, and Nixon got elected with less than one percent of the popular vote. And after all that, the war goes on."

"How can you blame them for *that*?" Eddie was incredulous.

"Because that's what happened. And now they're making a circus out of the Chicago 7 trial. And for what? *Vanity*." Billy saw Eddie's confusion, and grew more determined to make his point. He swiveled in his chair and drew his wallet and pulled out a piece of paper which he unfolded. "Here's what I'm saying. President Kennedy, the month before he was killed, went to a ceremony at Amherst College honoring Robert Frost. He delivered an address on Poetry and Power." He sighed, a little wistfully. "It's hard to imagine a president even talking about such things, now, I guess. But there were these lines in his address: *The men who create power make an indispensable contribution to the nation's greatness. But the men who question power, especially when the questioning is disinterested, make a contribution just as indispensable, for it is they who determine whether we use power, or power uses us.*"

"Right now, don't you think power is using us?"

"It always *has*, but that's not my point. The important part is that word, *disinterested*."

"Disinterested? I don't get it."

"It's the opposite of angry and selfish. It's the opposite of being all wrapped up in your own *shit*."

"No, I don't see—"

Billy leaned back and let the waiter set their food in front of them. The aroma nearly caused Eddie to swoon he was so hungry, and he fell on the meal like a starving man. "Why question power?" Billy said. "Why protest? Is it all about you, getting the chance to yell and march and get your anger out? Or is it about changing what makes you angry in the first place? Politics is not Gestalt therapy. *Disinterested* means instead of wasting time and energy on public tantrums, you apply it efficiently within the system to change what's wrong. You do what's effective, not what feels good, because in the final analysis it always comes down to who gets the most votes."

"So protest marches are a waste of time."

"Marches are great for meeting people and getting laid."

That made Eddie laugh. "I must've missed that pamphlet."

"Sometimes you have to march. But don't forget the cops are as angry as you are, and they have clubs and tear gas. And don't confuse one hour of marching with the months and years of hard political work within the system it takes to actually get something done. Our job as citizens is still to question power, and to keep reminding the government that they work for us, not themselves, especially now, when soldiers are dying on the battlefield."

"The battlefield. Yeah. Well, they may try and get me there yet."

"How did you do yesterday with the Army shrink?" Billy asked. Of course, that wasn't the real question.

"I told the truth." The meeting seemed like it was a year ago, now.

"And you came back 1-A."

"USDA Prime."

"We're still appealing your C.O. rejection. Maybe your lottery number won't get called. The law is, if you're not called this year, you're free."

"It's out of my hands now. But I didn't lie."

"Good. If you get called up, we'll figure out the next step."

Sitting through dinner had stiffened his body and limping up the street through the center of Toms River back to the courthouse was hard at first. Still, the vodka and food glowed in his stomach and he was quietly detached even from his own condition. Snowflakes out of the black sky were dropping heavier now through the spotlights shining up on Old Glory, coating the wreaths to the war dead at the base of the flagpole.

They took coffee from the urn in the prosecutor's office anteroom. Billy read the Asbury Park *Evening Press* and Eddie stared at the blank wall, calming himself by counting his breaths and praying silently to God and to all the divine and creative powers of the universe that, whatever was in that barrel, the soul of Kenny Rosenfeld was at peace, somewhere.

Heckendorfer's secretary, surly about working night hours, fielded phone calls. At ten o'clock she transferred a call from the Medical Examiner to the prosecutor. A few minutes later, he came out of his office. He padded heavily to a chair in the anteroom and slumped into it. "They opened it."

Eddie didn't need to hear more, it was on Heckendorfer's face.

"They have to check dental records and so on, but chances are, it's him."

"This'll be in the papers tomorrow, somebody should call his wife." Eddie said. He gave Sophia Rosenfeld's phone number from memory to Heckendorfer. He wished he could make the call and tell her in person.

"We've got the two men you left in the woods. Some locals down there handed them over to the State Troopers. We'll want you to I.D. them."

"When they had me in the car, I overheard the older one admit to Kenny's murder."

"That's Denardo, the one whose foot you cut off?"

"Yeah," Eddie said.

"Unbelievable," Heckendorfer said. He pushed himself to his feet. "Well, I'm done. I'd let you go home, but if I do the judge'll have my head on a platter."

"What time do we go before the judge tomorrow?" Billy said.

Heckendorfer asked his secretary for his calendar and examined it. "I've got a bail hearing on a drug case at ten o'clock in front of Judge Gordon. You're after that."

"Is there a typewriter around here I can borrow for a few minutes?" Eddie asked.

They let him sit at a secretary's desk in one of the outer offices. Billy sat back and finished reading the newspaper. Eddie rolled paper into the typewriter, using the back of a sheet of prosecutor's office stationery. He thought for a moment about how to write it. Was there any chance somebody other than Rosenfeld could be in the barrel? The killer himself had told him what happened. Pretty reliable eyewitness source. Nobody else had the knowledge he had, or could write it the same way, so the story, for tonight at least, was his.

TOMS RIVER — The body of development moratorium
proponent Kenneth S. Rosenfeld, 36, was recovered
yesterday from a building site in Lacey Township, and
police have taken one of his alleged killers into
custody.
County detectives pulled a steel barrel containing
charred human remains from beneath the front steps
of a home under construction in Roman Estates, a new

subdivision, yesterday evening. Dental record tests were pending last night, but officials had other reasons to believe the remains, which were burned beyond recognition, were Rosenfeld's.

They have officially labeled the case a homicide.

The development was partly owned by the late Matthew Esposito of Lakewood, who was found dead last Thursday, along with his son Tommaso and an associate named Anthony Notti, in the burning ruins of his Madison Avenue hotel, the Sunset Lodge.

Police were led to the burial site by this Independent reporter, who had been told by Esposito where Rosenfeld's body was buried.

At that time, Esposito said he learned where Rosenfeld's remains were buried by torturing Notti for the information, and he introduced Notti to this reporter as one of Rosenfeld's killers. Notti later confirmed that information to this reporter, though under duress from Esposito, who prosecutor Earl Heckendorfer last month labeled "The Rackets Boss of the Jersey Shore."

This reporter also gave the county detectives information that led to the capture of a man believed to be Notti's accomplice in the murder. Charges are pending a positive identification.

Heckendorfer said there would be no further statements while Rosenfeld's killing was being investigated.

Esposito was indicted on Dec. 23 for racketeering activities.

Incorporated one year ago, Rosenfeld's organization, Building Moratorium Now, had been rapidly gaining in membership and support in Ocean County's fast-growing townships, where the expense of building schools and providing services to newly-arrived residents and their children has burdened taxpayers to the breaking point.

Rosenfeld's call for suspending issuance of building permits for residential construction was widely denounced by business leaders as a path to economic catastrophe.

"I can't think of a quicker way to throw this area into a depression," said Roy McTierney, the county's largest home builder, in a recent interview.

He gave the copy to Billy. "Before you go home can you drop this off at The *Independent?*" Billy folded the pages and stuck them in his pocket, and they shook hands and Eddie thanked him. When Billy left, he went back inside and told Heckendorfer's secretary he was ready to return to his cell. A corrections guard came over from the jail and walked him back downstairs, this time without handcuffs. Locked up again, he was so happy to see a bed that he laid down without caring where he was or how bad it smelled and fell fast asleep.

When they brought him up from jail to the courtroom the next morning, he was looking forward to a quick dismissal of the subpoena and a late breakfast once he was free. He entered from a side door to an astounding sight: the courtroom was full. Behind him in the gallery was an overflow crowd of reporters, flashbulbs popped in his face, and when his vision cleared he saw two crews with lights and TV cameras being pushed out by the court officers.

Heckendorfer looked pensively out over the jammed courtroom and shook his head. Judge Gordon was visibly unhappy to see Eddie again.

"Mister Bonneville, I take it you still refuse to comply with the subpoena?" he said.

He and Billy both turned to Heckendorfer, who sat silently.

"Yes, Your Honor."

Heckendorfer stood and spoke briskly. "Your Honor, I ask the court to keep Mister Bonneville in jail until he complies."

Billy looked like he'd been slapped in the face. Eddie recoiled. "What?" he whispered to Billy. "I thought we had a deal!"

"That's history now," Billy stared at Heckendorfer and said under his breath, "He's obviously been spoken to." Billy was so angry he was turning colors. Heckendorfer stood calmly waiting for the judge to rule.

"Your Honor," Billy said, "under New Jersey's press shield law this subpoena was illegitimate before it was even served, and I ask the court to cancel it immediately. Unless the prosecution is willing to voluntarily withdraw it," he added. Heckendorfer ignored him.

"That may be, counsel," Judge Gordon said, "but until the court can acquaint itself with the exact status of the case law, especially with respect to a reporter who may have knowledge of illegality, I'm reluctant to rule on that right now."

Realizing he was going back to jail because the judge hadn't bothered to do his homework, Eddie stood. "Your Honor, in my defense—"

Judge Gordon pointed his gavel at Eddie. "I'm not the Supreme Court, son, I'm not listening to a lot of legalistic gibberish—"

"May I have a moment to speak with my attorney?"

The judge nodded and sat back.

Eddie leaned over to Billy. "We need the tapes."

"They're in my office safe."

"We need them here."

"What for?"

"They prove that I was working, so the First Amendment applies and so does the Shield Law."

"We don't need to prove that," Billy said. "Nobody's saying you're not a reporter."

"Enter them into evidence anyway. Or file them with the clerk or something."

"If I do, it's as good as handing them to the prosecution."

"But not under subpoena," Eddie said. "Isn't that the point, legally?"

"Well, yes. But once they're part of the court record, the other reporters—" He got the point, further words were unnecessary.

"Get them privileged."

"You know what you're asking me to do?"

"Yeah," Eddie sighed. "Yeah, I know."

Billy asked for a ten-minute break so some materials could be brought over from his office. Heckendorfer objected, and Billy said, "Pursuant to a discussion with the prosecutor last night, I had no expectation we would need these materials for this hearing, Your Honor. But it's clear now that we do."

Grudgingly, the judge granted the break. Billy called his office from the payphone in the corridor and told his secretary to bring the envelope from the safe to the hearing. She made it from around the corner on Sheriff Street just as Judge Gordon had started glancing impatiently at his watch.

When the hearing reconvened, Billy said: "Your Honor, we ask that these tape recordings be admitted into evidence as proof that Mister Bonneville was a working reporter when they were recorded, and therefore, is protected by the state shield law and First Amendment from complying with the subpoena."

"This again," the judge said through gritted teeth.

Heckendorfer looked puzzled, and wary. "Your Honor. They want to enter the tapes as evidence to protect the tapes from *me*?"

"No, from your subpoena."

"I assume these tapes are covered under the subpoena?" Judge Gordon said.

"They are, Your Honor," Billy said.

"Wait a minute," Heckendorfer said. "Your Honor, this still doesn't comply with the subpoena. He's still withholding his notes. He's still refusing to testify before a grand jury."

"That's true," Billy said. "Your Honor, on First Amendment grounds, we will not surrender the tapes to a subpoena, or his notes, or agree to a grand jury appearance. But to make our argument against compliance, we have no choice but to enter these recordings into evidence. The interview subject, Matthew Esposito, is dead, so all we have are these tapes to prove that Mister Bonneville was a working journalist when he did the interview, and therefore protected by the law from the prosecutor's subpoena."

"We all know he's a reporter! And if they're evidence, I get to listen to them anyway!" Heckendorfer said, looking agape at the judge, who seemed totally confused.

"That's true," Billy said. "Under the rules, the prosecution is entitled to review the evidence. So this compromise accomplishes the most important part of the purpose of the subpoena, but it also preserves Mister Bonneville's First Amendment rights. Everybody wins."

Judge Gordon looked relieved and impatient with Heckendorfer. "Isn't that effectively the same thing, Mister Heckendorfer?" the judge said. "Do you care by what method you get to listen to Mister Bonneville's famous tapes?"

"It's not as simple as it looks, Your Honor!" Heckendorfer snapped, losing it. Judge Gordon's face fell. He clearly thought Heckendorfer was calling *him* simple.

"Your Honor may still decide to send Mister Bonneville back to jail for resisting the subpoena," Billy said. "But we do have the right to submit evidence to support our position."

"Judge, they're trying to build a case for an appeal of your decision—"

Judge Gordon looked puzzled, and impatient to the point of pain. Then his jaw stuck out and his gavel cracked. "He can have his evidence. Mark them Exhibits A and B."

"No! Wait a minute, Judge, please!"

The judge gaveled him into silence. "I'm not afraid of anyone appealing anything I've done in my eighteen years on the bench. Enter the tapes, it doesn't change a thing here." Heckendorfer dropped, stunned, into his chair. "The subpoena is the issue. Mister Bonneville is still defiant, merely entering the tapes into evidence doesn't fully satisfy the subpoena. He is to remain in custody until he complies." Judge Gordon gaveled the hearing closed.

Eddie was handcuffed again. He saw a brief, mean look pass between Billy and the prosecutor. Eddie found a court officer on either side of him. Watching the bailiff bagging the two cassette tapes, Exhibit A and B, he was not sure he'd made the right move—the tapes might still become "lost"—but it was too late to turn back.

Judge Gordon stepped from the bench into a crowd of reporters.

"Your Honor, how soon will the tapes be available to the press?" one of them asked.

Judge Gordon scowled at the question. "Who said they ever will be?"

He heard Jackson's syrupy voice, warm and relaxed. "Your Honor, since the tapes are part of the evidentiary record, and they're privileged, the law allows the press to hear them."

"That doesn't mean you will," Judge Gordon snapped.

"And to write about them, if I'm not mistaken." A chorus of *That's right, You said it* from the reporters.

"Shall we have our lawyers call you?" one of the reporters said.

Judge Gordon's look shifted off the press pack over to Heckendorfer's killer gaze. He sighed and turned abruptly.

"The Bailiff will announce a time to play the tapes in my conference room—*once*."

The judge fled for his chambers. As they led Eddie back downstairs, he laughed at Heckendorfer's despair as he watched the reporters rush out to the pay phones in the corridor—and to get their own tape recorders.

He lay on the cot in his cell and closed his eyes. Down the corridor in another cell a drunk kept singing tunelessly, *I'm in the jailhouse, now.* He had no idea what would happen going forward, and there were only two possibilities. He would have to find the nerve and the patience to endure jail. He might be here for days, or weeks. Meanwhile, maybe hearing the Esposito tapes would provoke the other reporters to investigate, and maybe their coverage would vindicate his passion for this story, if not his clumsy reporting. He cringed, imagining the reporters around the judge's conference table listening to him interview the old gangster. Would they shake their heads and laugh at how young and clueless he sounded? And what would appear in their newspapers? Eddie 'Time Bomb' Bonneville would be in the middle of another embarrassing incident, except this time *he* got the crap beat out of him, first by gangsters, then by the court.

All night, wide awake and lucid and his mind agitated, he kept pulling himself back from the edge of panic. He assumed the lotus position on the concrete floor and began to meditate. Sitting with this anxiety was torture, but he kept at it and after a long time it eventually passed. There wasn't anything else he could do. Through his mind passed dead gangsters, the awareness of how parts of his body hurt, the vision of his good friend's remains aflame in a barrel, crushing self-pity, and shame that he wasn't as good a reporter as he thought, as well as intermittent rushes of whirling, nauseating vertigo.

Through it all, he sat calmly and counted his breaths.

Time moved slowly, as if it too had been beat up and had to drag itself forward. He wondered if he could request a visit from a doctor to check on his condition as a way of breaking the monotony. Would they allow him to read and write? He wondered when he would see Ivy again, and what she would do when she heard he was in jail indefinitely. She was in a hurry to leave town, for reasons she didn't care to explain. When she got her money from her parents, would she leave town without him if he was still locked up?

Gray daylight appeared in a glass square high on the wall above his head. The cinder block grid of the narrow cell slowly emerged from the dark.

Thursday morning, Ivy awoke to her mother—a tennis and golf matron named Peggy with a deeply tanned face—gently shaking her shoulder. "Darling?"

"Ma? Excuse me—mother?"

"There's a phone call for you."

"What time is it?"

"A little after seven. It's your friend David again." Her mother, silly woman, sounded exceptionally sunny. David must've turned on the charm with her.

"Oh. Okay."

Since they last spoke over a week ago he'd called twice but she'd been out. She was sure he'd found that annoying. Too bad he wouldn't let her call him at the townhouse. He never says when he'll call again, and she sure as hell wasn't about to sit at home waiting.

Ivy picked up the phone at her bedside.

"Hello?" she said with a huge yawn.

"It's me."

"Mother," Ivy yelled downstairs, "you can hang up now."

She heard a click on the line. "I'm off, dear," she called back. "Have a nice day."

"Good morning, Prom Queen. Hope I didn't wake you." His voice dripped sarcasm; what right did she have to sleep?

"Too late for that."

"Oh, too bad. I got a rude awakening myself yesterday. I went over to NYU to see exactly when you're supposed to be back. Told them I was your brother. They told me you withdrew. Took a leave of absence, or some shit."

"I told you I was going to do that," she quickly improvised, hoping he'd think he'd forgotten. *He called NYU. He checked on me.*

"Bullshit."

"David—"

"Bullshit. You got commitments up here. Just in case you're getting other ideas."

"I'll be back exactly when I said I will."

"How come you're never home when I call?"

"If you tell me when you're gonna call, I'll be here."

"I never know when I'll get the chance."

"Well, that makes communication difficult, doesn't it?"

"You never told me you were leaving school."

"David, I know you have a lot on your mind," she said. "It's not important whether you forgot I told you. The important thing is with school out of the way we can get down to some serious trouble making." Silence. "That's what we want, isn't it?"

"I don't know what you want, Ivy." She hated that sighing, disappointed way he talked to her sometimes. "You say you want a revolution, but only if your parents foot the bill. You say you're coming back to New York" —back to *me*— "but I'm beginning to think that's bullshit."

"School isn't my focus any longer," she said. "*You* are. You and our work together."

"The others are hassling me to do something about you."

"Do something like what?"

"Like come down there and drag you back to the city."

"What's their problem? They don't trust me?"

"They never trusted you. They trust *me*. I vouched for you, and now this shit's causing them to wonder whether I know what the fuck I'm doing. Plus you know too much, about our plans, about the house and what's in it, you know?"

"Just tell them I can be trusted. Can't you do that?"

"It's past that point. This shit's undermining my position. And I'm not sure *I* believe you any more."

Now's the time, she thought. Break up with him and get on with your life. But she needed money first. "That hurts, David. I can't believe you're saying that."

"You know the situation I'm in. That we're *all* in up here."

"What can I do to convince you?"

"Get back here."

"I will, as soon as I have the *money*. Look, I miss you just as much as you miss me."

"Oh wow. Hearing that makes me feel so much better."

"I'll be back soon. Another week at the most."

"Can't you forge the fuckin' check? You're never gonna see them again anyway."

"Patience, baby. The day I score, I'm on the train."

He hung up.

She struggled out of the blankets tangled around her. She couldn't free herself quick enough, and kicked them off and let them fall them on the floor. She got off the bed and looked around for her clothes. Her heart was pounding like she'd just run the hundred yard dash. She stood still for a moment, catching her breath, then forced herself to sit down and face the fact that while she was stuck here the situation in New York was getting out of control. Before she got the money, what if they came down here to get her? Or he did?

How she wished she could go to her parents, even if it took telling them of her trouble with David and his revolutionary comrades, and ask them to help her transfer to another school far away. What if, for once, they did their best for her? For once, no long disappointed faces, no heavy exasperated sighs, no reminders that she'd agreed to be good, no hysterical invocations of past broken promises, no more vows never to suffer this, or that, from her again. What if, for once, they loved her without criticism and gave her what she needed. If, for once, her father gave generously and wanted nothing in return. Believe that, she told herself, and you may as well go back to believing in Santa Claus and the friggin' Tooth Fairy.

Downstairs, the morning papers, the *Observer* and the *Independent*, were on the breakfast table, no doubt left by her mother so Ivy could read all about the latest mess Eddie had gotten himself into. When she found out that he was in jail, and why, and saw the photos of his battered face as he left the courtroom in handcuffs, she folded the paper with a sigh and tossed it aside and decided to get high before breakfast.

Friday morning Billy brought him coffee, a ham and egg sandwich, and the newspapers, then went to talk to the prosecutor. Weak and slightly addled with sleeplessness, Eddie sat on his cot and ate breakfast and read about himself. The follow-up stories about Rosenfeld's murder had been pushed to the inside pages by reports about his imprisonment. The *Observer* ran a picture of his battered face between pictures of Bobby Castellucci and Matty Esposito. He was uneasy reading about himself, the heroic reporter digging for the truth who got beat up by gangsters and jailed for defying the state. His fellow reporters still had no idea what a fiasco he'd made out of investigating this story.

"Let's go. You're out of here."

Billy stood outside the bars with a corrections guard, who unlocked the cell and left them alone.

"I'm free?" Unslept, confused, he thought he was somehow being rewarded for being painfully honest with himself.

"Heckendorfer will drop the subpoena. We went to chambers to ask Judge Gordon to vacate the order to remand."

"Why?"

"He has to. You're protected by the shield law. Believe it or not, Judge Gordon never even knew there was such a law. I'm sorry the technicalities took so long."

"You're sure I can go?"

"He has no legal grounds to hold you. He just doesn't like you. He wanted to see what he could scare out of you. Now, he owes you. You gave him Rosenfeld's body and identified his killers. He can't convict Denardo without your testimony. He's listened to the tapes, and he knows there's not much more he can get from you."

"He still hates me, I'm sure."

"He hates knowing you just made his career." Chuckling, Billy collected the newspapers off the cot. "The information on those tapes will give him ammunition for investigations he can ride right to reelection. At the same time, he can cut deals all over the Organization. Certain people will owe him for not investigating."

"I made that possible, and the prick still put me in jail for two days?"

Billy laughed merrily. "Is that a real question? People have been in jail for *years* for crimes they didn't commit. Throw a reporter in jail a few days, scare him into giving up his notes? No big deal."

As he was leaving jail, he called Ivy from a pay phone near the exit. There was no answer. He was too restless to go home and wait until she called. He drove down to the newsroom, empty because there was no Saturday paper. Only the advertising department was at work. He called Ivy again but there was still no answer. He sat at his desk and organized the notes he'd made from the Esposito interview. Even without the tapes he still had enough information to pursue the story—the right way this time, as soon as he was able.

Finally, fed up with jail, journalism, politics, gangsters, and feeling as beat up inside as he was outside, he went home. As he sat overlooking the ocean, longing for a moment's peace of mind, his conscience began to nag at him, reviving a debate he'd been having with himself for two weeks since he'd seen Rolly in the hospital. He was overdue for a second visit. Well, he decided, he'd avoided the discomfort of seeing Rolly long enough.

He drove over to Point Pleasant Beach, parked the car in the A&P lot on Arnold Avenue across from the Elks Lodge and used the payphone outside the store. He had no coins, so he pulled out a safety pin kept inside his jacket pocket for this purpose and poked it through the plastic cord of the handset. He touched the point of the pin to the coin return slot and after one or two clicks, he got a dial tone.

One of Rolly's sisters answered, he could never keep their names straight. She got Rolly on the phone.

"Hey-y-y-y," Rolly said. "I thought you left town or something, man, where you been?"

Eddie laughed. "Don't you read the newspapers?"

"Never. It's all bad news to me."

"Work has been pretty rough the past couple weeks," Eddie said. "I'm sorry. I just never know when it's okay to call."

"What do you mean?"

"I don't want to run into your father. He doesn't like me very much."

"Hey man." Rolly and his voice hit the roof. "It is *always* okay to call, you hear me? You call here any fuckin' time you please and don't let anybody keep you from talking to me, you understand?" It was as if he was yelling at someone in the room next to him. "I live in this house too, and I will not let anybody else keep me from doing what I wanna do." He sounded like he was continuing an argument he'd just had with somebody.

"Okay, okay," Eddie said. "I was wondering if now would be a good time to come over."

"Fuck yeah," he said. "You know the way."

On a street lined with tall oak and maple trees, the Rollins house was a large Dutch Colonial on the Manasquan River bank, with a big shady back yard that sloped down to a private beach and dock where a Boston Whaler and a cabin cruiser were moored. On his way to the front door, he found that Rolly's father had built a wheelchair ramp alongside the front steps, well-made out of two-by-fours and painted to blend in with the front porch railing. He wondered about Rolly and his father, whether this ramp was a bridge of another kind between them.

One of the sisters answered the doorbell and let him in. Rolly was in a wheelchair on the glassed-in rear patio overlooking the river, in a red and white Point Beach high school sweatshirt and red sweatpants. He lit a cigarette and focused all his attention on smoking it. He inhaled and exhaled with fierce intent and the room was hazy with smoke.

"I never knew you smoked," Eddie said.

"Something else I brought back from the war," Rolly said. In two weeks he had changed. He'd gained weight, and his manner of speaking now was clipped, intense, like he'd made up his mind about something. "I don't really like it, but it gives me something to do. I can't just sit around all day."

"Can you get out of here, take a ride?" He figured he could push the wheelchair up the street ramp onto the boardwalk, and they could hang out and watch the ocean for awhile.

"Not yet," he said. "Everything's *not yet*." Rolly finally noticed his battered condition. "Hey." He laughed his loony laugh. "What the hell happened to you?"

"I told you work's been rough lately. Monday night I got kidnapped, beat up and almost murdered. Then I spent the last two nights in jail for defying a subpoena."

Rolly tapped his cigarette in the ashtray more than necessary. "Are you okay?"

"I'll live," he said.

"Agh. Betcha been beaten worse in the ring," Rolly said.

"Only by you, my friend," he said, without thinking. Then, inwardly, he winced.

"Yeah, well," Rolly said. "We all know who won *that* fight."

They hadn't talked about the fight in two years. Eddie had hoped they would never talk about it. But now, like it or not, he'd blundered onto the subject. There it was, between them, inescapable.

"Nobody won, man," he said. "We both lost." He tried to steer the conversation in another direction. "But we got a pretty good friendship out of it anyway, right?"

"Yeah, I guess." Rolly stared out the window, not really here. For a moment Eddie thought Rolly didn't want to talk. "It really sucks, being forced to sit here all day. The worst part isn't being cooped up, or needing help with everything. It's thinking, sitting here all day stuck in my own mind."

"There's a meditation I'm gonna teach you," Eddie said, relieved they were no longer talking about the past, and eager to be helpful. "You sit quietly and focus on your breathing and just let the thoughts pass through your mind without grasping or getting stuck on any of them—"

Rolly seized the ashtray and with a sneer he flung it at the windows at the other end of the room. The ashtray shattered two jalousie window panes and glass and ashes and cigarette butts fell all over the terra cotta floor.

"Edsel," he said, grimly, "I doubt meditation will be enough." His sister came in, saw the broken glass and her brother's fury, stiffened, and retreated back into the house.

Quietly looking at him, Rolly began to cry. "What happened to me, man?" he said, in a small, quavering voice. "I'm not even twenty years old yet. How can I spend the rest of my life like this? I wish I'd died over there. This isn't the life I was supposed to have. What the hell happened?"

Eddie was so twisted up inside he was afraid to say anything at all. But his friend was looking at him, waiting for an answer, with big pleading eyes.

"*I* happened," Eddie said, "and I wish we'd never gotten into the ring that night."

Rolly made a face. "What're you talking about?"

"I know you didn't foul me on purpose. But I lost control, man. I hurt you bad."

"So?"

"So then your personality kind of collapsed. You started getting into all kinds of trouble. You got pushed into the Marines, that led to Vietnam, and that led you to here, now."

"And you think, what? You're to blame for that?"

"Of course," Eddie said, before he could stop himself. "Don't you?"

The idea annoyed Rolly. "Hey man, this is my life. Okay? It ain't yours to influence, or affect, or whatever you wanna call it. You ain't God. I'm not even sure *God* is really God, anymore. This is my life, and you're not to blame for it, okay?"

"If you say so," Eddie said.

"At least leave me *that*."

"Okay."

"You can't even manage your own life without getting your ass kicked," Rolly said. "You're not responsible for mine, okay?"

"Okay," Eddie said. But this would never get better, no matter what Rolly said.

Rolly's sister came in with a dustpan and broom and, ignoring them, began to sweep up the broken glass.

By the time he got home it was dusk, windy and cold under gray and purple clouds. He was surprised to find Ivy's white Corvair parked on the street. Slowly climbing the stairs, shivering in the wind, he saw the lights were on in his apartment. Through the window he saw Ivy standing at the stove cooking. He opened the door and limped in out of the cold and into the warm garlic and oregano aroma of ratatouille. There was a bottle of wine open and two places set at the table. Ivy put down the spoon, walked over to him and, mindful of his injuries, wrapped him in her arms.

THIRTEEN *Love is just a four letter word*

She didn't want to pressure him, but time was running out. During dinner, she watched him carefully, waiting for her moment. Afterward, she washed the dishes and he sat at the table staring out the window.

"So champ," she said, drying her hands on a towel. "How's that big story of yours going?"

"It's not mine anymore. Other reporters have heard the tapes. We'll see if anybody has the guts to pursue it."

"So you're done with it?"

Avoiding her eye, he said, "Uh, not yet."

"You're going to keep working on it?"

"I have to try." He lit a Lucky and blew out a long sigh of smoke. "After all I've put into it—" he waved a hand at his battered face—"I can't just let it go. Sorry if that bums you out. I know you want to get out of here."

"Never known you to walk away from a fight."

He seemed slightly ashamed at that suggestion. "Yeah, I guess."

"Don't worry about me. You have healing to do."

They stayed in Friday night, listened to music on WNEW-FM, played Beethoven records from Billy's collection downstairs and Bob Dylan's country and western record, *Nashville Skyline*. She let him nod off when he needed to. She helped him into bed, and he fell asleep without a word. Ivy curled up like a cat beside him, reading *The Group*, nibbling on pretzels and sipping tea.

Saturday morning she woke up alone. He was at his desk, smoking and writing. Billy knocked at the door, amused when Ivy peeked up over the blankets, and invited them to breakfast.

"How're you feeling?" he asked Eddie, once they were downstairs buttering toast and mixing nuts and raisins into their oatmeal and brewing coffee.

"Not too bad."

"When do you see a doctor again?"

"Monday, over at Community Memorial."

"Can you drive?"

"I'll take him," Ivy said. "Okay?" Eddie reached under the table and gripped her thigh.

After breakfast she and Eddie sat upstairs on the third-floor porch on a bench in a corner of one of the dormers, out of the wind and warm in the sunshine, talking idly, gazing out over the ocean. Eddie fell asleep again for awhile, sitting back in her arms. While he rested contentedly, she daydreamed, her fingers stroking his hair, biding her time.

They strolled on the beach in the late afternoon, but she held back again because he said he was tired. They went upstairs, and he gritted his teeth while she peeled off his bandages. She got a close look for the first time at the damage the beating by the gangsters had done to his body. It was worse than any fight he'd ever been in, and it nearly broke her heart. He took a hot bath followed by a cold shower.

While he was bathing, she called her parents and told them where she was, which didn't make them happy. Her father asked when she'd need her allowance, and she said she was expected back at college in a few days, so he said he'd write her a check, probably relieved she'd be getting away from Eddie and back to her studies.

He got out of his bath. She dressed the cuts on his face, knees and elbows with peroxide and gauze and tape. Bathed and clean and wearing fresh clothes, his spirits seemed to lift, so she decided the time was right.

"I'm getting almost a thousand bucks," Ivy said. "I'm getting the check on Wednesday."

He just nodded, buttoning his shirt.

"We could live on that money for awhile. Plus, you must have savings."

He looked wary. "Money I'm saving for college. Why?"

"Champ—" she cradled his face gently in her hands—"let's get the hell out of here."

"Couldn't we just live here?"

"I can't," she said. "I just… I've got to go."

He gave her a look she couldn't read. He shuffled over to the kitchen table and lowered himself carefully onto one of the chairs. She reached for his cigarettes. "Can I have one too?"

She lit two and handed him one. He slouched back and smoked, seemingly lost in thought, and didn't answer. She didn't like pressing him, but time was growing short. She almost postponed the conversation again, but then he said, "So, where would we go?"

"Anywhere but *here*." She stopped herself before she started mocking New Jersey again. It would only arouse his resistance. Instead, she tried to get him excited about the pleasures of the journey. "Y'know, out there just *moving*. Not *to* anywhere, exactly. Open to any place, any trip whatsoever. Just out on the road, diggin' America, man. *Free*."

"We can't live like that forever. I have to make a living. Also, you better realize, no matter where we go, because of the Draft, I have no way of knowing my future."

"All the more reason to see the world while you still can."

"We still need some *destination*, more than just a place to stop and change clothes. I've always wanted to see New Orleans. When's Mardi Gras?"

"It's soon, I think, like, next week. Wow, that's a great idea! Great music, great food, lots of street life, all kinds of interesting people."

"And after that, maybe the desert. I've always wanted to see Palm Springs."

"Palm Springs? What's out there? Old movie stars turning to beef jerky in the sun? Bob Hope? *Sinatra?*"

"Careful with that."

"Okay, okay. But see, that's the beauty of this trip, it's like, total freedom. To go anywhere, to not settle down in one place or another. Until, y'know, we're ready to." Did he hear what she was saying, would he be willing to go that far?

"Whatever the doctor says."

"Of course. Let's not do anything you're not ready for." A glimmer of hope, she thought, small, but bright. At least he didn't turn her down.

Dinner was exotic by their standards. She went out and got burritos from a new Mexican food place on Route 88 in Brick Township and a bottle of Burgundy she shoplifted from the liquor store attached to the Shop Rite. After dinner he fell asleep okay but the alcohol and spicy food in his stomach fired up his imagination and he was jolted awake by a nightmare, curled up defensively, sweating and sobbing but without tears. He'd been dreaming, he said, of being beaten up all over again. She held him in her arms until he stopped shaking. Healing the damage to his body would only be the beginning.

She went downstairs in the morning and picked up the Sunday *New York Times* off the porch. She made coffee and they read the paper lying in bed. After he decided he'd better try to move around they drove over to Point Pleasant for breakfast. The O-B Diner was crowded with people just out of early church services. Their heads turned at the sight of a limping, bandaged Eddie, his face still in the morning's newspapers. Ivy guided him to a booth in the back where they could ignore people's stares.

He wanted to see a movie, so she took him to a Sunday matinee of *Butch Cassidy and The Sundance Kid* at the Brick Plaza Cinema. On the way home he couldn't stop marveling over the ending: ambushed by the police in a Bolivian village, Butch and Sundance are trapped in a filthy little adobe room. They're bleeding and dying, hurting so bad they can barely reload their pistols, they know they're living the last moments of their lives, and what do they do? They argue about where to go next, as if they *had* a next, bucking up each other's courage, ignoring a little nuisance called certain death waiting outside in the dusty plaza.

At his apartment he laid back on the bed "just for a minute," and fell deep asleep. As late afternoon turned to evening, Ivy got restless reading and listening to him snore. She took a sunset walk on the beach, then left Eddie a note on the kitchen table.

She drove to her parents' house and smiled and gritted her teeth through Sunday dinner. When she was finished eating, they fought with her about going back to Eddie's. "He needs my help," she said. "He can't even dress himself he's so beat up." Her father shook his head and retreated to his Morris chair by the fireplace and her mother busied herself pouring two glasses of brandy at the bar in the dining room. Ivy went up to her room and pocketed her bag of marijuana and pack of rolling papers and was pulling on her jacket when the phone rang. Her mother called up the stairs, saying it was for her.

She expected Eddie, who probably woke up upset to find that she was gone. She waited until she heard the downstairs phone hang up.

"Hello?"

No greeting, just David bossing her around, and pissing her off.

"You're out of time. Get back here before it's too late."

He refused to accept that there was nothing she could do to get back to New York any faster. Even if she *was* going back to him, she would still be stuck here waiting for her allowance check. She wished she could put it to him, just like that.

"I've got good news," Ivy said. "I just talked to my father. That little friend I've been waiting for will be here on Thursday, so I'll be back Thursday night." Her father had actually agreed to give her the check on Wednesday; by Thursday she would be long gone.

"*Thursday*?" he groaned. It was strange, but she still didn't like lying to David.

"It's gonna take few more days. Something about my father transferring funds or something."

"That's not gonna satisfy the others," he said. "We had a meeting. The vote was unanimous. They're telling me I gotta do something about you."

"I hate that I have to do this, but I can't—"

"We got shit to do, y'know," he said, all high and mighty. "We can't wait on your social schedule, or your fuckin' father transferring funds—"

She wondered if he was calling from the town house and they were all sitting around watching him.

"I'm really sorry I'm causing people to worry," she said.

"Y'know, I don't understand why you turned so negative about our whole trip here, I mean the group—"

"David," she said, "listen to yourself." She didn't have to say, *whining*.

"Hey Prom Queen," he said. "Do you realize while you're down in your Daddy's fuckin' mansion—"

"Oh please!" She said, unable to listen to more, "Isn't that what turns you on about me? Isn't that what all this 'Prom Queen' shit is about? Admit it! I'm nothing but a sexual object to you! I'm a fuckin' trophy!"

"Listen to this, this bourgeoisie vanity—"

"You know David, you're never a bigger Bolshevik than when

you're jealous."

"Jealous?" he said. "It ain't that, you dumb bitch! You realize the pigs could pick up any of us off the street at any time?"

"David," she said, with icy calm, "that could happen whether I'm there or not. And if that really worries you, *stop bombing things*. I love you, I'll be back Thursday night, goodbye."

Driving back to Eddie's, she told herself she should've handled David better. If she'd been with David, the fight would have led to sex, and the tension resolved. Now he'd be furious and taking it out on the furniture in his bedroom. She should have put him falsely at ease. But she was sick of his complaining. She was sick of hearing about what the group wanted. He'd just have to deal with it, that's all. In three more days, none of it would matter.

On TV, she and Eddie watched Muhammad Ali on the Ed Sullivan Show. Ali, possibly facing the end of his boxing career, was brash, confident, loquacious, overflowing with soul and humor. Eddie hung on every word, entranced.

He nodded off when the show ended. She rolled a joint and found some candles in a kitchen cabinet. She lit them and placed them here and there, giving the room a honey glow. She took off her clothes and slipped into bed beside him. Tenderly, rhythmically, she woke him out of his slumber. When he was gasping uncontrollably, she paused, coming up for air, and said:

"How's your body feel now, champ?"

"Like a total car wreck."

"Well, maybe all you need is a firm hand on the stick shift," she said. "Let's take a little test drive."

She lifted a leg over him. Hands behind his head, he lay back on his pillow. She settled down on top of him, lit the joint and took a toke, then put it between his lips and he inhaled deeply. He let out the smoke with a deep sigh.

She held him down, astraddle him, telling him how excited she was to have him inside her. She rode him gently and slowly for a long time, prolonging their pleasure, touching him everywhere that made him feel good. Finally he came, convulsed into a full body muscle spasm beneath her, his eyes closed, then she came, endlessly, her warm moaning in his ear.

In the morning she had to help him out of bed and into a hot bath. When he stood up, he was unsteady and had to hold onto the shower curtain rod while she bandaged him again. She helped him pull on his clothes.

Outside, limping down the stairway, he held the banister with both hands. Halfway down, Eddie turned to her and took her hand. The day was bright and sunny, and the wind drove big white clouds across the deep blue sky. Down on the beach a fisherman in a heavy coat and hat and hip boots swung a fishing pole, casting into the rough surf at high tide, hoping to catch a late season striper.

At the hospital she sat in the waiting room while he was with the doctor. She picked up the latest *Time* Magazine, which featured a portrait of "The Man and Woman of the Year: The Middle Americans." The cover art was surreal, a New York illustrator's clichéd fantasy of life in the rest of America. On a blue background with white stars was a kind of Cubist portrait of Mister and Mrs. Middle America, their hair and complexion waves of red and white, over images supposedly representing America's heartland: a farmer on a tractor passing a little red schoolhouse, cigarettes in an ashtray, a plate of ham and eggs, a wrench, a couple of dollar bills. The article was a drag, in a different way. *Time* Magazine was declaring that after a turbulent decade the great mass of 'Silent Majority Americans'—frightened by inner city riots, insulted by their children and offended by their loose morals and dope, and heartsick over the loss of a better America that she suspected was mostly wishful thinking—these people, with their self-pity, resentment and anger, had become the dominant influence in America. And this was the country in which she would soon be traveling. Hopefully this backlash, starting with Nixon, would fade out fast. But wasn't that a Bob Dylan country and western record they'd been listening to lately?

The article made her even more restless. Time was running out. She was relieved when Eddie returned after thirty minutes and said the doctor told him he was healing nicely, though he still had a slight concussion.

They drove back to his house and parked in the car, gazing over the dunes at the beach and sea. Then he totally surprised her.

"When you came home this time," he said, "I had a feeling things would be different with me and you. Because, you know, we're not kids anymore. I thought maybe we could get a place, live together, have some kind of life—" She felt him holding back something he wanted to say, or ask.

"I've thought about it, too."

"You did?" He seemed surprised.

"And that's the life I want, if you do," she said.

"I do," he said, at once. "The question is, where?"

"How about if we drive across America? Maybe end up in San Francisco or L.A.?"

"Why there?"

"California's where everything's happening. We'll get a place at the beach. I'll transfer to a school out there. You can write for a paper. We'll live in the sun. Or would you rather hang around New Jersey waiting to get drafted or beat up again?"

She was ready for an angry reaction to that taunt. Instead, he looked at her coolly.

"I'm not saying I'm not tempted," he said. "Getting' out of here might be good for my head." He shrugged. "You really wanna do this, no fuckin' around?"

"Eddie, I'll be cool, I swear to you—"

"Don't make me any promises you can't keep."

"Look, I know I can be trouble—" Maybe if she showed some self awareness, he would trust her to control her impulses.

"Well, you're less trouble than the guys that did this to me," he said. "But I still don't know. I mean, why go someplace else when we could have a life right here? The *Press* offered me a job, the offer's probably still open."

"Eddie." She didn't want to do this, but… "I don't have a choice anymore. I have to get out of here. I want you with me, but if I have to, I'll go by myself."

"I knew something was wrong."

"Last fall I got involved with some people in New York. Political people. What they were into made a lot of sense at the time, and the people themselves seemed really cool."

"So what happened?"

"Well, now there's FBI warrants out on all of them. And they've got guns and bombs and shit."

"Really."

"Yeah. And I know too much about them. More than I ever wanted to know."

"Since when do you care about politics, anyway?"

"Hanging out with these people got me thinking about things. Most of our generation's just bopping along, enjoying our lives of white-skinned privilege, totally unaware of how other people on the rest of this planet live. But these people really want to change the things that're wrong with America, most of all the war. I mean, *somebody* better do something. The FBI's murdering the Black Panthers in their sleep, American soldiers are dying and we're bombing Vietnam back into the Stone Age. Nixon's out to destroy the antiwar movement, beginning with the Chicago Seven—"

"But here comes your friends to the rescue."

"Well, they had some good ideas once. Unfortunately, the only idea now is, cause more chaos. After a few bombings, the structure will start cracking. They think they can bring the whole thing down."

"And replace it with what?"

She shrugged. "Good question. These people can't have lunch together without playing mind games with each other."

"And what do Senator and Mrs. Porter think of their daughter joining The Revolution?"

"It's not discussed," she said. *Obviously!* "But that's an interesting question. What about my complicity? I mean, my father was a State Senator, that's part of the power structure. At the time I met these people, I just wanted to sit on my ass and pursue my little bourgeois education. They changed all that."

"And now you're running away from them."

"Because guns and bombs are not my thing. The trouble is, they're not gonna let me just drop out of this group."

"Well, what could they do?"

"See, I know where their safe house is, where they keep their weapons, who they are, how they operate. If I don't get out of here soon, and just disappear—"

"You're asking me to drop a story I nearly got killed trying to report," he said.

"You can get a job on another newspaper," she said, "and there'll be other stories."

"And the money, it's money I'm saving for college."

"We can live on my money, and when you find a school you can use your money for that." He stared at her. "Please?" She could see the struggle going on inside him. "I don't want to do this without you, but I will, if I have to."

"You mean that? You'd really go and leave me here?" *Again*, he meant.

"I don't want to. But I'm not safe here."

"Well, but what could they do, really—"

"Kill me."

"You don't really think—"

"No, I don't *think*. I already *know* of a guy a few months back they decided they couldn't trust. He tried to back out, too. Two of the men in the group killed him and got rid of the body. They were afraid he'd expose them. I know about that, too, and that's another reason they'll have to shut me up."

She was waist deep in bullshit, the worst lie she'd ever told him, but she had to get him to come with her. It was better if he believed politics was the reason she was leaving. If Eddie knew she was running away from another man, one she was afraid she couldn't leave, he might still go with her, but he'd be a sourpuss about it. "I'll be safer a long way away from those people in New York."

"You're serious."

"I've never been more serious in my life. It's been driving me crazy, waiting for my parents to give me my living allowance, knowing at any minute—"

He sat back staring out the windshield with a perplexed look. Finally he said, "Go home. I need to be alone for awhile to think about this. I'll call you."

They kissed, then she held him for awhile. "Don't take too long," she said.

In his rearview mirror, he watched her drive away. He hauled himself one step at a time up to his apartment. He sat down on the bench out of the wind, lit a cigarette, and stared out over the sea.

It all came down to what he really wanted—and what he was willing to lose.

It was time to admit to himself that his passion for the Esposito story was really about trying to earn back people's respect, so they no longer saw him as Eddie 'Time Bomb' Bonneville, Psycho Boxer and menace to society. Despite all he'd been through on this story, maybe it was time to abandon it. If he didn't, and stayed here, Ivy would be gone again, running from danger all alone. He might never see her again. High price to pay to stay in New Jersey, dig for the facts, and tell people there was corruption, as if that was *news*.

The trip wouldn't be only to escape, to roam through America's teeming cities and quiet little towns, the trip would be give the two of them a chance to find someplace to start over together. Wasn't that what America was all about? Isn't that why people came here from all over the world, to have a chance to start over in a place where they were free to make of themselves what they could? That's what going west across this vast and mysterious continent had always meant. A new beginning, new world, new life. Start fresh. Put it all behind you, and for God's sake, don't look back.

As the shadows lengthened across the porch and the sunlight turned from bright to golden, his indecision began to clear. Telling people about corruption was one thing, whether they cared about it, another. Lots of other reporters knew the Esposito story now. Well, they could have it. The woman he loved was in danger and she needed his help. Nothing else mattered.

The money he had in the bank was to pay for the education he needed, but education didn't only happen in classrooms, with books and professors. He wanted to meet and live among people different than those he already knew, people from other places who could offer the knowledge and wisdom that he, a loner by temperament, could never acquire on his own. He knew he was naive, and he needed experiences that would burn off his suffocating small town innocence and wise him up to the ways of the world. How could he ever write about the world unless he'd seen a lot of it first?

He let the phone ring in his apartment for a long time. Finally he got up and limped inside, sank into his desk chair, and picked up.

"So?" was all she said.

"Okay." Despite the time he'd taken it still seemed like a snap decision. "Okay. Let's go."

She became nearly breathless with excitement. "Okay, so… I'm getting the check Wednesday afternoon. That night I'll get my mother to bring me to the 10 o'clock train from Point Pleasant. It's the one I always take. She'll think I'm going back to New York. First stop across the river is Manasquan at, like, 10:05. I'll get off the train, hop in your car, and we'll be on our way. Which way do you wanna drive west?"

"Straight to the nearest motel."

"God, how exciting!" Ivy giggled. "This is going to be in—fuckin'—credible!"

He thought it would take awhile for the other newspapers to re-search, write, legally check, and publish stories based on his Esposito tapes. So he was surprised Wednesday morning when stories suddenly appeared. *Esposito Allegations Rock Ocean County… 40 Years of Crime, Corruption Alleged* one paper shouted. *Prosecutor Launches Probe of County GOP Machine* said another, less excitable. His favorite head-lines were *Officials Call Esposito 'Unbalanced…'* and especially *Judge Defends Evidence Admission, It Was 'By The Rules.'*

But the stories left him in a state of shock. None of the other jour-nalists had done the deep investigative reporting required. And in this way the stories were depressingly similar to his pieces that Frank re-fused to publish. Their newspapers may have printed the stories only because they were afraid of being beaten by the competition. It was a hot story about corruption and crime, hard to resist to begin with, and the public records privilege meant almost no risk of getting sued for libel. Very few names were mentioned, but the allusions to "a Trenton legislator" or "longtime county judge" or "county GOP bigwig" or "police chief of a major township" would be transparent enough to the right people. He imagined the stories and the rumors ripping through the county, arousing outraged cries over injured reputations and setting off quiet panic that certain arrangements might get exposed. But he felt no satisfaction at all. He hated to admit it, but Frank had done him a favor by spiking his stuff. Amplifying Matty Esposito's ranting and raving wasn't journalism. The only thing they had all accomplished was to start a lot of gossip.

That afternoon, Ivy stopped in at her father's law office in down-town Toms River to pick up her allowance check. With a quick kiss on the cheek she said, "Thank you Daddy," then rushed immediately to the bank and walked out with a pocket full of cash. At home, she stashed the money in her rucksack and finished packing. There was nothing more to do but wait until train time tonight, but she was too restless and excited to hang around the house. She got in her car and drove aimlessly for hours, wherever the wind blew her. At one point she drove past Eddie's, but his car wasn't parked outside so she kept going down the coast highway. She got back home a little after seven o'clock. She parked in the garage between her father's Lincoln Continental and her mother's Country Squire wagon.

Not quite ready to go in and face her parents, she smoked a cigarette sitting on the fender of her little white Corvair, her magic carpet to freedom. The afternoon spent driving around, taking a last look at things, had really done a number on her head. Her high school, where she'd spent four years of suffering, was now just a building, looking more like a factory than a place of learning. The Ocean Ice Palace, where'd she learned to skate in Girl Scouts. The Brick Shopping Center, the worst place in town to play hooky, where capture was almost certain.

The county park had been empty when she'd gone to sit under the evergreens on her bench by the lake. The bench was her refuge when bad shit happened in her life, and she would sit there alone for hours and days on end. Like when her mother discovered what her father was doing with her, acted like nothing happened, but treated her with cold hatred. Every day after school she'd gone to the bench by the lake instead of going home to a poisoned household. Like after Mister Angelo died. She never told anyone he threatened to kill himself if she reported him. Why bother? They blamed her for his suicide anyway. Instead, she sat beside the lake, telling herself that her teacher had been an evil, conniving man looking to get over on a young naïve girl, that he fell victim to his own emotional sickness, and that it was not her fault. Like, worst of all, when she came home from Puerto Rico and had to tell Eddie about the abortion and all the other stuff involving her father, and he wouldn't talk to her for a long time. She simply sat beside the calming waters and in time he came around. A bench by the lake was something she would always need no matter where she was, hers was just that kind of life. She crushed out her cigarette and pulled down the garage door.

Crossing the back yard, she inhaled the smell of wood smoke from the fireplace and the aroma of meat roasting. She came in through the kitchen door and kicked off her boots, deciding to shower before dinner and put on sexy underwear for Eddie. She hoped they could find a really raunchy, low rent motel to celebrate the first night of their journey together. As she padded into the downstairs hallway in her stocking feet, trying to remember whether she'd packed her French lace panties, the ones cut high on the hip, her mother breezed in holding a drink.

"Why, here she is!" she exclaimed toward the living room. "Where did you go? We've all been wondering about you."

Ivy hung up her coat and scarf.

All?

What she found in the living room was bizarre. Her father lounged in his favorite white cardigan in his Morris chair, his legs crossed, puffing his pipe. David leaned over the arm of the sofa, chatting quietly with her father, man to man. They were chuckling, man to man. David's appearance horrified her, so meticulously had he prepared his deception: his hair was cut short, parted and neatly brushed, he wore oxblood penny loafers and crew socks, khaki trousers, a white shirt and an argyle gray and blue crew neck sweater. She saw to her horror that her parents were clearly charmed.

"Here she is!" her mother announced. David turned to Ivy, with a big gleaming smile but dead behind the eyes. Her father snatched his pipe from his teeth, grinning broadly.

"Princess," he said, "you never told me you were dating a Nixon man!"

"Well, Daddy, " she chirped, "I didn't think you'd believe me! Hello David!"

"Hi, *princess*," David said.

He stood up and kissed her on the cheek. Close up, just between them, his smile vanished, and he gave her a cold, warning look.

"Sorry I wasn't at the, uh, station," she said, her eyes questioning David's sanity.

"Just a quick trip down and back," he said. "Had a couple stops to make. You know. Business."

"Oh, *business*," she said.

"Speaking of which, I need to get over to Lakewood and drop off some samples for a client. He should be home by now. Think you could drive me?"

"Actually, my car is acting up, a spark plug's missing or something, it stalled on me a couple times coming home—"

But her mother smiled sweetly. "Take the Country Squire, darling, you know where my keys are. Will you two be back in time for dinner?"

"Well, I'm not sure." Under the coffee table at David's feet was his blue canvas gym bag. Last seen, she remembered, at the townhouse in New York, full of high explosive. Suddenly her heart was pounding so hard she was afraid they'd hear it, or that it would make her voice shake.

"Should I still plan on driving you to the train tonight?" her mother said. She felt David stiffen slightly beside her. *Busted*. "Dear?"

"Yes mother, thank you. I'm sure we'll be back by then. Okay David, let's go." She took him by the arm.

"Thank you for your hospitality, Mister and Mrs. Porter," David said. "Very nice meeting you both."

"You two should come for a visit when you've got more time!" her father said.

"If I can tear her away from her studies!" David said, rolling his eyes and laughing.

Ivy knew she should go upstairs to her bedroom phone, call the police down on David, and be done with it. But she had to get him and his blue bag out of her parents' house, like, now. And if he was busted, she'd get hung up talking to the police and FBI, maybe get busted herself, and miss meeting Eddie tonight.

In the main foyer, he pulled on a heavy blue melton stadium coat. If he was any more Ivy League, she thought, he'd be wearing a fucking straw boater.

She said, under her breath, "Don't forget your bag."

He stopped. "Oops." He turned around and went to the living room and returned with the blue bag. "Almost forgot my samples," he said, chuckling.

Something woke Eddie up from his nap. It was after dark. What was that? A footstep, just outside the gabled bed chamber. Another, gritty-soled, like a boot. A gun hammer clicked back.

He reached out and turned on the bedside lamp. Esposito's missing girlfriend stood at his bedside pointing a revolver at his face.

"Hello," he said. "Sally?"

She stared at him. He lay perfectly still. Five feet away, he could smell desperate sweat through her cigarette smoke and heavy floral perfume.

Somehow, he managed not to sound scared. "I've been hoping to talk to you."

She looked scared but determined. Otherwise, she was just like he last saw her, jeans and her white rabbit fur jacket, her hair tied back in a blonde pony tail, no makeup.

"I want those tapes," she said in a shaky voice.

"I don't have them."

"Don't talk to me like I'm stupid."

"The court has them."

"The tapes you made talking to Matty from that night."

"The court has them."

"Fuck around with me, and you're making a big mistake—"

"They're evidence in a case. I was subpoenaed. I had to give them up."

"Those're the only copies?"

"Yeah."

"Don't fuckin' lie to me—" The gun in her hand shook.

"Read the newspapers. The story's out. I don't have them any more. If I had 'em, I'd give 'em to you."

"Why'd you give them up?"

"It's a long story."

"So how you gonna write the story you promised Matty you'd do?"

"I remember everything he told me. I've got notes. These aren't the kind of stories you forget. I don't need the tapes anymore."

"Well," she let out a long sigh, "I do." She backed up. "All right, sit up and keep your hands where I can see them." He pushed himself upright on the bed.

She pulled his desk chair over from across the room and straddled it, gun still pointed at him, and stared at him with a crooked, helpless smile. Tears ran down her cheeks.

"Sally. Put the gun away, please. You don't need it here, I promise you. Sally? Okay?"

She nodded, slowly. She eased the hammer down on her gun and put it in her jacket pocket, crossed her arms over the chair back and rested her chin on them. "I'm waiting for somebody. You mind if I hang out awhile?"

"It's cool." He sat up on the edge of the bed. She reacted but didn't reach for the gun.

"Try anything and I'll kill you."

"Just take it easy, okay?"

"I'm taking it easy."

"I can see you shaking from here. You're making me nervous with that gun and all."

"Yeah, well. I need it. After what happened to Matty, I mean."

"Just so you know, I don't have any weapons or anything here, okay? And I wouldn't hurt you, why would I? You seem upset. You wanna tell me what's wrong?"

She swallowed and shook her head, waving him off.

"Can I ask you something?" he said.

"Ask me what?"

"Don't get pissed at me, now."

"Ask me what?"

"Did you shoot Matty?"

"Do I look like the kind of person who could kill three men and set a hotel on fire?"

"Okay, okay. I had to ask, it's my job. But who do you think coulda done that?"

She gave him a blank look, reconsidered, sighed deeply, pushed a few stray hairs back off her face, and wiped her eyes. She got up, ran her fingers through her hair and sighed deeply. "I didn't kill him. I was in *love* with him." She reached for his cigarettes on the bed table, lit two, gave him one. "Okay, I mean, yeah, it started out as a job. For a working girl right off South Orange Avenue, it was a good job." She exhaled, making an O. "I just did what I was told."

"Told by Bobby Castellucci."

She nodded. "You know how it is. For me it was my ticket out of The Life. See, I'm older than I look, but I still got time for a shot at something if I make the right connections. So Bobby was like, 'I want you to meet this old guy down in Lakewood, play up to him, do whatever you gotta do, get inside. Find out whatever you can.' Yeah, right. I had just enough time to fall in love with him, then they put a gun in my hand and said, 'Do it.' I'm like, 'That ain't in the deal,' and they're like, 'It is now.' But I couldn't."

"Did you tell Matty about this?"

"How could I, without giving away how the whole thing got started?"

"You didn't have to tell him how it got started. You didn't have to tell him the whole thing."

"Yeah, well. That's always been my downfall. I'm too damned honest. Anyway, he didn't need no warnings about Bobby, believe me."

He wanted to believe her, despite the gun in her pocket. "Why didn't they kill you too?"

"I wasn't there. I was at the doctor's. Finding out I'm pregnant. I came back in the taxi and the place was on fire."

"Pregnant."

"Yeah. I couldn't wait to tell Matty." She closed her eyes and sobbed.

"Well, congratulations. Why a taxi? Couldn't Tommy drive you?"

"Matty had the car down in Lacey."

"So now Castellucci wants you dead, right?"

"*Very* fuckin' dead." He stared at her, at how defiantly she wore her hard life on her young and once beautiful face. She shook her head. "These *men*. These fucking animals, who call themselves *men*."

"Is there anything I can do?" he said.

"Those tapes, they're all that's left of my baby's father. I wanted him to be able to hear his father's voice some day."

"I would've given them to you gladly."

"Seventy years old! I think we're talkin' some strong genes, here. I'm sure it's a boy." She looked around at the apartment. "You got something to drink, maybe?"

He got a bottle of Smirnoff's from the freezer cabinet, poured some in a water glass, and offered it to her. She sipped cautiously, then put away a slug, deadpan.

"You been a reporter long?"

"Yeah. Well, a couple years. How'd you get mixed up with Bobby Castellucci?"

Sally swirled the liquor in her glass. "Bobby saw me singing in a place in Mountainside. Owned by a guy who's connected. He told me he liked my singing, I really liked his looks, long story short, we had a brief thing. He knows these guys from Vailsburg who hang with the Four Seasons. Introductions were gonna be made." More tears. He wondered if the drink was a good idea.

From down on the street a car horn tooted twice, and twice again. She stood and pushed the chair out of the way.

"You'll be okay?" Eddie said.

"This is somebody I can trust."

"You need any money or anything?"

"I'm cool. Thanks, though…" She slipped her handbag strap over her shoulder. He got to his feet. She hesitated, then reached out and hugged him, and planted a wet, warm kiss on his lips, her fingers light on the back of his neck.

Eddie gripped her hips, pulled her against him, and gave her a long French kiss, full on the mouth. She kissed him back. He was surprised at himself, he felt no guilt, just an overwhelming lust, pure and direct, crowding out anything more complicated. Reaching down, she touched him through his trousers. She made a sound in the back of her throat, surprised and approving, at what she found there.

"Hm, too bad I've got to go," she said. She reached back, and reluctantly lifted his hands off her ass. "I like young guys like you, full of pep. Maybe some other time."

"Some other time," he said, wondering what the hell just got into him.

"You be careful," Sally whispered. "You don't belong in this mess. You're too young and there's too much you don't know."

"Wait a minute! Like what?"

"Gotta go." He listened to her boot heels go down the steps outside.

He went to the window to see the car she got into. But he saw only red tail lights, turning on to the coast highway. Tires screeched as they pulled quickly away.

"We're going to Toms River, by the way, not Lakewood," David said, once Ivy had driven away from the Porter mansion and they were out on a misty wintry road, each house up on a hill on a large wooded lot. "You should have seen the look on your face."

"Nice acting job. Of course, they're easy to fool."

"Think I passed inspection, Prom Queen?"

"A *Nixon man*?" she said, chuckling at his cleverness. "What did you say to him?"

"'Peace through perpetual war,' 'free markets and free men,' 'the right to law and order before all others.' You know, the usual reactionary shit."

"And those clothes! David," she said. "This is too weird. What are you doing here?"

"The money you left me ran out—" He tried to make it sound like a joke, but it was also probably true. "You don't seem too happy to see me."

"I am, I am. But how could you sit there talking to my father with that stuff in the bag at your feet?"

"Didn't want to take a chance it'd get lost," David said. "That is one enormous fuckin' house you grew up in. I mean, all that for one family?"

"Uh, more to the point, why are you walking around with a bag of dynamite?"

"You never know when it might come in handy."

"Why'd you do all this, coming down here, disguised as a Young Republican or something—"

"I'm bringing you back to New York."

"You heard my mother, I was coming back tonight."

"You told me tomorrow night. Why didn't you call and tell me you were coming home tonight?"

"I thought it would be a nice surprise. You sounded so lonely on the phone."

"I—" He stared out the window, shaking his head, swallowing.

"Whatever you think, David, it wasn't easy for me, being down here without you." She said that from the small piece of her heart that still belonged to him, so it sounded authentic.

"Aw." His voice turned mean, intended to scourge. "I feel so much *better* knowing that you suffered too, down here in your Daddy's mansion."

"Okay, David." He was here uninvited, and being insulting, but she forced herself to stay calm. "So we'll have dinner, and we'll catch the ten o'clock train and go home. In the meantime, do you have to be this way? I'm glad you're here, and I would appreciate it if you didn't spoil that, okay?"

"Just drive."

She swung the car around the Laurelton Circle and turned onto Route 70, then Brick Boulevard. As the highway became Hooper Avenue, his voice broke the silence, his voice shaking.

"What made you think you could just pick up and leave?"

"What do you mean?"

"Leave the group. And leave me. Because obviously we're not gonna let that happen."

Before her fierce instinct to defend her freedom unwittingly confirmed his accusation, she caught herself. She sighed. "I don't know where you get this idea that I was ever going anywhere else but home to you, David. You're bumming yourself out over nothing."

"Yeah, sure." David unbuttoned his stadium coat. He drew an automatic pistol out of his waistband, checked the safety, and put it in his outer pocket. All to scare her, of course, but it worked.

"Why do you need a gun?"

"I'm wanted, remember? Keep your eyes on the road, please."

"You'd better cool it David," Ivy said, unable to keep her voice steady. "My father just about runs this county."

"I'm not afraid of your fuckin' father," he said. The face he turned to her, usually a bitter scowl from a hard-working class life, glowed with defiance and triumph. "Good thing you walked in when you did," he said. "I was about to shoot them both because I was running out of conversation." He shrugged. "The way you always talk about them, I figured I'd be doing you a favor."

At his kitchen table, Eddie finished writing a note. "I know you'll understand, in a way my parents never will. I'm not running away from anything. I'm running towards a new life, with the woman I love, who loves me for who I am. I need to find out what kind of man I am, and how well I handle things in this world. The one sure thing this whole mess has taught me is how little I really know about anything."

He folded the note into an envelope and sealed it. He addressed it to Billy Foster, Esq.

The old diner on the highway outside the village of Toms River was bustling at dinner time. She and David sat in a corner booth. He wore a Yankee cap and sat where he could watch the door, eating meat loaf with mashed potatoes and cut corn. She had coffee and blueberry pie, and a large side order of overcooked polemics.

"It occurred to me around Christmas, one night watching the news on TV," David said. "It ain't gonna happen next year, or the year after, or the year after *that*," he said. "We're at a very like, early stage. Anybody who's studied the history of revolutions will tell ya building grass roots support takes time, and..."

Inwardly, she cringed. Actually, she thought while he babbled, any *educated* person knows revolutions are never mass movements, David, they are usually driven by upper class elites, because people of *your* pathetic class are too filled with resentment and self pity to organize themselves effectively. Of course, David never allowed his ranting on history and revolution to be impeded by anything so mundane as facts or history. His political and intellectual intensity, which she had once found so sexy and inspiring, now was pretentious and ridiculous. He was full of shit, and he was insulting her by treating her like she was still gullible enough to believe him.

"So, what do you think we need?" she said, counting the minutes until tonight's train.

"Well, what we *don't* need is another one of these bullshit sessions about who's showing enough commitment," he said. Sore subject, because the other members of the cadre had accused him of being on an ego trip during one such powwow a few weeks ago at the townhouse.

"All that blah blah blah, the training and conditioning, petty fuckin' arguments and gut checks, what's really gonna come of all that?"

"A physically fit, ideologically pure, well organized cadre," she said, "freezing to death outside a meat packing plant in Des Moines, leafleting people who ain't gonna join The Revolution until everybody in it gets a haircut."

"Ha!" David loved that. "See, that's why I'm glad I came down here," he said. "I love that snotty attitude, and tonight I need your help."

Despite herself, she warmed to hear that he loved something about her. Careful with that, she thought. "Help with what?"

"Well, I'll tell you—what time is this train tonight?" he said.

"Ten o'clock. My mother'll take us," she said.

He glanced up at the clock over the lunch counter. "Perfect. It's 8:05 now," he said, lowering his voice and adding casually, "and we've got just enough time to bomb the Draft Board office before we leave town."

She managed to be nonchalant. "Punch line, please?"

David folded his hands under his chin. "Don't make me repeat that, it's crowded in here."

"You're serious?"

"Well—yeah." He stared, appalled at her for asking.

"Well—when?"

"Right now. I scouted the place this afternoon before I took a taxi to your parent's place. Walked around, checked the doors, locks, everything." He grinned and tugged the lapels of his stadium coat. "In this Ivy League get-up, nobody even looked twice at me. This is my disguise from now on," he said. "Joe College."

"David, I think we better talk about us," she said.

"Okay, let's talk about us. What duh'fuck you want me to say? You broke my heart. You used to be committed. Now I wonder if you meant it or you were just playing at revolution, just like you've probably played at everything else in your superficial, rich-girl's life."

Stung, she stammered, "That's not true."

"Sure it is. I'll bet right now you're sitting there wondering how you can get away from me." He stared at her, daring her to deny it. "Well, if you really want to go, go ahead. Get up. There's the door."

Ivy got up and reached for her coat hanging on a hook over the booth.

"And if you try to leave, I'll shoot you in the back." His face said he meant it.

"That won't be necessary." She took off her coat, hung it up, and sat back down. "David, I'm just wondering how doing a bombing will get us closer to ending the war, that's all."

"People don't feel the pain of this war in America yet. They're against it now, but they're not screaming from the rooftops to end it. After all that marching, the broken skulls, the jail time, America still isn't listening. So we need to give them a shock down on Main Street. Bring the war home. Give them a taste of the violence being inflicted in their name on the Vietnamese people. You and I are gonna do that." He waved for the waitress, grinning. "Two coffees to go, please."

Obviously, the war was beside the point. Her commitment to the revolution was being tested. He was forcing her to prove she was serious, and to join the rest of them as a wanted criminal.

"Look, I tried to make a constructive contribution," he said. "A cop in Mississippi gave me a fractured skull for my trouble. I want to make a *de*–structive contribution." He rubbed the half circle scar near the part in his hair—not from a Mississippi cop's nightstick during the Freedom Summer, like he told her and everyone else, but from a beer mug wielded in self-defense by his ex-wife. "A Draft Board office in small town America," he mused. "Wait'll you see it. Fuckin' Norman Rockwell all the way. It's the perfect target." He showed her a sketch of the courthouse layout in a pocket notebook. "Here's the Draft Board office, in the back corner. A few steps from a rear entrance that's hidden from the street."

"You actually think we can do this without getting caught?"

"The courthouse has been closed for three hours. The rear door and the office door are old. I can jimmy the locks with my Buck knife. Believe it or not, I didn't see any alarms."

Ivy leaned in closer, scared, not quite believing she was actually talking about doing this. "So you mean like, right now, on our way home?"

"That's the way it's done. Quick in and out. Timer set for an hour later when we're long gone."

"Suppose we kill somebody?"

David mopped his meatloaf gravy with a soft roll, and gazed up to where he always fixed his attention when accessing a higher truth. "How many people died at My Lai?"

"One hundred and nine."

"How many?"

"Too many."

"We're not going to kill anybody," he said. "We'll set the timer, we'll be long gone when it happens." He stuffed the roll in his mouth.

"Okay. Sounds like you've got it all thought out. So then—what do you need *me* for?" She winced at the weakness in her voice.

"I gotta have proof you really mean what you say, before we get back to New York, and the others put you through a real grilling."

She shrugged, as if to say *Okay, fair enough*. But she had wavered, and he'd said nothing, and he never passed up a chance to criticize her. Did he really need to impress her that bad? Some essential strength of his was missing, and in its place was weakness, a need to prove something to her. Since they would be handling dynamite in a few minutes, she wondered if that should worry her.

Eddie sped up the coast to Long Branch and went to The Inkwell one last time. He planned to eat dinner, but when he got there, he was too excited and too sad about leaving the Shore to have an appetite. So he ordered a double espresso and played the jukebox. That was all he had time for, and it wasn't nearly enough. He wanted one more night at The Upstage getting his eardrums tuned by the local rock n' rollers. He wanted one more thick chocolate milkshake from Jersey Joe's on the Freehold Circle, to body surf one more wave off Point Pleasant on a hot dry August afternoon, or sit in one of the wicker rocking chairs outside the cafe at Jenkinson's on the boardwalk and spend all day reading a novel. He wanted one more cold sunny autumn afternoon and another victory on the football field for the Brick Township High School Green Dragons, carrying silver-haired Warren Wolf on their shoulders around the stadium. He wanted one more summer Saturday night in Baywood watching the drag races on Mandalay Road and cheering for his Uncle George in his brilliant red Chevy convertible. He wanted to be five years old one more time and follow in his father's footsteps across Brick Beach to the surf, sit between his legs again as the waves rushed up and over them, unseated and almost sucked into the undertow except for his father's strong arms protecting him. Or to sit at the lunch counter at the Lakewood Public Service bus station and drink the chicory-flavored coffee and read paperbacks and pulp fiction mags borrowed from the racks behind him, watching people come and go off the Route 9 busses and writing verbal sketches in his pocket notebook, and hearing the busses announced—*Faw-ked Rivah!* He wanted to ride one more rattling rusty old Pennsylvania Railroad coach up to Asbury Park, walk down Cookman Avenue and through a bustling, sunny city to the St. James or Mayfair theaters, and sit in the dark universe of an immense movie palace and let himself be taken to another world. He wanted another night exhausted from dancing to Steel Mill on a fake I.D. at Pandemonium on the Asbury Circle. To park beside the ocean once more, waistband pressure on his wrist and his fingers slippery, a girl's warm breath repeating his name in his ear along with *Yeah, oh yeah yeah.* To wander through Ocean County Park, high on a Sunday afternoon in summer, and hear music in the birdcalls and shouts from the athletic fields, to feel the sun on his face, to hear a sigh in the wind, the tall evergreens nodding overhead, the sunlight like a handful of diamonds scattered across the surface of the blue lake roughened by the breeze. He wanted to swim one more time across the Manasquan River to Osborn Island on an evening at flood tide when the still waters were smooth as glass and the same silvery color as the twilight. Or to have another day to wander Island Beach State Park imagining how all this must have been before too many people came here. He wanted one more cold wet morning, smelling the mud in the gunning ditch off Twilight Road in Bay Head, to drink coffee with his father and uncles with the shotguns leaning in front of them, the dog's breath steamy on the frigid air, and the decoys, carved by his uncle, bobbing on the dark waters a few yards off, his father always the first to hear a covey of ducks coming in. He wanted one more day of cold, lead-colored ocean surf so stormy it tossed the mackerel and blue fish up on the sand to freeze before they could wash back into the sea, and he wanted to go walking along the beach in waders with his father frost fishing, picking up the frozen fish and dropping them into an apple basket. He wanted one more hour listening to Cousin Brucie spin the hits on WABC-AM radio, and one more Sunday night to lay in bed listening to Pete Hamill or Gay Talese talk with Howard Cosell on "Speaking of Everything," followed by "The Hour of Decision With the Reverend Billy Graham" and to fall asleep imagining God's eyes smiling upon him. He wanted to have a lot of things once more before he left town, but there wasn't time for any more of it now. Everything he loved would always be here. It was time to let all that go, and to venture into the unknown world, and find out what he was really made of.

David jimmied the lock to the Draft Board office. The lock yielded, and they slipped noiselessly inside.

Ivy stood motionless as her eyes slowly adjusted to the dark and the shapes of the furniture and filing cabinets emerged out of the murk. For a moment she heard only their hushed breathing. From down the marble corridors in the deep night-time quiet of the stone courthouse, the echoes of a far-off radiator clunking and hissing expanded her sense of the size and solidity of this old building that represented order, authority, law, society's structures—everything she detested.

Just enough glow came through the venetian blinds on the tall double windows from the lawn floodlights to allow them to move around.

"Let's do this and get out of here," she said.

He looked around the office for a moment. Against the walls at the back end of the room stood the filing cabinets.

"First things first." David rolled open all the drawers, exposing rows of file folders of military service records. They piled stacks of them on top of the cabinets.

"We can use that table back here," he said.

They moved the typewriter off a wooden table that stood at an angle to the board secretary's desk. They carried the table back to the filing cabinets.

"How big you wanna blow this fucker?" he said.

"Kingdom Come, motherfucker," she said, pumping her fist. Well, at least he couldn't say she didn't play her part to the hilt.

David opened the blue canvas gym bag on the table. He pulled out two wine bottles of gasoline padded in newspaper, a roll of wire, a roll of electrical tape, a battery and an old alarm clock.

"Tape one of these to each bottle," he said, handing her two sticks of dynamite. "This end up."

We're really doing this, she thought, totally incredulous. Not that she had any problem blowing up the Draft Board office, it was a legitimate gear in the war machine to attack. The bombing would destroy old and new Draft records, including, somewhere in those piles of files, one for Eddie Bonneville. It would strike terror in every small town in America. And it was a perfect goodbye to New Jersey. After talking so many times about working together, how weird they should really be doing it in the last couple hours before she dumps him forever.

As she taped a stick of dynamite to each bottle of gasoline, she came up with a plan for tonight she was sure would work. First, she would help David do the bombing. Afterward, her mother would drive them to the railroad station in Point Pleasant. Once aboard the train, Ivy would put David at ease. Just across the river, thirty seconds before Manasquan, she'd say she was going to the bathroom to put in a tampon, so he wouldn't bother her for a few minutes. She would take her backpack and walk through the train to the last coach. Just before the conductor called, "All aboard!" and the train began to move ahead, she'd step off, run like hell to Eddie's car, and be finished with David and The Revolution for good. She might even call the police, or have the FBI greet David when he steps off the train in New York. It was fun to imagine: a few stations up the line, David starts wondering where she is, searches the train, then it dawns on him that he's been dumped, and she's gone.

"Okay man," David said, placing the clock and battery on the table. "This is gonna make one helluva noise in that nice little world you grew up in, Prom Queen."

"I told you, I didn't choose to be born here," Ivy said, "and I don't like it, and it never liked me. There's nothing nice about it. And quit calling me that, will you? For your information, I never actually went to any fucking prom."

"Aw… Why not?"

"Me and my boyfriend were outcasts."

"You mean I'm not the first One Percenter you fell in love with?"

"'Fraid not."

David seized her arm. "I just got an incredible idea! Call your father. Get *him* to drive us to the train. Then we'll kidnap him! A State Senator!"

"And then what? Send a ransom note to my own mother? That's a little advanced for me right now."

"Aw," David said. "For his little girl, I'm sure your Daddy would come."

"*Lay off*, man." She jerked free of his grip.

He reacted badly to that. "'Course, then you'd never be able to sneak back to the lap of luxury when you get bored with The Revolution."

He would always treat her like that. It was her own fault. She was a rich girl who'd carelessly got involved with a charismatic loser, a guy who got a mean little thrill from mocking her. She should've been more careful. "The only thing that's boring me is you," she said.

"Whatsa matter?" he said. "Little too much honesty for you?"

This pretentious, *knowing* David, who wanted her to think that only he had the world figured out, made her angry. Too much honesty? How's this?

Sidling around the table she said, "Well, honestly, if it was just me alone, my father would *gladly* drive me to the train. My father gladly does whatever I want, because every time he does something nice for me, I pay him back with a first-class blowjob." At his astonished look, she laughed. "It's been going on since I was twelve."

There was shock and revulsion in David's eyes like she'd never seen before. "You mean the man I was just drinking and talking to?"

"Yeah, I know. *Evil*, right?"

David looked almost ashamed, then his eyes narrowed. "I've got a better idea. Have him drive us to the train. Then before we get on board, I'll blow his fucking brains out."

"Oh David—"

"I'm serious. I'll blow his fucking brains out."

"It's so nice to see you really care."

He stood there, breathing hard.

"Of course the arrangement has had it's benefits, too."

"God damn—"

"Pretty decadent, huh? He actually said to me, the first time he cornered me in the shower, 'Do you know what this is, honey? This is a pillar of the community.' Then he showed me how to make him happy. And what little girl doesn't want to make her Daddy happy, huh?"

He started to say something but was too shocked to speak. How touching, that he wanted to be strong and protective for her, but it was 'way too late for that—'way too late for everything.

"I told you I don't like coming back here," she said.

Eddie sat in the car smoking, up the road from his parent's house. The lights were on in the living room. Just go over, he told himself, and do what any decent person would do before leaving town. He crushed a third cigarette butt in the ashtray, then drove slowly away. He'd send the folks a postcard from someplace in America. But after a mile, he didn't like being a bad son, and turned around.

His father sat reading the *Press* spread out on the kitchen table. When he saw Eddie's condition the reaction on his face made words unnecessary. His mother came in from the living room, shaking her head in disbelief.

"We called the paper," she said, "but they told us you were off work and recuperating."

"We thought you were back in jail," his father said.

"The picture in the paper—"

"I'm sorry, Ma, I should've warned you."

"You look like hell," his father said.

"I'm all right."

"Who did this?" his mother said.

He put aside his long speech about the local underworld for another time. "We're still trying to figure that out."

"How many people would *like* to beat you up?" It sounded like she thought he brought this down on himself.

"I don't know, Ma. I haven't had time to do a survey."

His father would want to know everything but Eddie, thinking about the night of the gun, told himself to be careful.

"The hospital says I'm healing okay. And I'm out of legal trouble. I'm completely freaked out by what's happened, so I'm gonna get out of here for awhile. I got my stuff packed and money in my pocket. I'm going to do some traveling."

"All by yourself?" his mother said.

"No, me and Ivy. She's transferring to a college somewhere out West."

"You and Ivy," his mother said, her voice in that minor key that said, *How long will the melodrama between you and that tramp go on?*

His father shrugged. "I told you – well, never mind now…"

"I have a lot to learn about being a reporter. Maybe the next place I work I'll do better."

"Well dear," his mother said, teary-eyed. "I have to put the kids to bed."

"Give them each a kiss for me."

"You be careful, and call, *often*."

"I will." She hugged him, then left Eddie alone with his father.

It took a moment before Eddie could speak. He'd worked it out a dozen ways in his head until he thought he could say it right. Instead, what came out sounded like a helpless plea. "Look. All this fighting between me and you—"

"Yeah?" His father went back to reading the newspaper.

"Well, you have to admit, there's been a lot, like whipping me when I was a kid—"

"You're still a kid."

"—mocking my opinions, mocking my right to even *hold* any."

"So?"

"Kicking me out of the house—"

"Look," his father said, "if this is your way of settling things with me before you take off to see the world, it ain't working so well."

"I can see that." How fast he became angry and despondent! Trying to be reasonable with this man was murder on the nerves.

"So I gave you a whipping now and then? You know how many I got when I was a kid? Didn't hurt me any. And your opinions don't deserve the respect of any patriotic American. You're full of talk about what's right and wrong with this country, but when it's time to do your duty, you try to wiggle out of it. And kicking you out of here was the best thing that ever happened to you. You got a place of your own, and a job and it looks to me like you're doing fine."

"Does it."

"Yeah. So what's all this about?"

He knew he had to say it: "I just wanted to tell you I forgive you—"

"For *what*?"

Whatever he'd expected, or hoped for, it wasn't going to happen. The one thing he desperately wanted to do, to cry, was unthinkable. His father would crucify him.

"I forgive you, that's all. Don't ask about what. Just think about it. I want you to know I love you and it's all okay between us."

His father was impenetrable, but he let slip one rueful glance. It told Eddie everything he needed to know. In that glance he could see his father knew exactly what he was trying to do. It was what he probably never got to do with his own war-wounded and severe father, and, way of the world, he wasn't about to let Eddie do it either. What Eddie needed so badly was not in his father to grant; his inheritance, instead, was instability, a quick temper, and a violent streak he would spend the rest of his life struggling to control. Maybe it was childish, and even unfair, to expect so much from his father in the first place. He probably didn't know how to do anything else but pass on to his son the same wounds that his father had inflicted on him.

"I know you did your best, Dad." It came out weak, but he meant it. Somehow, he had to get past hating this man, even if his father wouldn't let him.

"Yeah, well." His father cleared his throat and turned the page of the newspaper. "I try."

This man had abandoned him in favor of his passion for politics, his struggle to save a losing business, his rigid sense of right and wrong, and his uncontrollable anger. Yet now, as he was abandoning his father, leaving him behind in a rundown rented house, in a job toiling for a paycheck from somebody else, in a political career in which the temptations of corruption kept challenging his sense of personal honor, he felt compassion for his father for the first time in his life.

"So where out west are you going?" his father said.

"We don't know, exactly. "

"And you got money?"

"Enough for awhile," he said.

"Well, we're always here," his father said. "Call if you need to." His father held out his hand and they shook. "And for Chrissakes, call your mother, she'll be worried to death until she sees you again."

David carefully placed the bombs and 12-volt battery in an open filing cabinet drawer. Two wires led to a cheap alarm clock sitting on the wooden table.

"So far, so good," she said. "Let's get out of here."

"Not yet."

Now what? He was really getting on her last nerve. He opened more filing cabinet drawers and pulled out handfuls of files and tossed them in the air, giggling like a friggin' child as the papers snowed all over the office. "They'll never be able to re-register all these men." He seemed disappointed she didn't share his zany mood.

"David, let's get out of here." She didn't have to be a hardened revolutionary to be shocked by his recklessness.

"By the time we get to New York tonight, this'll be national news, Prom Queen."

That really ticked her off.

"Hey man, are you fuckin' deaf?" she said. "I told you to stop calling me that."

He looked like a little boy who'd just had his wrist slapped. "It's just a nickname."

"Quit insulting my intelligence. Not that I even expect you to understand what I mean."

"Oh yeah?" Not so fast, his look said, his hands dropping to his sides. "Now who's insulting *who*?" It was risky to push back at him. She reacted without thinking and now she made him mad. "Spoiled little college cunt. Who do you think you're looking down your nose at?"

"David, let's talk about what a spoiled cunt I am later, okay? Right now, can we *please* get out of here, like, before the war's over?"

Sulking, with a few savage twists, David wound up the clock and checked his watch, set the correct time, nine-fifteen, and put it down quietly on the table, ticking.

"Fireworks at ten thirty," he said.

"Arm the bomb and let's boogie," she said.

"Not yet." He reached out and pulled her against him, and kissed her roughly, taking her by surprise. She resisted, but his strong fingers unsnapped her jeans and pulled the zipper down. He plunged his hand down her pants. She was shocked and offended, then aroused, despite herself. His hand was rough and dry, but not for long. "It's been really hard, living without this," he breathed in her ear.

"Feel that?" she said, referring to the state of affairs in her pants. "That's what you do to me just standing there. *So-o-o* sexy," she said, digging her nails into his chest. Well, he was asking for it. She would cock tease him now, make him all hot and eager to get her back to New York and in bed, then she would vanish off the train, leaving him with nothing but his fingers to sniff.

"C'mon. Right here," he whispered hoarsely. "Right now. Give it to me."

"Not *here*!" she said, caught off-guard.

"Yes, right here, right now."

"It's too dangerous. Wait'll we get home." She couldn't get his hand out of her pants.

"I don't wanna wait! It's been a month already! Right here! It'll be perfect!"

"Wait'll we get home!"

She held her jeans up. He tried to pull them down. His eyes were gloating so brightly she wanted to punch them out. Was she *really* impressed by him, with his bomb, with the balls it took to do this? He just *had* to celebrate his blow against the empire like a real warrior by fucking the rich Senator's daughter.

There was that little man again, she thought. Despite all of his strutting, his bullying and soapbox ranting, his showing off with his dynamite, he was really weak and helpless, unless *completed* by impressing a woman. Ugh…

She hauled off and smacked him across the face, meaning it, not playing their usual games. That got his hand out of her pants. They struggled, he slipped on the scattered files on the floor. As he fell on the linoleum, David grabbed her jacket and pulled her down with him. She kicked him away, which sent him sprawling on his back. David held his face, his eyes full of hot tears.

"God damn rich little—"

She rolled onto her knees, grabbed his jacket, then shoved him away, trying to keep from screaming: "Rich little *cunt*, right? Right? That's all I am to you! Go ahead, say it!"

He stared at her wide-eyed, a long time, then he blew her mind. "I really love you," he finally croaked, his throat thick with emotion. "Do you *know* that?"

"You don't love me, you love *having* me."

"No, no, it ain't like that. Look, I'm sorry, okay?"

"Well, why do you keep doin' this shit? I keep telling you I hate that nickname. And you keep saying it. Don't you get by now that it hurts me? That I hate being reminded of who I am and where I'm from, something I had no control over at all?"

"It's just me," he said. He sat back against the secretary's desk, clunking his head against it like he was punishing himself. "I've never been with nobody like you. My whole fucked up life the only women I knew I didn't respect, they aggravated me, and I was abusive and stupid. But you're different."

"Yeah. A spoiled college cunt."

"I'm sorry, I'm sorry I said that, I was pissed off because I thought you were calling me stupid."

"Because I keep telling you—"

"I know, I know, I'll never call you that again. I promise."

"The whole time I was stuck down here, missing you, you kept calling me up, pressuring me to come back, when you should've known I would as soon as I was able. How do you think that made me feel?"

"I know, I know—"

"And can I tell you something?" she said. "I really don't give a fuck what the others want, or what they think of me, okay? I don't care if I ever see them again."

"Tell you what," he said. "After this, we'll go back to New York, but just long enough to get my stuff. And we'll get the fuck out of there. Find another place to live. Or maybe just go on the road and travel around, me and you. Doing what we gotta do, we'll be a lot harder to track down if we keep moving. Pull into a town, blow something up and issue a communiqué, then get outa there."

"So long as I don't have to deal with the others anymore."

"The hell with them."

"They never showed me the slightest bit of respect. I was always the revolutionary dilettante, the phony, to them."

"I should've protected you from that. I'm sorry."

For the first time David wasn't acting like a macho asshole, he was being human and real, showing her a soul that felt desire and needed love, that missed her when she was gone and longed to be with her. And it was too late.

"Look," he said, "I know this is like the totally worst time to ask you this, but if I don't say it now, I may never have the guts to say it again."

"Yeah?"

"Do you think, once we're off on our own and we've been together for a little while—it's just that I've never in my life been with a woman as classy and smart as you—would you consider marrying me? Because I don't want to be with anybody else."

She wanted to cry, or laugh, or some inexplicable mixture of both.

"That's why I kept calling you and acting that way," he said. "Because I was terrified I was losing you, that you weren't just gone for Christmas, you were gone for good. I realized I'd been such an asshole and mean to you and scared you away. All I want is to be with you and take care of you and, well, be your husband. What do you think?"

"Ask me again," she said, "when we get to New York. Okay?"

Hollis Washington, the middle-aged black watchman on duty, strolled along the top floor corridor of the county courthouse, humming softly to himself in the dark emptiness and enjoying the echo.

As he passed a stairway, he thought he heard voices echoing upward. He stopped, and after listening a moment, he heard a man's voice from the lower floor. He backed up and crept slowly down the stairs, brandishing a foot-long flashlight like a club, pausing to try and locate the source of the sound.

On the main floor he stopped again. The voice was coming from the back end of the main corridor. He crept slowly that way, wondering if he should call the police first. The voice became clear once he rounded the corner. Hollis hesitated, listening, then heard a woman's voice.

"C'mon, it's almost nine thirty, it's late, let's go," she said.

David knelt at the table. One last time, he checked the fuses on the bombs in the open drawers. On the table, all you could see was two wires and an alarm clock. He rubbed his hands, held his breath, delicately slid the alarm switch on, and armed the bombs.

Light from the corridor came through the frosted window in the office door. A man's shadow loomed on the glass.

"Oh my God!"

Ivy whirled and looked at David. To her horror, David stared with a strange look at the door, and seemed unsure of what to do.

The shadow put a key in the door lock and turned it, the keys rattling on the brass lockset.

His hand plunged in his coat pocket but came up empty handed. "My gun!" David whispered. It must've fallen out when he was wrestling with her on the floor. It was too dark in the office to see and the floor was ankle deep in paperwork. He bent over kicking and groping noisily among the papers.

The door to the office opened with a squeak. The shadow reached in and switched on the lights. They came on bright and momentarily blinded them. A middle-aged black man in uniform had an incredulous look on his face.

"What are you people doing in here?" Hollis Washington said.

Retreating to the back of the office, shielding her eyes, Ivy slipped on papers on the highly polished linoleum floor, lost her balance and lurched into David. He fell against the table, jolting it, knocking the clock over. The alarm clock slid toward the back edge of the table.

"No no no *no*!" David gasped. He grabbed for the clock but clumsily knocked it over the table edge, armed and trailing wires.

"What did you *do*?" she screamed, crouching down.

He turned to her, his eyes pleading with her not to judge him.

The clock bounced off the floor, landed on its back under the table and lay there, ticking. David looked pathetic, sprawled over the table.

"Did you folks hear me?" Hollis demanded. "What do you think you're *doing* in here?"

"Would you step outside for a moment, sir?" Ivy said to him.

"No I will not." Looking at the floor covered in scattered files, Hollis demanded, "How'd this place get like this?"

David emptied his lungs in a huge rush. "Nothing happened."

She whirled on David. "Do you know what you're doing?"

"What do *you* think?" he snapped.

"Let's see some ID!"

"You don't wanna *know* what I think!"

"All right, shut up, I know what to fix," he said. He got on his hands and knees under the table, groping for the clock.

"We're past that point. Let's go."

Hollis shook his head, disbelieving. "Hey you, get out from under the table and let's see some ID."

"Please step outside, sir," she said.

"Don't tell me what to do." Hollis stepped closer and saw the bomb in the file cabinet drawer. "Jee-zuss Christ, get back, miss, and you, get from under there and quit what your doin'."

"David, don't touch it. Let's go, okay?" She wanted to grab his ankles and drag him out from under the table.

"We're cool," he said from under the table. "I got it."

"It doesn't *matter* now." To hell with him, with his bomb, with his revolution, she had a train to catch, and a rendezvous with the man she really loved, but David had the car keys in his pocket. "I only have to fix one thing."

"Both of you stay right here," Hollis ordered, backing away and picking up the secretary's desk phone. "I'm calling the police."

Ivy stepped on something under the papers, reached down, and picked up David's gun, the last damned thing she cared about. The watchman saw the gun, dropped the phone and raised his hands fearfully and began stammering.

"Oh no, don't do that, please. I got a wife, I got kids."

Oh my God, she was frightening the poor man, how terrible. She looked around for someplace to lay down the gun. "No-no-no sir, it's okay, see? It's okay." She turned and said over her shoulder, "God damn it, David, *come on*."

"One of the wires came off," David said. "I just have to—"

Eddie stood beside his car in the parking lot of the Manasquan train station. Cold rain began to patter lightly on the Impala's roof. The 10:05 train to New York pulled in, and his heart lifted. People got on, people got off. The train pulled slowly away. The disembarked passengers dispersed until only a wisp of somebody's cigarette smoke hung in the air.

No Ivy.

Was she in trouble, or has she made a fool of you again? Either way, no reason to hang around here. Slowly, as if something might still happen to restore the beautiful dream that had driven the last three days, he got in the car and put his hands on the wheel. Where to? He had his life packed in the car, ready to transplant someplace new. But leaving town tonight without knowing what happened to her was unthinkable, and he was too baffled and angry to do anything except go home.

The traffic on Route 71 south was heavy and slow, and the rain on the windshield made it hard to see. The house downstairs was dark. Billy's parking space was empty. He retrieved his letter from the kitchen to get his key back. Halfway up the stairs, he heard the phone ringing. He looked at his watch, it was almost ten thirty. With a sigh, he ran up the stairs, unlocked the door, and grabbed the phone. He imagined her at the other end, about to offer any number of excuses.

"This better be good," he said, ready as ever to be the tolerant, patient lover.

He raced to Toms River, broke every speed limit and ran every red light, and he didn't see a single cop. They were all downtown on Washington Street. The county courthouse was surrounded by dazzling red, white and blue lights from the emergency vehicles. He parked his car two blocks away. Police posted at sawhorses held back pedestrians and detoured traffic north and south on Hooper Avenue. From where he stood in the crowd, he could see a gaping hole in the rear corner of the courthouse building where the Draft Board office used to be. Glaring work lights inside the crime scene revealed blackened ceiling and walls, and the furniture, filing cabinets, light fixtures, venetian blinds and the red brick wall shattered by the blast lay scattered across the lawn. The shrubbery and bare trees were littered with thousands of pages of paper being collected by men in raincoats.

He identified himself and a cop moved the barricade to let him pass. At the courthouse entrance he showed his press card to a State Trooper and was allowed inside. Halfway down the main corridor, a crowd of reporters and photographers were squeezed together behind the police tape, held back by a State Trooper who was ignoring Bobbi Ann's charms. Jackson was there, looking lost with no politicians to interview. The far end of the corridor was littered with shattered glass and blackened wood, and the smoke from blasting powder, burnt plaster and paint still fogged the air.

He found Goldy pacing at the tape, frustrated and not hiding it. "They won't let us into the scene."

Eddie walked up to the tape where a State Trooper in blue uniform and high leather boots barred the way. Eddie showed him his press card. "Officer, can't we get our photographer back to the scene?" he said. "We're getting close to our deadline."

"Orders from the FBI, sir," the trooper said.

"See?" Goldy shook his head disgustedly. "Good thing Frank pushed the deadline thirty minutes for this."

"Yeah. Thanks for the call."

"I figured it'd be good news, maybe your file went *poof* and they'll forget all about you."

"Was anybody inside? Anybody hurt?"

"They won't say," Goldy muttered.

"Any arrests?"

"They won't say that either. Here's the agent running things."

The FBI special agent, tall and bald and wearing a green plaid raincoat with a black moustache and piercing black eyes, came out to the tape to face the media.

Camera flashes went off and the press pack pushed forward. The Special Agent briskly confirmed that an explosive device, not a gas leak, caused the blast. When he said three bodies had been recovered, a gasp went through the press corps. Next of kin for two of the deceased had been notified, he said. The night watchman, Hollis Washington, of South Toms River, had been identified by his shoes and parts of his uniform. The other two victims, believed to be the bombers, were identified by the remains of identification they carried and by a vehicle they parked nearby; the FBI agent named Margaret Ivy Porter, a local resident, and David Andrews, of New York.

"Porter?" the *Press* guy yelled. "Did you say Porter?"

Eddie felt the floor beneath his feet drop away and he was falling, falling for an endless moment. He put a hand on the wall beside him to steady himself. His hearing disappeared, leaving him in a zone of shocked silence. He could see the reporters around him yelling questions and the Special Agent's mouth moving as he answered. He saw Goldy out of the corner of his eye looking astonished and trying to see his face.

At the end of the corridor, an ambulance crew emerged from the bombed office pushing a gurney with a sheet-covered corpse. The gurney's wheels crunched on the broken glass in the silence as they came toward the police tape.

"Holy shit…" Goldy scrambled for position. He jumped up on the bench across the corridor and took aim. The photographers fired away as the trooper lifted the crime scene tape and the ambulance attendants rolled the gurney past. Goldy yelled to the trooper at the tape, "C'mon, man, you gotta let us into the scene, one minute, sixty seconds, how long is that—"

Another ambulance crew emerged pushing a second gurney with a corpse covered with a white sheet. Alongside trudged Senator Porter, disheveled, hastily dressed, one hand gripping the rail of the gurney.

Eddie tried to back away, but the reporters and photographers pushed forward against him. The reporters yelled, "Senator! Senator!" The Senator, his face rigid, shocked Eddie by reaching out and gripping his shoulder gently, neither pushing him away or pulling him along, one small gesture acknowledging their mutual loss.

The body on the gurney poked up under the sheet in all the wrong places.

Goldy lowered his camera. He came over to him and stared in disbelief. "You all right?"

His reply blew out of him in a high-pitched whisper: "No."

"She's your girl, right?" Goldy said. "The one you're always with?"

He turned to Goldy and shrugged helplessly. "I don't believe this." He put his notebook and pen in his pocket. "You got enough?"

"Yeah," Goldy said, looking surprised at the question.

"What happened to Bobbi Ann and Jackson?"

"She said she was going back to the newsroom. He's around the corner at the payphone."

"Let's go, it's thirty minutes to deadline."

At the *Independent,* Goldy went back to the darkroom and started developing pictures. Eddie began writing his story at five minutes before deadline. He was causing Frank a conflict with the stories from Jackson and Bobbi Ann, but he didn't care how Frank sorted it out.

TOMS RIVER — A powerful explosion destroyed the Ocean County Draft Board office last night and killed a night watchman and the two people that FBI agents believe detonated the bomb.

The dead were identified as Hollis Washington, 54, a county employee for eighteen years, married and the father of five children; Margaret Ivy Porter, 19, a local resident home on leave from New York University, and David Lloyd Andrews, 34, believed to be an associate of Miss Porter from New York.

Former State Sen. Thomas Porter, the deceased woman's father, came to the scene of the explosion and accompanied his daughter's body to the county Medical Examiner's office.

The FBI special agent at the scene confirmed that a bomb caused the explosion at approximately nine thirty. It destroyed the outer wall of the Draft Board office and damaged the rear wall of the county jail.

The explosion blasted office furnishings, filing cabinets and thousands of pages of documents over the courthouse lawn. Draft Board officials were not available before press time to assess how many local Selective Service records may have been lost.

Pieces of the explosive device are being analyzed by the FBI crime lab.

He left the newsroom and returned to the scene of the bombing. The acrid smell of fire still hung in the cold air over the courthouse grounds. Most of the emergency vehicles were gone and a small team of investigators were bent to the work that would probably go on until dawn. He stood on the sidewalk and watched as FBI agents sifted and collected evidence under the work lights. Around midnight, a heavy rain began falling, carrying ashes and charred bits of paper into the gutter. He went inside and stood again at the police tape with the other reporters. Around midnight, a trooper and an FBI agent escorted the reporters and photographers past the tape for a quick tour of the scene. Just a black, charred room, a gaping hole where the wall blew out all over the lawn, and bright rain drops falling through the work lights in the open air. Investigators out on the frozen lawn in streaming rubber raincoats stood and smoked and talked. The cold night air backed up into the scene, carrying the aroma of the bombing into the courthouse corridor.

He inhaled it, and the effect was paralyzing. He could barely breathe. Ivy had died here a few hours ago, a few feet from where he was standing. With their trip across America that was to have started tonight, how could she have done this? She said she was running away from these people. So how did she get here? Knowing nothing about David Andrews, Eddie hated him, because he got Ivy killed, and would forever be linked with her in infamy. Her last moments on earth had happened here. He desperately clung to the fantasy that her spirit or soul was still around, and would whisper something in his ear, something final and forever. Standing at the police tape, exhausted and with nothing more to learn, he kept telling himself to go home. Yet for a long time he couldn't, because it felt like abandoning her, something he once promised her that he would never do.

FOURTEEN *And now, the news*

All night he kept falling asleep, then jerking awake, afraid to surrender to unconsciousness. Near daybreak he lost the struggle, only to be jolted awake again, thrown into the deepest sorrow he'd ever felt by a nightmare he couldn't remember. He sat up in bed, still dressed in yesterday's clothes. He tossed the blankets off and stripped out of his sweaty, wrinkled shirt and trousers. He smelled coffee from downstairs. He showered and dressed quickly. He desperately wanted the warmth of Billy's kitchen.

Outside the rain had stopped. Shafts of cold sunlight broke through gaps in the low gray clouds and streaked the dark, rolling sea with silver. When he came through the kitchen door, Billy sat at the head of the table. Dressed in a suit and tie for the office, he would also have been properly dressed for a funeral.

"I'm sorry, Eddie. I know it's not enough to say that, but I don't know what else to say." He looked down at the morning *Independent* with her face on it. "This is just unbelievable."

"It's all right. I'm just glad you're here."

His face ashen, Billy went back to eating. Eddie poured a cup of coffee and they sat silently for awhile.

"I'm trying to understand how this could have happened," he finally said. "How could she have done this?" And then he couldn't stop talking. He poured out the doubts that were plaguing him. She'd talked him into hitting the road together. They'd planned to leave last night, to wander across America. Now he wondered if she'd been running a number on him from the start. Had she been planning the bombing all along, from that first phone call on Christmas Eve? Did she come home planning to seduce him and use him as her alibi? Maybe she just needed a driver and a way to vanish after the bombing? Did Andrews kidnap her and force her to join him, or had she been willing? Would she have reunited with Andrews and dumped him later, somewhere in the middle of America? *You know me better than anyone else*, she once told him. Did she secretly laugh at him as she said that? Were the past four weeks a lie? Eddie, totally consumed by Ivy for three years, now wasn't sure how well he'd really known her.

"So?" Billy said, when Eddie wound down. He'd shown no reaction during Eddie's lament. "What do you think?"

"I don't know," Eddie said, head hung, looking bewildered. "What do you think?"

"How the hell would I know?" Billy shrugged. "I wasn't fucking her, you were." Billy turned back to his shredded wheat and yogurt.

Shame, like a lick of heat across his face. "Okay, forget I asked—"

"Asked me what? Whether I think Ivy was running a number on you?"

"Look, I'm sorry I asked—"

"Well, I just think it's too bad you didn't know your own girlfriend."

"I thought I did," Eddie said. "She told me she was running away from those people. I believed her."

"Well," Billy said with a sharp, cruel laugh, "if there's anything we know about Ivy, it's that she could get you to believe anything."

"Hey, what *is* this?" Now he was angry too. "What are you trying to do?" He came to breakfast looking for a sympathetic ear, not this. He reached for a cigarette, but he'd left his Lucky Strikes upstairs. Billy held out one of his filtered Parliaments, bland, but at least it wasn't menthol.

"You're wondering if she was conning you?" Billy said. "I'm wondering, when did she ever *stop*?"

After a sleepless night, Eddie didn't have the strength to survive one of Billy's 'reality checks,' especially about Ivy. But the other choice was a silent, empty apartment, to be alone with a brain full of bitter, woeful voices, all his own. "She's not even buried yet, and you're sitting there—"

"I'm not passing judgment on Ivy," Billy said. "I'm pissed off at you. *Somebody* better tell you what's real and what isn't, because you're a pussy when it comes to love."

"*What?*"

"Always ready to fight for her," Billy said, "always ready to listen to her pain, always ready to believe her, and always ready to come back to her after she's played you once again for a fool." Eddie's shame couldn't have been worse, but Billy wouldn't let up. "Time to learn the facts of life, pal. A man can't be a pussy at the game of love. Women already have a pussy. They don't need another one. They need a *man*. Somebody who knows how to play the game like a man."

"I hope I never get as cynical as you about love."

"Oh, grow up! You want to learn how love and romance *really* work? Trying being a gay man for a while. Guaranteed to cure all romantic illusions." He stirred milk into his coffee, grinning coldly with one corner of his mouth. "Ivy really knew how to play the game. She was smart enough to wrap any guy she wanted around her little finger. I'll bet your heart isn't the only one broken this morning." He took a slow sip of coffee and stared at Eddie, calculating the effect his words were having. "To answer your question, was she setting you up as her get-away driver, was the bombing all she really cared about—"

"That's what I was asking, yeah," Eddie said, in a voice as small as he felt.

"Maybe. Maybe not."

Why was Billy was making this as hard as he could?

"After three years, if you're wondering how well you knew her, I can't help you. Keep in mind, though, that nobody can really know another person, not totally. Do you know how she ended up with Andrews last night?"

"I never heard of him until last night."

"I'm sure she wanted to drive across America with you. Not because she needed a getaway driver. That's just a doubt you dreamed up to torture yourself with. She loved you. I'm sure she did. As much as Ivy could love anyone, you were it."

"I think she was involved with Andrews," Eddie said. "I just can't believe he came down here, kidnapped her, forced her to—"

"Man, what is with you?" Billy said. "Isn't losing her terrible enough? Why are you looking for more misery?"

That stopped Eddie cold. "I'm not looking for—"

"Yes you are. Try being honest with yourself for once. You want another reason to feel terrible?" He jabbed at her face in the newspaper. "An innocent man is dead because of Ivy. A man with five children and a wife who's now a widow. Your girlfriend killed that man. It doesn't matter whether she was willing or unwilling."

"No. That only matters to me."

Billy's voice rose to a taunt. "Because you're too fucking childish to care about anything but getting one last chance to feel sorry for yourself."

He knew Billy was right, and he couldn't look him in the eye. After a moment, got up and walked out.

He climbed back up to his room, sat at his desk and rolled the last page of his journal into his typewriter, and stared out over the rooftops. He put his fingers to the keyboard, and began to think through them, hitting the keys.

Why *was* he looking, once again, for a reason to be her victim, duped and cuckolded? Despite all his toughness, was he really a weak youth who needed to be humiliated that way? If so, his love affair with Ivy had been perfect, a three-year roller coaster up and down ecstasy and betrayal, and he'd played the part of the gullible faithful boyfriend perfectly, right up to the night she blew herself to bits. She had let him see the aching hopelessness, deep inside her, and he had tried to take care of her, make things better, even to save her from herself. But now he saw how lame that was, requiring Ivy to stay messed up so he could be strong. Sudden clarity hit him with a shock: two confused kids, attracted to each other's suffering, joined in a passionate confusion of illusion and hormones they thought was love. Was that all it was?

Much later, when time had passed and he could look back on it, he would consider that day the most important of his life because of the decision he made that morning. Billy came upstairs and brought him a fresh cup of coffee, apologized for being so harsh with him but emphasized it was what Eddie needed, then drove off to work. Eddie sat on the front steps, drinking coffee, smoking Luckies and staring at the Impala, which had never looked so beautiful, its sky-blue flanks and top and chrome accents gleaming in the sun.

Everything he owned was packed in the trunk of that car. All the money he had in the world was in the pocket of his jeans. The one and only love of his life was gone, leaving him without even the consolation that it had been real, true love, only unanswered questions and constant sorrow. The biggest story in his reporting career, he mishandled, then abandoned. If his situation had ever been lower, he couldn't remember when. There seemed to be only one solution—get out on the road and just go.

His life had been torn loose, he was floating free, and he could take himself anywhere at the turn of the ignition. He'd never been anywhere or seen any of the country in whose name the government would soon try to force him to go to war. If he just got in the car and began to drive, he could get away from this mess he'd made of his life.

He grew more and more excited. Was it the places he could go, New Orleans, Los Angeles, San Francisco? Or was it that in a new place he would find the freedom from his past to become a new man? Freed of the ties binding him to this life as a small-town fool, from a nowhere place, who never got anything right, he could remake himself and create a new life in the West. He could get in the car, turn the key, and escape the past, shedding this life like an unwanted skin.

But before he'd had a chance to enjoy this fantasy, reality crept in like a curtain going down. He shouldn't forget, after all, that he was still the same loner he'd been in high school. He worked too many hours at reporting when he wasn't holed up at home writing in his journal trying to figure himself out. He had lots of associates, but just about no close friends. He'd only dated one girl in the past three years, and he wasn't too suave at meeting new ones.

Just get in the car and drive away from all this. Finally, he realized he had no business driving a car. He stayed seated on the steps, because he was certain that in this state of mind he wouldn't care if he drove to San Francisco or straight into the nearest brick wall at high speed. Unhappily giving up his new man fantasy, telling himself to get real, he was suddenly certain that if he drove thousands of miles away it would only be to recreate the same life in the same rut, in some new town where he would soon be just as unhappy. The same hassles and frustrations, the same mystery that was himself, would be there at the end of his journey, the first things he would unpack. Better to stay here and deal with this mess where it began, in his family and his hometown.

He emptied the car trunk and got his boxes out of the garage and moved everything back up into the apartment. Before long, the place was like it had always been, only tidier. Outside on the porch, he stood and smoked and watched the surf break and softly slide on and off the beach in the sun. At lunchtime he went to the bank and put the thousand bucks back in his college tuition fund and crossed the street to the tobacco shop and bought cigarettes and the newspapers.

The morning tabloids, with only a couple hours between the bombing and their deadlines last night, put up large-type bulletins with huge headlines and full pages of photographs. KILLED BY OWN BOMB, said the *Observer* story. DRAFT BOARD BLAST KILLS 3, said the *Independent*, with Eddie's story in a box surrounded by Goldy's photos. The largest picture showed Senator Porter beside his daughter's gurney gripping Eddie's shoulder, and the look on Eddie's face staring down at the sheet-covered body. He wasn't identified in the caption.

Reporters from the Asbury Park *Evening Press* had all night to cover the bombing and their stories contained more detail. The main story reported the facts that had been officially confirmed, and there were sidebar stories on the innocent victim, Hollis Washington, and on the terrorist bombers, David Andrews—described by the FBI as having ties to the violent Weatherman faction of SDS—and Margaret Ivy Porter, portrayed as a spoiled rich girl rebelling against her wealthy, Republican ex-state Senator father. She was named by the FBI as an accomplice in the bombing and in Hollis Washington's death.

That night the stories on ABC, NBC and CBS national television news carried a story about the arrests of the people that David Andrews and Margaret Ivy Porter had associated with in Manhattan and the recovery of a large cache of weapons. The radicals were paraded in handcuffs in front of the news cameras and the weapons laid out on a table. They used an old mug shot of Andrews and the high school yearbook picture of Ivy that she'd hated. They used all three names, Margaret Ivy Porter, like they would with a presidential assassin or infamous criminal. The television Ivy, Eddie did not recognize. One side of her personality, rebellious and reckless, had been grossly inflated to become the only Ivy Porter the world would ever know.

While he and Billy were watching the news, Frank Devlin called.

"How you doin,' kid?"

"The doctors say I'm getting better." Nice of Frank to check on his recovery.

"Good, good. Sorry about the Porter girl. I didn't get a chance to say that last night. Good job on the story."

"Well, there's a lot more to it—"

"Well, ain't that always the case in this business?" Frank chuckled nervously.

"So, I'll be back to work in a couple days," Eddie said.

"No, you won't."

"I think it's the best thing for me."

"Oh, you do?"

"The doctors gave me the okay."

"I don't care. I just spent half a day getting my balls busted by McTierney and his lawyers over you. We're letting you go."

"I'm fired?" Hearing this across the room, Billy shook his head and laughed silently.

"The lawyers are working overtime to keep us out of court with all the people the Esposito stories pissed off."

"But I didn't write any stories. None that got *printed*, anyway."

"Yeah, but thanks to you and your lawyer, everybody else did. Besides, it's come to our attention you've accused Roy McTierney of attempted murder, so I think under the circumstances—"

"I don't believe what I'm hearing."

"Believe it. Even if I wasn't under orders, I don't want you back here. I told you to drop the story and you didn't listen."

"You weren't talking as my editor. You were talking as a pal to gangsters and as a bagman for crooked politicians."

"And you're a self-righteous little cocksucker who'd rather believe a crook like Matty Esposito than me. I gave you a job and what gratitude did I get? A punch in the mouth."

"You deserved it."

"Yeah well, the lawyers'll send you a letter."

"Shove it up your ass."

"See? That's the attitude I'm talking about—"

"And to think I once wanted to be like you," he said. "Thank God I woke up before it was too late."

"You'll never make a good reporter. You know why? Because—"

"Fuck you." He hung up.

It didn't end there. The next morning Eddie came downstairs for breakfast, shaky after a second troubled night. The blustery day was sending long rolling breakers up out of a gray sea to thunder onto the beach. The cold wind whistled through the beach grass and dune shrubs and chased him across the porch and through the front door. The warm kitchen held its comforting aroma of coffee and cigarette-smoked walls, with hints of garlic and curry.

Billy was dressed for work, finishing his black coffee, sitting up straight and tense. The *Independent* lay folded by his elbow on the table.

"How are you, Bonneville?"

"Lousy."

"Is that all you're having?" he said, indicating the cup of coffee Eddie brought to the table.

"This and a little o' this," he said, shaking a Lucky Strike from the pack.

"Good. Get nice and fortified."

"Why?"

Billy leaned over and lit Eddie's cigarette. He handed him the morning's *Independent*.

The lead headline said USA GETS NEW PRIORITIES, over a wire service picture of President Nixon, grinning wolfishly in the well of Congress after delivering last night's State of the Union address.

Billy pointed to the bottom corner of the front page, to a small picture of Eddie's battered face and an editorial teaser that said, "An Apology." He tore open the paper. It was the only editorial in today's *Independent*. He immediately recognized Frank's style.

The task of the mentor is never an easy or simple
one. Yet the passing of knowledge and experience in a
particular craft is often best done from one person to
another. In learning the skills and techniques needed
to become proficient at a trade or craft, in this case
journalism, the relationship that grows between the
novice and the mentor is an essential part of the
process. The key factor here is passion, a shared love
for working in the craft in which both are engaged.

Often as the novice begins to form his personal
style, and he strives to define himself as a
professional, conflicts develop with the mentor. This
is a natural part of the process. Too often just
when the mentor hopes to hear a word of gratitude or
receive some gesture of appreciation for passing on his
valuable wisdom, the novice responds with a betrayal
that signals the end of the relationship, and the
beginning of independence.

Sometimes this painful passage marks the birth of a
mature professional. We only wish that this were so in
the relationship that is the subject of this editorial.

Ever since the demented rantings of the late
gangster Matty Esposito became public, we have been
deluged with letters and phone calls taking us to task
for the role our reporter, Eddie Bonneville, played in
their release. Bonneville tape recorded an interview
with Esposito on assignment from this newspaper.
But the sinister accusations Esposito made in that
interview were so sensational, so potentially libelous
to scores of people, and so unsubstantiated, that they
were judged unfit for publication without extensive
investigation and checking. We call on the State
Commission on Investigations to take on such a probe
at once. It may be the only way to undo the damage
that has been caused to so many people of heretofore
impeccable reputation.

We tried from the outset to discourage our reporter
from pursuing his investigation. We felt with only one
year's professional experience, he was not qualified
to investigate such sensitive, highly inflammatory
statements without the mature grasp of human nature and
political reality that can only come after years of
reporting. He forged ahead anyway without authorization
and attracted the attention of criminal elements in our
community with whom Esposito was intimately familiar
and was badly hurt and nearly killed.

Our reporter not only refused to stop his
investigation when ordered to by the *Independent's*
editors. Subpoenaed for his notes and recordings by the
county prosecutor, he and his lawyer contrived to have
the tape recordings entered into evidence, where they
became available to other reporters, resulting in the
lurid headlines of the past week.

It is to those persons who feel they have been
maligned or their reputation impugned that we address
this editorial. We apologize, sincerely, for the
reckless and self-aggrandizing behavior of Eddie
Bonneville, who no longer writes for this newspaper. We
apologize for not recognizing sooner that a notorious
incident two years ago, in which he nearly beat an
opponent in the high school boxing ring to death,
signaled a severe mental and emotional immaturity that
made him unfit for the responsibilities of professional
journalism. We apologize for the damage his attempts to
get a scoop and glory for himself have done to decent,
upstanding members of our community. We apologize
for failing to supervise a young and impressionable

reporter who let sensational gossip from a notorious gangster go to his head and ended up aiding and abetting character assassination. We would like to apologize, finally, for our failure in the education of this young and impressionable reporter, who did not respond to our best efforts to mold him into a seasoned professional.

My God. Eddie was pounding with anger from head to foot. *My God.* Keeping his cool, he looked up at Billy.

"It's pretty bad."

Eddie shrugged. "Nobody reads the Friday paper anyway." *I've been fucked. Fucked in public.*

"Well," Billy said, "some of what it says there is true, isn't it?"

"*No.*" Eddie saw himself in the window beside the table. He looked quickly away, but that meant looking at Billy. "I don't know, maybe."

"As a lawyer, I did what was right for my client," Billy said, evenly. "But I'm not proud of the results."

"Neither am I. I guess I could've burned the tapes." Except that, as Frank was telling the readers of the *Independent* that morning, he had believed Esposito's story and never questioned it. Why? He'd never stopped once to ask himself what he was doing. Why not?

"By the way, that's one of the most gutless, ass-covering editorials I've ever read," Billy said. "They wasted no time blaming you."

"Look at this," Eddie said. On an inside page was a story written by Bobbi Ann Nelson headlined *Esposito Crime Empire Exposed*, quoting law enforcement sources saying the old man had been the malignant center of crime and racketeering at the Jersey Shore. The piece was illustrated with an editorial cartoon of Esposito as an evil octopus with tentacles labeled prostitution, gambling, labor racketeering, loan sharking, murder—though none, he noticed, for official corruption. In a boxed story at the bottom of the page, the *Independent* announced an upcoming public service series by a new young reporter—actually a nephew of the McTierneys—that would explain, like a civics lesson, the way government worked, using the "well-oiled machines" of local county and municipal government as examples.

The letter Eddie wrote in reply to their editorial was not printed. Nor did they take his one suggestion that wasn't profane, that the *Independent* change its name.

He'd never lost anyone before, not even a pet. He knew nothing about handling death. He'd never endured such empty days or felt such desperation as afternoon darkened into evening.

Like so many times before in his life, there was no-one he could talk to, so he tried to handle it alone. He sat down and searched through his diaries and journals, hoping to recall a loss that had a powerful impact on him, to see if he'd learned anything useful. He was looking for the memory of loss, and of feeling utterly lost himself. Well, the assassinations of Dr. King and Bobby Kennedy had been terrible. But he'd been too busy arguing with his father on those occasions, so he'd written nothing.

Then he found a diary entry he had written at age thirteen that brought up the same desolation. Beside the date he had written in his own neat handwriting: *Death can happen when you least expect it, while you are busy living.* Six years ago, a 13-year-old boy had pulled out his pocket notebook while going home from school and had written that thought. Then he went on to live his life and forgot he ever had that insight. The memory of the death that caused that realization, however, was as fresh as if it had happened yesterday.

It had been November, a cold, sunny autumn day, a Friday, a report card day. Around noon, Eddie's eighth grade English class was reading aloud from *The Adventure of the Blue Carbuncle*. It was nearly Eddie's turn to take up the reading. He didn't want to read aloud, he was bored and surly and worried about his first report card of the year. After a descending cascade of B's and C's there was a handwritten note from his teacher Mister Bissinger, a fortyish bachelor who drove a green MG sports car and had elaborately coiffed red hair: "Dealing with Edward's behavioral problem has become a major obstacle to the class's progress. He is constantly disruptive and argumentative. He incites conflict and encourages it between the other students. Please schedule a meeting with me and the vice principal to discuss demoting him back to the seventh grade." He could picture the inevitable scene later. His father would read the note, fling the report card aside and tear off his belt, and he'd get a whipping.

Dread of this had settled like dust in the back of his throat. He was afraid he would have to read that way. Then the principal's voice came over the intercom, the same way he led the Pledge of Allegiance to the flag every morning. He said the President had been shot by somebody a short time ago in Texas. He put the intercom microphone up to the television in the main office and the events were broadcast on CBS News while the whole school sat silently listening. Details tore through disbelief like fragments of shrapnel from an explosion: President Kennedy definitely shot, how seriously nobody could say, a sniper from an upper floor of a building in Dallas, then a race to the hospital, Walter Cronkite saying the President was dead, nobody in the classroom able to look at each other for a long time. A few minutes later, the principal announced that in light of the national tragedy school was dismissed and WJLK radio in Asbury Park would announce the reopening.

Eddie went home, his father read the report card, looked at him sadly, tossed it on the kitchen table and said, "You're on your own," and went back to watching the news. While the whole world huddled around television sets that weekend, the weather turned wintry and the cold gray heavens settled over the Jersey Shore, dark clouds so low it seemed you could reach up and touch them.

There was nothing useful he could learn from that day except this: life just *hits* us, and we make the best of it, like Billy once said. And it was the same with death. It was always there, waiting, a sudden wind that extinguished life as easy as blowing out a match. Just an everyday, normal part of life. After all, the death that made him write the note in his diary happened on a day that started out like any other, a beautiful autumn day, the oak and maple trees around the school red and gold and tan and over the green football field the sun shining bright. Then came the shocking news, and the strangeness of leaving school in the middle of the day, everyone either crying or just looking numb, bewildered. And from that day on, people seemed to feel a deep fear and uncertainty that became permanent—if the President wasn't safe, then who was? His 13-year-old mind had written, but even now it was hard to accept, that death, whether close and personal or one that shook the world and plunged millions into grief, could strike without warning, out of a clear blue sky, on a perfectly ordinary day.

That afternoon his phone rang as Eddie was meditating.
"Is this Eddie?"
"Who wants to know?"
"Tom Porter."
Well, well. "Senator."
"I uh, wanted to speak with you. Do you think I might be able to

buy you a drink later?"

"Sure, why not?"

"Yeah, why not?"

Because when I see you, I just might kill you, he thought.

He met Ivy's father on a rainy afternoon in the bar of a seafood restaurant called the Olde Anchor in Point Pleasant Beach, on the ship channel where the fishing boats docked. The shingles on the place were gray, Rheingold and Budweiser neon beer logos gleamed in the windows, and a big rusty anchor was embedded in cement by the front door. Inside, picture windows overlooking Gull Island magnified the white winter daylight, blackening the corners of the room and turning the glasses of beer on the bar to gold.

They took a booth against the back wall. Before anybody recognized the Senator, he turned his back to the room, loosened his tie, and tossed his black overcoat over a chair. The Senator dropped heavily onto his bench and leaned forward on his elbows, his head bowed and his hair falling over his forehead. He and Eddie shook hands for the first time in three years. The Senator's face was drawn and pale.

"Thanks for coming, Eddie," he said. "There wasn't much chance to talk the other night."

"No, there wasn't," Eddie said. Nor was he eager to talk now, but Ivy's father had made the call.

It was hard for the Senator to get started. "My wife and I were just at Hollis Washington's funeral," he said. "I don't know how those people do it, the blacks, I mean. They've put up with so much shit for so long, then something like this happens, and they just come together and—" He sighed raggedly, and his cigar breath put a punk odor in the air that Eddie dispelled by lighting a cigarette. "I didn't know what the hell to say except I was sorry. I'm thinking when the time comes, I'll offer to put the kids through college or something."

"That'd be nice."

"Doesn't make up for losing a father, but it's the least I can do. And Hollis was a sweet, sweet man. To think that my god damned daughter killed him—" All he could do was shake his head in sorrow over how all this was hurting him. He was so wrapped up in his own self-pity he didn't seem to sense how much Eddie hated him for cursing Ivy.

The Senator ordered a double Old Grand Dad from the waitress. He drank half before setting the glass on the table. Eddie sipped a glass of club soda, slowly. He caught the Senator glancing at him distastefully.

"You really don't like being here with me, do you?" Eddie said.

"I've never liked you," the Senator said.

"Then why'd you ask to see me?" Obviously not to offer his condolences. The Senator had apparently gotten over the generosity of spirit with which he'd touched Eddie in sorrow the night Ivy died.

"For the aggravation you've caused the Organization," the Senator said, "I shouldn't even be seen talking to you. But I need to know certain things—for reasons of my own—"

"I was surprised to hear from you," Eddie said. "Considering the past."

Senator Porter rubbed his eyes with his fingertips. "Can we let the past stay in the past?"

"That'd make this conversation nice and easy for you, wouldn't it?"

"Look," Ivy's father said, almost snarling, "to talk to you, do I have to apologize for every injustice you think I inflicted on you and my daughter?"

"I don't care whether you do or not." He was tempted to mention the child that the Senator did not allow to be born, but then he would not be able to continue the conversation nonviolently. "The person whose forgiveness you should be asking is gone."

That sent the Senator back to sneering into his whiskey. Eddie was sure there was no way he could know that Ivy had told him everything. Would it matter if he knew? Eddie doubted that this man, so powerful in politics and government and so helpless against the evil within himself, had ever given a second thought to his own sins. He had probably assumed his power would protect him, and that nobody would have the nerve to confront him. Now he'd found out how little his power mattered.

"What do you want from me?" Eddie said, growing impatient. "Why should I be of any help or comfort to you?"

"Because I'm asking you to," Senator Porter said. "Because I need you to tell me what you know."

"About what?"

"About my daughter. My own daughter died a total mystery to me." He clearly thought this was a great injustice that life had inflicted upon him.

"It might be better to leave it that way."

The Senator shook his head. "You'll be a father one day," he said, "and then you'll understand."

Did he really say that, with no irony whatsoever? Did this man have no memory? It was less than two years ago. Of course his daughter was a mystery to him. The man couldn't see past himself. His blindness was total and complete, almost childish. Yet along with the contempt he felt, Eddie saw how utterly pathetic Ivy's father was. Instead of following his instincts and attacking, he gave the Senator what he was asking for.

"Ivy said at first she agreed politically with Andrews and those people in New York," he said. "Then she looked around one day, and they had guns and bombs and she wanted out. But they wouldn't let her leave, not with all of them wanted by the FBI. She knew too much."

"She was afraid they'd come after her?"

"She was sure they would."

"You know, they found a gun in the rubble. I'm convinced he kidnapped her and made her help him," the Senator said. "My daughter was wild, but I don't believe she would willingly bomb a public building. Even if this was some crazy stunt aimed at embarrassing me—"

"She had more important things on her mind," Eddie said. "That night she was only gonna take the train as far as Manasquan. We were gonna meet, and drive across the country, and live someplace out west. We had planned, once we were settled, to get married—"

"Yup, that's Ivy," the Senator cut him off, aggrieved. "Didn't say a word to her mother or me about any of this, of course. She would've taken her allowance and called two months later from California to say, 'Hi, sorry I've been so out of touch'." The fact that Eddie had lost so much, that his life was shattered, clearly meant nothing to this son of a bitch. "If she was planning to run off with you, I think that proves she was not a willing accomplice. Andrews was a punk, a petty thief and a con man. The FBI showed me his criminal record. Real white trash." He gave Eddie a furtive glance and hurried on. "He had me believing he'd been an organizer for the Nixon campaign. Ivy was nervous when she saw him in our house, but I thought it was just something romantic between them." Senator Porter sighed. "My poor daughter's had the worst luck with men."

"Yeah," Eddie said. "Right from the start."

Senator Porter sat back looking down his nose at Eddie. "I don't know if you realize it, but *you're* the only one who ever meant anything to her," clearly proving her bad judgment, he meant. "I know Ivy really loved you, because we fought over you constantly." The memory of those battles seemed to occupy him for a moment, then he sighed. "Agh, shit. I guess I ought to try and be grateful for whatever happiness she had with you."

The Senator was trying to make himself feel better. It had the opposite effect on Eddie. "If that's an apology, it's too bad she never got a chance to hear it."

"You're much too young to be so bitter, my boy."

"I don't need your fucking advice," Eddie said. "Get to the point."

"Can you shed some light for me on what happened?" the Senator said. "In some ways, you knew her better than I did."

"Don't be so sure of that, because I'm not."

"I was hoping you could help me understand where I went wrong."

He couldn't stop himself. "You went wrong when you dragged her down to Puerto Rico and forced her through an abortion."

"There was no other choice."

"You didn't leave *us* a choice at all, did you?"

"You were kids. Too young for a decision like that. It was for your own good."

"*Our* own good?"

You went wrong when you starting taking showers together. He wanted to say it, but he stopped himself. He sat back and took his time lighting a Lucky.

"Ivy and I had no secrets from each other, you know," he said. "None."

Her father's blank stare, a politician's professional poker face, told him he'd been heard. So he didn't need to speak the ugliest truth of all. *Our own good? You were afraid the baby was yours.* Would it matter now? It would accomplish little, only the momentary satisfaction of mortifying the Senator by telling him that Ivy had betrayed him and revealed his obscene secret. And what good would that do him? Just more bitterness, more rage, and more of his life stuck in a past he couldn't change, a past from which he could only free himself through the most difficult way of all—compassion and forgiveness for the monstrous hypocrite sitting across the table.

So Eddie said what he knew the Senator needed to hear, because it served his purpose. To speak the words wasn't easy, and to actually mean them, impossible. Yet it was his only choice if he wanted to outgrow the past three years and be free. So he would say it now, because he had to, and work on actually feeling it later.

"Look, Tom," he said, "whatever's happened in the past, whatever you may think of me, I want you to know despite the heartache you've caused me and Ivy, I forgive you. We've both lost something precious and irreplaceable. I'm feeling pretty bad, but I'm heartbroken for you and Mrs. Porter."

Undoubtedly, Senator Porter hated to hear that this kid he loathed could forgive him. "Well, I don't know what to say, Eddie." What Eddie wanted to hear, he knew would never be spoken: *You're a better man than I am, son.* But he knew that already.

While he had the advantage, he asked something he needed to know from the one man who might actually know the truth.

"Listen, there's something maybe you can help *me* understand."

"Well, I'll try."

"Do you think Matty Esposito was off his rocker?"

Senator Porter seemed relieved at the change in subject. "No, far from it. Matty Esposito was a man of many talents. In any field, he would have been a top guy."

"He told me he got into crime because it paid better than playing the trumpet."

Senator Porter shrugged. "I'm sure he was a better gangster than musician. But it wasn't money that turned him." The Senator emptied his glass and sat back. "When Matty was twenty-five, his mother was killed by a drunk driver in Toms River. The driver was a frequently drunk member of the local bar and a Republican, and he was speeding. Clear cut case of vehicular manslaughter. But because of who he was, there was no mention of alcohol in the police report, and sobriety tests barely existed in those days, so no evidence about DWI was introduced at trial. He was allowed to plead to careless driving and let off with a fine and a slap on the wrist. When the Espositos tried to investigate, they were told to get lost, and when they sued, they found the defendant had dispersed his assets and was essentially broke and dying of heart disease. Matty told me his father worshipped his mother. Losing his wife killed his father long before he died. Bruno lived another forty years, brokenhearted and hating every day that God forced him to live without the woman he loved."

Picturing an aging man, stricken by the loss of love, living in inconsolable grief where a great romance once filled his life, unexpectedly brought Eddie to tears. He could scarcely imagine Matty's tortured life as the son of such a man. He shook his head and said, almost offhandedly, "All those payoffs over the bar all those years, and it bought him no respect."

The Senator pretended he hadn't heard him. "Losing his mother and being brushed off by the authorities left Matty bitter and vengeful. He went off and started bribing, blackmailing, bullying and murdering until he organized the local underworld. What little there was. He set up the rackets, he controlled the unions, he forced everybody to deal with him, and nobody was ever able to lay a finger on him."

"At least while Colonel Ted was alive," Eddie said. "Right?"

The Senator rewarded this worldly remark with a nod. "I feel bad I wasn't able to reconcile things before he, uh, left us."

Either the Senator works out a deal, or this ain't gonna end so good, Esposito had told him. Now he wondered what the Senator knew about Esposito's murder; more than he'd ever get him to admit, he was sure.

"How'd you get to be Esposito's lawyer?"

"He called me. That's all I can really say."

"He told me the Organization was trying to put him away so a new guy they liked better could take over his rackets."

The Senator just looked at Eddie.

"And all the stories he told me, the Colonel Ted Tax, all that?" Eddie said. "Were they all true?"

"Who knows?"

"If anybody does, you do."

"Me? I'm just a small-town lawyer."

"Yeah, okay." Suddenly Eddie wanted to be out of there. The useful part of the conversation was over. They finished their drinks. The Senator gave him his business card, in case he ever needed anything, a private number hand-written in the corner. When they shook hands, the Senator held on a moment longer.

"I'll have my office call you when the services are scheduled," Senator Porter said. "I hope you'll come."

Ivy was buried on Wednesday, January 28, on a windswept hillside on a bright, frigid morning. At the Porter family's request the graveside service began with a prayer for the soul of Hollis Washington and to ask for God's mercy on his family. The Senator and his wife and her sister, a real estate broker from Tuckerton, stood to one side of the coffin with their heads bowed while the reverend prayed. Eddie stood at the back of the crowd of family and friends. The wind snatched the words from the reverend's lips, and all he heard was his voice droning up and down, as he stood there on the hard packed earth with numbed ears and toes.

It was the cold ears and toes that brought back a memory. After Ivy had broken up with him last fall, one night when he'd found it impossible to sleep or to accept that it was over, he'd driven sixty miles up the Parkway and Turnpike and through the Holland Tunnel into Manhattan, intending to find her and beg her to take him back. He'd parked on the east side of Washington Square Park, and stood at a street corner where he could see the window of the tenement apartment off University Place she shared with two girls. He stood there for hours, undecided, smoking, freezing, staring at the window, trying and failing to get up the courage to cross the street and ring the doorbell and risk that she'd turn him away. He had hoped she would walk by and find him standing there so he wouldn't have to act. He couldn't stay away, and he couldn't go ring the doorbell, even after the wind froze his ears and toes. Had that been love? Not the liberating, enlightening love of the pop songs, but a love that brought as much misery as joy, a love that wouldn't let go, a love whose germ was deep in his blood.

He turned and left. He didn't want to see the coffin lowered into the ground. The reporters and photographers covering the burial caught up to him as he was getting in his car.

"Eddie, do you think Ivy Porter was a willing revolutionary? Or was she kidnapped by this guy David, like her parents say?"

With no hesitation he said, "I didn't know her that well." He dropped behind the wheel of his car and got out of there.

In March, the first day of spring was a day of chilly rain showers, the first day that you could smell spring rising from the earth. Under a soft gray sky, the chicken farm field in Cassville was staked out with twine that crisscrossed in a grid. In a light rain, two and three man teams dug several holes around the field. Another pair of men removed soil from the last chicken coop. On the dirt road in front of the house, police cars, press vehicles, and a hearse were parked. Under a broad tarp, a crowd of police officers, medical examiner's assistants, reporters, and photographers smoked, made small talk, and waited, taking paper cups of coffee from an urn on the tailgate of a sheriff's department station wagon.

After saying his hellos, Eddie stood slightly apart from the crowd under the tarp and observed the proceedings. He wore a two-button brown suit, blue shirt and black tie and black oxfords. His hair, newly barbered and brushed back, didn't quite touch his collar. On his jacket pocket hung a press card from the Asbury Park *Evening Press*. His enthusiasm for his new job was so high that wasn't offended when the *Press* editors, who called him enterprising and aggressive and a good writer when they hired him, dismissed his tabloid years and said working for the *Independent* was not real professional experience. But not to worry. Every new *Press* reporter was broken in by the editors in the city room in Asbury Park before they were deemed a good enough representative of the paper to be given a steady beat somewhere.

He took a folded *Press* from his jacket pocket. Eddie read again a page 2 story in the Ocean County section. Sally Meglio, part time club singer and companion to the late rackets boss Matty "The Mule" Esposito, had appeared recently before a grand jury hearing murder charges against local cocktail lounge owner Robert Castellucci. She'd agreed to testify in exchange for protection from Castellucci's criminal associates. No doubt Sally had considered the baby she was carrying and was determined to give the kid a decent beginning in life. So Matty Esposito, in some form, would live on.

He tucked the paper back in his pocket and finished the coffee. One of the diggers came out of the coop, his knees and elbows dirty. He looked around and called out to the Assistant Medical Examiner. Police officers and the assistant M. E. and reporters and photographers trooped out from under the tarp, marching around the edge of the staked-off field, their umbrellas bunched together like a black bouquet. After a moment, Eddie tossed his empty cup away then followed, while out in the field the digging continued.